An impossible escape from the jaws of death. . .
The secret of a Biblical prophecy revealed. . .
A loved one brutally attacked. . .
Forces of terrifying evil empowered. . .
A man of surprising courage is tested and proves ready
to become a much-needed hero for our times. . . .
And that's just the beginning. . .

RANDOM HOUSE

LARGE PRINT

BABYLON RISING

BABYLON

RANDOM HOUSE
LARGE PRINT

RISING

TIM LAHAYE
AND GREG DINALLO

Copyright © 2003 by Tim LaHaye

All rights reserved under International and Pan-American Copyright Conventions. Published in the United States of America by Random House Large Print in association with Bantam Books, New York, and simultaneously in Canada by Random House of Canada Limited, Toronto. Distributed by Random House, Inc., New York.

The Library of Congress has established a Cataloging-in-Publication record for this title

0-375-43237-x

www.randomlargeprint.com

FIRST LARGE PRINT EDITION

10   9   8   7   6   5   4   3   2   1

This Large Print edition published in accord with the standards of the N.A.V.H.

Dedicated to:

GENERAL LEW WALLACE, whose nineteenth-century classic Ben-Hur, subtitled *A Tale of the Christ,* taught me that fiction could be both thrilling and instructive at the same time and could appeal to both a secular and a Christian audience. With more than six million copies in print and a stage play seen by more than half a million people by the turn of the century, the book had an international audience and was made into three movies: first, for the silent screen; second, in black and white; and then in 1959, William Wyler's color classic, starring Charlton Heston, which elevated this story to one of the best-loved movies of all time.

JERRY B. JENKINS, my co-author and partner in writing the Left Behind® series, which has turned into a publishing phenomenon, who worked with me to bring to the printed page my vision of a fictional portrayal of Bible prophecy based on the book of Revelation. Together we proved that fiction with a message was still possible in the twentieth century.

GREG DINALLO, my co-author for this book, who has helped to shape my vision of a fast-paced action thriller for the twenty-first century that is based on Bible prophecies not covered in the Left Behind® books.

And to the HEBREW PROPHETS, who saw, under divine inspiration, forecasts of world events so necessary to know for those living in what they called "the time of the end," or what some modern historians call "the end of history," which could occur in the early part of the twenty-first century.

A MESSAGE FROM TIM LAHAYE

Dear Reader:

Welcome to my new prophetic fiction series, Babylon Rising. I hope you will come to share my tremendous enthusiasm about this first novel, which bears the series name, whether you are one of the millions of readers who have read my Left Behind series (coauthored with Jerry B. Jenkins) or you are a first-time reader of my fiction writing.

I am more excited about *Babylon Rising* than *any* of my previous books. My prayer is that it will have the same effect on the lives of readers as have the Left Behind® books.

The fantastic popularity of the Left Behind series (54 million in print and growing) convinced me that fiction is a powerful way for me to share with readers some of what I find so completely fascinating about end times prophecies. Happily, readers were stimulated by the combination of great adventures and important revelations.

Babylon Rising is my newest attempt to create another uniquely satisfying combination of suspense and substance. I base this exciting story on the single most important prophecy in the Bible regarding international events, one that is having an incredible impact on our society today.

Bible prophecies and their interpretation are clear signs of what our present and future hold for this world, and they are a continuing basis for all of my writing. In the Babylon Rising series, you will find some truly fascinating and important material based on my continuing rescarch on the prophecies of the Bible.

My hope is that you will not only find *Babylon Rising* a fascinating read, but that the series will help you understand that end times prophecy could be fulfilled in our lifetime, and that it will help you make sense of "the signs of the times" that we see being fulfilled internationally almost every time we watch events unfold on television or read a newspaper.

The setting for Left Behind, as you probably know, starts with the rapture of the church and then takes the world through the tribulation period, the millennial kingdom of Christ, and on into heaven. Babylon Rising starts in our present time and moves forward to the rapture, one of the most exciting periods in the history of the world.

To really make this a "grabber" of a novel, you will find *Babylon Rising* features a hero who faces many of the challenges of our day that are familiar to all of us. That hero, Michael Murphy, is one of the real appeals of this series for me. I like Murphy so much, I named him after my son-in-law. There are many wonders in our world, but many dangers as well, and I wanted to center this series on a hero who I think is very engaging yet very real, and someone who is up to the task of confronting a rising tide of danger throughout the books.

Murphy is a scholar in both archaeology

and Biblical prophecy, but unlike other scholars, he is also a complete adventurer and risk-taker when he is on the trail of ancient artifacts that can help to further authenticate the truth of the Bible. Murphy is a man of action and a man of faith, a true hero for our times—which is a good thing, because as you will see right from the start of this series, Murphy will begin to confront a profound evil. An evil force he will soon discover has ensnared him in a countdown to what the Bible calls "the time of the end."

I thank you for your interest in my work. Starting with this volume, my hope is that you come to feel as I do that Babylon Rising is a real page-turning series that manages to be both a totally absorbing story and extremely relevant to our times.

Wishing you a great reading experience, I now give you *Babylon Rising*!

BABYLON RISING

ONE

EXACTLY THIRTY-THREE HOURS and forty-seven minutes after he had last been in church, Michael Murphy was hurtling through a terrible dark abyss. Prayer had never seemed more necessary to him than at that moment. In pitch blackness, with the only sound the *whoosh* of his body falling through the air, Murphy had no idea where he was heading.

Except down. Quickly. All six feet three inches of him.

Just a moment ago, Murphy had been standing on the rooftop of what appeared to be an abandoned warehouse on a desolate street in Raleigh, North Carolina. It was an unusual place for him to be on a Monday night during the university semester, when he normally would be preparing for his next day's lecture.

Yet it took only one word to make him drop all normal activities and race to this dank and deserted height. Granted, that word was in Aramaic, one of the many ancient languages Michael Murphy could read with some fluency.

The Aramaic letters had been penned with elaborate style in a bright blue ink that had seeped deeply into a thick, expensive ivory-tinted paper stock that had been wrapped with great care and tied up by a translucent ribbon around a heavy stone.

A stone that came crashing through the lower window of Murphy's campus office late that afternoon.

Whoever threw the stone into his office had disappeared by the time Murphy got to the window. As he unwrapped the paper and translated the single word that appeared there, he first stared, then began to count.

Thirty seconds until his office phone

rang. He knew what voice he would hear at the other end of the line, although he had never seen the face to go with that voice.

"Hello, Methuselah, you old scoundrel."

There was a high cackling laugh in answer, a sound Murphy would recognize anywhere. "Oh, Murphy, you never disappoint me. I take it I've piqued your interest."

"And cost me a replacement window." He looked down again at the single word on the paper. "Is this for real?"

"Murphy, have I ever let you down?"

"Nope. You've tried your weird best to kill me several times, but let me down, never. When and where?"

The cackling now was replaced by a tongue-clucking. "Now, don't rush me, Murphy. My rules. My time. My game. But trust me, this will be the best ever. For me, anyway."

"Then, I assume that, as before, no sane man would take you up on this challenge?"

"Only an eager lad like yourself. But as always, you have my word. You survive, you get what you came for. And trust me, you'll want to survive for this prize."

"I always want to survive, Methuselah. Unlike yourself, to me life is a precious thing."

The old man snorted. "Not so precious that you won't come sniffing like an eager dog after this bone I've just tossed you. But enough chatter. Tonight. Nine-seventeen. Be on the roof of the warehouse at Eighty-three Cutter Place in Raleigh. And take my advice, Murphy boy. If you do come, and I know you will, make the most of these last few hours."

With another cackle, the line went dead.

Murphy shook his head, put down the receiver, and picked up the paper. He double-checked his translation. This time, the name he read set his mind racing even faster than before.

For Michael Murphy, a scholar who could not confine himself to library stacks of dusty, ancient tomes, an archaeologist dedicated to hunting and rescuing artifacts that could authenticate events from the pages of the Bible, this was the name of the prophet who was guaranteed to intrigue him more than any other:

DANIEL

For the rest of the day, Murphy could think of little else besides speculating about his nighttime rendezvous with Methuselah. It had been approximately two years since Murphy had first been contacted by this eccentric figure. Each time, without warning, and without ever showing his face, Methuselah would get a message to Murphy, always a single word in an ancient language that would turn out to be the name of one of the books of the Bible.

This would be followed within a minute by cryptic directions, always to some deserted location, where Methuselah would watch from a secure hiding place and taunt him while Murphy would try to survive some very real, very deadly physical challenge.

The risk of death was very high and very real each time. Methuselah was seemingly as serious about his sadistic games as he was about the scholarship behind his finds. And apparently he had enough money not only to sponsor the acquiring of the artifacts but to indulge his wildest ideas to lure Murphy into the most elaborate death traps. Would he actually allow Murphy to die if it ever came to that? So far, each time Murphy had come extremely close to losing his life, and each time he had no doubt that Methuselah would have let him die.

Yet, despite two broken ribs, a fractured wrist, and too many scars to recall, Murphy had so far somehow managed to muster all of his considerable abilities to stay alive long enough to claim his prize.

And what prizes they had been. Three artifacts Murphy never would have seen in any other way. Each proven with laboratory tests to be genuine, yet Methuselah never uttered a word about his sources. There were lots of issues that plagued Murphy about these mad, whirlwind chases, but each time Murphy went public with the artifacts, no organization, government, or individual collector had come forward to claim they had been stolen.

So, however and from where Methuselah was getting his occasional treasures, they had proven to be just that.

Methuselah remained a complete mystery to Murphy. To say he was eccentric would not begin to explain his actions. The man was clearly a scholar of ancient artifacts, yet Murphy could find no trace of where he came from or how he found these artifacts that any archaeologist would drool for. It was especially mystifying why Methuselah did not keep these treasures for himself, or for a museum, or why he chose his really strange games to give Murphy a chance to claim them.

As a man of high integrity, Murphy believed he could overlook some potential gray areas regarding the source of these artifacts. Some wealthy, connected, but truly mad collector was as close as Murphy could come to an explanation of who Methuselah was. However, there was the troubling religious aspect.

Methuselah was clearly not a religious man. Quite the opposite. A good deal of the pleasure Methuselah seemed to get from these challenges was to taunt Murphy about his faith. So far, Murphy had been up to every challenge, and he had to admit that in addition to getting the artifacts, part of what drove him was the chance to defy Methuselah's nasty verbal insults about Murphy's faith.

Which was hardly a justification for his risking his life, Murphy realized. However, pride, temper, stubbornness were all high on the list of Michael Murphy's imperfections. Probably Murphy's greatest reservations about his Methuselah adventures were a result of his deep religious faith, which made it far more difficult to justify the extreme risk to his life and limb.

Justify the risk not merely to himself, but to his wife, Laura.

So far, his passion for the quest for artifacts had been a real test of Laura's passion for Murphy. It certainly helped his cause that she held a degree in ancient studies herself. However, there were many arguments after the fact, many pledges that he would try to resist the next Methuselah temptation, but Laura knew there would always be another insanely dangerous Methuselah trap. All he had to do was to dangle another artifact before her husband.

It was that understanding that caused Murphy to dash off a quick note to Laura before he left for Raleigh that evening. She was at a conference in Atlanta and would not be home for another night, and Murphy wrote down what little he knew about where he was going. He left the note on the mantel in their living room. Just in case.

Murphy kept a touch light on the accelerator all the way from Preston to Raleigh to make sure he did not get a speeding ticket. That was one risk he could definitely avoid for the night. The address Methuselah had barked at him was for an eight-story building on an empty street in a deserted neighborhood. When he got to the rooftop, Murphy looked for some sign for a next move.

Without warning, the very roof beneath his feet opened, and that was when he found himself dropping through the building.

Free-falling.

In the fleeting seconds after he started his descent, his multitasking mind flashed on how beautiful Laura had looked yesterday afternoon before she left for her plane, he offered up a quick prayer, and he forced himself to focus on his years of martial arts training, specifically on the best position for his body to be in when he finally landed.

Assuming he had to land eventually, it would not be pretty.

He settled on the combination he had come to call Cat's Last Gasp, his own poor interpretation of a Tibetan landing maneuver. He thought of it as the moves a cat in its ninth life would make to land safely. Murphy loosened every muscle, fighting the natural instinct to tense up in anticipation of what was bound to be one fearsome impact.

Instead, he bounced. In the pitch-black space his body hit what felt like a huge net, and Murphy bounced up and down, rapidly making him more disoriented than the falling had.

Feelings that were intensified by a blast of bright light that completely blinded Murphy.

"So good of you to drop in, Murphy."

Methuselah. Though Murphy still could not see, there was no mistaking the cackling laugh that filled the space. Murphy also knew that even if he could see clearly, Methuselah would be well hidden, as he always was.

"You're probably still getting your bearings, eh, Murphy, so you can't appreciate what a great old building this is. They built that chute to go through all the floors so they could drop things from the roof down to the main work floor here. I had my people set this up especially for you, but I took pity on you at the last minute and provided the net. I'm getting soft. Let's hope you're not."

Murphy finally stopped bouncing and rolled himself to the edge of the net. His sight was beginning to normalize, but there did not seem to be much to see inside this building. There were white walls enclosing one giant floor space. The ceiling, if there was one, must have been several stories high, but the combination of gloomy darkness and now the piercing glow from spotlights mounted on the walls made it impossible to be certain.

The netting was strung up at one end of the floor space. It was made of thick rope in a crosshatched pattern. The net had been stretched between four heavy wooden poles that were bolted to the floor and stabilized by heavy bags of what Murphy guessed was sand. At the opposite end of the vast room, what looked like a sliding door of shiny silver corrugated metal stood closed.

Surrounding the floor was a raised work area that was protected by heavy glass. That was where Methuselah must be, Murphy thought, but he could not make out any specific figure up there. His head was clearing and his breathing was starting to normalize.

"That was certainly worth the trip from home, Methuselah. Now, may I claim my prize and get back there?"

"You call that earning your keep, Murphy? That was just my special way to get you inside the tent. Get ready for the real show. Right now."

For the first time, Murphy heard an ominous sound, a low rumble that filled the empty space, but he was not sure what he was hearing. "Aaah, I see, Professor Murphy, by your perked-up ears, that you are ready to meet your match."

Murphy sighed. *So, now it really begins,* he

thought. Then came a second, much more ominous sound. Something crashed against the metal door from the other side. Something that Murphy suddenly realized was about to come shooting out that metal door, heading directly for him. "Say, um, Methuselah, aren't you going to tease me first with a look at your latest artifact? So I at least know what it is that will make you try so hard to kill me."

"Yes, you do know I love to have my sport with you, Murphy. I actually wish you could live to get this one. It's hot stuff. Tell me, what made you so excited about seeing the word 'Daniel' from me today?"

Before Murphy could answer, there was another, even louder banging against the door. Murphy could not help but flinch where he stood and looked anxiously at the rattling metal.

"Up to now you've put into play some amazing artifacts from Biblical times, Methuselah. I don't know how you got them, but I never would have found them on my own. And Daniel, well, you know he was the most important prophet of all. I have studied him for years. Let me at least get a good close look at whatever Daniel artifact you've gotten your hands on."

"No. Enough talk, Murphy. You're about to get a closer look than you'll want. Because tonight you're not going to *study* Daniel, you are going to *be* Daniel."

With a metallic clang, the sliding door at the other end of the room was raised.

A full-grown lion stood roaring in the doorway. Murphy could not help but marvel at the tawny color, the tensile muscles along its flanks, its full mane, and the way the bright floodlights from the walls made the claws practically sparkle.

The lion, however, was wasting no time admiring Murphy. With a roar that echoed from every wall, and a propulsive spring of all four powerful legs, the lion bore down on Murphy as if he were an easy meal for the taking.

On pure instinct, Murphy threw himself to the floor, landing with a jarring thud just to the left of where he had been standing but close enough to smell the full hot blast of foul breath from the lion's mouth.

"Come on, Murphy, don't run. Make a fight of it, be a man."

The lion's claws braked on the wooden floor as its roaring head swept from side to side. Angry flecks of saliva pelted Murphy. After the first landed on his face, Murphy was already moving again, rolling twice and scrambling to his feet. Without stopping, he reached one of the wooden poles of the netting and swung himself back up into the net. The lion was in close pursuit and swiped its front paw within an inch of Murphy's leg. Having missed once, the lion swung the razor claws again without resting, and again just missed. The third swipe ripped Murphy's left sleeve to shreds.

Before he could get raked again, Murphy bounced up from the net. He landed a few feet away, back on the ropes, and without stopping, he bounced up again. The lion swatted at the rope again and again, but looked frustrated and confused by this bouncing prey.

Between the wooden floor, which was slippery to its back claws, and the netting, which was tangling his front claws, the lion writhed and roared in frustration. Murphy kept bouncing as far from the lion as he could get each time because he knew that the moment the lion connected with him, even with a glancing blow, it could be his last moment on earth.

"Murphy, stop playing popcorn and come down and give the pussycat a chance to really play with you."

I'll come down, Murphy thought, *but not the way you're thinking.* He reached into his pocket and pulled out his army knife. He did not wish to intentionally take another creature's life, even though the beast had four paws full of blades to his one. Instead, as the lion clawed and tried to jump up toward him, Murphy stumbled to one of the poles in four bounds. There he slashed the rope holding the netting to the pole.

"Murphy, that's not fair," Methuselah screamed.

"Don't talk to me about fair, you maniac."

Murphy was bounding to the next pole. The lion swung furiously but seemed to be tiring, much like a heavyweight boxer in a middle round. Or maybe that was just wishful thinking, Murphy realized, but the lion definitely looked confused by Murphy's rapid movements.

As the second side of the netting fell away from Murphy's knife, the lion realized too late that he should have moved out from under it. Its two front paws were now hopelessly tangled in the heavy rope. Murphy slid more than jumped to the floor, careful to stay out of range of the lion's claws.

Or so he thought, until an intense pain seared his left shoulder when a back claw struck him as it jerked free from the ropes. Murphy forced himself to run toward one of the two remaining ropes holding the netting, able to run faster on the floor. Best case, he had maybe another ten seconds before the lion pulled himself free of the ropes that had already fallen around him.

The pain in his shoulder told him he would have to lift himself back up with only his right arm, and he was grateful for the hundreds of pull-ups he forced himself to do in the gym each week. He raised himself up and swung around, then bounced again to grab the pole and slashed the third thong just as the lion was twisting away from the heap of ropes it had torn away from its body.

Now with this new batch of netting en-
trapping him, the lion momentarily collapsed on the floor. It roared through
ragged, heaving breaths, still trying to slash
free with its claws. Murphy rolled to the
floor but made sure to stay completely out
of the range of the lion.

"Aw, Murphy, you spoiled everything."
Methuselah was fairly sputtering. "But you
got fight in you, boy. For a useless Bible
teacher, you got moxie, I'll give you that."

Murphy was breathing almost as rapidly
as the lion. He managed to gasp, "How
about giving me my artifact instead?"

"Well, you earned it, I guess. Only it's
not going to be what you think."

Murphy straightened and looked up at
the platform. "What are you trying to pull
here, Methuselah?"

"Shut up and listen. It's right there in
front of you. You just have to grab it."

"Grab what? Where?" Murphy was getting a bad feeling.

"Oh, your body's still prime, Murphy,
but I swear all those digs have turned your
brain to dust. Look at the lion's neck." Sure
enough, Murphy noticed for the first time

that there was a thin leather strip tied around the lion's neck. Attached to the strip was a red tube approximately the size and shape of a very large cigar holder.

"Oh, no, Methuselah. You think I'm going to fight this lion again just to get at that thing around his neck? That's too crazy even by your standards." Murphy paused, sensing his opportunity slipping away. "Besides, what's in the tube?"

Methuselah started his cackling laugh again. "Oh, Murphy, I've put the fever in you good tonight. You can't resist. I know you too well. You'll go back at him; you can't stop yourself. And this time...heh-heh-heh, your curiosity's going to get the cat to kill *you* for sure."

Murphy looked at the knife in his hand and was tempted, but he folded it back and pocketed it.

"Ooh, ever the good Boy Scout, Murphy. Going to make it a fair fight."

Murphy shook his head as he walked over to the pole nearest the downed lion. "No, Methuselah, not exactly fair, but I can live with it. I'd never kill that lion any more than I'd kill you tonight, and Lord knows you've given me more pause for thought than he has. But that won't stop me from taking advantage of him when I get the chance."

He picked up the heavy bag that was weighting down the nearest pole. He needed both arms to hoist it, but his bleeding shoulder made him shout with pain, and he almost dropped the bag on his foot. Instead, he dragged the bag over to where the lion was still tearing at the rope netting that hopelessly tangled his paws.

"This is definitely going to hurt you more than it hurts me," Murphy grunted, and he dropped the heavy bag right on the lion's head. The lion dropped in an unconscious heap.

Murphy watched thc stilled beast take several shallow breaths before he reached slowly for the leather cord that held the red tube to its neck. He held his own breath and yanked the tube free of the lion's mane.

He grasped his prize. It was so light, he feared it was empty. "What gives here, Methuselah? This better be something besides a cigar."

At first, Methuselah did not say anything in response. Then the metal door rolled up. "You won, Murphy, now get out. Enjoy your spoils of this war on your own time. However, I will tell you these three things, because a warrior in victory does deserve some respect. First, like I told you, this one is hot, really hot."

"Hot as in stolen?"

"Never mind how I got it. Like the others I've given you, there's no angry owner going to come hunting you. But there is somebody who will want to come after you once they know you have it. I don't know who they are or why they're so interested, but I cover my tracks very well, as you know, and I've picked up several hints that somebody is desperate to get this, and will stop at nothing—and I mean nothing—to get it."

"But get what? What's in here?"

"That's the second thing. The tube doesn't have the artifact. The tube has the key to finding the artifact. And what the key is and what the artifact is you'll have to figure out for yourself. But I think you're maybe one of a handful of people alive who can figure it out. And I also know that if you do figure it out, it will get you the find of your life. If you live."

"But Daniel, it's got something to do with Daniel?" Murphy was getting exasperated now.

"That's number three, and then that's all I'll say. The connection's not going to be obvious to you, but I swear to you, I'm certain it's the real thing, and it will make you the reigning king of your precious Bible circle. I guarantee it. Now get out."

"Come on, Methuselah, you can't leave me hanging like this. What is it?"

"Can and will, Murphy. Get out. I'm a sore loser and you know it."

Wincing with one last painful look over his wounded shoulder at the lion, Murphy walked toward the door, clutching the tube tightly. "Good-bye, then, you crazy coot. And thank you, I guess."

Just before Murphy was through the doorway, Methuselah growled, "Murphy, don't get overconfident with your Bible-boy heroics. I'm telling you to be careful with this one. If somebody's going to kill you, I want it to be me in one of our little contests."

Murphy looked up at the platform. "Ever the sentimentalist, Methuselah. Thanks for the warning, but so far, the way I'm scoring, it's Christians one, lions zero."

TWO

Babylon, 604 B.C.

THE SCREAM PIERCED the Babylonian night like the howl of a great beast in mortal pain. It rang through the stone corridors and could be heard even beyond the palace walls, in the moonlit market square, in the mazelike alleys where the beggars slept. Even the waterfowl at the edge of the great river squawked in disturbed response to the cries, then burst into flight over the mighty banks upon which the city was built.

The scream was followed by a silence that was, if anything, even more chilling.

Then the thrashing, the writhing, the uncontrolled rolling of eyes that were shedding real tears over the most horrible of dreams. Unearthly surroundings, swirling chaos, images and noises from a realm between wakefulness and sleep.

The ruler of the greatest power on earth was powerless to resist this relentless assault from within his own mind.

A dozen of his elite royal guards, strong men whose powerful legs were pounding the great stone flags, shouted orders back and forth. The light from hastily lit flaming torches illuminated helmeted faces constricted in fear as they raced to confront whatever dire threat they had failed to foresee.

Short swords drawn, the guards poured into the king's bedchamber, eyes frantically searching the flickering shadows for the gleam of an assassin's dagger. The bedchamber shadows revealed no threatening figure, but there was no sense of relief, for each of the guards would rather have faced an assassin than turn his terrified gaze upon the body of the king.

Nebuchadnezzar, ruler of the Babylonian empire, conqueror of the Egyptian army at Carchemish, destroyer of Jerusalem twice in a decade, whose name struck fear into the hardest of hearts, now sat bolt-upright on the great ebony bed, eyes wide, mouth trembling, the skin of his torso a ghostly pale. The royal pillows were soaked with sweat.

"My lord." Arioch, commander of the royal guard, took a step closer, knowing that to approach too near the king's person was to invite death. But he had to be sure. The king's body appeared unmarked, and surely there had been no time for an assassin to make his escape. Had he been poisoned, then? The king's breathing came in ragged gasps, a hand fluttering at his heart. Though stunned, he didn't seem to be in pain. If it had been poison, he would be clutching his belly in agony by now.

Steadying himself, knowing he had to calm his panicking men by example, the captain waited.

"A dream."

The king's voice was a whisper. The usual thunder reduced to a breath of wind.

"A dream, my lord?" The captain's eyes narrowed. This could still be dangerous. Sent by a sorcerer with true knowledge of the black arts, a dream could kill as surely as a blade.

"Forgive me, sire. What manner of dream was this?" The king whirled to face him. "For surely it was most terrible," he added quickly.

The king closed his eyes in thought as if trying to recall a forgotten name or bring the face of a long-dead friend to mind.

"No," he said finally, grimacing in anger. His

voice rose to something approaching its normal timbre as he grasped the earthenware wine jug beside the bed and dashed it to the floor. "I cannot tell. I remember nothing!"

"Speak!" The king gripped the arms of his golden throne, his fingers kneading the elaborately carved lions' heads as he surveyed the men standing before him.

They were a strange sight. Two Chaldeans with shaved heads and hooded eyes, naked except for linen loincloths and the sacred amulets hanging around their necks. A black-skinned Nubian with a cheetah's pelt around his thin shoulders. An Egyptian, whose simple cotton shift was offset by a startling ring of black kohl around his eyes. And a Babylonian, a priest of Marduk himself, bringer of plagues.

"Bring me the best of the sorcerers this day" had been his decree. "Gather them from the four corners of Babylon, for my spirit is anxious. I must know the meaning of my dream."

They stood in a half circle below the king's throne, faces gleaming with the sweat of fear as the king bellowed once more.

"Speak, you dogs, or I promise your worthless

carcasses will be food for jackals before the sun sets."

They had no reason to doubt his words. Since his dream, the king had thought of nothing else. His nights were an agony of sleepless agitation and his days were spent in a fruitless quest to recall the smallest fragment of the vision.

Now it was up to the soothsayers to recall it for him. If they could not, the stiff line of soldiers ranged behind the king's throne, short spears held at the ready, made it clear what the consequences would be.

As the silence stretched on agonizingly, Amukkani, leader of the Chaldean sorcerers, cleared his throat and attempted an ingratiating smile.

"Perhaps my lord has been granted a vision from Kishar himself—a vision only you are worthy of. Perhaps the god has taken away your memory so that you may not tell it to ordinary men."

He bowed low as Nebuchadnezzar fixed the Chaldean with his piercing black eyes. "What is the sense in that, you fool? To give me a vision and then to take it away. If it is meant only for me, then I must know what it is!"

The king fingered the oiled ringlets of his beard and turned to Arioch. "Be sure your spears *have sharp points. These so-called wise men are as slippery as eels."*

The commander of the guard grinned. Like most Babylonians, he feared the power of sorcerers almost as much as demons. It would be good to see them skewered on the end of a spear. Sensing that time was fast running out, the Egyptian gasped theatrically, as if a sudden thought had come to him. "My lord! I see it! My mind is filled with light, as if a thousand torches burned. And there in the midst of the flames is a river of fire, and upon the river—"

"Silence!" the king's voice boomed. "Do you think to trick me? Do you think I am one of the foolish old women who pay you to tell their futures? When someone tells me my dream, I shall know it. And I shall know when some mangy cur pretends to know it. Enough! A bellyful of iron will put an end to your lies!"

He raised a hand, signaling the spearmen to prepare.

"Wait! I beseech you, lord." The second Chaldean had stepped forward, as if in his terror he were about to lay hands on the king. "Spare us and I swear you shall know your dream."

Nebuchadnezzar let his hand drop. He regarded the speaker with an amused smile. "None of you has told me anything except lies and evasions. If I spare you, what will that profit me?"

The Chaldean swallowed, his mouth dry. "We cannot tell you your dream, lord. That is true. But I know of one who can."

The king leaped to his feet and the soothsayers cowered as one. "Who, then? Who is this man?"

"One of the Hebrews, lord," the Chaldean continued. "Brought from Jerusalem." He stood straighter now, half believing that he would live to see another sunrise.

"This Hebrew, he is named Daniel."

THREE

SHANE BARRINGTON WAS a man
who had never known fear. As a kid growing up on the dog-eat-dog streets of
Detroit, he had quickly learned that survival
meant never showing weakness, never letting your opponent know that you were
afraid, no matter how much bigger and
tougher he was.

And the lessons of the streets had served
him just as well in the boardrooms of corporate America. Barrington Communications was now one of the biggest media and
technology giants on the planet, and its success was built as much on Barrington's mer-

ciless destruction of his competitors as on his near-genius ability to manipulate numbers.

Now, as his private Gulfstream IV neared the Scottish coast, he stared out into the icy darkness and felt a chill that went right to the bone. For the first time in his life, Shane Barrington was afraid.

For the hundredth time, his eyes scanned the printout, now crumpled and stained with sweat. For the hundredth time, he read the columns of figures, the little rows of numbers that could spell the end of everything he had worked and schemed and lied for. Little rows of numbers that could destroy him just as surely as a bullet in the brain.

He had already given up trying to figure out how the evidence of Barrington Communications's creative accounting practices had leaked out. Custom-made, state-of-the-art data encryption systems, combined with the threat of dire consequences for anyone who dared to cross him, had kept his secrets safe for twenty years. Surely none of his employees was smart enough—or dumb enough—to betray him. One of his former business rivals, then? A gallery of names and faces presented themselves, but he dismissed them all. One was now a burned-out alcoholic; another had hanged himself in his garage. All of them had been thoroughly broken in one way or another.

So who had sent him the e-mail?

He would find out soon enough. As the first glow of dawn became visible on the horizon, he checked his Rolex and calculated the jet's arrival time in Zurich. A little before his blackmailer had demanded. Just a few more hours and they would be face-to-face. And he would discover just what the price of survival would be.

By the time the Gulfstream had taxied to a halt on an outlying runway near Zurich, Barrington had showered, shaved, and changed into a dark blue suit tailored to perfection to hint at the athletic frame beneath. Surveying himself in the bathroom mirror, he saw a face too hard to be genuinely handsome, thin lips, and severe cheekbones lit by flint-gray eyes still burning with the intensity of youthful ambition.

The softening touches of gray at his temples, he knew, were what saved him from looking like the coldhearted corporate warrior he was.

He had used the last hours to compose himself, drawing deeply from the well of self-belief at his inner core to concentrate his energies. As he stepped down onto the tarmac, he felt focused, alert, like a warrior about to do battle. One thing was certain, he wouldn't go down without a fight.

A gleaming black Mercedes was parked next to the plane. Beside it, a uniformed driver with sallow skin and blank eyes stood at attention in the frigid morning air, opening the rear door as Barrington approached, and wordlessly motioned him inside.

"So, where are we going?" Barrington asked as the Mercedes eased onto a twisting mountain road that seemed headed directly into the clouds. In the rearview mirror he saw only a tight-lipped smile from his driver.

"I asked you a question. And I expect an answer. I *demand* an answer." The icy threat in his voice was unmistakable, but the driver didn't flinch. He held Barrington's gaze for a moment with those blank eyes before turning his attention back to the road as it wound ever upward.

In an instant the rage Barrington had held in check for the last twenty-four hours burst to the surface. He leaned forward and gripped the driver's shoulder as he snarled, "Speak to me now, or I swear to God you'll live to regret it."

The driver smoothly brought the car to a halt in the middle of a hairpin bend that hugged the mountain. Slowly, he turned his face until he was looking directly into Barrington's eyes. He reached for the car's overhead light, flicking it on. Then he opened his mouth to reveal that he had no tongue.

As Barrington slumped back in his seat, his own mouth open in shock, the car accelerated once more, the only sounds the steady purr of its engine and the relentless thumping of his heart.

The castle seemed to grow out of the mountainside like a malevolent gargoyle clinging to a church steeple. Its massive granite walls, topped with spiked turrets, reached into the cloud-laden sky as if embracing the darkness, while a handful of ancient leaded windows emitted a flickering, sickly light.

It was nearly midday by Barrington's watch, but as the sky opened and the rain drummed on the car roof, it seemed like night. And in the gloom ahead of them, the castle seemed like something out of a nightmare.

While Barrington was still trying to adjust to this medieval apparition of rain-blackened towers, the driver was already opening the rear door, holding a large old-fashioned umbrella and beckoning him toward the castle's massive iron entry.

Taking a deep breath and silently telling himself that it was still day, that he was in a modern, civilized country in the twenty-first century—whatever his senses were telling him to the contrary—Barrington followed.

He was hardly surprised when the heavy door folded silently inward and he was ushered into a cavernous hall stretching into the shadows beyond. What startled him was the sudden shaft of light illuminating a section of wall to his left that appeared to be gleaming steel. Was this where he was supposed to go? He turned toward the driver, but the gloom had swallowed him. Barrington was alone, and despite the unearthly chill, he felt a trickle of sweat run down his spine.

Willing himself forward, he walked toward the steel door, which opened at his approach with a gentle hiss. As he stepped into the elevator and the door whispered shut behind him, he came as close as he had ever been to uttering a prayer.

By the time the elevator disgorged him, Barrington felt as if he had sunk into the very bowels of the mountain, and the unearthly silence engendered a moment of breathless panic, as if he had been entombed alive.

The booming voice brought him to his senses.

"Welcome, Mr. Barrington. We're so glad that you could make it. Please be seated."

Stumbling like a zombie, Barrington felt his way through the shadows toward the ornately carved wooden chair to his right. Easing himself gently into it, as if it were an electric chair that would take his life, he raised his head, hoping to lock eyes with his tormentor at last.

Instead, he saw the stark silhouettes of seven people seated at a massive obsidian table that seemed to draw the remaining light out of the chamber.

Illuminated from behind, each figure remained black and two-dimensional, like the moon during a solar eclipse, betraying no features he could discern.

The voice spoke again. It seemed to come from the figure seated in the middle of the seven. It no longer boomed, but beneath the smoothly articulated vowels was a grating harshness that made Barrington think of fingernails scraped down a chalkboard.

"Your presence here indicates that you understand the gravity of your position, Mr. Barrington. There is hope for you, then. But only if you do exactly as we command from this moment on."

Barrington felt light-headed, like a frog mesmerized by a viper, but this was too much.

" 'Command'? I don't know who you

people are—I'm not even sure where I am anymore—but one thing I do know: Nobody *commands* Shane Barrington."

His words echoed in the darkness, and for a moment he wondered if he had scored a victory, altered the balance of power a little. *Okay, let's go on the offensive,* he thought.

Then the laughter started. Softly at first, then gaining momentum until it cascaded through the chamber like a tumbling brook. It was a woman's laughter, and it came from the last figure seated on the left.

"Oh, Mr. Barrington. We knew you had no morals. But we did think you had brains. Don't you understand? You belong to *us* now. Lock, *stock,* and barrel. And we would use the barrel to carry off your soul as well—if you had one."

She was clearly enjoying herself as she paused to let her words sink in. "The information we have about Barrington Communications's business practices over the past two decades would be enough to send you to jail for the rest of your life—if it were all to be made public."

Again, she paused for effect. "That is, if

your angry shareholders, whom you have cheated so thoroughly, did not storm your corporate offices and beat you to a bloody pulp first."

A new voice rang out of the shadows, a voice with deep tone and a distinct British accent. "Make no mistake, Mr. Barrington, our invitation to you was brief by necessity, only the very tip of a massive accumulation of your business transgressions. Like an iceberg, an iceberg of financial wrongs, sir, which could sink you so horribly, it would make the *Titanic* look like a tub toy."

Barrington rose out of his chair, mustering the last shred of his arrogance. "Impossible. You bought off some people to get a little dirt, I can see that, but you could not possibly have more than a few embarrassing manipulations of funds that I can make—"

The British voice cut him short. "Do not take us for fools, Mr. Barrington. We have it all—the capital expenditures that have been listed as profits, the offshore companies set up to look like assets when they really concealed liabilities. Not to mention the threats to your competitors, the intimidation. Why, even in these impressive times of ill-gotten gains, you, sir, have been a Guinness Book–caliber corporate sinner."

So this is it, at last, Barrington thought. *Payback.* He'd always thought he was too smart, too ruthless, for any of his sins to catch up with him. Now, despite himself, the faces of people he had ruined on the way to becoming one of the world's richest and most powerful men began to flash into his mind. The grieving widow of a former business partner he had driven to suicide. The old folks whose pension funds he had decimated to cover his debts.

"So, you're going to turn me in?" Barrington croaked weakly.

A new voice answered. It was a male voice, Hispanic, with a sharp edge like the squawk of a bird of prey. "We did not summon you here to give you a Better Business Award from your chamber of commerce, Señor Barrington, but, no, we have no interest in exposing you to the authorities."

A gleam of understanding flashed in Barrington's eyes. "Oh, I get it. This is all about your getting a *taste* for yourselves."

His mouth snapped shut at the sound of a powerful hand clap, which was all the more startling when Barrington realized it had come from the woman. "Sit down, and stop your jabbering."

Barrington sank back down into the chair.

"A taste? This is no Mafia shakedown. Don't you get it yet? We *own* you, Barrington."

There was a throat-clearing cough, and then the British voice spoke again.

"Now that I see you understand your position, let me offer you an alternative to a life behind bars—short as that life would no doubt be."

Barrington could almost see the sneer on the darkened face. "We have chosen you, Mr. Barrington, because of what you can do for us. How you can help us in our...endeavors. We are prepared to inject a minimum of five billion dollars into Barrington Communications, enough to wipe out the debts you have so cunningly concealed, enough for you to continue to swallow up your remaining competitors.

"Enough to make you...*numero uno* in the business of global communications. Except, of course, that you will be working for *us*. The Seven."

Barrington was suddenly dizzy. He felt like a condemned man who had been counting out the final seconds and then the governor had come through with a re-prieve—*and* a check for billions of dollars. With a smile, he realized he'd do anything—*anything*—that was asked of him.

"Well, I think I'll go with option two," Shane Barrington said, his composure quickly restored as a hot buzz of adrenaline flooded his veins. "Just tell me what it is you want me to do."

Outside, the clouds seemed to embrace the castle walls even more tightly as a biting wind danced around the ramparts. Amid the keening of the elements, the castle lay cold and black and silent.

In the impenetrable silence of the subter-ranean vault, the thud of the castle's iron door as it clanged shut could not be heard. Nor could the Seven hear the subdued roar as the Mercedes began its journey back to the airport. But they knew Barrington was on his way, his mind afire with his new mission, their choice vindicated.

Soft lighting from hidden spotlights restored the Seven from their shadowed specters to a normal human appearance. However, even as they allowed themselves a measure of relaxation in their complete privacy, each of them exuded a fearsome aura. Third from the right, a round-faced man with a silvery mane of thinning hair adjusted his half-moon glasses and turned, smiling, to the man whose booming voice had first broken the silence.

"Well, John. I must offer my apologies. Barrington was indeed an excellent choice. I'm almost surprised he hadn't volunteered for the cause before now. He seems to positively relish his new duties." His lilting English cadences dwindled into a soft chuckle.

Unsmiling, without turning his gaze from the chair where Barrington had moments before been sitting, John Bartholomew spoke, and his tone remained chilling. "The time for self-congratulation lies far ahead of us, I think. Our great project is just beginning, and there is much yet to be done."

"But, John, John! Surely what we have started cannot now be stopped. Is it not written?" continued the Englishman. "I bow to your superior wisdom in the realms of finance. But as a man of the cloth, I think I can claim some special understanding of, let us say, the spiritual dimension. Think of Daniel, think of Nebuchadnezzar's dream. Think of what it means!" In his excitement he gripped Bartholomew's arm. "Surely with the plans of us Seven, the true power of Babylon—the dark power of Babylon—*will* rise again!"

FOUR

MURPHY WASN'T SURE which was worse, the red-hot streaks of pain that criss-crossed his shoulder or the fiery blast of anger his wife was directing at him. At least the anger would burn itself out eventually. He hoped.

"So, Michael"—it was always *Michael* when he was in the doghouse—"tell me why I'm so special."

He grunted as she swabbed his shoulder with antiseptic. A little harder than was strictly necessary, he thought.

"Other wives come home unexpectedly in the early hours of the morning to find their husbands in bed with another woman, or betting the kids' college fund in a poker game, or just plain old dead drunk." She paused to shake out some more of the antiseptic liquid onto a fresh cotton pad. "But *me,* lucky old me, *I* come home to find my husband has been half killed by a *lion*!" She stopped working on his shoulder for a moment and smiled sweetly at him. "Please explain exactly what have I done to be so blessed."

Not for the first time, Murphy said a silent prayer of thanks that he'd managed to find such a wonderful woman, and that miraculously, or so it seemed to him, she had agreed to be his wife. He was taking a verbal beating from her now—and that wasn't a first either—but he knew that was only because she cared. And, as ever, it was well deserved.

It was also providential, to say the least, that she'd arrived home when she did. The last day of her conference on mapping lost cities had been canceled when the star of the show, Professor Delgado from the Mexican Archaeological Institute, was taken ill, and with a mix of disappointment at missing out on the great man's legendary stories and excitement at cutting short the time spent away from Murphy, she had hopped on the first plane out of Atlanta.

"I was hoping to surprise you," she'd said wryly. "But I guess I should have known. I'm the one who gets the surprises around here, right?"

She finished taping the sterile pads in place, and Murphy could see her in the bathroom mirror, nodding at her handiwork, before she helped him ease a clean T-shirt over his head. They both knew he couldn't have fixed himself up alone.

Downstairs she settled him in one of the rockers, then went into the small kitchen. She came back with two steaming mugs of tea.

"Okay, Professor Murphy, it seems you're not going to die of your wounds. Your wonderful, long-suffering wife has therefore calmed down sufficiently to listen to whatever cockamamie nonsense you're about to tell her. So sit there and try not to go off your rocker for the second time tonight and let me hear your sorry story."

Murphy sighed. She wasn't going to like it.

"It was him. Methusaleh. I got a message while I was in my office. Very attention-getting."

"And you just dropped everything and went wherever this madman told you to go?" She rolled her eyes. "Oh, but I was forgetting, you're Michael Murphy, the world-famous archaeological adventurer. No assignment too dangerous. And the crazier the better."

She was just shaking her head. He waited until he was certain she was done. She finally took a sip of tea. The signal for him to go on.

"He said *Daniel*. The Book of Daniel. How could I not be interested?"

"Ah, hence the lion's den. I get it."

"Exactly." Murphy put down his mug on the little coffee table between the rockers and leaned toward her. "One of the most important books of the entire Bible. The mother lode of prophecy. It's all there, Nebuchadnezzar's dream, the statue, everything." In his excitement, the throbbing in his shoulder was forgotten. "Methusaleh was offering me an artifact that related to the Book of Daniel. Such hard evidence would certainly cause skeptics to think twice before dismissing Daniel as mere fiction. Imagine!"

Laura sat back in her rocker, out of reach. "And all you had to do to get it was to go three rounds with a man-eating lion." Her tone was icy.

"Now, sweetheart, it could have been worse," Murphy said with a grin. "If it had been the Book of Revelation, I could have been going head-to-head with the Beast himself."

The look she gave him was icier still. Not funny. Not funny at all.

Murphy tried a different tack. "Honey, the point is, Methusaleh may be crazier than a bucket of snakes, but he always plays by the rules—"

"*His* rules," Laura interrupted. "The rules of a crazy mystery man who has nothing better to do with his money than to lure you into risking your life. And you've fallen for it each time!"

"Yes, because his rules say," Murphy continued, unfazed, "that if I win his game, I get the prize. Look, we've talked this over before, Laura. I know this sounds insane, but it's true. I'm just not a half-measure kind of man. I love my work full tilt, I try to love God full tilt, and above all else, I love you full tilt. It's a package deal, sweetheart, even on nights like this, when you feel the prize package you're stuck with is the booby prize."

Laura frowned in defeat. She'd said her piece. She knew Murphy could no more resist the lure of Methusaleh's artifacts than decide not to breathe. And though she was not about to tell him, Murphy's fearless passion for bringing the truth of the Bible to light was a big part of why she loved him.

She dragged it out for ten more seconds and gave in, reaching around to hug him. "Michael Impossible Murphy," she whispered, calling him by the middle name she had given him several years earlier, "you know too well that the most impossible thing about you is still the fact that I can't stay angry with you for longer than it will take you to get into trouble the next time."

He nodded toward the table. They both

looked down at the red tube as it lay innocently, like an unexploded bomb, between them. "Okay, then, Murphy." She smiled her sweetest smile, and he wondered what was coming as he saw her smile turn into a worried frown. "This bleeding is worse than I thought. That lion got deeper into your shoulder than it looked. I am driving you over to the hospital to get you stitches. No argument."

Though he had rejected her earlier insistence on getting him to the emergency room, now Murphy did not even offer the meekest resistance.

Laura softened again. "Hey," she said, wrapping her hands around Murphy's good shoulder, "since you went to all the trouble of getting this thing, tomorrow, after your lecture, how's about I come to your lab and help you look at what's in there?"

FIVE

"SO, YOU PUT your life on the line every day?"

"That's right, my friend. One slip, and *splat*!"

The bartender, who stood just close enough to his only customers to hear their conversation, shook his head and kept flipping through the newspaper. Here on a slow Tuesday afternoon in this dingy neighborhood bar in Astoria, in the shadow of a not-too-distant Manhattan, he felt a million miles away from the excitement of the big city.

He had been listening to these two guys

rattle on for twenty minutes and with only one beer between them. That was for Farley, the big hero, one of his regulars.

The other man was a stranger. He would have to be, to be talking to Farley this long. Every other regular knew that Farley was a bore who would talk on and on about how risky his job was. The guy was a window washer, not a combat marine! The bartender eyed the stranger again. He would have thought the man must be deaf to listen to Farley drone on, but the stranger was lapping it up. And he wasn't even drinking anything stronger than water.

When the stranger had asked for a water—not even sparkling water—the bartender had started to give him his standard rebuke about this being a bar, not a public drinking fountain, but there was something about the stranger's manner that stopped him. Not because he looked threatening. Farley was a drab-looking, doughy kind of figure, and if anything, this stranger was even plainer-looking—gray-haired, clunky glasses, a thick, pockmarked nose, a pronounced slouch to his stance. However, while Farley was a threat only to bore you to death, there was something about this meek stranger that made the bartender not want to challenge him.

"Hey," he heard the stranger ask, "you want to go get a burger?" Then, showing that he was a quick study, since everyone knew Farley was the cheapest man in all of Astoria, the stranger added, "I'm buying."

As the bartender watched the two men shuffle out of the bar, he knew better than to check to see if Farley had left him a tip, but raised an eyebrow when he saw a five-dollar bill sitting next to the stranger's empty water glass. *Man,* the bartender thought, *I hope I see him again soon.*

He had no way of knowing he would never see either man again.

Outside the bar, the stranger said, "Why don't we take my car? It's just around the corner."

Farley nodded and followed him. "Say, friend, tell me your name again."

"I didn't tell it to you the first time." He

stopped in front of a dark green Jeep, and Farley paused, a puzzled look on his face.

"Hey, that's right. So, what *is* your name?" The stranger gave him no notice, darting his head from left to right to survey the deserted street. Then Farley saw the stranger make some quick movements around his head. "Huh?" Farley looked even more puzzled.

Only then did the stranger turn to look at Farley. But the face that Farley saw before him now was an entirely different one. Gone were the gray wig, the glasses, and the nose. "You'll never need to know it."

Almost too quickly to see, the stranger swept his right hand in front of Farley's throat. A thin line of blood appeared there before Farley could cry out. Now, as he tried to make a sound, nothing came out.

"You'll never need to know anything again." He reached over to grab Farley and threw his limp body into the car. "Now that I know the only things you knew that were worth knowing."

The stranger got behind the wheel. He wiped some blood off his right index finger on the shirt of the dead man beside him. Farley would not mind, he thought. He took out his cell phone and looked at the index finger in the greenish light from the phone panel as he dialed. The finger looked like a normal index finger until you looked more closely and saw that it was an artificial digit, carefully sculpted and tinted to look real. Except for the very tip, where the nail should be, which was honed to a deadly edge.

His call was answered with a single word. "Status."

The stranger replied in a cold, deadpan, accentless voice, quite a change from the hearty tone he had used with Farley. "I am ready to proceed at your order." He straightened in anticipation.

"Go," he was told. "And, Talon, do not fail—and do not fall."

The man known as Talon clicked shut his phone, taking a split second to make sure all of the blood had come off the digit that gave him the name he went by. He pushed Farley down below the car window sight-line and headed for the spot where he would dump the body. A place where it would never be found.

He allowed himself a grim smile. Failure or falling were not options for him any more than breathing would ever again be an option for Mr. Farley.

SIX

THE KING AND the captive of Judah looked each other in the eye, and the king was intrigued to find that the slave held his gaze. True, there were no guards at his side to intimidate the man with their swords and murderous looks. But wasn't his royal presence alone, the majesty and power of Nebuchadnezzar, whose name made kings and princes quake, enough to terrorize a humble Jewish slave?

And yet the man seemed calmness itself as he waited patiently for the king to speak. It was strange indeed. These people had a reputation for cleverness. Yet this man seemed not to understand that his own life would be forfeited if he could not *give the king an answer. An answer the wisest men in the kingdom had so far not been able to provide.*

The king took in the simple woolen robe, the relaxed posture—neither arrogant nor submissive—and the blank, patient gaze, and wondered if this could really be the man to reveal his dream. If he failed like all the others, then one thing was certain: Daniel would be only the first of many to feel his anger. The gutters of Babylon would be awash with blood before his wrath was spent.

The king shifted in his carved cedarwood chair and broke the silence. "Well, Daniel." His pronunciation of the slave's Hebrew name was mocking, as if he had alluded to some shameful secret. "No doubt I do not need to explain why you are here."

"I am here because you commanded it, my king."

Nebuchadnezzar scrutinized him for signs of impudence. His tone was as maddeningly neutral as his expression in the flickering torchlight.

"Indeed, Daniel. And I'm sure in your wisdom you understand why I commanded it. And what it is I would have you do."

Daniel bowed his head slightly. "You have

been troubled by a dream, my king. An awesome dream that stirred your spirit, and yet when you awoke, not a fragment, not a shred of it, remained. Only an empty echo, like the sound of a word in a strange tongue."

Nebuchadnezzar found himself gripping the amulet of Anu he wore around his neck. By the gods, how did this man know his inner thoughts so well?

"Yes, yes, all of Babylonia knows of this. But can you tell me the dream, Daniel? Can you restore it to me?" He realized with alarm that his voice was breaking, his habitual tone of command replaced by the fretful whine of a child.

Daniel closed his eyes and took a deep, slow breath. The moment lengthened and Nebuchadnezzar felt his nerves stretch to their breaking point. At last Daniel opened his eyes, now bright with a new intensity, and spoke.

"The secrets which you have demanded cannot be declared to the king by soothsayers, magicians, astrologers, or sorcerers. Only the God of heaven can reveal such secrets." Daniel silenced his voice as he concentrated deeply.

"Yes, yes, do not stop now," Nebuchadnezzar shouted.

Daniel would not be rushed. Finally, he

looked calmly at the king and spoke slowly and loudly so there would be no mistaking his message.

"The God of heaven, in this dream, has revealed to you, King Nebuchadnezzar, things which are to come in the Latter days."

SEVEN

AS HE WALKED purposefully toward Memorial Lecture Hall B, Michael Murphy looked like an unlikely academic. Sure, he had the slightly ruffled look of someone who cared more about ideas than outward appearances—the tie slightly askew over a creased denim shirt, an old canvas jacket worn at the elbows, and a pair of sneakers that clearly had some serious mileage on them.

But if you looked a little harder, you could tell from his measured, economical stride, the calloused hands, and faint scars that neatly highlighted his handsome features that this was no ivory-tower dweller. This was a man who was happier outdoors than in—and happiest of all when he was dealing with tough physical challenges.

For just a moment, Murphy found himself wishing that he would be suddenly called away to complete such a physical challenge. *Any* physical challenge would do. Usually not a man plagued by lack of confidence, all during his brisk stroll through the Preston University campus in the late August heat, he had been getting ready for an embarrassingly low turnout.

Biblical Archaeology and Prophecy had been a late addition to the curriculum. Murphy's regular lectures drew an enthusiastic audience, but it was a small one. There just weren't that many students in a university like Preston who wanted to devote themselves to the study of the past—let alone the Biblical past. Then, at the end of last semester, some of the wealthy alumni had put pressure on the university president to have more Bible-based courses for the general student body.

Bless them, Murphy thought, although it could turn out to be a mixed blessing indeed. The two most troubling negatives were that he would have a lot of explaining to do to the donors if nobody showed up to take the course, and that Dean Fallworth of the Arts and Science faculty absolutely hated having another Biblical archaeology course.

Murphy tried not to be a vain man despite his growing notoriety for his discovery of Biblical artifacts. So far, he had starred in three cable television specials about his work, which had attracted some corporate funding for the department and some revenue-enhancing exhibits at the university museum.

All of that attention brought on the jealousy and anger of Dean Fallworth. There had been several veiled comments by the dean that struck Murphy as being antireligion, but Dean Fallworth was both direct and vocal when voicing his opinion that what Murphy studied and taught was neither worthy science nor credible history.

This from a man, Murphy had pointed out to Laura last week, whose most recent published scholarly paper had been "Button Materials of the Eighteenth-Century Georgia Plantations."

The positives of getting to teach the new Biblical Archaeology and Prophecy course were that Murphy loved teaching and these additional funds would allow him to wing it with a new course that he had described in his posted syllabus as "Studying the Past, Proving the Bible, and Reading the Signs of the Prophets."

Here for the first time was an opportunity for any student, no matter what their major, to take one of his classes. His plan was to liven things up by incorporating some of the background video that had not made it onto his television specials, and he figured he would also include viewings of some of his most recent finds.

Still, he had been leery about checking the enrollment before this first class. He had hoped for the best, but a nagging voice said, as it sometimes did when he allowed the real world to crowd in on his frequent thoughts about his studies of the ancients, *It's the twenty-first century, does anybody care about Hittites in a hip-hop world?*

"Well, I do," Murphy said out loud, not meaning to. "I'm going to have a great lecture even if it's just me and my slides who show up."

As the excited buzzing from within became audible, he took a breath and strode into the lecture hall. To his amazement, every seat was filled, several students had taken up position against the walls, and some were even squatting on the floor below the lectern.

Murphy clapped his hands and the chattering came to an abrupt halt. "Okay, people, let's get started. We're dealing with thousands of years of history here, and we've got only forty minutes, so there's no time to waste." He scanned the rows of faces and wondered what they were hoping for. What were they expecting? And would he be able to deliver it? Spotting Shari Nelson's bright eyes and eager smile in the first row brought a half-smile to his own lips. At least he had one friend in the audience. If they started to throw things, maybe Shari could calm them down.

"It's great to see so many of you here, so

let me just check that you know what you're letting yourselves in for. This class is called Biblical Archaeology and Prophecy, and according to the prospectus it's the study of the Old and New Testaments with an emphasis on archaeological evidence that supports the historical accuracy and prophetic nature of the Bible. Anybody who just got lost on their way to the seminar The Matrix: Movie or Blueprint for Our Future, now's your chance to sneak back out."

A few snickers, but no one got up to go. Okay, they were still with him.

"So, what does *Biblical archaeology* mean? Well, let me ask you some questions: Did Noah really build an ark and fill it with two of everything?

"Did Moses really part the Red Sea with a wave of his staff?

"Did a man named Jesus really live and breathe and walk around the Holy Land two thousand years ago, teaching and healing and performing miracles?

"How can we truly know any of this for sure?"

A slender hand went up at the back of the

hall. It belonged to a blond girl with long, straight hair and big, round glasses he had seen once or twice in the university chapel.

"Because the Bible tells us," she said in a quiet but confident voice.

"And because Hollywood tells us," another voice interrupted. It belonged to a chunky, dark-haired student with his arms folded across his Preston sweatshirt and a smug smile on his face. "If Charlton Heston believes it, it's got to be true, right?" That got a few laughs, even a little ripple of applause.

Murphy smiled and waited for the students to calm down.

"You know, when I was your age I was a skeptic too. Maybe I still am. Christians are supposed to take the truth of the Bible on faith. But sometimes faith needs a helping hand. And that's where Biblical archaeology comes in."

He pointed to the still-smirking young man in the row just behind Shari. "What would I need to do to prove to you that Noah's Ark existed? What would convince you?"

The student looked thoughtful for a moment. "I guess I'd have to see solid proof, you know?"

Murphy seemed to chew that over. "Solid proof. Sounds about right. Well, let's see, when it comes to scientific research, you have to be willing to go wherever the evidence takes you. In just the last one hundred fifty years, there have been more than *thirty thousand* different archaeological digs that have unearthed evidence supporting the Old Testament portion of the Bible alone.

"For centuries, skeptics scoffed at the idea of there being a Hittite nation, as recorded in the Bible, until archaeological evidence unearthed irrefutable proof of the Hittites' existence. Likewise, the mere mention of the city of Nineveh used to bring laughter and ridicule to the lips of nonbelievers until the entire city was discovered near the Tigris River by the great archaeologist A. H. Layard.

"And yet, to date, *not one piece of evidence has been unearthed that disputes the Bible's authenticity.*"

"Whoa! That's impressive!" someone called out from the back. The student looking for solid proof still was not satisfied. "I'd still want to see, like, Noah's rudder if you want to sell me on the Ark being real."

Murphy smiled. "Well, no one has yet found the rudder of the Ark. But here's something you might find interesting."

Murphy clicked his first slide onto the large screen behind the lectern. It showed a box covered by a sheet. The next slide revealed a pale stone box with an overlapping lid beneath the sheet. About twenty-four inches long, fifteen inches wide, and ten inches deep, it still bore the marks of the primitive tools that had been used to carve it out of a solid block of limestone.

"Anyone know what this is?" Murphy asked.

"How about Fred Flintstone's lunch box," came a now-familiar voice.

Shari turned and gave the speaker a withering glance before offering her own answer. "Is it a sarcophagus? A child's sarcophagus, maybe?"

"Good guess, Shari." Murphy gave her a warm smile. "It's a coffin all right—a bone coffin. What we call an *ossuary*. Thousands of years ago, it was a common practice in some parts of the world that after the flesh of the buried dead had decomposed, the bones were dug up, wrapped in muslin, and placed in one of these."

"So whose bone coffin are we looking at here?" came a voice from the back. "Russell Crowe's, maybe?"

Murphy ignored the laughter. "Well, let's take a look." The next slide was a close-up of the box's side panel showing its worn and faded inscription. "It says here, James—"

"Hey, Jimmy Hoffa, we was wondering where y'all got to!"

Seemingly lost in thought, Murphy didn't hear the comment or the sniggers that followed. He was somewhere else. Somewhere far away in time. He clicked to a greatly enlarged close-up of the ossuary panel and began to read from it.

"James . . . son of Joseph . . ."

A hush had descended on the hall.

". . . *brother of Jesus.*"

He let the silence stretch, then turned back to his audience. "In this little box you see here—which I have actually touched—lay the bones of Jesus' brother.

"Normally, only the name of the father

of the deceased would be inscribed on an ossuary *unless* the deceased had another relative who was extremely well known. And no one was more famous, or infamous, than Jesus in that part of the world during that period.

"What is significant here is that this ossuary not only confirms the historicity of Jesus—that is, that He truly was a real figure in history—but it confirms that He was of such notoriety that the family of James identified his dead brother with him. Once this ossuary is proven to be legitimate, it will prove that Jesus not only lived during this time period, but was a prominent person in His day. Just as He is presented in the Bible."

As he did every time he looked at pictures of this stone box, Murphy was experiencing a strange, disorienting feeling, as if the thousands of years separating him from this long-dead man had been swept aside, as if they were somehow present together in this timeless moment.

His mood was abruptly shattered by a voice from close to Shari.

"Maybe it says that on the box, but how do we know it isn't a fake? You know, like all those saints' relics that used to be churned out in the Middle Ages like cheap souvenirs. Like the Shroud of Turin. That's supposed to be a fake, isn't that right, Professor Murphy?"

Murphy looked intently at the questioner. He seemed to be a skeptic all right, but he seemed more serious, more thoughtful, and better informed than the class joker who'd been hogging the spotlight up to then. He noticed Shari had turned to give him a cool appraisal too.

"You have a good point there..."

"Paul," the student offered, then started to blush, clearly not seeking this much attention in the hall.

"Okay, Paul. Some experts have concluded that the Shroud of Turin probably is a medieval fake. I am not convinced. So, how can we tell the fakes from the real thing? What makes me think that this ossuary really contained the bones of Christ's brother?"

"Carbon dating?" The response was quick and confident.

"Thanks, Paul. Anytime you want to step up and take over the lecture, let me know.

It seems you have all the answers," Murphy said with a smile.

Paul blushed again, and Murphy quickly realized he'd been too tough on him. This guy wasn't trying to give him a hard time, he was just that much sharper than the average student.

"Yes, carbon dating is how we can tell almost to the year when an artifact was made or when it was in use," Murphy continued. "Carbon-fourteen is a radioactive isotope found in all organic objects. Since it decays at a known rate, the amount of C-fourteen remaining in an object can tell us its age."

Paul looked more sheepish now. He clearly didn't relish being in the spotlight. But he couldn't keep his questions to himself either. "Um, Professor Murphy, wouldn't carbon dating just tell us when the original stone was formed, not when the box—the *ossuary*—was carved out of it?"

"You're absolutely right, Paul. But inside the box, embedded in minute cracks, we found bits of muslin and fragments of pollen that carbon date to just after the time of Christ—around A.D. sixty. And not only that, the inscription was written in a form of Aramaic unique to that time. And if you want *more* proof, microscopic examination of the patina that formed on the inscription proves it wasn't added at a later date."

Murphy paused and noted the attentive faces. Nobody having private little conversations at the back. No text messaging on handheld devices. Nobody goofing off. Even if they weren't convinced, at least he seemed to have gotten their attention. Now for the real test.

"All very well and good, ladies and gentlemen, but everything I just told you is a bucket of hogwash. This box is a complete fake."

The class erupted in cries of dismay and confusion. *So much for sedate old archaeology,* Murphy thought.

"Make up your mind, man."

"That's right, this ossuary is a fraud. That's what more than one body of scientists and scholars have said. I, however, have been impressed by both the carbon-fourteen testing, which we will examine in a later class, and by the writing in Aramaic that was limited to the first century. This is a relatively new find, so there will be lots more study and debate over this ossuary in years to come. I raise all this as we get started on the journey of this course for a reason."

Murphy paused. "I'm a scientist, the people who have challenged the authenticity of the ossuary are scientists. I'm very proud to be a serious, practicing, full-tilt, believing Christian as well. I suspect the scientists who are crying fake might be motivated to challenge this very important discovery because it could force them to change their preconceived doubts about Christ. Is my religion clouding my thinking; is their lack of religious belief distorting their judgment? Folks, these are just some of the interesting extra issues that an archaeologist searching for proof of the Bible faces. I look forward to exploring all of this and more with you in the coming weeks."

Just his luck. He noticed Dean Fallworth pacing the back of the hall. How long had he been back there? Murphy wondered. "Now, not to leave you in suspense, let me assure you that the question of whether Jesus of Nazareth was a bona fide person in history does not rest on the authenticity of this ossuary. We will study some of that body of evidence in this course. But when the ossuary is proven to be authentic, as I believe it will be, this will be further evidence for those who do believe in Jesus that He once walked among us."

Murphy checked his watch. "Now, let us go over the course reading list before I ramble us out of time."

"Hold it, Murphy!"

A bony hand grabbed Murphy by his backpack as he left the hall. "Dean Fallworth. What a fine example you set for the students by monitoring my lecture."

"Can it, Professor Murphy." Fallworth was as tall as Murphy but cursed with a library-stack pallor that would make some mummies look healthy by comparison. "You call that a lecture? I call it a disgrace. Why, the only thing separating you from a Sunday tent preacher is the fact that you didn't pass the plate for a collection."

"I will gratefully accept any donation you

wish to make, Dean. Did you need a syllabus, by the way?"

"No, Mr. Murphy, I have everything I need to get the university board to begin accreditation hearings for this evangelical clambake you're calling a class."

"Temper," Murphy mumbled to himself. "Dean, if you feel my work is unprofessional in any way, then please help me to improve my teaching skills, but if you want to bash Christians, I don't have to stand here for that."

"Do you know what they're already calling this silly circus around the campus? Bible for Bubbleheads, Jesus for Jocks, and the Gut from Galilee."

Murphy couldn't help but laugh. "I like that last one. I'm intending this to be a quite intellectually stimulating course, Dean, but I confess I did not post an I.Q. requirement for taking it. The knowledge will be there, I promise you, but I will likely fall short of your apparent requirement that the only acceptable instructional method is to bore your students to an early ossuary."

"Mark my words, Murphy. Your hopes

of this course surviving and your hopes of tenure at this university are as dead as whatever was in that bone box of yours."

"Ossuary, Dean. Ossuary. We're at a university, let's try to use multisyllabic words. If it doesn't turn out to be legitimate, maybe I can get it for you cheap and you can keep your buttons in it. Now, if you'll excuse me, I have a new artifact to begin work on."

EIGHT

CLOSING THE LAB door behind him, Murphy breathed a sigh of relief. This was his inner sanctum, a place where bloated egos and petty academic infighting had no place. The only thing that mattered here was truth. Fittingly, the pristine space was painted pure white. Bathed in halogen light, the room was lined with high-tech lab benches and chromc-plated equipment racks, the only sound the quiet hum of computers and high-tech environmental control systems.

In the middle of the room was a table

specially equipped for photographing arti-facts, with two halogen strobes for shadow-less and colorless lighting and scales for size reference. Perched on a tripod was a state-of-the-art digital camera. Shari Nelson, in a clean white lab coat, was hunched over it, loading a diskette.

"Hi, Shari," said Murphy. "Thank you for clearing your schedule to help me this after-noon. Laura's going to try to get away, but let's get started, because I'm sure she has her office full of huddled masses of youths yearn-ing to complain for free."

"Professor Murphy, sometimes I think you were never young."

"I wasn't. I have an ancient soul. Just ask my mummy."

"Ancient jokes, anyway." She looked up and gave him a radiant smile. "I've been here an hour, getting everything ready. I mean, it's so exciting!" She pointed to the metal tube clutched tightly in his hand. "Is that it?"

He placed it on the table in front of her. "I don't want you to be too disappointed if it turns out to be nothing, Shari. Until we look at it, I really have no idea what it is."

"But you think it could be something big, right? You said so. I mean, I could tell from your message how excited you were."

She was right. At three in the morning, half delirious with pain and exhaustion, Murphy had been convinced he was holding something of monumental importance, and his slightly manic e-mail message to Shari had reflected that. Now, in the cold light of day, doubts were creeping in, along with a throbbing pain in his shoulder.

"I hope it is, Shari. But you remember the first law of Biblical archaeology?"

"I know, I know," she chirped. "Always be prepared to be disappointed."

"Right. Don't let your hopes cloud your objectivity." She knew the drill, but it did not sound as if she had really taken it to heart. He hoped for both their sakes that the tube had more in it than a handful of ancient dust.

Before he and Laura had finally fallen into a fitful sleep, they'd examined the tube minutely, and discovered the almost invisible seam in the middle. It looked like the two halves screwed together precisely to form a perfect seal.

Shari seemed mesmerized as Murphy took the tube in both hands and prepared to unscrew it.

"Wait!" Shari shouted. "Isn't there something we need to do first?"

Murphy looked puzzled. "Oh, you mean X-ray it? Shari, you're a credit to your old professor. You're right, normally we'd want to get some idea of what's in there before we expose it to the air and potential damage. But I'll bet you lunch that what we have here is a papyrus scroll. It's the only thing that could be that small and light and still contain the clues that I was told were in this tube. And if it is papyrus that has survived for a couple of thousand years or so without rotting, that means it's pretty well dried out, which also means as soon as you've taken your photographs—"

"We have to rehydrate it!"

Murphy couldn't help smiling at Shari's enthusiasm. Even though she was still a student, she was probably the most level-headed person he'd ever met. But the prospect of a genuine Biblical find had her bouncing on the balls of her feet like a hyperactive two-year-old. "Exactly. So, you all set? Okay, let's do it."

As Murphy tightened his grip and began to exert pressure on the seal, Shari slid a white plastic tray onto the table beneath his hands. The tray would catch any debris that came loose from the papyrus, fragments that could be used for carbon dating. The background hum of the machines seemed to increase in volume as they concentrated intently on the tube. With a pop the seal gave way. He was pretty sure that Methuselah must have already opened the tube to verify what was in there, but he had somehow sealed it up as perfectly as the original owner had. Now the two halves slid apart, revealing a faded papery scroll. Murphy tipped it gently onto the tray.

"Lunch is on me, I guess, Professor," said Shari breathlessly. "I'd say that was genuine papyrus." She hesitated. "Isn't it?"

Murphy didn't seem to hear her at first. He was leaning close, already trying to decipher the faint marks on the surface of the scroll. Ink? Or just spots of decay? Was that a man-made shape or just a stain? After a moment he grinned and patted her on the shoulder.

"I'll have my usual, please, Shari. Chili cheeseburger with extra pickles."

"And a root beer," she added happily.

They set to work, Shari alternately taking pictures and sucking dust and debris from the tray with a flashlight-sized vacuum, while Murphy scrutinized the scroll from every angle. When she was done, Murphy carried the tray over to what looked like an oversized microwave, complete with windowed door and electronic control panel on the side. He slid the tray inside the hyperbaric chamber, latched the door, and keyed in the settings for humidity and barometric pressure.

With luck, the scroll's ancient fibers would gradually absorb moisture until it was supple enough to be unrolled without disintegrating. If not, then the photographs Shari had just taken would be all they had to unlock its secrets.

Together they gazed through the opaque glass like new parents anxiously watching a baby in an incubator.

"And now," said Murphy, "we wait."

As Shari Nelson left Professor Murphy's lab, Paul Wallach had to quicken his step to catch up with her. He was at risk of losing her as she strode briskly through the maze-like corridors of the history building.

"Excuse me. Can I talk to you for a moment?"

Shari turned, and Paul was surprised to find her smiling at him. With her jet-black hair tied back in a short ponytail, and dark blue jogging pants and sweatshirt, she looked as if she didn't work on the way she looked. But the effect, especially with those sparkling green eyes, was captivating. Paul was suddenly at a loss for words.

"Look, I ... I know you work with Professor Murphy, and I just wanted to apologize for what I said back at the lecture. I didn't want you to think I was trying to be a wise guy or anything."

She tilted her jaw as if she were weighing his words in the balance.

"You raised an important question. Isn't that what they keep telling us we're sup-posed to do here? Ask questions?"

"I guess. It's just that I noticed you

were ... you know." His eyes went to the simple silver cross at her throat.

She frowned and he felt himself blushing. She was being nice, and now he'd offended her. If he was so smart, how come she made him feel so dumb?

"Christians can ask questions, too, you know. So, here's one. Who are you?"

He blushed even deeper. "Paul Wallach. I just switched to Preston this semester."

Shari held out her hand. "Shari Nelson. Nice to meet you, Paul. And I didn't think you were being a jerk, not at all. Actually, when it comes to the really big questions, maybe it's the *atheists* who don't like to ask them." She laughed. "Sorry, I'm sure you didn't come to Preston to be lectured by *me*."

"Well, no, I mean, it's fine, you can ..."

He took a deep breath to compose himself. *Come on, get a grip here.*

"I'd certainly like to ask you some stuff, if that's okay. If you have time. About the lecture and Professor Murphy. I've heard there are some doughnuts in the cafeteria that are in urgent need of carbon dating. What do you say?"

"So what's he like, Professor Murphy?" asked Paul. "He seems like a cool guy."

"For a Biblical archaeologist, you mean?"

Paul and Shari had been chatting for twenty minutes. One ancient-looking doughnut sat uneaten on a paper plate in front of them, alongside two now-empty mugs of coffee, and as far as he could tell, she wasn't getting bored with his company. But she still had this unnerving ability to make him feel like a total bumbler.

"No, I didn't mean that. Really. I meant cool for a professor."

She gave him a smile to show she believed him, or maybe that she'd just been teasing him. Either way, his sigh of relief must have been audible.

"Murphy is cool. And he's the best at what he does. I've learned an awful lot from him."

"You said he lets you work in his lab sometimes, on his finds. Is that right?" Paul asked.

"That's the best. I'm so lucky. Sometimes I can't believe he trusts me not to drop these things—really important historical artifacts, you know?"

She looked at Paul with those green eyes that he now realized could be as intimidating as they were enticing. Maybe she'd told him more than she'd meant to.

"Okay, Paul, that's enough about me and enough about Professor Murphy." She looked him up and down. "You haven't told me a single thing about yourself yet. Hmmm." She put a finger to her chin. "Judging from the pressed slacks and shirt, neat haircut—not to mention those shiny loafers—I'd say you weren't exactly typical of Preston's student body. In fact," she continued in a lower tone, leaning over the table toward him, "I'm not sure you're a student at all."

He winced, choking on a reply, and Shari instantly realized she'd gone too far. She'd been enjoying herself at his expense, and that was wrong.

"Look, I didn't mean—"

"No, you're right," he said, his eyes fixed forlornly on their empty mugs. "I don't really fit around here. I'm not sure *where* I fit in anymore."

"Why do you say that? You must have had some reason for transferring to Preston this year."

Paul was deciding whether he should launch into his story. He really liked Shari, so he did. "Well, you asked for it. I transferred here to Preston from Duke."

Shari was taken aback. "Wow, not a lot of students give up Duke to come here."

"No, and I didn't really do it the easy way. You see, my dad was pretty hard-driving. He never went to college; he built up the family business, a printing business, the hard-knocks, old-fashioned way. He drove away my mom when I was pretty young by working day and night, and pretty much all the time he ever had for me was to tell me how I had to go to college and learn business the 'fancy way,' as he called it. He made enough money so he could send me to boarding school, which is where I got in the habit of dressing up for school, plus there were always servants around our house who really raised me, and they were pretty strict. I went to Duke to study business because that's where my dad always dreamed of going. Then, last winter, my father died of a heart attack—bam!—no warning."

Now Shari instinctively reached across the table for Paul's hand. "Paul, I'm so sorry. That had to be rough."

Paul was trying hard to concentrate on talking and not on how nice it felt to have his hand touched by Shari. "You know, I never really knew my father much, so as lousy as it sounds, I didn't really miss him when he died. The rough part came when the accountants and attorneys started going over his business and discovered that he had been drowning in debt. I took a leave from Duke to try to help sort things out, but it was hopeless. By selling the business and our house at a fire sale, I could pay off the debt, but I couldn't afford to go back to Duke even if I wanted to. I liked the area, though, and I realized it's as close to a home base as I have now, and I thought I could afford Preston. Or at least I will if I can get a job."

"And why did you register for business administration courses here if you hated them at Duke?"

"All those years of having it drummed

into my head by my dad, it's still what seems like my destiny. I want to finish college, I'm trying hard not to just fall apart, and business is as close to a plan as I ever had. I did promise myself I would try to audit a few other courses just to try them out, and Professor Murphy's seemed interesting."

Shari smiled. "I know. I felt the same way. I certainly never dreamed about being an archaeologist."

Paul looked again, inadvertently, at the cross around her neck. "Well, you at least had some religious background. I don't even have that. Religion was on the long list of things my dad never had time—or use—for."

"Neither did my parents while they were alive, but the great thing about our church is, you can start anytime."

"I guess so. But first I think I'll worry about my business major. I feel like an athlete who's been training, then doesn't get to go to the Olympics. It's all my dad had me concentrate on, but I really hate it."

Shari looked at her watch. "I have to run to my next class, but I bet that being pretty new to campus, you could use a home-cooked meal. Why don't you come over for dinner one night this week and we can talk some more?"

Paul did not hesitate. "You don't have to ask me twice."

NINE

UNLIKE SO MANY big-city high-rise luxury-apartment dwellers who pay a kingly fortune for a terrace but seldom take the time to go out to admire the view, Shane Barrington made a point each morning of studying the dazzling urban skyline that surrounded his penthouse. Much like the lords of the manors of old, Barrington felt that he would one day own everything in his sight.

Most mornings, Barrington was lost in his own plans for short-term and long-term business conquests and was left undistracted by any street noises from sixty-two stories below. On this particular morning, he was disturbed from his scheming by a repetitive sound that he could not place at first. It sounded as if something were being pumped.

As a shadow momentarily fell across the front of the terrace wall, Barrington turned to see what was coming up behind him, which led to the surprising sight of a large peregrine falcon swooping out of the sky and landing not more than five feet from him on a wrought-iron table on the penthouse deck.

The bird was majestic and haughty in its bearing, much like Barrington himself. The two predatory beings eyed each other with a chilling respect.

Barrington's stare broke away first as he became aware of something in the forward claw of the falcon. He realized the bird was clutching a pair of very compact, ultrasophisticated-looking binoculars. Now, having noticed that the binoculars had registered with Barrington, the bird dropped them and they clattered lightly onto the table. Barrington waited until the falcon stirred its wings again and flew away over the rooftops before he reached over and picked up the binoculars.

As the falcon slowly began to soar majestically into the sky just above his head, Barrington was further surprised to see a small banner unfurl from the bird's other claw. Barrington quickly trained the binoculars on the cloth to read the words that were written there:

ENDICOTT ARMS 14th FLOOR
12 MINUTES

Curious now, Barrington sought out the Endicott Arms apartment building diagonally across from his own building and counted up fourteen stories from the street, then put the binoculars to his eyes. The meticulously crafted lenses chipped but did not crack when Barrington dropped the binoculars, so shocked was he by what he saw through those lenses.

For through the windows on the fourteenth floor of the Endicott Arms was a face he instantly recognized. It was not exactly the face of an acquaintance he saw regularly;

in fact, he had not seen the individual for some three years. But the face bore many similarities to a face Barrington had seen as recently as that very morning, and every morning of his life—his own.

There through the binoculars, Barrington stared at the face of his twenty-five-year-old son, Arthur. The only offspring of his short-lived marriage, the son had grown to be a good-looking, younger version of his father. Barrington had had little interest beyond child support and perfunctory holiday visits through most of Arthur's childhood, especially once his ex-wife moved to California with her new husband.

Barrington did have his secretaries keep tabs on both his ex-wife and Arthur over the years as a defense against their coming to him for financial support. So he was not surprised when Arthur was thrown out of his fourth art school and relocated to downtown Manhattan with every intention of having his wealthy father set him up as a sculptor.

The elder Barrington was therefore prepared when his son showed up in his office with purple hair, ripped leather pants, and a pierced tongue to demand money to open a sculpture gallery. Arthur Barrington got a one-minute-thirty-second angry lecture from his father about there being no money forthcoming for "a loser freak freeloader," and those were the last words that had passed between them as security guards hustled him from the offices of Barrington Communications.

Now Barrington was able to recognize his son instantly through the binoculars, but his son could not see him from across the street and many floors below. However, his head was turned in Barrington's direction. He was held forcibly to face his father, by a figure standing next to him in the window.

That figure was clearly squeezing the young man's head very hard with one gloved hand, while the other gloved hand held a very long, very menacing knife blade to the young man's throat. The final image that registered with the elder Barrington before the binoculars slipped from his shocked hands and crashed to the deck was the handwritten sign hanging around his son's neck:

FATHER, YOU HAVE
11 MINUTES, 30 SECONDS
TO GET OVER HERE TO APT. 14C
OR THIS MAN WILL
KILL ME

"Are you people homicidal maniacs?" Shane Barrington was screaming with what breath he could muster after his race out of his penthouse and across Park Avenue to the fourteenth floor of the Endicott Arms, as instructed. It had taken him only eight minutes to arrive, and in just the three minutes since, his world was once again collapsing in on him, much as it had in the castle in Switzerland.

The Seven.

He was yelling at the man who had been holding the knife to his son's throat just minutes before. The knife was no longer in sight, but Arthur Barrington was now stretched out on a bed, seemingly unconscious, his face attached to a breathing mask which in turn was hooked to a rather complicated machine that was lit up and beeping.

"Mr. Barrington, I'm honored that you accepted my invitation. But no warm welcome for your long-lost son?" The man's voice seemed to have a hint of a South African accent, but there was no trace of human emotion in it.

"Who are you and what are you doing with Arthur?"

"I am the man the Seven told you would be contacting you, Mr. Barrington. I don't believe they mentioned my name, however. I go by many different identities, as my work requires, but you can call me what the Seven call me: Talon."

Barrington's anger, and now fear, would not subside. "Talon? What kind of name is that, a first name or a last name?"

"It makes no difference. I use it because it is a tribute to the one serious wound I have ever gotten in my life as a warrior. The first falcon I raised and trained as a boy in South Africa, the last thing I allowed myself to grow attached to, turned on me one day and ripped my index finger right out of my hand."

He removed the glove from his right hand, and it took a moment for Barrington to realize what he was being shown. At initial glance, Talon's hand looked perfectly normal, but he noted that the index finger had been replaced by some kind of hard flesh-colored material shaped to look like a finger, except where the fingertip should have a nail, the whole tip was honed to what was certain to be a deadly sharp point. "I killed the falcon, and carry this to remind me of what happens when you get soft or careless. And it comes in very handy in situations where a weapon is not convenient. Which, you can appreciate, being a man of the world, happens more often now that we live in such nervous-making times."

"So, am I to believe that the Seven want me taking orders from you?"

"Correct, Mr. Barrington."

"But what does my son have to do with any of this? I haven't seen him in years."

"Three years and two months, to be exact. He's just a little exercise we need to go through, to satisfy the Seven and to convince me that you are truly ready to do what will be asked of you. No matter what. So although you are not the picture-postcard family, I figure you must have some baseline feelings for him, even if it's just as one human being to another."

"Feelings for him in what way? What have you done to Arthur?"

"It's a little late for fatherly concern now, isn't it, Barrington? But actually, that's a reasonably convincing act. And I say that as one heartless man to another." Talon moved to the plastic tubing attached to the breathing mask covering Arthur Barrington's face.

"I don't get it. Why is he lying there unconscious? Is he sick? Did you do something to him?" In spite of himself, there was desperation in Barrington's voice.

Talon gripped the plastic tubing in his right hand. "You see, Barrington, I'm going to be giving you your marching orders for occasional, very specific actions the Seven will need you to undertake. Some may be illegal, some may be unpleasant, all of them will come when I decide to give them to you directly, and you will act upon them instantly, without asking for explanation, without making excuses, and without fail."

"I know. I already agreed to all that in that castle in Switzerland."

Talon's eyes cut right through Barrington as sharply as his index finger now cut into the tubing, causing a sudden hiss of air to shoot out. The bedside machine started bleating a high-pitched alarm, and four different red lights flashed urgently. "Yes, it's easy to pay lip service to your pledge when there is nothing immediately at stake, Barrington. But show me you have what it really takes."

"Got what it takes for what? What's happening to my son?"

"Don't pretend some great sudden love for this kid. Granted, he's a life, but he's not much of a life. No real friends, no purpose, nobody will miss him when he's dead."

"Dead? What are you talking about? Why should he die?"

"Because I say so. Right here, right now. That's our test. It's completely arbitrary, senseless, brutal. Just like many things the Seven will make you do. That I will make you do. Things you will either do—or you will die."

Barrington lunged toward Talon. "Why, you're—" Talon grabbed his arm, stopping him instantly.

"Don't even think about it, Barrington. Not for one second. Oh, I'm not completely heartless. If you tell me to save your boy, I will." With his index finger he covered the spouting airhole cut into the tubing. The hissing stopped immediately; the alarms ceased. After a few seconds, he lifted his finger and the air shot out and the alarms restarted. "Yes, I will stop for a few seconds. Just long enough for me to slash *your* throat." He held up his razor-sharp finger just an inch from Barrington's eye. "Then I'll kill the boy."

Barrington collapsed on the bedroom floor but could not stop his eyes from moving from his son to Talon. After two minutes, the machine emitted a long, continuous beep and the graph on its monitor flatlined.

"Congratulations, Mr. Barrington. The Seven would be proud of you. I'm proud of you. You did the right thing when it counted. Now, just keep doing the right thing every time I contact you and you will be successful and powerful beyond even your wildest dreams." He threw a sheet of paper down at Barrington. "Here are your first instructions. Some information I need."

"What will happen to my son?"

"I assumed you wouldn't feel some be-lated familial tugging of your heartstrings to bury him in the family plot, so I will take care of disposing of him and no one will ever know. Actually, that's only partly true. People will actually know quite a bit about Arthur Barrington and his death. There is, as always, a plan. You do not have to know the next parts of the plan for now. That will all be revealed to you when I am ready. For now, just get that information. Show your-self out."

TEN

LAURA MURPHY WATCHED the young man with the shaved head and the baggy jeans loping down the hallway, and shook her head, smiling. She remembered enough about her own student days to feel a rush of sympathy whenever a student turned up at her door with red eyes and chewed nails, looking as if they hadn't slept or eaten for a week, and while today's young men and women seemed to find it harder than her generation had adjusting to the big, bad world, she didn't judge them harshly.

Negotiating that tricky no-man's-land

between childhood and adulthood had never been easy, and there were certainly more temptations and distractions nowadays for them to deal with. When you considered all the disturbing images and messages being pumped out daily on TV and in the music they listened to, she sometimes felt it was a wonder any of them turned out as well as they did.

Even if their taste in clothes was still occasionally beyond her.

And if she could play a small part in helping their transition to adulthood, she was more than happy. She had been the university's student counselor for two years now. While some people close to her—notably her father—had berated her for throwing away a potentially glittering career as a field archaeologist just so she could listen to some acned teenagers "whining about their grades," she had no regrets. She knew few professional triumphs that could match the sense of achievement she felt when a formerly suicidal English major she had helped was able to get a book of her poetry published and then start her own creative writing seminars, helping others channel their inner emotional turmoil into something positive.

Besides, Laura was still able to find time to work on her own book on lost cities. It might not hit the best-seller lists or spawn a hit movie, but when she proudly handed a copy to her dad, she would at least have created an archaeology artifact of sorts of her very own.

She also shared fully in her husband's work, not just acting as an unpaid diplomat in his frequent brushes with authority, but adding her considerable expertise to his in the quest to search out and authenticate Biblical artifacts.

Which, she realized with a keen shiver of anticipation, was what she was supposed to be doing just then. She had missed Murphy's day-after initial scroll investigation because of a typically jammed office of students, but now it was time to see if the rehydrated scroll was ready to reveal some wonderful secret about Daniel.

She closed her office door behind her, adjusted the sign that read I KNOW I SAID MY DOOR IS ALWAYS OPEN—BUT I'LL BE BACK SOON, I PROMISE! and walked briskly down the corridor and out of the building. After a few minutes, she arrived at Murphy's door, knocked smartly, and walked in.

Murphy was seated at a workbench, denim sleeves rolled up, hair awry, peering at something through a magnifying lens, and seemingly lost in thought. *That's the Murphy I think I like best,* she thought with a smile, *the so-absorbed-in-his-work-he-wouldn't-notice-the-building-is-on-fire Murphy.* The Murphy who had called her with such buzzing excitement a few minutes before to shout that the scroll was ready.

She gave his hand a squeeze, said hello to Shari, and turned her attention to the hyperbaric chamber. "So, you think the scroll's properly rehydrated?"

"I reckon it's as plump and juicy as one of your mother's Thanksgiving turkeys," Murphy declared. "Actually," he added, "it may even be slightly juicier."

"I know, I know, and probably tastes better," said Laura, rolling her eyes.

Murphy put on a pair of white cotton gloves, opened the door to the chamber, and carefully removed the scroll. "Let's see what we have baked," he said quietly.

Gently he began unrolling the papyrus over a plastic tray. Laura held her breath, amazed at the steadiness of his hands, considering he was holding something that had been made in the reign of Nebuchadnezzar, the time of Daniel. *Right now,* she thought, *in this room, we three living, breathing people are linked to the Biblical past through this impossibly fragile object that could crumble to dust at any minute.*

But the ancient papyrus didn't crumble. Like a butterfly emerging from a chrysalis, it slowly unfurled, intact and beautiful.

"Will you look at that," said Murphy as line after line of ancient cuneiform appeared. Solid triangles with linear tails, and V shapes like birds against the sky, crammed together in narrow columns. Fully unrolled, the sheet of papyrus measured about nine inches by fifteen. It was scarred by long creases across its tobacco-brown surface, the edges were tattered, and much of the surface had flaked away. But more of the lettering remained than Murphy had dared to hope.

"I'd say that was Chaldean."

Laura couldn't bear to look away from

the strange geometrical symbols, in case they faded to nothing in front of her eyes. "That makes sense. In Nebuchadnezzar's day, half the priests and sorcerers in Babylon were Chaldean. Can you read it?"

Murphy tilted the scroll slightly to get a better angle. "Well, I'm not exactly fluent. I can order a salad or ask directions to the post office, but anything more complicated than that..."

Laura gripped his arm. "Be serious. I've seen you doodling in Chaldean. What does it say?"

"Well, that's the funny thing." Murphy squinted intently at the letters. "I can definitely make out the symbol for 'bronze,' and here"—he pointed to a barely legible smudge—"is the symbol for 'serpent.' And look, there they are again, with the symbol for 'the Israelites.' "

They were silent for a moment, and Shari watched as it seemed both Murphys' minds were racing to make sense of the images before them. "What does it all mean?" she asked.

"The Brazen Serpent," whispered Laura.

"Exactly," said Murphy. "Made by Moses thirty-five hundred years ago..."

"And broken into three pieces by King Hezekiah in seven fourteen B.C."

"But, ladies, this doesn't make any sense. Methuselah said this prize was an artifact that had to do with Daniel. He lived in the time of King Nebuchadnezzar—which was almost a hundred fifty years after the time of King Hezekiah."

Murphy pushed his chair back and started pacing. "It doesn't make sense. What would a Chaldean scribe be doing writing about the Brazen Serpent? And what's the connection to Daniel?"

Laura peered at the scroll to see if she could make out any more details. "Any chance of asking the crazy person who gave it to you?"

"*Gave* it to me?"

"You know what I mean."

Murphy shook his head. "Methusaleh likes me to figure things out for myself. That's part of the game." He snapped his fingers. "But there's no reason I can't ask for a little help. Come on, let's take some photographs. I know someone who practically speaks Chaldean in her sleep."

Laura folded her arms and gave him a stern look.

"Not," he added quickly, "that I know from personal experience. In fact, I've never even met her."

"Relax, Murphy. I know you love only me—and anything that's been lying in the ground for two thousand years. Who is this oracle?"

"You're not going to believe me, but her name," said Murphy, pronouncing each syllable carefully as if he were ordering an exotic bottle of wine in a fancy restaurant, "is Isis Proserpina McDonald."

ELEVEN

THE PARCHMENTS OF Freedom Foundation was one of hundreds of private organizations headquartered within the very official-looking stone buildings in Washington, D.C., that many citizens automatically assumed must be government offices. The plaque on the door of the office on the second floor of the PFF building read simply DR. I. P. MCDONALD and only initiates would have known that behind the door was one of the smartest living experts on the subject of ancient cultures.

Nor would anyone passing by this office make the connection between the study of dusty, forgotten civilizations and the very loud, persistent commotion coming from behind the closed door.

The noise of books thudding to the floor one by one was followed by the gentler swish of cascading paper, then a crash as a heavy object (a lamp? a paperweight?) connected with something solid. It was lucky for the perpetrator of the chaos that few people ever did pass down this particular corridor.

The small, windowless office was lined with bookshelves on three sides, but many of the volumes—some irreplaceable, almost all of them rare or at the very least out of print—now lay in a sprawling heap on the faded brown institutional carpet. Standing in the middle of the carnage, a petite, lithe figure was scanning documents from a large pile on an antique rolltop desk and furiously tossing them aside.

"It must be here. It *must* be," rasped a voice as a tottering column of academic journals was heaved onto the floor. Now the desk's drawers were exposed and these were systematically rifled, but judging by the hiss of anger that accompanied the search, the desired object was not inside.

The figure stopped suddenly, head cocked toward the door. Footsteps. High heels tapping their way down the corridor. In the office all was still. The footsteps continued, coming nearer. Then stopped. A pause. Then a knock, soft, tentative. Then another, louder, more insistent.

"Dr. McDonald? Do you need any assistance?"

The prim young woman in the neat navy blue suit hesitated. Sometimes when Dr. McDonald didn't answer, she was simply concentrating so hard on a manuscript that she literally didn't hear you knocking, and woe betide you if you marched in without being invited. One thing she'd learned early on was that Dr. McDonald didn't take kindly to being interrupted in her work. It was a little like sleepwalkers, she thought to herself—if you woke them up, they could get terribly confused, violent even. Best to leave them well alone until they found their own way back to the land of the living.

But this was different. She'd distinctly

heard several loud crashes as she turned the corner, and as she neared the door there was no doubt in her mind that someone was trashing Dr. McDonald's office.

Fiona Carter wasn't brave. The thought of any sort of physical violence made her nauseated with fear. But if there was one thing she feared more than a confrontation with a determined burglar, it was trying to explain to Dr. McDonald why she had allowed someone to decimate her precious library.

Her hand shook as she slowly turned the knob and pushed the door.

It swung open gently, revealing a slim female figure in a tweed skirt and a shapeless fisherman's sweater standing ankle-deep in tattered journals and manuscript pages, a few of which stirred briefly in the sudden draft. The figure glared at her.

"Dr. McDonald!" Fiona took a step forward and almost tripped over a hefty black volume. "Are you all right? I heard such a noise—I thought there was an intruder. I thought someone was—"

"I can't find the blasted poem of Charybdis! I was looking at it only yesterday, and now it's disappeared. Fiona, have you been interfering with my manuscripts again?"

Fiona stifled a nervous laugh. How could anybody, however ill intentioned, make Dr. McDonald's office any more chaotic than it already was?

"The poem of Charybdis? Is it possible you were consulting Merton's *Early Coptic Literature* while you were reading it?"

Dr. McDonald looked dubious. "Possibly. I suppose."

"In which case perhaps you put the poem inside the book for safekeeping?" If she remembered correctly, *Early Coptic Literature* was bound in dark green cloth with red lettering on the spine. It wasn't in its usual place on the shelf against the far wall. Very little was. She looked down at the book-strewn floor.

"Is that it? Over there, next to Eliade's *The Sacred and the Profane*?"

Dr. McDonald turned in the direction Fiona was pointing and scooped up a fat green book. She riffled nimbly through its pages and a single sheaf of parchment fluttered to the floor. The poem of Charybdis.

Dr. McDonald turned back to Fiona, beaming. With her matronly clothes and permanently severe expression, it was easy to miss the fact that Isis Proserpina McDonald was a stunningly beautiful woman. It was only her rare smiles that gave it away. Not that you were likely to see her smile if you called her by her given name.

"Clever girl. How on earth do you put up with me?"

Before Fiona could frame an appropriate answer, they were both frozen in place by a sudden ringing. Turning instinctively to the empty desk, they then scanned the floor, trying to pinpoint where the sound was coming from. Fiona pushed back a pile of journals and picked up the phone.

"Hello, Dr. McDonald's office, Fiona speaking. Oh, good morning, Professor Murphy." She turned back to Dr. McDonald, who was still standing amid the rubble of her library, furiously shaking her head and mouthing *no*.

"No, she's not busy at all, Professor Murphy. I'm sure she'd love to speak with you." Fiona smiled sweetly and held out the phone.

Isis sat at her desk, arms folded, lips pursed, and waited for her computer to register an incoming e-mail. While she had been standing in the wreckage of her office, listening to Professor Murphy and his rather wild story about a Babylonian scroll, she had hardly noticed as Fiona began the laborious task of restoring order. Now almost everything was, if not in its place, then at least off the floor and in neat-looking rows and piles. She'd even done her best to rearrange Isis's collection of ancient pottery figures—her goddesses—in the correct chronological sequence on the top of her one filing cabinet.

As Isis's eye traveled over the dear, familiar forms, beginning with a bloated fertility goddess from the Neander valley in Germany and ending with a graceful Sumerian moon deity, she felt a tear welling up and quickly blinked it back. The little figures were a precious legacy from her father, another Dr. McDonald and one of the most eminent archaeologists of his day, the result of a lifetime's digging around the Mediterranean and Near East.

"For my own little goddess, worshiped

and adored above all others," he'd said when he'd presented her with the big, square cardboard box done up with ribbons. To her thirteen-year-old eyes, the little figures, some missing an arm or a little hand, all grooved and pocked with the dirt and dust of civilizations long disappeared, were better than any Barbie doll. The gift marked the beginning of her own passionate commitment to the secrets of the past.

Unfortunately the goddesses were not the only legacies of his obsession that her father had passed on to her. There was also her name.

She supposed there were girls called Freya who had never been teased at school. She knew a Greek paleontologist called Aphrodite who didn't seem in the least self-conscious about it. And wasn't there that tennis player called Venus? No one gave her a hard time because she was named after the Roman goddess of love. But *Isis Proserpina* was a different matter. It was like being born with a circle of stars around your head. Or writhing snakes instead of hair. It made it rather hard to blend in.

At the little Highland school it had been

Issy or *Posy,* both of which she loathed. Why couldn't she be a Mary, Kate, or Janet like the other girls? In the museum, in the haven of her office, at least she was able to insist on *Dr. McDonald.* But with friends it was a little trickier. Which was perhaps one reason, she supposed, she didn't really seem to have any.

She drummed her fingers—narrow, elegant, with nails bitten down to the quick—on the desk, impatient for the promised pictures of the scroll. A watched kettle and all that. She frowned.

Professor Michael Murphy had seemed something of an oddball. Very concerned with Biblical prophecies. Babbling on about the Book of Daniel. But the scroll did sound intriguing. Could be a forgery, of course, or just turn out to be something rather mundane—a three-thousand-year-old shopping list or a form for a hyena permit. God knows, those Babylonians could be a bureaucratic lot.

Over the years, as her reputation as a philologist had grown, the trickle of ancient enigmas in need of her language skills had become a steady stream. If you dug up a shard of pottery with a puzzling inscription or discovered a scrap of papyrus covered in a meaningless scrawl, eventually you would turn to Isis McDonald. And nine times out of ten, even if it took her six months and she nearly drove herself to distraction in the process, she would solve the riddle, crack the code, or unravel the linguistic knot that had had the rest of the experts stumped. It was her unique gift.

Her father, happily watching her career begin to bloom as his faded, had speculated that it was a matter of memory rather than expertise. Surely only someone who had been an Egyptian priestess in a previous existence could have such a facility with their sacred hieroglyphics. Ridiculous, of course. But it was the sort of silly thing he said toward the end. Probably just his funny archaeologist's way of saying how much he loved her.

She blinked the memory away as the screen began to fill with images of the scroll, and she turned with relief from the troubling world of emotion to the much more straightforward one of ancient Babylonia.

What she saw instantly got her attention.

And kept her staring at the screen and scribbling furious notes for the next two hours.

He was jolted back into the present by the phone.

"Professor Murphy? Dr. McDonald. I've been reading your scroll."

He gently put the Bible aside. "Good to hear from you. And please, the name's Michael. Though most people make do with Murphy."

There was an awkward pause.

"Well, Mr. Murphy, it seems you were right. We're definitely dealing with the Biblical Brazen Serpent—"

"But the scroll dates from a period a hundred fifty years *after* the Serpent was destroyed." He could sense her frowning at his impatience. "I'm sorry. This thing has got me wound a little tight. Please go on."

"Well, the scroll appears to be a sort of diary written by a Chaldean priest named Dakkuri. As far as I can make out, the Serpent was indeed broken into three pieces, as in the Biblical account, but someone apparently forgot to put the pieces out with the trash. The pieces must have been stored in the Temple, and when the Babylonians came to sack Jerusalem, they found them somewhere in the Temple and obviously thought they were worth taking back home."

"And when the pieces got to Babylon, this priest, Dakkuri, put the pieces of the Brazen Serpent back together?"

"I think so, yes. But that was just the beginning. I think Dakkuri believed this Serpent had far greater value than as a handsome bronze sculpture."

Murphy's mind was racing ahead. "So, what you're saying is that the Babylonians heard the stories in Jerusalem about the Serpent's healing powers when Moses first made it and they felt it was worth letting Dakkuri see if he could get it working again."

Isis was not pleased with Murphy's interruptions, and she realized she would have to be just as pushy if she was ever going to get through her piece. "Actually, Professor Murphy, my point is that I think Dakkuri tried to use the Serpent as part of a cult."

"You mean Dakkuri had his Babylonians

worshiping the Serpent just like the Israelites in the time of Hezekiah?"

"Not many of them. The scroll seems to indicate that there was some kind of priestly inner circle led by Dakkuri that surrounds the lines of power that are drawn from the Serpent symbol."

"And then doesn't it look like the Serpent-worship turned out to be a big mistake for the Babylonians, as it did for the Israelites back with Hezekiah?"

"Well, there is some reference to trouble with the Serpent, but there's some damage to the scroll at a crucial point." Isis made it sound as if this were due to carelessness on Murphy's part.

He let it pass. "It looks like that trouble, as you call it, was big trouble. The king symbol is there, which could mean that Dakkuri's cult of the Serpent was banned by Nebuchadnezzar himself, right?"

"Yes, I'm sure you don't need me to teach you your Bible, Mr. Murphy," Isis said smugly. "According to the Book of Daniel, Nebuchadnezzar built a great statue with a golden head, a likeness of the one in his famous dream. And all the princes from far and wide were ordered to bow down and worship it at certain times. When they heard the sound of the cornet, the flute, the harp—let me see, what else?"

"Sackbut, psaltery, and dulcimer," said Murphy without hesitation.

"Thank you. Yes, *psaltery* and *dulcimer*— how poetic the King James can be. Takes me right back to Sunday mornings in our little kirk in Scotland." The memory seemed to derail her for a moment, but she quickly got back on track. "Anyway, the long and the short of it was, God made the king mad as a March hare as a punishment for his arrogance, and when he finally re- gained his sanity, Nebuchadnezzar got the message that idol-worship was evil. So he banned it."

"Right, and, of course, the ban would have included the cult of the Serpent."

"So I would imagine."

Murphy tried to put it all together in his head. "So this priest—Dakkuri—gets the order to stop worshiping the Serpent, to get rid of it."

"But I'm beginning to think this Serpent is rather hard to get rid of. Nobody who possessed it ever wanted to just melt it down and recast it."

Murphy bolted out of his chair. "Yes! That's it! The reason for the scroll. Dakkuri isn't taking the trouble to write all this down just to let people know he's been a naughty Serpent-worshiper. No. He made it look as if he broke it again and got rid of it, as ordered by Nebuchadnezzar. He wasn't stupid. But he hid the three pieces, and that's what he's telling us in this scroll, isn't it, Dr. McDonald?"

"Better than that, Mr. Murphy. I believe what Dakkuri has written here is not just that he hid the pieces, but the beginnings of how to find them."

Murphy sank back in his chair as if he had been deflated by her last comment. "What do you mean, 'the beginnings of how to find them'?"

"The last part of the scroll is really in two parts. Part one continues Dakkuri's report of events. It looks like he picked three of his acolytes to scatter the Serpent pieces far and wide within the Babylonian empire."

"But does he tell us where they went to hide the pieces?"

Isis was getting good at talking past Murphy's interruptions. "That's the second part of the end of the scroll. It looks like Dakkuri was setting up a kind of high priest's scavenger hunt for the Serpent pieces, and the last lines are a key for where to find the first piece. Then it looks like he's indicating that once you find the first piece, that will lead to the rest of the Serpent."

Murphy stared at the blow-up of the scroll in front of him. "And based on this pattern here, the curve with the ridges at the bottom, this first piece must be the tail, right?"

"The tail of the Serpent gets my vote."

"Dakkuri sure went to a lot of effort to save this Serpent, yet made certain that it would be awfully hard for somebody to find the pieces."

Isis found talking to Murphy brought into full play her twin drives of scholarship and competitiveness with smart men. "Not hard for somebody smart enough to work out his clues."

Murphy felt every archaeologist's bone in his body starting to quiver with excitement. "This means that we can find the Brazen

Serpent made by Moses! Better still, if we do find the Serpent based on this scroll, it proves that it was still in existence during Daniel's time!"

A particularly unladylike laugh escaped Isis's mouth before she could stop herself. "Forget this 'we' business, Mr. Murphy. I can barely find things in my own office. I don't go on expeditions. However, you are free to charge off in search of the first Serpent piece. Nothing could be simpler. So long as you know the location of the Horns of the Ox."

TWELVE

HORNS OF THE OX.

Horns of the Ox.

Murphy kept replaying the phrase in his mind and marveled at the seeming ease with which Isis McDonald had come up with that site from the symbols at the very end of the scroll. As hard as he had stared at those same symbols, he had not come close to making that connection.

Of course, now that she had given him her interpretation, it seemed crystal clear. With more than a bit of both his professional and male pride rebounding, Murphy did note that here was where his field experience could put Dr. McDonald's bookish linguistic skills into operation.

The Horns of the Ox would have to refer to a fairly prominent landmark reasonably close to the old Babylon. Dakkuri probably would have chosen a natural landmark as opposed to a man-made one, because he could not have known how long it would be before this Serpent piece would be dug up.

For a few hours he pored over his map texts, but he realized that nobody knew the ancient landscapes better than his own wife. Her studies of ancient cities gave her an encyclopedic knowledge that he now needed.

Desperately.

Murphy finally tracked Laura down in the faculty lounge. "Honey, you've got to get out all your books and maps. I think I've found the location of the Serpent."

"Murphy, really, you figured out where the Serpent is?" Instantly, Laura shed her counselor's cloak and was one hundred percent archaeologist.

"Well, it was really Dr. McDonald. And it's only the clue to where the first piece of the Serpent is hiding. According to her, the scroll is a kind of Chaldean treasure map, with the Serpent piece as the treasure."

"How exciting!" Laura said. "But where is it?"

Murphy knelt down and showed Laura where he had written *The Horns of the Ox* and sketched out several rough pencil drawings of landscapes that could have inspired that nickname. They all had two high vertical points curved like horns, straddling a mound of land that could be seen as the ox's skull. "This is about as far as I got. The truth is, I need your ancient-map-reading skills. It's been a while since Dakkuri wrote down the directions, and I think the neighborhood's changed a little in the meantime."

Laura laughed. She took Murphy by the hand and they started off down the hall.

"I don't know, Murphy," she said, shaking her head. "Why is it men just can't read maps?"

As soon as he'd shown Laura the partial translation of the scroll, she had gone into overdrive. Within minutes their already cluttered living room had become a stormy sea of paper, as maps, reference books, and computer printouts had been laid out on the floor. Laura sat in the middle of the chaos, grabbing maps, throwing them aside, scribbling furious notes while she hummed a tuneless ditty to herself.

As she put it, it wasn't like looking for a needle in a haystack. It was like trying to reconstruct a two-thousand-year-old haystack, figuring out where each individual piece of hay had originally fit before being bumped around by a couple of millennia of winds, floods, and earthquakes—and then trying to find the needle.

Dakkuri's directions—assuming Murphy and Isis had correctly deciphered the scroll—to the final hiding place of the Serpent's tail had been pretty specific. Laura gave a more refined interpretation to Horns of the Ox than Murphy's crude sketches, saying it most likely referred to a particular geographical feature—probably a curved ridge ending in two sharp promontories. Maybe with a big hump of rock or a prominent hill lying behind it—the "body" of the ox. And the whole thing was likely to be visible from some distance, so the surrounding area might well have been relatively flat.

But the landscape Dakkuri had had in his mind's eye was ever-changing. Sea levels advanced and retreated, erosion moved hills around like pieces on a chessboard, the courses of rivers and waterways could be diverted, turning desert into pasture and vice versa. And on top of that, earthquakes could shake things up like a kaleidoscope, totally changing the picture from one year to the next.

To see things the way Dakkuri had, it was necessary to reverse the process. To somehow look at the modern landscape and see the ancient one beneath.

Such a task required an uncanny ability to read relief maps in three dimensions, a detailed knowledge of ancient geography, and an intuitive sense of geological transformation through time—not to mention a kind of sixth sense that you couldn't put a name to.

Luckily Laura was one of only a handful of people on the planet who had the full skill-set. As Murphy watched her pore over her papers, he marveled at these unique and powerful skills. Finding the tail of the Serpent at the Horns of the Ox was going to test those skills to the limit.

THIRTEEN

IT WAS THE second punch that Murphy regretted. No one was fighting him; he was hitting a heavy bag in the Preston University gym. The first punch, a sharp right jab, felt good to him, so good that he quickly snapped his left hand with a pop against the bag that sent a jolt from the boxing glove straight up his shoulder. The shoulder he had momentarily forgotten was still throbbing from the clawing by the lion.

When Murphy dropped both arms to let the pain ricochet around his upper body, the burly figure next to him let out a gruff snarl. "Come on, Murphy, no coffee breaks.

This isn't government work, it's supposed to be a workout." Levi Abrams pushed Murphy's shoulder to get him started again. His left shoulder.

Now Murphy had to double over to keep the pain from shooting around his torso. "Levi! Didn't you hear me say I had to take it easy today with that shoulder?"

"Suck it up, Murphy. Intensity. Focus. Do you remember nothing of your army time? Train, train, train some more. That's the only way to keep yourself from decaying like one of your desert mummies."

Murphy had to laugh as he looked over at the six-foot-five Israeli who was always so serious about their training sessions. Actually, Levi Abrams was serious about everything he did, as far as Murphy could tell. He had been recruited to the United States by the high-tech companies in the Raleigh-Durham area as a very highly paid security expert. So highly paid that he could afford to take an early retirement from the Mossad and relocate his family to Raleigh.

However, Murphy was certain that Levi had not completely retired. He would never ask Levi directly, and Levi was far too seri-

ous and closemouthed to say anything, but
he remained extremely well connected in
the Mideast, in the Arab countries as well as
in Israel. So much so that Levi had been able
to help Murphy on a number of occasions
with expediting papers to get himself and,
more important, some objects out of the
Mideast.

For his part, though you would never
guess it from his always stern expressions
and no-nonsense conversations, Levi seemed
to respect Murphy. Like Murphy, in his way
Levi was a natural instructor, though if
Murphy worked his students the way Levi
worked him, the university would have him
brought up on abuse charges.

They had first met by eyeing each other
before sunup on the running track two
years earlier, when Levi was overseeing the
security needs for a high-powered computer system being donated to the university by his current tech firm. Eventually,
Levi offered to expand Murphy's martial
arts skills, which led to high-intensity training sessions whenever they could fit them
in. With Levi, Murphy always pushed himself way beyond the effort he put in on his

own, and he normally pushed himself hard. Right now, getting so carried away had brought on the pain that kept him doubled over.

This morning Murphy would have skipped working out altogether to let his shoulder heal, but he had an urgent reason to get together with Levi. He decided to get to it while he was waiting for the pain to subside.

"Levi, my friend, I have a major favor to ask. I've gotten a lead on something really huge, an archaeological find that I need to jump on."

"Another of your dusty knickknacks?" Levi's respect for Murphy as a fighter did not exactly extend to Murphy's choice of profession. "Let me guess, you need, as my son has taken to saying, 'wheels'? Transportation to somewhere dicey in the Mideast?"

"You know me all too well, my friend. Levi, all I need is to get Laura and me into Samaria ASAP, try to find the hiding place for this piece we're looking for, and bring it back to Preston and have no hassles with officials or customs. Oh, and have it cost me no money."

Levi gave a long, low whistle. "What, you're not going to make time for a round of peace talks as long as you're in the neighborhood? Let me see what I can do. How soon can you get away?"

"We have most of next week off for independent study, and I've just about got all my students covered, so I can leave immediately. Laura's getting her office hours covered as well. I really owe you, Levi."

"Let's see if I can deliver first. In the meantime"—Levi punched Murphy's shoulder—"your coffee break is over. Get back to the bag."

FOURTEEN

"WE ARE TWO men, but we make an interesting couple, Professor Murphy, do we not?" Murphy nodded deferentially to his host, Sheikh Umar al-Khaliq, but he wondered where he was going with this conversational opening. They sat drinking strong Arabic coffee in al-Khaliq's beautiful home in Samaria, after a day of traveling, all arranged by Levi Abrams with amazing rapidity.

Laura had gone to their guest bedroom, saying that she was exhausted from her flight, but privately she pointed out to

Murphy that she was sensing the sheikh was no believer in women as being worthy of inclusion in any serious discussion. "Typical," she said, "of so many Arab men of his generation. In fact"—she jabbed Murphy with her finger—"typical of so many men of every country."

"Hey, don't point that finger at me. It's loaded," Murphy said. "I'm clean."

"But you could help bring the sheikh into at least the nineteen hundreds."

Murphy sighed. "I agree, dear, but could we not offend the generous hand that has made this trip possible? At least until the trip is over. Then, I promise, I will leave you behind to enlighten him. You will be my very special gift for the Samarian host who seems to have everything else."

"Murphy, it's a good thing I have my maps to study. Because tomorrow, when we set out exploring, I'm going to pick out a really great place to leave *you* behind. Don't stay up too late with your manly man talk."

Actually, Murphy was pretty certain what the sheikh might want to talk about, thanks to Levi Abrams, who had connected him with the sheikh. After working his cell phone for fifteen minutes while Murphy finished his workout, Levi said, "I think I've made a perfect match for you, my friend. Sheikh Umar al-Khaliq."

"And he's perfect because . . . ?"

Levi sat Murphy down. "This may sound like the last thing you would expect me to know about the Mideast, Murphy, but did you know that there are more and more Arabs who are seeking out *your* God?"

"I had read a little bit about the Christianity movement among Muslims, but I honestly believed it had to be about as likely as their coming to your God. No offense."

"None taken. At any rate, al-Khaliq is wealthy beyond belief, still enjoys diplomatic status for his fleet of private airplanes, and somehow, I guess, it was not enough. I had heard that he was putting out some discreet feelers to some of the Christian missionary groups in the region. As you can imagine, such seeking is not a popular extracurricular habit in the Mideast, no matter how powerful you are. So I told him that you would be happy to counsel him in return for round-trip passage and supplies for a little digging."

"Levi, you are a genius. Can I trust him?"

"I helped the sheikh out years ago with a messy situation with some trigger-happy Bedouins who were making it a little awkward for him to fight back against them on his home turf. I would trust him."

"Thank you, Levi. I owe you big-time."

"You owe me nothing. Take care of that wonderful wife of yours. You, I would miss not so much. Her, I would miss. And, Murphy, trust the sheikh, don't necessarily trust anyone else who's working with him. But you know the drill, so to speak, about digging in strange lands."

Now, two days later, Murphy sat across from the sheikh, waiting for him to explain in his sometimes tortured English why the two of them made such an "interesting couple." The trip could not have gone more smoothly. The sheikh's main adviser, Saif Nahavi, had made all of the travel arrangements, and al-Khaliq's wealth and diplomatic status had eased all bureaucratic hurdles.

Of course, as Laura had pointed out, "Murphy, your trips are always a lot like prison, a whole lot easier getting in than getting yourself out."

Certainly, Murphy had a lot to be thankful for due to the sheikh's generosity, and he wanted to live up to his part of Levi's bargain by counseling al-Khaliq about any and all aspects of his apparent interest in Christianity. However, his many trips to the Mideast had taught him that he must wait for the sheikh to bring up the discussion of such a sensitive topic in his own way. If he broached it at all.

"Professor Murphy, you are a Christian man who comes to my Muslim land in search of something that has been lost for centuries, something you feel is still vital today. I am a man who has every modern possession tenfold, but I feel I am seeking something even more ancient, more simple than you seek in your journey here."

"Sheikh, I respect your courage in your search. Are there questions you have?"

"So many questions, Murphy, but it is enough for me to meet you and help a man of your faith. In my position, as long as I stay here in the land of my ancestors, and despite all I can afford to do, I do not have the freedom that you enjoy, you who come here with your hat in hand."

Murphy had to suppress a laugh once again at the sheikh's unintentional knack for the embarrassing phrase.

"Let me just say, Sheikh, that I am at your service at any time of the night or day. I am indebted to you for your generosity toward my work and on such short notice. But after tonight, I realize that I am doubly blessed, because you have reminded me of how lucky I am to be an American and to be free to pursue any religion I wish."

"It is I who must be thanking you, Murphy. Someday perhaps we will be able to discuss many things in your land."

"Are you sure we must wait for that time, Sheikh? I'm sure we do not have time tonight for all of your questions, but how about giving me the two that are of greatest concern at this time?"

The sheikh smiled. "I see, Professor, that you are good at your digging. All right. Tell me, what do you see as the main difference between Allah and your God? Many people think they are the same."

Murphy sat forward. "There are several similarities. We believe our God is the creator of all things, and you agree. But we also believe in a triune God, one God made up of three divine personalities who have individual works. He is a merciful heavenly Father and sovereign sustainer of the universe who loved mankind so much, He gave His only Son to die on the cross for our sins so that we can have eternal life. He sends His Holy Spirit into our hearts to create a new spirit in us and lead us through life."

The sheikh sighed. "There is so much to try to understand. My second big question is, what would I have to do if I wanted to become a Christian?"

"According to the Bible, a person becomes a Christian by believing that Jesus Christ is not only the Son of God who died for the sins of the world, but that He rose again on the third day and will save all who call on Him by faith."

"That is all? It seems too easy, too simple."

Murphy nodded. "Yes, it does. That is one reason so many people miss it. But the truth is, it was not easy for Him to die one of the most excruciating deaths in history. As you know, Sheikh, those of your faith believe He was simply a good man, a teacher, or even a prophet. But Jesus was much more than that. The fact that He then rose from the dead shows that God the Father was pleased with His sacrifice and is willing to save all who call on Him by faith."

The sheikh looked tired. Murphy gently added, "Sheikh, what I have explained tonight is a matter of the heart. In the quiet of your own thoughts you can call out to the Father in the name of the Son, and the Holy Spirit will save you and give you eternal life."

"Thank you, Professor Murphy, for not squeezing me on this." Murphy winced again at the torturing of the language. "And thank you for your answers to my questions."

"You are welcome, Sheikh. I will pray that you make your decision soon. One thing I would ask: When you do, please drop me a note and inform me. Here is my card. You can reach me by phone or e-mail."

"Fine. Now you must get your rest, Professor. Tomorrow, my aide, Saif, will escort you through my land and see that you return to your land—with as little interference as possible."

An hour after the sheikh had retired and half an hour after Murphy had turned out his reading light in the guest quarters, the sheikh's right-hand man, Saif Nahavi, slipped unnoticed to the marketplace. It appeared that he was securing last-minute supplies for the Murphys' excursion the next morning.

As Nahavi passed an electronics store that was closed, a low voice called out, "Nahavi. Behzad. Do not turn around. Just look in the window."

Nahavi did as instructed. Behzad spoke from the darkness of the recessed doorway of the store. "Are you ready for tomorrow?"

"Yes. The regular driver has already

taken ill. You, Behzad, will be our last-minute replacement driver. It will be just the Murphys and me. They are traveling light, to say the least."

"And what are they seeking?"

"I do not know what Murphy is hunting in our country. I have to believe that because he has been so secretive, it must be worth a lot of money."

"It had better be." Behzad's cold tone was not one to be dismissed lightly.

"Do not doubt me, Behzad. We have never worked together, despite all the times you have tried to convince me to use my position with the sheikh to steal things for you to sell on the black market. But I know value, and whatever the Murphys will find tomorrow will be worth a fortune. Plus, there is the not-insignificant matter of my gambling debts, which this month have finally gone beyond what I can free from the sheikh."

"You, with your mighty position with the sheikh, are always looking at me like dirt, Nahavi. I always figured you were a thief like me."

"You are the professional thief, Behzad,

which is why we are doing business tomorrow. But remember, we do this my way. It must look like a robbery by strangers. I will not jeopardize my position with the sheikh."

"Yes, Nahavi, I will take care to protect your precious innocence in all this. As long as the money comes from the black market for what I take from the Murphys."

"The money will come, Behzad. Half for you, half for me, and just to be fair, if you do your part right, two full shares of death for the Murphys."

FIFTEEN

MURPHY WIPED HIS sleeve across his forehead, squinted through the glare toward a distant line of dusty hills, and breathed in a deep lungful of hot desert air. It felt good to be home.

In fact, he had never before set foot in this particular region of Samaria, but as his sneakers crunched over the dry ground and a ragged herd of goats scuttled past him, leaving the clatter of bells and a sharp, musky scent on the air, he knew this was where he was meant to be. The first Christians might have walked here. Perhaps one of the apostles had rested awhile in the shade of that large boulder perched on the escarpment. For all Murphy knew, he might literally be following in the footsteps of Jesus.

He grinned at his own flight of fancy. Maybe that was a stretch. But there was no doubting that this was the stage where some of the key events of the Bible had unfolded. And he was convinced that this seemingly dead and empty landscape could tell a miraculous story, if you knew how to read it.

That, unfortunately, was the tricky part. The official cover for the Murphys' visit to Samaria was to shoot some test footage for an upcoming television special. So, while Laura continued her methodical searching of the landscape, Murphy kept raising and lowering his digital camera, pretending to be doing the main work.

Through his camera monitor Murphy watched as Laura paced slowly back and forth, scanning the low ridge to the south, checking it against a handful of maps stuffed into the pocket of her cargo pants, suddenly turning one hundred eighty degrees as if she'd suddenly remembered something—

then turning back, frustrated, as if the memory had eluded her. Murphy knew better than to crowd Laura when she was in the zone.

The other members of their party, provided by the sheikh, were Saif Nahavi and a driver named Behzad. Both men remained down below with the Land Cruiser, watching for intruders but seeming to be paying no attention to either Murphy. They had told Nahavi nothing about what they were seeking other than the general vicinity to which they wished to be driven. Going beyond Levi's warning to him, Murphy did not tell even the sheikh about the Serpent's tail.

They were otherwise alone in their little corner of the desert, a natural semicircular amphitheater formed by the curving horns of the ridge. The goat bells had faded in the distance, and the only sound was the whisper of sand being gently blown up from the desert.

After her map study the previous night, then early that morning, Laura had been fairly dizzy with excitement and strong Arabic coffee. She was convinced that she had nailed it. After staring at the countless hills and gulleys, not allowing herself to be distracted, Laura had stabbed a finger at the map spread on the kitchen table. "That's it! I'm sure of it. Just north of the old riverbed, before you reach the wadi. There!" And Murphy had hoped she was right. After all, she was a natural.

Now, he could tell, that sense of certainty had disappeared, evaporating like the dew under a fierce desert sun. Laura had her head down, shoulders sagging like a defeated athlete as she picked her way through the boulders and little outcrops of rock toward him.

And then, in an instant, she was gone.

SIXTEEN

MURPHY STOOD OPENMOUTHED for a moment, like a member of the audience at a magic act who could not figure out where the girl in the suddenly empty box had vanished to. Then he broke into a run.

Laura had been about fifty yards away, he figured, when she'd disappeared. Heart hammering, he felt the soft ground sucking at his feet as he pounded through the sand toward the plume of dust marking his last sight of her. It was like one of those dreams where you are running from a monster but your legs don't seem to work. He suddenly had an image of Dakkuri, dark eyes gleaming with malice, and whispered a silent prayer.

He stumbled, righted himself, and finally crested the shallow rise that had divided them. There, where Laura must have been, was a gaping hole some four feet wide, sand pouring into it like water down a drain. He threw himself down, leaning as far into the hole as he dared. He remembered rescuing a classmate who had fallen through the ice one winter, hoping the ice would take his weight as he inched closer. Did desert sand behave the same way?

He thought he heard something, a muffled cry that might have been Laura, and leaned farther over. Suddenly, the solid ground beneath him gave way and he was plunging like a kid down a park slide. He landed with a thump, and rolled onto his side, choking on a mouthful of sand. As he spat it out, the dust began to clear and the world came into focus again.

On three sides were rough-hewn walls of dark, uncut stone. The fourth was buried in the tidal wave of sand that had sucked him down with it. And there, seemingly oblivious of the chaos around her, was Laura.

Murphy scrambled to his feet and reached out for her.

"Laura, are you okay? Are you hurt?"

Her cargo pants were shredded at the knees, a dark stain seeping through, and sand seemed to be falling off every inch of her. But as she shook a big swirl of sand from her hair, Murphy could see that she was smiling.

"You see—I was right! It was right under our feet the whole time. No wonder we couldn't see it."

Murphy wrapped her in a bear hug and laughed with relief. "I never doubted you for a second, sweetheart." He stood back to make sure she really was still in one piece, then followed her gaze to the far wall.

Their eyes were adjusting to the mix of light from the holes they'd fallen through from above with the shadowy, mostly stale-aired gloom of the underground sand cave in which they had landed. They saw that the sand actually started to give way fifty yards ahead to some stone. The stone formed steps, and the steps led to the entrance of what appeared to be the kind of natural stone cave they were used to seeing when hiking through North Carolina.

They stumbled through the sand to the steps, where they could move more swiftly to the entrance of the cave. Both Murphys took their flashlights from their pants now and swept the cave entrance in twin arcs.

"What are we looking for?"Laura asked.

"Probably an amphora."

Laura drew up her mental image of the ancient clay jars that were bulbous in shape with two handles that stuck out like ears from their narrow necks. Amphoras were used to store grains, dried fish, water, wine, and valuables. She spotted a piece of one that was lying in the sand and handed it to Murphy.

"Yes, this certainly looks like the 'vessels' the Bible speaks of, what we call *amphoras,* the kind the Babylonians took when they sacked Jerusalem. If I'm right, the tail of the Serpent is in one of these." Murphy turned the clay jar upside down. Something horrible and snakelike crawled out of it and slithered away. "But not this one."

Laura shuddered and jumped aside as the

slimy thing skittered past her. She lost her balance, went stumbling backward against the cavern wall, and fell through a narrow vertical fissure.

Murphy heard her scream and whirled around with his flashlight, searching the darkness for her. But Laura was gone.

"Laura? Laura, where are you?" he called out, staggered by a surge of anxiety. "Laura?"

"Over here, Murph," Laura finally replied after what seemed like an eternity had passed. "Over here. I think I found it!"

Murphy was relieved to hear her voice but still couldn't see her. Tense moments passed before he saw the beam from her flashlight through the narrow fissure. He dashed toward it and slipped between the gap in the cavern's walls that had swallowed Laura.

Murphy found himself in another cavern, considerably smaller than the first. "Laura, you have got to stop trying to disappear on me."

Laura was standing there, sweeping the beam of her flashlight across what she had discovered. "Look, Murph!" Laura exclaimed in amazement. "Isn't that in-credible?"

Murphy trained his flashlight beam alongside Laura's, and both of their mouths dropped open.

"Murph, do you see what I see?"

"After all this, it's almost too good to be true."

The neck of a large stone jar was sticking out of a mound of dirt and sand as if it were just waiting for them to open it.

They approached it together, like hunters stalking a buck they feared would bolt be-fore they could get it in their sights. Silently, they knelt down and scooped the dirt and sand away from the jar. It was about eigh-teen inches high and the neck was just wide enough to get a hand through.

Murphy was bursting with anticipation, and he raced to pick it up. Trying not to think of scorpions, vipers, or other stinging creatures, he reached inside. Laura, being the more cautious of the couple, trained her flashlight beam on the floor of the cave be-tween where she stood and the amphora, to make sure there was nothing crawling be-fore she moved another step toward her husband. The path looked safe and she was about to join her gleefully shouting spouse when, just to be sure, she shined her flashlight against the far wall of the cave.

There was nothing crawling there either, but what she saw instead made her heart sink. "Um...Murph...we have a problem."

SEVENTEEN

THE REST OF the cave was filled with amphoras. Hundreds upon hundreds of amphoras. Amphoras of all shapes and sizes.

Murphy put down the one he had been cradling, the one that only seconds before had seemed like the certain hiding place for the Serpent's tail.

The floor was flat and free of water, which was why the amphoras had likely been stored there many centuries before. Stored and forgotten. "Great," Murphy groaned. "This must be where amphoras came to die. I wasn't planning on spending the next six months down here."

"And I was doing so well."

"Yes, you were, sweetheart. You got us this close."

"Any idea how we know which one is hiding the Serpent's tail?"

"Hmm...I wonder if that sneaky high priest Dakkuri pulled a clever trick here. What if he instructed his minions not only to bury this piece of the Serpent but to go one step further and kind of bury it in plain sight?"

"Yeah, kind of like looking for the needle in a stack of other needles instead of a haystack."

"Maybe not as bad, Laura. You know this stuff better than I do from your research—how did they use these amphoras?"

Laura began sorting through her vast knowledge of ancient artifacts. "They usually sealed them with plugs made out of cork, clay, or wood, if they were sealed at all," Laura explained. "But something this important, we should be looking for one that was sealed with wax."

"If we find one full of pennies, we'll definitely know it's a fake."

Laura took one side of the cavern,

Murphy the other, and they began examin-
ing amphoras by the dozen. Most were
empty. Some held animal bones, others
primitive household tools and personal
items. Every one of these amphoras, let
alone their contents, was an ancient artifact
that under different circumstances would
have had Murphy, or any archaeologist, doing cartwheels.

They searched amphora after amphora
and were at their wits' end, when an idea
struck Murphy. "Hold it," he said in that
tone he used when he couldn't believe how
blind he had been to something. "If you
wanted to hide a piece of the Serpent,
which is presumably long and thin and hard,
you wouldn't put it in one of these fat ones
so it could rattle around, calling attention to
itself every time it moved. You'd wrap it in
something soft and slip it into one of these,
right?" He picked up a tall, narrow amphora that resembled a flower vase. "Find
one like this that's sealed with wax and
we've got it."

Most of the amphoras in the cavern
were of the potbellied and bulbous variety.
Murphy's moment of insight had eliminated

every one of them. He and Laura quickly picked out the potential candidates, and just as quickly eliminated those not sealed with wax.

"How about this one?" Laura soon asked, showing Murphy one whose mouth was sealed so tightly, smoothly, and totally that the plug had to be made of wax.

Murphy began digging at it with a knife, first placing all of the wax he removed in a plastic bag for future study. The plug soon popped out with a dull *thwack*. His eyes were wide with anticipation as he reached inside and removed something wrapped in a coarsely woven cloth.

What he found when he unrolled it was a perfectly preserved piece of cast bronze about twelve inches long and two inches in diameter. It was tapered snakelike at one end and broken off at the other. Murphy had no doubt he was holding the tail of the Brazen Serpent in his hands.

EIGHTEEN

"MURPHY, WE'VE FOUND it. Let me hold it." Laura marveled at the weight of the bronze snake's tail in her palm. "Imagine, Murphy, Moses made this!"

"Amazing. We are blessed today. Now let's try to get out of here so we can live to tell about it tomorrow."

They retraced their steps but realized they would not be able to climb back out of the holes they had fallen into to get to the underground cave. There were two passageways leading back in the opposite direction from where the cave entrance was. Murphy chose the one that was least sandy.

After several hundred yards, the sand was turning into dirt and the ground was even a little damp, indicating that water would be nearby. A few yards farther, and there were roots of trees and shrubs showing through some of the soil, and Murphy was able to hoist himself up on a combination of rock and roots and poke his head aboveground. "Honey, I think we can squeeze through here."

"Murph, I'm stuck!"

Murphy whirled to see that Laura's foot was caught in the network of snarled roots. He crouched down and worked it free, having to break off a knotted clump in the process. He was about to discard it, when he noticed a small shoot growing out of it in the shape of an almost perfect cross. He snapped it off and handed it to Laura.

"For you, my amazing wife. A souvenir of your visit here to the Brazen Serpent attraction."

A thin shaft of daylight from above was passing right between them. The tiny cross was struck by the light. It gave off a sparkling aura that seemed providential.

Murphy and Laura were speechless. She hugged the cross to her chest as Murphy wrapped his arms around her. They stood in the shaft of light, embracing, both forgetting where they were for the moment. But they were suddenly reminded of where they were when the first bullet slammed into the rock two inches from Laura's cheek.

The second bullet hit an overhanging branch just above the hole in the ground through which Murphy had poked his head. They were both peppered with pieces of bark.

Murphy threw his body in front of Laura's for protection, pushing them both back against the rock wall.

"Murphy, what's happening?"

"Bullets. Somebody isn't fooling around. Unless we can backtrack in hope of finding an amphora full of guns and ammo, we've got to move. Now."

Laura had never been shot at before, but she quickly got the message. The third bullet, kicking up sand at Murphy's foot, helped to get her moving. They started running farther underground but hit a full wall of sheer rock. "We're going to have to risk coming up out of the hole. And whoever is shooting at us knows it. Come on."

Murphy led Laura back to the clumps of root in which she had gotten her foot tangled, since it afforded the best protection from the gunfire. It wasn't much, but at least they weren't out in the open. "Stay here and stay down."

"Murph, where are you going? Don't leave me!"

Murphy ran to the rocks just on the far side of the hole. "Shh. I've got an idea that might work, but it's going to get noisy." Whoever was firing was able to shoot down the hole but would not be able to establish much range unless he stuck his gun inside it. Which was what Murphy was counting on.

There was quiet for a moment as the gunman was reaching that conclusion on his own once he no longer saw the Murphys running underneath the ground hole. First, the tip of the barrel of an AK-47 showed itself in the hole, then the rest of the barrel.

As it was being pushed through the hole, it was firing dozens of rounds of ammunition at the ground, making a deafening racket and breaking the ground into a furious cloud of dust, dirt, and sand.

Murphy hoped his timing was correct as he leaped for the gun barrel while it was still spitting out round after round and yanked it downward. With a horrible shout, the rifle and the man who held it came hurtling through the ground hole. Murphy straightened, positioning himself to pounce on the gunman once he hit the chewed-up ground into which he had been firing. Murphy figured he had, at most, a split second to take his only advantage, the momentary element of surprise.

In the end, the surprise was greater. For the gunman did not actually hit the ground for long. He fell right through and just kept falling. The bullets had torn up the ground to such an extent that they loosened centuries of sand, dirt, and stone that had provided only a relatively shallow covering—for a deep pit of sand way underneath the ground.

As Murphy looked on in wonder, the gunman finally stopped with a soft thud. Since the rifle was still in Murphy's hands, he assumed the gunman had nothing else to fire at him. Murphy peeked over the new, much-deeper hole. He need not have worried about the gunman. Or what was left of him.

As Murphy tried not to listen to the horrible, high-pitched scream, he could make out the body of the gunman being buried alive. Tons of sand that had not been touched by humans for centuries, if ever, rushed to cover his body within seconds of landing. Even if he had wanted to, there was nothing Murphy could have done to save the shooter. In fifteen more seconds, there was only a mound of sand where the head had been in the sunken chamber.

Before it disappeared completely, though, Murphy recognized the head as he shined his flashlight beam on it. Bezhad, the driver.

Gun still in his hands, Murphy whipped around, ready to fire, when he felt a hand on his shoulder. "Hey, Murph, take it easy. It's me."

"Oh, sorry, sweetheart. Let's get up that

hole in case this whole floor collapses."
Then to himself, so as not to scare Laura, he
muttered, "And since that was our driver
trying to kill us down here, I wonder what's
waiting for us up there."

NINETEEN

BLOOD OOZED OUT at them. Murphy
and Laura had pulled themselves out of the
ground hole after Murphy carefully surveyed the opening, rifle at the ready. It was
blessedly quiet after the roar of gunfire underground. They had worked their way
down the ridge to where the Land Cruiser
was, calling for Saif.

When they reached the car, they realized
why Saif had neither answered nor helped
them. He was slumped in the front passenger seat with his head bleeding from what
looked like a blow from a heavy object.

"Is he . . . dead, Murphy?"

Just as she asked her question, Saif gave a weak groan and his body stirred. "My professional opinion is no, Laura, Mr. Saif is not dead." Laura glared at Murphy.

"Get out of the way, wise guy, and let me look at that wound." She reached for the bottom of her shirt, which was as close to a clean cloth as she saw in the vicinity. "Mr. Saif, can you hear me? Somebody hit you. Probably Behzad, the driver, the goon who came after us. Did you see *anything* before you were knocked out?"

Saif opened one eye, then the other, and moaned. "Aaah, Mrs. Murphy, you are all right. Did you...are you...praise Allah, you are safe. I believe that substitute driver must have been a robber. He overpowered me and must have come after you. I am so sorry. The sheikh will be outraged. I am sorry the robber stole your object."

Murphy looked at Saif warily. "What do you mean, Saif? We were attacked by the same driver who knocked you out, but he didn't rob us. And he won't be robbing anybody ever again."

Saif tried to look relieved. "Then you got what you came for?"

"Yes, and a lot more—mostly bullets. Let's get to the airport now."

Two hours later, the Murphys were settled safely aboard the sheikh's jet, heading for home. "What a day, Murph!" Laura snuggled beside her husband, her eyes closing quickly despite her coursing adrenaline.

"The first piece of the Brazen Serpent."

"And my first time getting shot at. But I'm so impressed by the Serpent that I almost forgive you for nearly getting me shot to death."

"It may take a little longer for me to forgive myself." Murphy turned and put a hand to her cheek. "Sweetheart, if I'd had the slightest idea I was putting you in danger..."

Laura smiled and put her hand on his. "I know, you'd have left me at home to do the dishes and darn your socks. Now that it's all over, I can just savor the bragging rights I'll have next week in the faculty lounge."

"And I don't think I'll ever forgive or forget our friend Saif."

Laura shot Murphy a puzzled look.

"What do you mean, Murph? The poor guy was practically killed himself."

"Yeah, 'practically' being the operative word. I'm no doctor, but have you ever seen a more perfect head wound? Nice amount of blood to get our attention, but nowhere deep enough to cause any head damage."

Laura bolted upright in her chair. "Oh, no! Murphy, I was too scared and deaf from the bullets to realize it at the time, but when he opened his eyes, there was no way he was coming out of unconsciousness. Those pupils were clear as the dunes."

"Yes, I noticed that. I think Saif was in on the whole thing and just trying to make it look like he was a victim, too, just in case we survived, but we were never supposed to get past the goon driver to see Saif's faked act."

"But how did he know we were looking for the Serpent?"

"He didn't. He couldn't. Nobody over here knew. I think he knew the sheikh was helping us find something of value. He didn't care what it was, he just wanted to steal it from us. I don't think the sheikh had anything to do with the scam. But once we land, I'll be letting him know just what a scheming skunk he has working for him."

"Now, Murphy, the sheikh was our host. Don't lose your famous temper with him on the phone."

"Not at all. I just believe he would like to know the truth. Speaking of the sheikh, what do you say we take a closer look at what we almost got killed for today?" He reached for the sheikh's diplomatic pouch and removed the cloth-covered metal piece.

No longer struggling with her exhaustion, Laura smiled. "What took you so long?"

Murphy began to loosen the knots, half expecting the tail of the Serpent to slither away between the seats with a hiss. He pulled back the cloth and held it up to the light. It had been forged thirty-five hundred years before, but the rich bronze surface seemed undamaged by the corrosive forces of man or nature.

The expertly cast texture of the Serpent's skin was intact. Each reptilian scale had been faithfully rendered, and Murphy recognized the unmistakable pattern of a venomous sand viper.

"Moses made this," he whispered. *"Moses actually held this in his hands."*

Laura reached out and touched it with a finger. "In obedience to God, they put their trust in Him and were healed. It was a symbol of their faith."

Murphy could see there were goose bumps on her arm. "But after Moses was done with it, what did this Serpent become? That has been the question all these centuries since."

Murphy tilted the tail of the Serpent so the light from the window raked its surface, making the scales glitter and dance. It almost seemed alive. "Hey, sweetheart. Did you see this?"

Laura leaned closer. "What do you mean? It's just the—" Then she saw it. Another set of markings. Barely visible, as if they had been crudely engraved, almost scratched into the bronze. But once she focused on them, they were strangely elegant—and instantly familiar. Triangles with linear tails and V shapes, like birds seen against the sky.

"Chaldean cuneiforms," Laura gasped. "Just like the scroll."

"Yep. I'll bet this is Dakkuri's handwriting too." Murphy turned and pressed his face to the window. Thirty thousand feet below, the desert rippled toward the distant horizon.

"You know, whatever this high priest Dakkuri was up to, it looks like he made good on the promise in his scroll. He did leave something here on the first piece that looks like it can lead us to the rest of the Serpent."

TWENTY

"SO, ANYBODY DO anything interesting last week? Me, I was in Samaria."

There was only a mild stir of interest among his students. *Tough crowd,* Murphy thought. He resisted getting their attention the easy way by adding, *Getting shot at by an Arab.*

Instead, he reached into his backpack beside the lectern. "And look what I found."

"A shower pipe?" someone called from the back of the hall.

"No, but the next wise guy is getting sent to the showers. This amazing foot or so of bronze, ladies and gentlemen, is a snake."

Vermont?" Their voices, that were only shrill, sounded mocking to him. Startled by his mistake, he slipped his clutch, brought his car roughly to a stop, remembered that he could neither back out nor turn around, flung his lever into low speed with a grinding of nervous gears and started forward. The children, sharp-faced and mournfully knowing-eyed, stopped their play again to stare at the jerking car. He read derision into their silent gaze and nettled vanity wet his forehead and began to crumple his collar with sweat. Still gripping the steering wheel too hard, stooping his tall frame to peer through the low windshield for a possible traffic light, he all but ran into a pushcart loaded with empty crates, left standing by the curb. Wrenching at the wheel and careering to the left to avoid this, he saw with horror that he had gone by a red light, and strained his ears guiltily for an angry whistle. But for once no traffic cop was near.

The rest of the trip downtown was a series of crises inexpertly met; he parked too far from the curb at the hotel; the doorman lifted his eyebrows at the three-year-old Ford; the hotel clerk was disdainfully silent when he said he'd have one of the cheapest rooms. Out of moral cowardice he grossly over-tipped the bell boy who showed him to his dingy cell. Left alone he looked into the mirror and saw that his collar was not right, and that he must start the next day with a visit to a New York barber to efface the rusticity of his Clifford haircut.

"I must come to the city more often, by God, I must!" he said aloud, his bruised vanity throbbing like a stepped-on corn. How shabby his ancient pigskin bag was now, which only an hour before had looked upper-class and "county," with its mellow saddle-soaped leather, compared with the dented pasteboard suitcase of the Barney girls.

It was late, he went to bed, but as he closed his eyes a mob of cars bore down on him with all their headlights glaring, and every time he turned restlessly over to avoid them, he saw only two young provincials with hats that were uncouth because they showed an amount of forehead that was right last year, not this year. But he was tired and finally fell asleep. And during this sleep his mind took charge, opened the right switch and shunted him back from the Clifford to the New York rails and from the quivering dramatic miseries of adolescence to the monotonous, unexpectant, self-confidence of maturity. When he woke up he was an old New York boy back in New York.

And glad to be there, relieved to have the tiresome mechanisms of daily life run invisibly by people of whose membership in his own race he need not be reminded. His cheap room was dingy, yes, but it was an anonymous back that bent to shovel the coal into the fire that kept it warm. That back could ache with overwork, could break in exhaustion, but because he would never know whose back it was, he would be safe from the nagging summons of moral responsibility. How restful city life was! The plumbing in the battered bathroom was old-fashioned but if the pipes froze or burst, it would be a figure in blue jeans whose face he need never see, whose wages might be fair or unfair for all he knew, who would toil till the repairs were made. In the morning when he let himself out of his door the man in the next room was just entering his. T.C. reveled in the stony indifference with which their eyes crossed. He might be going out to jump in the river; the other man might be going in to cut his throat—and no intrusive interest taken by either one. Neither would ever know or care. Nor anybody else. It was delightful to breathe in this rarefied air of irresponsibility, compared to the unremitting density of the rural consciousness that everybody else is human. The old city boy walked with a light step through the bell boys in the lobby, who would, no matter how disagreeable to them he made himself, give him accurately the service he had cash to pay for; he glanced at the opaque face of the waiter who came to take his order for breakfast and thought, "Your wife may have been killed in an automobile accident last night, or have run away with another man, but *I* don't have to take on your troubles in addition to my own." What a vacation it was to get away from the crowding closeness of country life to the decent isolation and privacy of the city. Yes, I must really plan to come more often, he thought, opening his morning paper like a civilized being at half past eight in the morning instead of like a hick at half past four in the afternoon.

He had meant to take at least two days, perhaps three, for his various errands, remembering his old city-scorn of country people who crammed too much into a short visit, and then blamed for their fatigue and bewilderment—not their own bad planning but New York ways. But it had been evident that a single day had seemed an almost sinful extravagance to the Barney girls with Delia's college years to be financed. He had hastily revised his trip to suit them, planning to do by letter or telephone many of the things he had thought to do in person. Even so, the day ahead of him was formidably full. After a shuddering glance at the headlined news of Fascist bombing of civilians in Spain and yet more Nazi savagery in Germany, he laid down the paper to plan his comings and goings. His city lore about subways, elevated trains, and busses came freshly to his mind, and with it the unsurprised city acceptance of the need to spend large sections of each day in being hurled from one place to another. After breakfast he stepped out to a branch of the same shop where he had bought his clothes when he was in college, bought some new collars and a smarter tie, and coming back to the hotel put them on with preoccupied confidence in their rightness, giving only his usual forty-five-year-old glance in the mirror to see that they were in place. In the barber's chair he sat somberly dreading his call on Mr. Wheaton, rebuking by his inattention the barber's urban grin over the length and odd cut of his hair. And when, close-trimmed and clipped and shaven, he stood up to go, he tipped the man, firmly, unapologetically, a dime and nickel, no more. Shrugging his overcoat on absent-mindedly, he looked at his memorandum to verify the address of the chic hotel where he was to meet a Jewish mother who had written to propose her son as a student.

In the subway as he gazed at the wooden faces of the people opposite him, he gave himself another moment of city elation that he need feel no responsibility for their welfare, and then set his mind to work on the first call he was to make. Of course the fact that Mrs. Bernstein wanted her boy to leave the expensive New Jersey prep school and enter another, even before the end of the first semester, meant that something was the matter with young Jules. But it might turn out to be something which a needy rural academy could afford to overlook. He wondered how anyone living in a Park Avenue hotel had ever heard of the Academy. Clifford was by this time so far away that he himself could barely remember that it existed. Well, there had been, of late years, off and on, a few

141

Several of the heads in the front rows re-coiled. "Relax, it was never alive, but it has had several lives, all of them more interesting than any real live snake ever had."

Murphy clicked his slide projector to life. "Now, these Biblical names and kingdoms are mouthfuls, I know, so I'm going to try to help you keep them straight by flashing them up on the screen. All of these gentlemen ruled way before they could be on the cover of *People,* so I don't have big, glossy color photos to help you remember them.

"Now, this slide shows a decrepit-looking document, an ancient papyrus scroll that came into my possession not too long ago. However, as is often the case for archaeologists, I had no real context for what I was looking at. It would be a lot easier if these artifacts already came with the background audiotape you get at the museum for the walking tour, but I haven't found one yet that does. So we have to discover all those facts ourselves."

The next slide was a close-up of the scroll. "Don't worry. Those of you who think you're hungover, that's not English up there. Not even close. It is a language

Jewish students at the Academy. Perhaps one of them had mentioned Clifford. Although, he thought fifteen minutes later, looking around the department-store elegance of the private sitting-room, certainly none of those former students ever lived in any such expensive hotel as this.

The door opened, Mrs. Bernstein came in. All of T.C.'s Scotch blood curdled, and all his New England experience bared its teeth at the first sight of her—too handsome, too fashionably dressed, too articulate, with an aroma of fluent insincerity that was almost innocent so open was it, as if she lived in a world where it was taken for granted, like the law of gravity. She assumed at once the manner of intimate friendship. With a reflex he could not control, the obscure schoolteacher from Vermont grew more frosty as she waxed more cordial. He was shocked by his own bad manners. He would not have spoken to the town drunkard in Clifford as curtly as he put the necessary questions to this opulently beautiful woman, nor fixed so insolently cold an eye on any human being in Windward County.

He wanted just one thing from her, to know what was the matter with Jules; and as he expected, that was the thing she had no intention of telling him. Had Jules passed all his examinations? "Oh, yes, *indeed,* Professor Hulme, you'll find him a very bright student. Why, I've had teachers tell me that they never *had* such a—"

Silent and saturnine under the flood of her quotations from the many teachers who had thought Jules the very brightest boy they had ever seen, Professor Hulme waited, at first for the end of her monologue, then only for the end of a sentence, and finally waited no longer but interrupted her flatly with his request to see the boy's report card.

"Oh, I have it right here, Professor Hulme. I knew that with a careful person like you that would be the first thing you'd ask for." The card came out, warm and perfumed, from a petit-point bag on her satin lap.

He gave one look at it. "But, Mrs. Bernstein, there are no marks on it for the before-vacation examinations."

"Ah, trust your experienced eye, Professor Hulme, to see that at a glance. Ha! Ha! Ha! Anyone can see that you know all about . . ."

142

known—or, these days, mostly unknown—as Chaldean, dating back to the time of Nebuchadnezzar, the greatest king of Babylon."

Murphy clicked the king's name up on the screen, followed by a map of Babylon. Then he forwarded to the figure on the scroll that he had interpreted as representing the king. "Again, this didn't come with an instructional video, so how did I know that this lovely artist's rendering is of King Nebuchadnezzar? By knowing the period of the writing and knowing my succession of kings, which is to say, folks, eat your vegetables, say your prayers at night, and study, study, study. There are no Hollywood shortcuts in this business.

"Now, here's why this scroll is so exciting. A lot of what archaeologists have found from Babylonian times are storage receipts and ordinary everyday records, because the Babylonians were the early-day versions of college administrators. They loved to write everything down."

He clicked on the next slide. "Now, that might look like an eyelash on the projector lens, but it is the cuneiform symbol for a snake. Combining that with this next symbol, which we believe to stand for what we call *bronze,* I began to get excited. And then when I pieced together enough of the rest of the scroll, I started to realize this was no Babylonian grocery list."

That was his last slide, so Murphy turned off the machine. "I'm going to come back to some greater detail about methods for interpreting ancient writing in a later lecture. For now, let me skip all the way ahead, past what I learned by reading the scroll, and how that led me to find my snake friend here." He pulled the bronze Serpent tail out of his bag once more. "Because the point I wanted to get to today is about having the courage to make some leaps of logic and knowledge, because it's oftentimes the wild, crazy, impossible notions that lead even boring old archaeologists like me to discover new truths.

"This bronze piece, I believe, once we test it out in the lab, will prove to be the tail of the Brazen Serpent, which in your Old Testament was made by Moses in fourteen fifty-eight B.C. The Israelites started complaining about wandering around in the desert for so long and began acts of 'unbelief' against God. As punishment for their rebellion, God sent down poisonous serpents to bite the offenders. That got everybody back on track and they prayed and asked Moses for help. He prayed to God, who took mercy on the Israelites and told Moses, 'Make a fiery Serpent, and set it on a pole; and it shall be that everyone who is bitten, when he looks at it, shall live.'

"Moses interpreted 'fiery' as bronze, because he made this Serpent figure and held it up before the afflicted, and those who repented were healed. All of this Serpent symbolism, of course, is a very potent direct line back to the Serpent tempting Eve in the Garden of Eden, which started the world down the road of sin and judgment. And one of these days I'd like to come back and talk about what healed the Israelites. Was it some magical dark power in the bronze snake, or was it the fact that the Israelites recommitted to their faith in God? But Dean Fallworth will start accusing me of being a tent-show preacher if I dare to wander off into issues of faith. Plus, I want to get to my real investigative point today.

The flood poured down again, on and on, flattery, cajolery, side-issues without end. Professor Hulme waited, looking stonily out of the window, writing grimly on his bony face, "The answer to my question, if you please!"

Finally when she could ignore his expression no longer, "Well, the point really is, Professor Hulme, that at Brentwood they don't give the boys examinations before they go home for the winter vacation. They don't think it good for the adolescent nervous system to have to go through such a strain, just when"—the faucet opened yet more widely—"modern psychiatrists . . . the defeat complex . . ."

Timothy waited again. No break at all occurred in the barrier of talk this time. He looked rudely at his watch. She talked more rapidly. He held it to his ear, with no effect. At last he broke through by raising his voice to say, "Well, then I'd like to see his report card for the last year."

"Oh, really! I'm so sorry, I never *dreamed* you'd care to see that. Let me see. I don't believe I have kept it. Or if I have, I wouldn't know where to find it. Living in a hotel . . . you country people with your great roomy houses and attics, you can't imagine how hard it is for us poor city people with no place to . . ."

Letting the fluent words pour on and on past his ear rather than into it, T.C. looked up to the ceiling and considered. Then, making no pretense that he was not interrupting her, he said, "Mrs. Bernstein, I'm afraid I'll have to telephone to Brentwood to get your son's record. They always keep complete records, I know. I could get it in a few minutes."

With a stirring of her sleekly corseted body that was not so much a flutter as an uncoiling, she said in agitation, "Well, I'll see —I might be able to find it."

After a moment of search in the desk drawer she drew the missing card out and reluctantly showed it. It had, of course, a record of the results of examinations taken before the last Christmas vacation. Professor Hulme laid it down on the elegant little desk and looked at Jules' mother—from the North Pole.

She threw herself on his mercy. She was a widow, she cried brokenly, giving her whole life to her fatherless boy. All she wanted was his happiness. If she had tried to deceive the pro-

"There are two places in history that are recorded in the Bible where this Brazen Serpent makes an appearance. The first is in fourteen fifty-eight B.C., when Moses forms the Serpent for the purpose of healing the Israelites. We then fastforward to seven fourteen B.C., to the only other time it's mentioned in the Bible, in II Kings 18:1–5, where, contrary to the First Commandment, the Brazen Serpent becomes a special object of worship.

"The young King Hezekiah, who was one of the most devout kings of Judah, discovers that his people are beginning to adopt the practice of idolatry, which was common among the neighboring tribes. Evidently, this Brazen Serpent had been secretly preserved and used as an object of worship. Some people even attributed mysterious healing powers to the Serpent.

"When Hezekiah discovered the people of Judah bowing down before the Serpent in worship, worship that belonged to God alone, he was so enraged that he smashed it into three pieces.

"And that, as far as the Bible goes, is the last we see of the Brazen Serpent. Until this

fessor, it was as any mother would lay down her life for her child, for . . ."

After a time, "What *was* the matter with Jules' examinations this year?" asked Mr. Hulme.

Pressing a handkerchief against her eyes, she implored him, "Don't hold this against Jules! He'd kill himself if he knew that his poor mamma had . . . He's always telling me that . . ."

Mr. Hulme cleared his throat formidably. It was a pedagogical feat he found useful with parents.

She conceded everything. "I'll let you talk to Jules himself. But"—she put both hands over her face—"before you see him, I'll have to confess that . . . I've been ashamed to tell you before . . . I simply can't pay your full tuition rates. . . ." Her face still buried in her hands, she laid her head on the table. "It's absolutely impossible, because I . . . the depression has wiped out . . . not a single . . . my poor, poor boy, he is . . ."

After all the schoolteacher from Vermont was a man; this was a woman, a handsome woman young enough to be provocative, and she was a widow distracted with anxiety about her only son. For the first time Mr. Hulme felt a decent discomfort about his clammy Northern suspiciousness. The difficulty might really have been money all the time. That *would* be, of course, what would seem to a New York woman the thing to be ashamed of. This expensive suite, her elegant toilette, her costly handbag, they might really, as she was incoherently protesting, be all that was left after one of the typical New York débacles of these ruinous years. His nerves stirred in sympathetic response to her agitation as in an involuntary reaction to the near-by throbbing of a drum.

She moved her forehead distractedly to and fro on the table, she turned her head slightly, and between her fingers he caught a keen cool eye fixed on him with a canny scrutiny of his expression. It brought him to his feet raging at the detestable New-York-Mediterranean haggling code which counts it mawkish impotence not to pay less for a thing than its price. He thought of poor Eli Kemp's dignified refusal to make one of the pennies he so sorely needed by getting more than its value for what he was selling. He reached silently for his hat and turned towards the door.

144

scroll set me on the trail of some connection to the Serpent's being around in the time of the greatest empire of Babylon, during the kingdom of Nebuchadnezzar. That's a long time and a long way from where the Bible leaves the Serpent lying in three pieces at Hezekiah's feet."

Murphy paused. "So, because archaeologists look for some way besides time machines to explain how artifacts may survive leaps of time and distance, I have a theory, and that theory helped me to find this piece of the Serpent last week. I believe that when Hezekiah ordered the Serpent destroyed in Judah, it was broken into three pieces and placed in the old Temple. Back then, even if the king told you to destroy an idol, you didn't just throw away a three-foot piece of perfectly good bronze. About one hundred forty years later, when the Babylonians stormed through Judah and sacked the Temple, they took back to Babylon anything that looked like it was worth something, and somebody eventually rescued the three pieces of the Serpent.

"Now, some of the writing is missing from this scroll I uncovered, so some greater speculation than usual is in order, but we have pieced together enough of the message to reveal that some high priest among those idol-worshiping Babylonians put the Serpent back together, probably believing that it had great powers.

"In my next lecture, I will begin to talk about prophecies, and how Nebuchadnezzar got his fear of the true God and ordered idols destroyed left and right—and there goes the Brazen Serpent on the chopping block again. Except the high priest who wrote this scroll wanted the Serpent saved again and split up the pieces with instructions on this scroll for finding them to put them back together. Which, if I have any luck reading what's written on the bottom of this tail here, I will endeavor to do. So, while I dash off to do that, class dismissed."

A student called out, "Professor Murphy? Nobody got healed when you held up the tail, but don't you think that if you do find the other two pieces and Lego them all together again that you will be able to heal people?"

"That is the big question, yes. Or just as

possible, according to believers in the so-called dark arts, who have sought out the Serpent for centuries, if the pieces are ever connected, you could wield this Serpent for evil."

"Wait! Wait!" cried the woman behind him, and ran out past him into the hall, calling, "Jules! *Jules!*"

Out of a door at the other end of the long hall a tall, thin, stooped lad of fourteen emerged and came slowly towards them over the long strip of red carpet. He held himself badly, he walked clumsily. His mother ran to meet him, enveloping him in an emotional embrace. Over her head he looked at the visitor out of melancholy hazel eyes. He said wearily—but gently—in a little boy's treble not yet changed for all his height, "Now, Mamma, now there, Mamma . . ." and with a mild gesture of patience put her to one side. He had a swarthy ugly face, sensitive and sad.

"Hello, Jules. How do you do?" said Mr. Hulme in the first natural tone he had used. He stepped forward, holding out his hand. The boy took it in a nervously taut grip. He tried for a manly bluffness with a "How do you do, Mr. Hulme," but his eyes cried, "Oh, rescue me! Help me to escape!"

They turned back into the expensive sitting-room and sat down.

"Which ones of your last exams did you flunk?" asked the school-teacher.

"All of them."

"What was the matter?"

"One of the kids in the dorm had a 'cello his mother made him take to school and I got to fooling around with it, and never studied a lick for a month." His voice cracked ludicrously from treble to bass on the last phrase, and he blushed.

His mother flung up her hands, opened her lipsticked mouth to cry out, and was cut short by Mr. Hulme's saying, "All right, Jules, come along to Vermont. If you'd like to try us, we'll give you a try."

Going out of the hotel he looked at his watch. Less than an hour since he had come in. And enough drama to fit out a Clifford month. He made a calculation of distances and decided to use the subway to reach Mr. Wheaton's office.

On the dirty stairs that led down into the earth, the schoolteacher from Vermont saw a shawled old working-woman with sunken tragic Celtic eyes. She was struggling with a heavy pasteboard suit-case, her lips moving as if in prayer or sorrow. She tugged the

145

heavy carton up a step at a time, collapsing on it to get her breath, her face paper-white. The city crowd streaming down, pouring up the stairs, avoided her as they would have turned aside from a tree or post. They passed so close to her that they brushed her limp black skirts; the wind of their speed stirred the strands of her straggling white hair. Their eyes, steadfastly fixed on what they were about to buy or sell, saw her not. Timothy Hulme thought of Aunt Lavinia. He turned, went back up the stairs, took off his hat to her and smiling kindly, laid his hand on the suitcase. "Won't you let me help you with this to the street-car, or wherever you are going?" he said in his gentlest voice.

His hand was struck away with a blow that made it tingle. The old woman screamed at him, "L'ave my bag alone! I know what you're up to! I've seen the likes of you before now!"

For an instant he was too much astonished to stir. The people passing up and down the stairs found their urban sense of humor tickled by the comic sight of kindness taken for malevolence, and turned their heads to grin—without slackening speed. The old woman pushed her face up toward T.C. with a hideous expression of hate and fright, crying, "Lay so much as a finger on that bag an' I'll call an officer!"

He ran on down the stairs, his cheeks burning, dropped his nickel in the turnstile and got into a subway train. Some of the people in the car, evidently among those who had passed him on the stairs, recognized him as the man who had made a fool of himself, and grinned to see his face still red. "I should have known better than to show common humanity on a city street," he told himself, breathing hard.

The train drew into Times Square station. He leaped up to change to the shuttle. Scurrying along the underground burrow with the other termites, trying to close his nostrils to the lifeless, thrice-breathed air, he thought, "I'd dismiss on the spot any teacher or janitor who'd let the air in a schoolroom get a tenth part as foul as this." The tempo of the scurry rose as those in front saw that a shuttle train was about to leave, and Timothy, although he saw what they all saw, that another train was waiting ready to move up at once, ran poundingly over the concrete, and hurled himself into the departing train just before the doors slid shut.

146

TWENTY-ONE

SHANE BARRINGTON WAS forcing himself to not think of his son. Naturally, even for a master at turning the coldest of mental shoulders toward all the vicious acts and ruthless business sins he had perpetrated in his life, Talon's murder of Arthur while he had just stood by helpless was proving to be a difficult memory for Barrington to ignore completely. Especially with no idea as to what Talon had done with the body, despite his cryptic promise that he had some further plan.

Odd, he thought, how after cutting his son out of his life completely for so many years, now, in death, Arthur kept coming to mind. Not that Barrington was in any danger of suddenly becoming sentimental about family. Other than his ex-wife, who had been paid off more than two decades earlier, Arthur had been his only living relative. And he had no need of nor interest in something as pedestrian as a friend. Associates, staff, servants, yes; friends, no.

Nor did Barrington have a great attachment to places. There was nowhere he would really call home, though he owned luxurious houses on three continents. The place he came from certainly held no sentimental value for him. It was a place you escaped from if you were lucky, not one you dreamed of going back to. As for the attractions of magnificent architecture or priceless works of art, that was for weaker souls. The truth was, he was happiest when he was on his way somewhere, in a plane or a fast car. Moving, at speed, feeling the world shrink under his feet. And with the state-of-the-art systems Barrington Communications manufactured, he could make things happen wherever he found himself.

But if he had to choose one place where

he felt most at ease, as if he were standing at the very center of the universe, it would be here, in his penthouse, watching the vast, jagged landscape of towering steel and glass come alive in the growing dawn. However, after that horrible moment of seeing Arthur tortured by Talon from his terrace, Barrington had not even looked out his window, let alone used the terrace.

Now, with four minutes before his guest would arrive, he told himself it was time for the great Barrington willpower to come to the fore. He forced himself to open the draperies and part the sliding glass doors to the terrace. He would not be like every weak creature he had conquered in the past. There was no room for guilt in the Barrington game plan. He strode toward the railing and looked down at the Endicott Arms. For a second, he shuddered, then he wiped his mind clean.

Immediately, he started to feel the return of total command, as if he were a barbarian king standing on the piled-up corpses of his vanquished foes. Barrington Communications had recently become billions of dollars richer and had never been stronger than it was now. The gaping holes in its financial structure had been shored up, leaving more than enough to bankroll further expansion, further conquests. Any business magnate foolish enough to think he could stand toe-to-toe with Shane Barrington was about to discover the error of his ways.

He put his hand to the glass and smiled. All this, and how little, really, they had demanded in return. Now to initiate his second assignment from the Seven. As with his first assignment, this task seemed odd, arbitrary, and unconnected to any big master plan, and had been delivered in terse fashion, with no supporting explanation. However, like obtaining the checklist of U.N.-related security information, it was something he could accomplish from his position of power with ease.

He checked his Rolex. The meeting had been scheduled for seven o'clock. Late enough to have forced her to cancel any plans she might have had for the evening. And he had made her wait a further ten minutes. Long enough for confidence to drain away and be replaced by fear. Cheap tricks, perhaps, and hardly necessary any-

He was a little late for his appointment with Mr. Wheaton but this gave him no concern, part of the Wheaton technique being to make callers wait—those who were not moneyed. After rising twenty-four stories in a Gothic elevator and finding his way through marble-lined corridors to Mr. Wheaton's velvet-carpeted Italian Renaissance outer office, he sat looking down at his hat on his knee, meditating on the atmosphere of high urban civilization in which he had been moving since he left his hotel, and bracing himself for the encounter before him.

"Mr. Wheaton will see you now, Mr. Hulme."

With an inward, "Oh, he will, will he!" Professor Hulme followed the streamlined and thrice-lacquered woman secretary into The Presence and was placed in a Louis XV armchair (which had cost, he had often calculated, as much as two months of his salary) between the rich old man in flesh and blood, and the rich middle-aged man in a life-size Sargent portrait, flattered about five thousand dollars' worth, which all day long looked back at the original behind his mahogany desk. The two men, silently despising each other, shook hands and exchanged pleasant greetings. Timothy Hulme was thinking that no late-Roman vulgarity could equal putting up a portrait of yourself as an ornament for your own office. Mr. Wheaton was thinking that a man of T.C.'s ability, education, and personality must be really a half-wit—or have some secret vice —to continue accepting such a salary as that of the Principal of Clifford Academy.

Then the Principal got to business, began his report, and in a moment was being told that he had made an enormous mistake in admitting a Jewish boy as student. "You don't realize the danger, T.C., safe in those blessed green hills, you don't *realize* that the only way to handle that problem is ab-so-lute exclusion. The world's no place for a dewy idealist like you. Let in Jews, and they'd make one mouthful of you. Admit just one—and the ghetto pushes in after him. We old-Americans must stand solidly against the flood of them that's pouring in from Europe!"

For the second time that day the schoolmaster waited, his ear cocked for a let-up in a pouring spate of words. But when on this subject, Mr. Wheaton refused to let anyone else speak till he had presented loudly his usual number of run-of-the-mill formulae.

147

Some of them contradicted the others, but they were all equally dear to him.

"You may think you've found one of them who's decent, but take your eye off him for a single instant and he'll . . . I don't deny that once in a while you'll find *one* who's as good as a white man. It's his family you have to look out for and they all bring their families wherever . . ."

One of these formulae always shook Timothy in a clap of inward laughter almost beyond his control. He waited for it today. Here it came, "There never was a Jew knew what we American business men mean by honesty." Timothy coughed loudly, choked, put his handkerchief to his mouth, blew his high nose.

"Now *I* know them, T.C., and you don't. I've done business with them for forty years." ("Heaven help them!" thought Mr. Hulme, glancing at his watch.)

Time was going fast. He recognized the harangue now going on as Oration No. 5, knew it to be lengthy and decided to try to shunt the speaker on towards the later paragraph of the speech. Without waiting for a break in the eloquence, he cut in with a reminder that the Academy had for the last thirty years or so had an occasional Jewish student from outside, or from one of the Jewish families in business in Windward County towns, "We've never had the slightest trouble with them or their families. They are exactly like any other Vermont boys and girls. Our basketball team owes a good many of what victories it has to the goal-shooting of one of the Hemmerling boys. And the Junior class that Rosie Steinberg was elected president of . . ."

Mr. Wheaton's lips twisted in an ugly grimace. "Their very names make me sick!" he said. "Think of a Rosie Steinberg in our dear old New England school! She's not there with *my* O.K., I call you to witness! You never let in one with my consent, T.C.! Not—with—*my*—consent! And because you've run a risk once without getting caught is no reason for putting your head in the noose again. My dear old Academy may be a poor school, but it is anAmericanschool-thankGod, and will be as long as I have anything to do with it!"

T.C. said in a rather loud voice, to run no risk of not being heard, "This particular boy I've just accepted struck me as very likeable, and—for a boy—civilized. In my opinion it is a good thing

148

to give our isolated Vermont young people some contact with natures that have good points different from their own."

But no, try as he might, he could never bring out an opinion as the successful Wall Street operator did, with the authentic ring of finality. In years past, thinking that if he could learn to use it he might turn it back on its practitioner, he had tried to analyze the Wheaton intonation which announced with bluff, manly plainness that when he had set forth his opinion of a matter, it was a womanish waste of time to discuss it further. But T.C. had long ago realized that the authority in that voice, whether it was laying down the law about education, painting, politics, the position of women, or sexual morality, was unshakeably based on successful speculating with profits made in manufacturing and selling carpets. Of course it was something no mere schoolteacher could acquire.

"Howdoyoumean—civilized?" Mr. Wheaton challenged him. "One of those precocious, smart-aleck, Jewish bookworms, I suppose."

"Here's where I get his goat!" thought the schoolteacher, yielding to a cheap temptation, and aloud, with a poker face, said seriously, "I wouldn't say he was bookish. I was referring to a certain sensitive fineness of personality—he was gentler to a tiresome mother than any Yankee boy would be—and he has a living perception of musical values. To come in contact with these qualities would be very wholesome for the esthetic ignorance and blunt roughness of most of our Vermont students."

This was a success. Not having made money and not being always surrounded by yes-people, he could not, it was true, present an opinion of his as all there was to say; but he knew which ideas could be counted on to make the lion's den resound. He sat back, smiling inwardly, listening to the roars, looking up at the broad blunt nose of the portrait, adroitly flattered but still recognizable, at the hard blue eyes, larger and bluer than in life but faithful to the stony coldness of the original. To push one of the buttons which made Mr. Wheaton go into the air gave Timothy Hulme a malicious pleasure he was not proud of, but could not resist—the pleasure of contempt. For when the successful speculator was aroused to indignation, the veneer of semi-civilized catchwords over his ordinary conversation cracked and showed a Yahoo, Black

149

Legion savagery, the baseness of which made up to the teacher for his own economic inferiority.

"Let me tell you, T.C., LET—ME—TELL—YOU, that we want no effeteEuropeanartyideas corrupting our American he-boys into—"

"Well, well, you wouldn't believe it if you didn't hear it with your own ears," thought the schoolteacher, wallowing richly in his scorn. "Really Sinclair Lewis is a phonograph record! When you read him, you think he's laying it on too thick. Not at all. He doesn't exaggerate a hair." The roars began to die away for lack of breath. Mr. Hulme looked down at his memorandum and prepared to take up the next item on his list.

But the trouble with making Mr. Wheaton roar was that the sound of his voice, no matter what it said, always tuned to a higher pitch his certainty of being right. What he was shouting about the value of plain old-American-stock characterbyGod compared to the slippery Oriental superfluities of the arts, pleased him so much that by the time he stopped to pour himself out a glass of water from the silver-mounted thermos bottle he felt a mellow man-of-the-world compassion for the poor teacher from the backwoods. Without help from a sensible man he would be lost, poor simp, in the rough-and-tumble of the world of men, and the Academy with him.

"Well, let all that go for this time, T.C.," he said. "Did you and old Dewey knock together some kind of a budget after Van and Swettinger blew up if I'd had my way we'd-have-sold-those-bonds-long-ago."

They talked figures for a while, Timothy Hulme trying to force himself to an expression of what he felt at such times, a wistful admiration for Mr. Wheaton's grasp on the complications of investment and finance. He knew that not to recognize this superiority openly, put him on a level with Mr. Wheaton's monstrous ignorance of what magnanimity is. But apparently he could not claim to live on a higher level, for he could never bring over his lips a single word of appreciation for what was invaluable help. He hoped this was because he knew the air about the financier to be so poisoned by adulation that in it the plainest sincerity turned into flattery. He feared it was because he was not man enough to acknowledge ability and power of any kind in a man he personally disliked.

On this occasion, when the time came for the usual hand-to-hand

more. But the exercise of power, however petty, was what gave him pleasure, and if he could not indulge himself in that, life would surely be very dull indeed.

He turned away from his shadowy reflection and spoke into a microphone woven into the lining of his jacket. "Send her in."

Stephanie Kovacs, Barrington News Network's up-and-coming star reporter on the national beat, willed herself not to check her hair, her makeup, one more time as the cropped-blond receptionist behind the desk motioned her toward the door with a curt wave of her perfectly manicured hand. Here she was, Stephanie Kovacs, ace TV investigative journalist, fearless exposer of the crooked and corrupt, a woman who'd been shot at, slashed by a knife-wielding maniac, and threatened by slavering attack dogs—who had always stood her ground and kept her head while facing down men twice her size and ten times as aggressive—here she was, nervous as a kitten just because her network's CEO summoned her to a meeting.

What was the worst that could happen? Okay, he could fire her. That was the thought that had been racing around her brain for the last five minutes, forcing her to flip urgently through her mental Rolodex. *Who would I call first? Who was that executive who said at the awards dinner, "If you ever think of leaving the show..." Which network needs a new face to boost the ratings? Which news program is desperately seeking some credibility?*

But finding a new job in TV wasn't really the point. She was successful and respected enough in the business not to worry unduly on that score. What was eating away at her and making the butterflies in her stomach do loop-the-loops was the certain knowledge that when Shane Barrington fired you, he didn't just let you go. He made sure you were finished. Career over. If that was what he had in mind, she'd be lucky to be standing in front of a camera in a month's time and talking about the unseasonable June rainfall's effect on the soybean crop.

She paused at the door, patted a stray hair into place, and walked in, hoping he wouldn't see beneath her practiced veneer of confidence.

"You asked to see me, Mr. Barrington?"

Shane Barrington seemed taller than in photographs and the rare pieces of TV footage, but the harsh features and dark eyes were ominously familiar. Without a word or a change of expression, he gestured toward the dark leather couch against the far wall. He remained standing as she seated herself, forcing her to look up at him from below.

"Miss Kovacs," he began. "Stephanie. I'm so pleased you could spare me a few moments of your valuable time. I hope I haven't kept you away from an important investigation. I'd hate to think some wrongdoer got off the hook because I'd distracted you from your work."

She tried to laugh. "Well, there's always more fish in the sea. That's the great thing about this job—you never run out of worthwhile targets."

Barrington looked at her without smiling. "Sure. I know exactly what you mean." He turned and sat behind the long, smoked-glass desk in the center of the room. She couldn't help noticing the absence of a phone or a computer. In fact, there was nothing on the desk to mar its perfect crystalline surface.

"Sometimes I hear people say I don't really pay attention to this part of the corporation. That I'm not really interested in TV. Like it's old technology, a thing of the past. And Shane Barrington is always interested in the future, right?"

"Right," she found herself saying.

"But that's not true at all, Stephanie. I pay very close attention to what goes out on the news channel. And I've been paying particularly close attention to your reports. To your fearless investigations."

It seemed to her the word *fearless* was his way of mocking her. If anyone else had used that sneering tone, she would have gone for their throat instantly. No one trivialized her and got away with it. But to her own surprise she continued to smile meekly, as if she were a dog being stroked, not a lamb being lined up for the slaughter.

Barrington's eyes seemed to lighten a little, as if he were enjoying her discomfort. "You really know how to stick it to the bad guys. No mercy. No quarter. I like that."

He made her sound like a prizefighter, not a reporter, but if he liked her style, that was fine with her. She still wasn't sure where he was going with this, but her anxiety level was beginning to drop just a little. Maybe she wasn't going to get fired after all.

"People also say I'm a hands-off CEO. I don't tell the producers at the station what to do. As long as it gets the ratings, what do I care, right? Make a program about anything you like. Killer cockroaches, grandma serial killers. Whatever rings your bell."

Better and better. He liked her news judgment. He believed in editorial freedom. What was she worrying about?

Barrington leaned back in his chair and laid his hands flat on the desk. His eyes darkened again. "But sometimes people just can't be trusted to do their job. Sometimes they need a little direction." He smiled humorlessly. "From above."

Okay, not so good. The conversation, if you could call it that, had just taken an ominous turn.

"I've decided that someone ought to do an investigation—a ruthless exposé, no holds barred—on a certain group of people who pose a major threat to this country—to the world. Someone needs to expose them for the dangerous fanatics they are."

He paused. *Uh-oh, here comes the punch line,* she thought.

"The group is evangelical Christians. And that someone is going to be you."

Whew, she had not seen this coming, not where she thought this conversation was heading at all, but Stephanie Kovacs had not risen past the other bright, desperately eager TV talent by being slow on the uptake. She recovered from her puzzlement quickly by flashing a humble smile. "I am honored by your confidence in me, Mr. Barrington. I will try not to let you down."

"See that you don't. I will be watching."

TWENTY-TWO

THE MAN CALLED Talon paused in his labors, allowing himself a few seconds to take in the part of Manhattan that lay below him. In fact, there was only a narrow railing and some ropes keeping Talon from dropping down to the street.

He stood ten stories up on the window-washer platform descended from the top of one of the most recognizable structures in the world: the Secretariat Building of the United Nations.

Talon turned back to one of hundreds of windows that made the outside of the U.N.'s tallest building look like a towering wall of glass. There were thirty-nine floors, but Talon had done his calculations carefully and he was interested only in floors five through twelve. That would make enough of a statement for his purposes.

Shane Barrington had come through as instructed and managed to get Talon some of the security-defying access he needed to carry out his task. He had told Barrington what he wanted and left it up to Barrington, whose many subsidiaries designed communications, security, and utilities systems for thousands of businesses, to figure out how to get him what he required.

Talon had not needed too much because the very boring Mr. Farley had given him endless details about his window-washing routine. And Talon had lifted all of Farley's personal identification before disposing of his body. Which he did only after relieving Farley as well of the necessary body parts for the fingerprint and retinal scanning he would have to pass through to gain access to the U.N.

Now, in makeup that transformed him into the late Mr. Farley, and having padded his body to fill out his uniform, which said

EXECUTIVE BUILDING MAINTENANCE, Talon consulted the paper in his hand. It was a meticulously rendered grid he had drawn for himself of every window of the Secretariat Building. If he could continue to raise and lower himself on the motorized window-cleaning platform at this swift pace, everything would be in place well before zero hour.

TWENTY-THREE

MURPHY'S EGO AS a proud male and a proud professional archaeologist was taking quite a pummeling. "Shari, I have to admit, I'm stumped. For the life of me, I don't know what's written here on this tail."

Shari wished there were something more she could do to help. They had already performed as many dating tests as they were equipped to do in their lab, and she had taken careful digital photos from every angle. They were looking at the enlargements now. "I don't think I can blow them up any larger, Professor Murphy, or we won't be able to see anything besides smudges."

Murphy rubbed his hand through his hair in distracted frustration. "No, whatever tool Dakkuri used to etch this message into the tail, he made it last pretty much intact for all these years, and seeing it is not my problem. I just can't make head or your proverbial tail out of this. Because he didn't have a lot of room, he must have used some kind of ancient shorthand. And I suspect Dakkuri must have been trying to be more than somewhat cryptic beyond that, because he was giving directions for uncovering the next piece of what he believed was his most powerful icon."

Shari drew a deep breath before saying what had been on her mind for several minutes now. "Umm...Professor Murphy... have you thought about—"

"Don't even finish the sentence. I know when I'm beat. I've got to get Isis Mc-Donald back on the phone."

"Wow, Professor Murphy, that's some whopper of a tale...er...story." Isis Mc-Donald looked back over her hastily scrawled notes and shifted the phone receiver to her other ear just to give her neck a chance to uncramp. "But tempting as it is, I can't do what you ask."

"Why not? Look, I know we haven't met, but you've got to know I'm not a crackpot and I usually know my stuff. You backed me up on the scroll and it seems to have been proven right. This is the next step now. I'm closer than anybody has been in thousands of years, presumably, to finding the entire Brazen Serpent."

"Yes, yes, Professor Murphy. That's all very well and good, but I'm a philologist for the Parchments of Freedom Foundation, not a starry-eyed, glory-seeking archaeologist, and I've got a deskful of my own research I'm behind in. Actually"—she craned her neck to look around her—"it's more like an office full of things I should have finished months ago."

"Please, Isis. Believe me, I don't want to ask for your help, but I can't wait on this— and I also hate to admit that I'm just not smart enough to figure this out and you are."

Isis sighed, but, to her surprise, her lips were forming a smile. "Oh, Professor Murphy, I can see how you bull your way to all these breakthroughs. You are skilled in the ancient art of flattery."

"I am a licensed professional. Will you help me, please?"

"Look, Murphy. Here's what I'm willing to do. I have to be here for foundation review meetings for the next few days, and you're a busy man as well. However, the good thing about the foundation is that resources are generally not in short supply. Which is why I need to be here for our review meetings, since you are not the only skilled practitioner of necessary flattery. But I will dispatch my very able, very trustworthy secretary, Fiona, on our foundation jet to pick up your Serpent's tail and bring it to me."

"Whoa! That's very extravagant, but I can't let this out of my hands. How can I be sure it would be safe?"

"Murphy, you're there in what I'm sure is a quaint, perfect-little-tiny-town school and I'm sitting here in the world's largest privately funded historical research center with state-of-the-art systems and security. Who are you kidding?"

Once again, Murphy knew when he was bested. "Point taken, Isis. Before I scurry off with my tail between my legs and lick my wounded small-town pride, let me just say thank you, the Serpent's tail is yours for as long as you need, and when can Fiona be here?"

Murphy surprised Laura in her office. He was holding a small box.

"Murph, what are you doing here? Did that mean old dean send you here for detention again?"

"Sweetheart, I was sitting and moping in my lab because I had to call Isis McDonald to take the Serpent's tail because I'm clearly not smart enough to figure it out. Then I realized I was still good for something, so I dug this out and fixed it up. I've been meaning to give it to you ever since we got back from Samaria."

He handed the box over to Laura. She looked as eager as a five-year-old on Christmas morning as she ripped the lid off. "Oh,

Murph, it's the cross formed by those root branches in the cave. I was wondering where it went."

She held up the now-polished wood to admire it. It was approximately an inch and a half long and a half inch wide. Murphy had drilled a tiny hole through the top, then burnished the finish with a few drops of oil, which brought out the grain and enhanced the color of the wood. At the meeting point was a rounded burl from which the four tendrils of root that formed the cross had grown. It shone like a hardwood gemstone.

"I've strung it on my very best leather moccasin lace. No expense has been spared to keep you in jewelry befitting your status, m'lady." He bowed before her.

Laura bent down and hugged him hard. "Arise, you noble lad. Your queen has greater things in store for you. Come, take me home, let me show you why it is good to be the king."

TWENTY-FOUR

PAUL WALLACH WATCHED as Shari dipped a spoon into the sauce. She took a quick catlike sip, gave a little nod as if to say *Not bad, if I do say so myself,* and went back to stirring the pasta. In the cramped kitchen, the steam made her look flushed, as if she'd been running and hadn't had time to change. To him the sheen of perspiration somehow made her look even more beautiful.

She turned and caught his abstracted gaze. "Hey." She frowned. "You're supposed to be watching closely. How long did I say the pasta had to cook?"

"Five minutes?" he offered. "No—fifteen."

Her frown stayed in place and her grip on the spoon tightened.

"Oh, I know," he said. "Trick question. Until it's, you know, whatever the word is—al dente."

She brushed a damp strand of dark hair from her forehead and turned back to the steaming pots. "Hmm. I don't think you've been listening to a word I've been saying, Paul Wallach. I mean, you're the one who said he lived on cans of tuna and takeout pizzas and wouldn't it be great to learn how to cook a meal once in a while that actually tasted of something. I know this isn't exactly duck à l'orange or anything, but you could show a little more appreciation."

He quickly put his glass of Coke down on the counter and adopted a sincere expression. "I do appreciate it, Shari, I really do. And it smells incredible. It's just that I find it hard to concentrate on things that don't really interest me—"

"You'll be interested enough in eating it, I bet," she interrupted.

"Sure, yes, you're right. What I mean is,

I don't think I'll ever be any good at it. However hard I try, I don't think I'm ever going to be a great cook."

"Just like you're never going to be the next Bill Gates, right?" she said, glancing quickly over her shoulder to make sure she hadn't upset him.

He sighed. "Exactly. I feel like I've spent my whole life trying to be good at things I'm not. Pretending to be interested in stuff I couldn't give a . . . give a fig about. I mean, I wanted my dad to be proud of me and all. I didn't want him to think I was, like, a failure, or whatever. And it turned out he was the failure."

Shari had promised herself that she would let him talk without interrupting him, but she turned from the stove to face him. "Paul, you can't think of your father that way. He may have failed at business, but he provided a good life for you for a long time."

"Yeah, some *good life*. I'm not sure which he was a bigger failure at, business or being there for me."

"Paul Wallach, let me tell you something I discovered when my parents were killed in a car accident years ago. You can blame them for anything you feel is wrong in your life, you can feel guilty about things that went unresolved while they were alive, but at some point, good or bad, you have to live your own life, whether they've given you a good foundation or not, and stop making them an excuse."

Paul slouched in his chair. "Oh, I keep telling myself things like that. That's why I pushed myself to go back to college here at Preston, because I didn't want to just sit and mope about my tough luck. At least my dad gave me the example of working hard. But it's tough working hard at stuff when your heart's not in it."

Shari handed him two steaming plates of spaghetti and red clam sauce, and for a moment he was distracted by the rich, warm smell.

"Wow!" he said. "I mean, really. Wow! You must let me have the recipe sometime," he added, grinning.

"Ha-ha," she said, shooing him into the little living room, where she'd set the table. "Sit down and eat. And then you can tell me what it is exactly that your heart *is* in."

"Thanks," Paul said, handing Shari a mug of coffee. "And not just for a delicious meal. Thanks for listening to my problems like this. I feel bad taking up your time with this stuff when you could be, I don't know, doing more exciting things."

She smiled. "I like helping people, Paul. And I know from my own experience that someone just listening can be a big help."

He'd hoped she was going to say something else, something a little more personal. Something that indicated she was interested in him. He wanted to be more than just her good deed for the day. But maybe he was hoping for too much. Or maybe it was just too soon.

"So," she said, "the first thing you've got to do is be honest with yourself. You no longer have to live your life for how your dad feels. If you don't think you're cut out for high finance, then find something that does interest you."

"I think I've found a subject I want to study."

"Great." She beamed. "What is it?"

He hesitated. Would she think he was

faking an interest just to impress her, to worm his way into her affections? He didn't want to blow everything.

"It's about as unbusinesslike as I can get. Biblical archaeology," he said, watching her expression.

She looked steadily at him for a while. Not smiling, but not quite frowning either. As if his sincerity were being weighed in the balance and the scales hadn't quite come down one way or the other. Finally she said, "I guess you know how *I* feel about it. I can't think of anything more fascinating, more worthwhile. And if you want to get into it, well, that's good. But are you sure you totally understand what it's all about? I mean, it's not just about digging up artifacts and finding out where they came from. That's what regular archaeologists do. It's about proving the truth of the Bible."

Paul started to frame an answer, then stopped himself. He did have an answer, at least he thought he did, but he wasn't sure he could put it into words. No, he couldn't claim to be a fully paid-up member of the Christian faith. He wasn't even sure what it was exactly he believed in. But when he'd seen Murphy's photos of the ossuary in the lecture hall, when he'd heard him read the inscription, he'd felt something deep inside that he'd never felt before. All he knew for sure was that he wanted more of it.

A loud buzzer broke the awkward silence. *Saved by the bell,* he thought.

"I don't know who that could be," Shari said with a trace of real annoyance as she got up from the table and went to the front door. She pulled the latch, there was a moment's silence, and her hand flew to her mouth. Standing in the doorway was a young man with an unruly mop of dirty-blond hair, a couple of days' stubble, and an unpleasant grin. He shouldered his way past Shari and planted himself in the middle of the room.

"I don't see balloons. I don't see ticker tape." He scanned the room, looking straight through Paul as if he weren't there. "I definitely don't see booze. I gotta say, you don't do a great homecoming party, sis."

You just never know about families, Paul thought as he walked back to his apartment.

Here he had been unburdening to Shari about his turmoil over his father issues and his future, and she seemed like this peaceful, perfect, wise person who had it all figured out. Then—*boom*—that awful guy comes barging in and it turns out he's her brother who had been in prison for burglary and got released early and surprised her.

Some surprise. Chuck Nelson didn't stay long. Just changed his clothes and stormed back out. Shari seemed really upset, so Paul ended up staying for another whole hour, talking, only this time about her. Paul was even more impressed when he listened to her.

"My parents were killed instantaneously in the crash when Chuck and I were teenagers. They had never taken us to church, so I did not know Christ personally. However, I started going to a Bible-believing church with my friend's mother and it was there that something wonderful happened. I received Christ personally as my Lord and Savior and He changed my life. Salvation gave me something to hold on to when I needed it most. But Chuck went bad fast."

Paul shook his head. "He must have, to have ended up in prison."

"Chuck fell in with the worst elements from the surrounding area, committed crimes from stealing to drug dealing, and eventually got caught. He would never listen to anything I had to say and refused to put me on his list of visitors in prison, so I stopped going to see him. I've never stopped praying for him, though."

"What will you do now?"

"I don't know. You know as much as I do. You saw him storm in and out. I guess he thinks he's going to live with me here, and I would never throw him out, but I will not have him fall back into his wild life. I'll need some help here. I think Laura Murphy and Pastor Bob at the church will be good to talk to. And you, Paul, you've been really great to listen."

Paul blushed. "Hey, you listened to me, I listened to you. That's what friends do. And, hey, I guess that means we're friends."

Shari gave him a friendly pat on his hand. "Well, friend, you'd better be getting home. But I tell you what, why don't you join us for church Wednesday night. The Murphys will be there, and I'd like you to meet Laura. She can help you too. And you should get right in the spirit by coming early and helping out in the basement, sorting clothes for the church clothing drive. Say, six-thirty Wednesday?"

I think I'm going to like it here at Preston, Paul thought as he whistled the whole way back to his apartment.

TWENTY-FIVE

THE NEARLY TWO hundred flags of the members of the United Nations were flapping in a light evening breeze coming off the East River. At six P.M., as twilight was passing rapidly to full darkness across Manhattan, the U.N.'s brilliant night-lighting beams switched on.

There was an immediate burst and flash, thousands of lights turning the thirty-nine stories of the Secretariat Building into one of the jewels of the New York City night skyline.

Since it was not completely dark yet, the lights did not create their full dazzling effect.

However, the explosion of attention was immediate.

Horns honked as passing cars screeched to a halt along First Avenue. Pedestrians gasped, shouted, and pointed up at the glass facade of the U.N. And by 6:02 P.M., the first of numerous phone calls sounded in the office of the head of United Nations Security in what was going to be a very long night.

For painted on half the windows from floor five up to floor twelve of the United Nations Secretariat Building, in a bright red that took on an otherwordly glow in the night lighting, all the world was now reading:

J 3 16

Within a half hour there were even more lights trained on the Secretariat Building.

The premises were cleared, as were the surrounding buildings and streets, except for dozens of official vehicles. The mobile units of what seemed like every television and radio station in the world were also now jammed as close to the U.N. as they could get.

It was a full-disaster reaction scene without any apparent disaster. Preliminary search and evaluation teams could find no victims and no damage to any of the U.N. buildings. Except for what appeared to be meticulously applied blood that had cascaded down eight floors' worth of windows on the Secretariat Building front. If the writing on the windows was some kind of warning about an impending explosion or attack, no further clue had been found, though it would take many hours to complete a thorough search.

Because the U.N. was technically on eighteen acres of international property, the United Nations security chief, Lars Nugent, was in charge of the operations that night, but the New York City police and FBI and other federal emergency teams were swarming all around, lending services and giving advice.

By nine-twenty, Nugent had gathered together Burton Welsh, senior FBI official on the scene, along with the police commissioner of New York and the undersecretary of state for the United States, who had flown up from Washington to try to coordinate the many government services that would be called upon if there was an attack on the United Nations. Despite its official international status, it would be both a danger and an embarrassment for the United States if the U.N. was in any imminent danger of an attack of any nature.

Nugent, a man who looked more distinguished than many of the diplomats he protected, said, "Let me summarize what we know. The message was painted on the outside of the windows on floors five through twelve. We need to do some real testing, but we've determined it is paint, not blood, as those TV reporters have been speculating. The paint that was used is some kind of chemical that goes on clear and takes on its color only when really bright light zaps it, some kind of super glow-in-the-light chemical."

The police commissioner interjected, "How did it get on there?"

"We assume it was done from the window-washing platform. It was up and running today on those floors, but so far everything checks out normal with the washer and all the security screenings. The police are trying to round up the regular window washer, a Joseph Farley, lives in Astoria. No luck yet, but he's been on the job for ten years and has nothing unusual on his record either here at work or with the police."

The undersecretary looked up from his notes. "It's almost one hundred percent certain that whoever painted this up there wanted to make a statement for the world to see. The U.N. is obviously *the* world organization. So far, though, we have no communication from any terrorist group taking credit."

Burton Welsh shook his head. He unzipped his FBI windbreaker before speaking. "We're not necessarily looking foreign on this."

The undersecretary raised his eyebrows. "You mean domestic terrorists? Like Oklahoma? What would be their beef with the U.N. that would make it worth trying to crack one of the tightest security systems in the world?"

Nugent waved his hand in disgust. "That

security doesn't seem to have done squat today. What's the latest analysis of the markings?"

Welsh picked up the book in front of him. "Pretty crude, pretty basic." He opened the book. "We're assuming it refers to the Bible, New Testament, 'J' for Book of John, 'three' for Chapter Three, 'sixteen' for Verse Sixteen, and I quote: 'For God so loved the world that He gave His only be-gotten Son, that whoever believes in Him should not perish, but have everlasting life.'"

Nugent nodded. "Yes, it's maybe the most famous quote from the Bible, but why here, why now?"

Welsh reached for his cell phone. "We've got some thoughts, but if this is the call I'm expecting, we'll be getting the benefit of some outside help."

TWENTY-SIX

MURPHY WAS STILL trying. The symbols were starting to wiggle in front of his eyes, he had been staring at the cuneiforms for so long. They seemed to be moving to a regular rhythmic beat, until Murphy realized it was his office phone that was ringing.

He shook his head to try to clear it as he reached for the receiver. It was Laura, from the house. "Murph, thank God you're still in the lab."

"A fine thing to be saying to your husband in the middle of the night."

"Murph. An FBI agent was just here looking for you."

"FBI? Why me, and why me at this hour?"

"He's coming to the lab to get you, Murph. The FBI wants you for questioning."

FBI agent Hank Baines sat in Murphy's office twenty minutes later, holding Murphy's extension phone against one ear while Murphy paced. Laura had told Murphy to turn on the TV in the department lounge and he had watched the BNN update live from the U.N. Murphy was completely dumbfounded, like the rest of America, by what he saw.

Agent Baines had been ordered by Washington to race from the Charlotte field office to Preston to wake up Professor Michael Murphy for questioning. The questioning, however, was not to be undertaken by Baines; he was merely ordered to get Murphy situated for a conference call with Burton Welsh, head of the New York office.

"Mr. Baines, this makes no sense. What does this have to do with me?"

"I do not believe it is about you, sir."

"It is now if you've sped down here to question me."

"Like I said, Professor, I am not going to question you."

"That makes even less sense. If all this is about is my getting a phone call, what are you doing here? Do you shoot me on the spot if I answer a question wrong?"

Baines spoke into the receiver. "Agent Baines in position, New York. I will put Professor Murphy on the phone directly." At Baines's nod, Murphy picked up his desk phone.

"Professor Murphy, I'm Burton Welsh, senior FBI agent on site here at the U.N. We have you on speakerphone with the U.N. security chief, Lars Nugent. Thank you for taking the time to talk to us."

Murphy frowned, then said into the receiver, "Gentlemen, I don't know what you think I can do for you."

"Mr. Murphy, I'm sorry to disturb you, but we've got a situation up here at the U.N."

"I've just seen the TV coverage. What do I have to do with any of this?"

"Sir, we're quite familiar with your expertise with all things having to do with the Bible."

"Hogwash, Agent Welsh. I've never dealt with you guys before, but I always figured the FBI would be straight shooters in every way. There are dozens of experts you could have called who know more about the Bible than I do, including lots right there in New York, so you wouldn't have had to roust Agent Baines here to babysit me."

"Sir, could I ask you to tell me what you make of this message, J three sixteen."

"Welsh, I'm an expert in ancient Biblical history, not modern graffiti."

"Take a whack at it anyway, Mr. Murphy, if you would."

Murphy took a deep breath before answering. "John Three: Sixteen, as I'm sure you know, is the verse many Christians believe is the most important verse in the entire Bible."

"Because?"

"Because it tells us that through faith in God's Son, Jesus Christ, we will receive the gift of eternal life."

"So, you think this is the work of some religious fanatic," Nugent interjected.

"Whoa, gentlemen! *Religious fanatic?* You mean because it refers to a Bible quotation? Look, *fanatic* would seem to be a fair conclusion, because somebody obviously went to a whole lot of trouble to paint it all the way up there on the U.N. But there're many millions of people, myself included, who think about that quotation every day of their lives and would take offense at being described as *religious fanatics.*"

"Look, Murphy." Agent Welsh's official tone of moderation had disappeared. "I don't have the time to argue semantics with you. You've got to admit there are a lot of fringe evangelical Christians in this country."

"So, now I get it. You called me because I must be the only Bible expert who popped up on your computers as a known evangelical Christian. *Religious fanatic* is your definition for *evangelical Christian,* is that it? That's the kind of ugly cliché thinking I would have thought had no place in the FBI."

"Come on, Murphy, we've got files and

files on fringe Christian groups that are ranting and raving about the U.N. Don't you agree this looks like one of them on the warpath here?"

Murphy looked over to Baines, who was listening in on the extension, but the agent was rubbing his eyes, perhaps to avoid Murphy's stare. Murphy's voice actually got much quieter as he waited an extra few seconds to try to regain his composure. "And I don't consider myself fringe, crackpot, reactionary, nuts, or any other code words you want to tar me with because of my faith. So I don't see how I can help you."

"Can't or *won't*?" Welsh fired back.

Before Murphy could answer, his office door opened and Laura came charging in. "Murph, what's going on? What does the FBI want with you and this crazy U.N. business?"

"Sweetheart, for the life of me, I don't know. But it's beginning to smell like a smear that's bigger than what's covering those windows up there." Into the phone he said, "Welsh, my wife's joined me. She shares my faith as well. You'd better call in backup for Agent Baines here—the religious fanatics now outnumber him. I'll put you on speakerphone."

Laura looked first shocked, then puzzled by her husband's outburst.

"Professor Murphy, Mrs. Murphy, hello, I'm FBI agent Burton Welsh up in New York. Look, we just seem to have pushed each other's buttons—"

"I'm pushing the hang-up button, Welsh. I don't see how I can help with any of this, and I've got some writing that's a few thousand years old that I can do something useful with. So, unless you want Agent Baines here to arrest me and my wife, and then round up our entire church, I'm going to go."

Welsh bristled in his chair in New York. "You can go, Mr. Murphy. Just don't go far."

"What's that supposed to mean?"

Agent Baines reached over and disconnected the call before Murphy could get an answer. "I'm sorry, Professor Murphy. Things seemed to get a little out of hand here tonight." He paused, and Laura sensed an awkwardness behind his hesitation.

"Agent Baines, is there something else we should know?"

"No." He looked away from them both.

"Baines, you can talk to us. We're not monsters, no matter what New York thinks."

"No, ma'am, I know that. Agent Welsh is a fine man and a superior agent. I saw him in action at Quantico. But...I'm from down here, and I know how funny some big-city folks get about religion. I just wanted you to know, we're not all like that at the FBI."

Murphy shook his hand. "Agent Baines, thank you. It takes a special man to stand up for both his God and his job sometimes. You seem to have figured that out, and I admire that. I could probably have used some of your balance tonight."

Laura put one arm around her husband and gave him a loving squeeze. "You, choosing balance over temper? If Agent Baines could teach you that, we'd give him tenure here at Preston. Agent Baines, it was good meeting you, even if the circumstances were bizarre."

"Hey, I'm just a messenger in all this, but I'm glad to be out of the frying pan, whatever is going on up there."

Laura put both her arms around Murphy. "That FBI man can't possibly think you had something to do with the U.N. thing, can he, Murph?"

"No, I think he's just desperate to make some sense out of why somebody would leave a big Bible quote on the U.N., and like a lot of people, he looks at all of us believers as some vast conspiracy opposed to individual thinkers. Still, he is right about one thing. Somebody went to a lot of trouble to paint that up there."

Murphy reflected, as he had for the last half hour, on the possible reasons why. The entire message of the Bible was condensed into this one tiny sentence by the Holy Spirit, who had inspired John to write it down. The Scripture itself had crept into the mainstream a few years back when an individual started a habit of holding up a crude cardboard sign inscribed with a big black JOHN 3:16 at countless televised sporting events across the country, always in direct view of the cameras.

Sometime later, the Scripture survived the silliness of a pro wrestler's using a variation as part of his act. But now things were about to turn really ugly. Just based on tonight's hyped-up coverage, Murphy sensed that the media was poised to use the same Scripture, the most beautiful and poignant of all Scriptures, which had brought hope to countless millions down through the ages, as part of a smear campaign, a conditioning process against evangelical Christians. The irony was not lost on Murphy.

"John Three: Sixteen is a pretty good message to get out there," Laura said.

"Yes," Murphy agreed, "but something tells me it wasn't some Sunday-school teacher who put it up there."

TWENTY-SEVEN

SHANE BARRINGTON WATCHED his own BNN network's live coverage of the U.N. events alone in his apartment after he had been alerted to tune in by the president of the news division, who had a standing order to call Barrington's personal hotline whenever there was important breaking news.

Of course, his network news head had no idea that Barrington had been peripherally involved. *How could he?* Barrington thought. *Even I'm not certain I was involved.* These people he was now working for, these *Seven,* along with their creepy thug, Talon, were a strange lot. He dared not ask them questions, and he had no way to contact them even if he had wanted to. They seemed to know everything about his business, however, and he assumed they would know about his personal life as well, if he had one.

Most nights, like this one, he would be poring over reports and figures by himself in his apartment. With the financial security assured by the Seven, Barrington was even further empowered in his greed, so he was driving every division to expand, to look for takeovers, to seek new ways to crush his competition.

The Seven's backing also allowed him to pay off the few trusted lieutenants within his organization so that he could be assured there would be no betrayals or sellouts. Except for the moles who were obviously reporting to the Seven, but he didn't mind about them now because he was not planning on trying to cross the Seven in any way in his business dealings. They knew what they were getting when they aligned with him: a ruthless, hard-driving, take-no-prisoners bottom-line business mogul.

He just wished he had some better idea of who these people were, these Seven. What was their goal? Other than making money and building an ever-larger and controlling communications systems and electronics empire, what was his role in their plan?

Take this U.N. stunt, for instance. He had gotten his specific instructions from Talon to find some ways to circumvent some of the U.N. security systems and he had been able to do so in a complex round of maneuvers that could never be connected or traced even under the tremendous focus that would now be brought to bear on the U.N.

However, once he transmitted the information himself to Talon, he never heard another word about the U.N. until that night. He just assumed that somehow Talon and the Seven were behind the deed, but to what end?

Barrington marveled, as he always did, at the quickness and cleverness of his network producers, who had already come up with one of their trademark alarmist names for this latest crisis: *U.N. VIOLATED.* However, this painting of the message on the front of the building looked more like a high-school prank than a world-shaking security threat.

His phone rang. Expecting his news president on the other end, he answered, "Jim, what's the latest?"

"You're not going to be getting the news tonight, Barrington, you're going to be making some." *Talon*. Despite himself, Barrington froze at the sound of his voice.

"You're going to give your lady news star, that Kovacs woman, the big scoop of the night."

"I am?"

"Just listen and write this down. It's a house at One Hundred Sixty-fourth Street and Seventy-sixth Avenue in Queens, a house rented by Joe Farley, one of the regular window washers at the U.N. It's not where he lived, it's a secret place he kept. So secret, in fact, he didn't even know he rented it, if you get my drift. Tell Kovacs that one of your big lawman buddies tipped you that the FBI is about to bust in on the place. The FBI doesn't even know that yet, so she's got a jump on the story."

"So what's the big deal? Is this guy Farley hiding out there?"

"The 'so what' is that this guy kept this other house, which is full of crazy rants and Bibles and all sorts of religious-nut papers— and plans to blow up the U.N."

"How do you know this? You couldn't have gotten this from the information I supplied you with."

"Let's just say that all this is information I supplied myself."

"You mean you've planted the evidence to frame this Farley? When the FBI finds him, won't it be clear that somebody set him up?"

"But the FBI will never find Farley. Nor will anyone. And trust me, *never* is sooner than anyone will find you if you ever ask me another question. Just get Kovacs on the phone, give her her scoop, and tell her to get over there with her cameraman and start broadcasting. She can make up some excuse later for breaking in. Then tomorrow tell her to redouble her efforts on her assignment to investigate these evangelical Christian crazies. Why, it's a disgrace what they could do to an international treasure like the U.N."

Barrington was unsure whether he should laugh, but the line went dead. As he punched in Kovacs's speed-dial phone number, he decided he would use those very words on her.

TWENTY-EIGHT

"THIS IS STEPHANIE Kovacs, broadcasting a live world exclusive for BNN. I am now standing on a deceptively quiet street in Queens, New York City. Here in this seemingly ordinary two-story brick house you see behind me, the apparent mastermind behind tonight's shocking attack on the United Nations had his secret terror cell."

Talon watched from his hotel room and gave a grim chuckle. *This woman is good,* he thought. *She may have more ice water in her veins than her boss, Barrington, has.*

He would have to keep an eye on her for future use.

In U.N. Security headquarters, Burton Welsh broke in on Nugent and turned on the television.

"Look at this, will you? That BNN reporter Kovacs is broadcasting from the window washer's secret hiding place."

Nugent swore. "How did she get there?"

Welsh shrugged. "My people say all she's said is 'street sources.' And we'll probably never be able to sweat it out of her. But look at what she's found there."

He turned up the volume on the set. "...Although there is no sign of the alleged renter, Joseph Farley, here at this house, BNN has confirmed that he was a regular window washer at the U.N. who would easily have been able to perpetrate tonight's shocking attack. And we have confirmed that he was new to this neighborhood, which is not his legal residence, but at least one neighbor told me she has seen him coming in and out of this house at strange hours."

The camera now panned away from Kovacs, and in the harsh brightness of the TV lights it zoomed in on piles of books and papers on the table in what looked like a dining room.

"Here is what BNN has found, as we are the first on the scene of the Farley-the-Fanatic house. Bibles that appear to be marked up with key passages about Christ and the resurrection. Floor plans of the United Nations also marked up for what I fear could be a terrorist attack."

Nugent swore again. "How long until the NYPD are over there and get her off the air?"

Welsh held his cell phone to one ear while cupping his other ear. "ETA a minute and a half. I'm getting myself patched through to her as soon as they arrive. This is turning into a night at the circus."

Talon did not want to take the time to wait until Kovacs interviewed the foolish old woman who lived next to the house he had rented in Farley's name. He knew Kovacs was too good a reporter to miss the half-blind but fully nosy Mrs. Sorcatini, who Talon had made sure would see him when he made his two late-night forays dressed as Farley to set up the house.

No, he had seen enough of BNN's very satisfying hyped-up news coverage. Apparently, so had his contact at the castle. By the second ring he had unlocked his security-scrambled phone. As expected, the voice was John Bartholomew, his main contact from the Seven.

"I tell you, Talon, if Christ had the miracle of twenty-four-hour satellite television, there would be no need for evangelicals. I suppose we could say that tonight you have actually begun to do the same thing, using that TV newswoman to begin destroying them."

"I don't know about that, sir," Talon replied. "This is just a flash in the pan. Nothing is going to stand up when the authorities investigate, and they will never be able to produce Farley to prove anything."

"Now, Talon, this is no time for false modesty. You've established a great worldwide media event. That's what news is these days. Nobody cares about the fine points, the correction, the follow-up—they'll be on to the next scandal by then. But people will remember that some Christian nut job, as they say on the talk shows, was going to blow up the U.N. I'd say that's a good night's work."

"If you're happy, I'm happy. Do you want me to step up the next wave?"

"No, Talon, just keep doing your prep work. My colleagues and I must decide which paths to pursue and on what timetable. We want to do this right so that we can remain in control. Chaos is a noble pursuit if properly orchestrated. Otherwise, it is just that, chaos, unless you can manipulate it to your advantage. I will be in touch."

Stephanie Kovacs held her cell phone a foot from her ear as Burton Welsh screamed at her. The network had gone back to the anchor desk for the hourly update. "Mr. Welsh, you know I'm not going to reveal my street sources for how I beat the police—and the FBI—to the Farley house."

Welsh refused to lower his decibel level. "All the freedom of the press in the country is not going to save you from a breaking-and-entering charge, Miss Kovacs. You had no right to bust into that house tonight, and you know it."

Kovacs spoke in her most innocent voice. "Why, Agent Welsh, I was watching this house from my news van because of my tip, when we thought we saw smoke coming out. We were just doing our duty as citizens to save whoever was inside from the fire."

Welsh snorted. "Fire, my foot. There will be fire coming, I promise you, when I fry your fanny in court!"

Kovacs smiled. "Mr. Welsh, don't you feel that one psychopath threatening violence is enough for tonight? Any further questions you have can be referred to the BNN legal department. Good-bye, FBI."

TWENTY-NINE

"OH, TALON, I swear it is enough to make one believe in a higher power." John Bartholomew's usually somber voice sounded almost jolly on the secure phone line. "The next phase of our plan has fallen into our laps. Pack your bags."

Talon, as usual, exhibited no emotion whatsoever. "Where am I heading?"

"You will be strengthening your inspiring new devotion to evangelical Christianity, young man."

"This time I hope I will actually get to follow through with something bigger than paint cans."

"I believe you will, but you will need to exercise some patience, Talon. We have somebody else doing the heavy lifting for us at the beginning of this next phase. Only he doesn't know it yet."

Talon sounded wary. "Who? Our agreement was that I was to be in complete control of any U.S. actions."

"And so you shall be, you suspicious boy. You are just going to monitor our unsuspecting helper while he rises to his challenges. He has a skill-set that even you cannot match."

"What skills are those?"

"Finding things. Old things. You're going to Preston, North Carolina, to keep tabs on Professor Michael Murphy."

"I hunt things, I kill things. Why do you want me watching a professor?"

"You are a man of few words, Talon, but such clear, colorful phrases. You see, one of our sources in the Mideast has alerted us that this Murphy has stumbled onto something we want very badly."

"Then let me just go take this thing you want."

"Oh, you will, but it's not that simple. We've had it checked out, and what we want is actually in pieces, pieces that probably no one else in the world could find."

"That's preposterous. You've demonstrated that you have power and money enough to do almost anything you want."

"Murphy cannot be bought. He's got morals, principles, things you wouldn't understand. And he tries to be a very good Christian, something you *certainly* wouldn't understand. And yet, surprisingly, he is also a risk-taker, much like yourself, a man of action, sometimes foolish action. Which is why I wish I could be there when you finally do battle with him, Talon, because that should be something to see."

"You're not frightening me."

"I'm not trying to. I am warning you that this is not some flabby window washer in Queens you're going to be tracking. He's smart, he's capable, and most of all he is the only person in the world who has such a unique combination of knowledge, courage, and drive to recognize the value of these pieces we want and to go find them."

"What are these pieces he's finding for you? He finds old Biblical junk, doesn't he?"

"So eloquently phrased, Talon. Yes, he finds ancient artifacts that have helped to validate events in the Bible as real historical events."

"Why is that of interest to you? I thought you all hate religion of any kind."

"No, we do not hate all religion. We will one day soon have a new religion, and only one religion. To help lead all of those millions of Christians toward our one religion, we want to lure them over with some of their own symbols from their own Bible. If we can show that we have been entrusted by their God with these symbols, it will make us seem that much more legitimate and will help to distract them as we wean them away from their old God to our new God."

"What do you need the real artifacts for? Why don't you just make your own?"

"Because there are people like Murphy in the world who would be able to spot a fake. Besides, this particular artifact he's hunting has been rumored for centuries to have some real power all its own. The Brazen Serpent of the Bible."

"You mean to tell me that you Seven have all the power that money can buy and you still believe in some Bible souvenir?"

"Well, Talon, when Murphy finds the three pieces of the Serpent and puts them together, we'll just see. Whether it has a darker power or not, we will eventually use it as a centerpiece to rally believers to our religion. So, you are going to keep close tabs on Professor Murphy while he finds the other two pieces, and then take them all for us. Got it?"

"I'll need something besides babysitting to do down in North Carolina."

"Ah, great minds do think alike, Talon. You know how we have been considering what our next moves should be in our other goals, such as stirring up general fear and distrust in all of the world's organizations and institutions. Our focus has been on the urban centers, but we have decided to combine several of our goals for your next action. We're going to take the terror to a small town. And continue our drive against our dear evangelical brothers and sisters."

For the first time in their conversation, Talon sounded more energized than usual. "Let me guess. The small town is Preston, North Carolina. And the evangelical church is Murphy's."

"Very good, Talon. You go right to the head of the class. In fact, you're ready for the university."

THIRTY

NEBUCHADNEZZAR COULD stand to wait no longer. Daniel seemed to be straining to hear an inner voice.

Finally he spoke again. "You saw a great image, O King. You dreamed of a statue—"

"A statue! Yes! I see it!" The king was on his feet, smiling from ear to ear like a blind man who had just had his sight miraculously restored.

Daniel continued, taking no heed of the king's excitement.

"The statue you saw in your dreams, its splendor was excellent in form, awesome. A mighty statue that towered fully ninety cubits above you.

"The head of the statue was of gold, wondrously bright, like molten fire, the chest and arms of shining silver like the moon when she is full." He paused as the king stepped forward and gripped his shoulders fiercely. It was as if the statue were standing before them under a great black veil and Daniel was pulling the veil away inch by inch with his words.

"The belly and thighs of the statue were of bronze, the legs of iron, the feet of clay and iron mixed." He paused, and the king became still, not daring to move or speak in case the vision was lost.

Nebuchadnezzar sat back on his cedarwood chair and drank deeply from a cup of wine. The exhilaration that came with remembering his dream was intoxicating but short-lived. Now he was filled with a gnawing hunger to discover what meaning might lie behind such an extraordinary vision.

He looked up, and Daniel seemed to sense his question before he asked it.

"The four portions of the statue represent four empires. First gold, then silver, then bronze. Each empire less mighty than the last. Until the final empire of iron, which will be the weakest, for its foundations, the feet of iron and clay mixed together, shall likewise be divided."

"Four empires," the king mused. "And only four?"

"Yes, there shall be only four world empires until the Latter times. This is how the people will know that only the God of heaven can accurately reveal history before it comes to pass. Then, in the Latter days, ten kingdoms of the world will join together in an attempt to rebuild a world kingdom similar to yours, O King. After that, the end shall come."

It was extraordinary. Nebuchadnezzar lived in a world where lies were common currency. Even those closest to him—perhaps especially they—could not be trusted. He had long ago concluded that only a man bound and chained and who sees the red-hot iron in the approaching torturer's hand could be relied upon to tell the truth.

Yet, he had no doubt, not the smallest shred, that every word Daniel spoke would come to pass. For the first time in his life he, the ruler of countless nations, felt there was no solid ground beneath his feet.

Once again, the Hebrew slave anticipated his next thought.

"And what of Babylon, what of Nebuchadnezzar in all of this?" Daniel looked the king in the eye once more, and his deep, resonant voice seemed to fill the chamber.

"Here is the dream's interpretation. You have been chosen by God to be the ruler of all things and all men. The God of heaven has given you a kingdom, power, strength, and glory. Before the coming of the kingdom of God, yours shall be the greatest empire the world will ever know. You, my king, are the head of gold of the dream's statue. When the fourth kingdom arises, it shall be as strong as iron. That kingdom will break into pieces and crush all other kingdoms."

"Break into pieces?" the king shouted.

"That is the rest of your dream. You watched as a stone was formed without hands. The stone struck the image with great force and shattered the feet made of iron and clay. The image came crashing to the ground. Its iron, clay, bronze, silver, and gold were all crushed together and became like chaff from the threshing floor. Then the wind came up and blew them all away so that no trace could be found. And the stone that struck the image grew to the size of a mountain and enveloped the whole earth."

The king arose and began to pace with agitation.

"My king, the feet which you saw, made partly of clay and partly of iron, they indicate a divided kingdom, both strong and fragile. As you are aware, O King, iron cannot mix with clay. And in the days of this divided kingdom, the God of heaven will set up His own kingdom, which shall never be destroyed. It will not be ruled by ordinary men. It will consume all the other kingdoms and stand forever."

Daniel then concluded, "The God of heaven has made these things known to you, O King. The dream and its interpretation are certain."

King Nebuchadnezzar then commanded his men to present an offering of gifts and incense to Daniel. He placed his hand on Daniel's shoulder.

"From this day forward, you shall be ruler over this entire province and chief administrator over all of the wise men of Babylon. For you, Daniel, serve a God which is greater than any other."

THIRTY-ONE

CHUCK NELSON FISHED in the pocket of his jeans and pulled out a handful of crumpled bills. He looked at them sourly. Ten bucks, give or take. Enough for a burger, maybe some chili. He swept a hank of greasy blond hair out of his eyes and squinted at the bills, as if looking harder was going to change anything.

Nope. The same ten bucks he'd had in his pocket when the cops had pulled him over in the stolen Chevy. Just like he was wearing the same oil-stained jeans with the tears at both knees, the same stained green sweatshirt and muddy sneakers. At least they'd laundered his clothes. Didn't look like they'd done the same for his money.

His stomach began to rumble and he tried to remember when he'd last eaten a meal that was fit for a human being rather than a hog. A big bowl of chili would sure go down easy. And he needed a drink right now.

He'd need every cent, unless they'd passed a free-beer law while he'd been away, that is. It was only a couple miles into town. And hey, maybe somebody would pull over and give him a ride. But he doubted it. He knew he looked like what he was. Trouble. And the oh-so-good folks of Preston always liked to avoid trouble if they possibly could.

He pulled his old Preston High jacket closer as he felt the first spatters of rain, and started marching down the two-lane country road.

First get that beer. Then settle a few scores.

Two hours later Chuck was sitting at a table in Mooney's Tavern and shaking the last drops out of an empty pitcher. He had a little buzz going now, but his money was all spent and the barman, some new guy probably straight out of bartending school, had refused to run him a tab. He slammed the pitcher down and spat on the floor. How much money had he spent in this lousy dive over the years, drinking their lousy watered-down beer? Math wasn't his strong suit, but it had to be a lot. And now the barman was eyeing him like Chuck was something nasty he was fixing to scrape off his shoe. He could feel the rage mounting, that tingling feeling at the ends of his fingers as if a fuse had just been lit.

A screech followed by raucous laughter diverted his attention from the barman, and he swiveled to see a pretty blonde choking on a beer, while another girl thumped her on the back and the two guys sitting across the booth slapped the table, whooping.

He didn't need to see the words "Preston University" on their sweatshirts to know they were students. And probably underage too. He'd been getting drunk in this place when they were still wearing braces, and now he was the one the barman was giving the evil eye to.

He sauntered over and put his hands on the shoulders of the two guys. "Hey, boys, don't you have a class to go to? I think your little friend here could use a beer-drinking lesson." He grinned and gave them a friendly pat.

The blond girl wiped beer from her mouth with her sleeve and glared at him as the two guys shook off Chuck's hands and jumped to their feet. They were both an inch or two shorter than he was and looked out of shape. Too much time reading books and not enough working out, he guessed. He could see they didn't want to look bad in front of their girlfriends, but the worried look in their eyes told him they weren't going to give him any trouble.

"Tell you what. You boys buy me a pitcher of beer and I'll give you a free demonstration. Show you how it's done. What do you say?" He gave them his best good-time grin and winked at the girls. They were still glaring at him like wildcats. *Hey, it ain't my fault if your boyfriends are such wimps,* he thought.

He was about to press the point when he felt his jacket being yanked from behind.

Off balance, he staggered backward and fell heavily against a table. Before he could regain his feet, someone pinned his arms behind him and started shoving him toward the door.

"Hey, get your hands off me." He managed to wrench himself out of the armlock and whirled around. The barman stood smirking, arms folded. Next to him was another man Chuck had never seen before, heavier set, unshaven, with faded tattoos on his forearms. *Must have come out of the kitchen,* he thought. The man stepped forward, getting right in Chuck's face.

"Get out. Now. Before we decide to get nasty. We don't want scum like you in here no more."

Chuck reckoned he could take the barman, no problem. But the kitchen guy looked like he meant business. No point getting all busted up for a pitcher of beer, no matter how thirsty he was. He brushed himself off and did not look back.

A few minutes later, the man known as Talon left an untouched beer on a corner table and walked out of the bar. He scanned the street. No sign of Chuck in either direction. No matter. It wasn't exactly hard to predict his next move. He sniffed the air, then turned right. Toward the river.

As he walked through the town, past the little corner drugstore, then the thrift shop with its display of teddy bears in the window, he wondered how long his work would keep him in Preston. Long enough to make a lasting contribution to the place, he felt sure. To make a few changes that would be remembered. He stopped at the Hey Preston! magic shop with its hand-painted sign depicting a rabbit peering over the brim of a top hat, and smiled. Oh, yes. He'd show them a few new tricks before he was done.

Another ten minutes and the cute little shops and family restaurants began to give way to boarded-up storefronts and vacant lots. Even Preston had its bad part of town, where the street lighting wasn't so good and the picket fences were missing a few slats and a coat of whitewash. He began to search for a likely spot.

He found it almost at once. An alley between a Chinese takeout place and a liquor store. A good shortcut if you weren't afraid of the shadows and anybody who might be lurking there. Somebody who might be badly in need of some cash and didn't care how they got it, for instance.

He peered into the gloom. There was a powerful stench of rotting vegetables. No doubt this was where the restaurant dumped its garbage. The scraping and scurrying sounds told him he was not the first to figure that out. He took a few steps into the alley and listened. Just in time. He walked another ten yards through the discarded boxes, then ducked behind a Dumpster and pulled out his cell phone.

Chuck kept the little man pinned to the wall with one hand while he tried to flip through his wallet with the other. The guy was so terrified, he probably could not have run, let alone fight back. But the lessons you learned in jail stayed with you. Never turn your back. Never let your guard down. And never assume your opponent is down for the count unless he's actually stopped breathing.

The other rule was to listen hard. You might not see trouble coming, but maybe you could hear it. And right now Chuck could hear a siren. Hard to tell how far away, but it seemed to be getting louder. Time to finish his business and get on his way.

Suddenly a flashlight swept across the alley, blinding him for a moment. Behind it stood a cop, nightstick at the ready. "Stop right there," he shouted. "Step away from the wall with your hands out front, where I can see them."

Chuck shoved the wallet into his jacket and let go of the little man, who crumpled against the wall and slumped to the ground. Now what? He didn't have a weapon and the cop was advancing steadily. He'd be on him in a second.

If he didn't think of something quick, he'd soon be back in Cell 486, and this time they'd throw away the key.

The cop found his target again with the flashlight, and now Chuck couldn't see a thing. Then suddenly there was a crack, a sharp cry of pain, and the light veered off into the shadows. As his eyes adjusted again to the gloom, he made out a dark shape—a tall man standing over the cop with what looked like a piece of two-by-four in his hand. The cop wasn't making a sound now.

The man turned toward Chuck and he saw his face. Bone-white features and blank eyes that made him shiver. He beckoned Chuck forward with a gloved hand.

"His friends will be here in a minute or two. Time to ship out, Chuck."

Chuck froze in place, uncertain what this ghoul had in mind. His brain had shut down.

The ghoul seemed to sense his fear. He flung the two-by-four into a pile of boxes and held both arms out to the side. "You have nothing to fear from me, Chuck. Quite the opposite. In fact, you could say I'm your savior." He laughed, though Chuck couldn't see the joke. It was a harsh, animal sound, not really a laugh at all.

The sirens were loud now. Only a few blocks away.

"Come on, I have a place where you can

get cleaned up. Money. I even have a job for you. Unless you'd rather go back to jail, of course."

Chuck's brain unscrambled itself enough to figure out he didn't really have any more choices.

"Okay, mister," he said. "You're the boss. I guess you better lead the way."

THIRTY-TWO

STEPHANIE KOVACS FOUND herself gazing out the window for the third time in the last half hour, wondering how she had gotten stuck talking to one of the most boring men in the world while researching a story that to her great surprise was one of the hottest of her career. Since her worldwide exclusive at the home of Farley the Fanatic, the U.N. window washer who still had not turned up, Stephanie's media star was rising at BNN even faster than before.

Of course, it did not hurt that Shane Barrington himself seemed to be following this story with keener personal interest than he had exhibited about any prior news story. From the moment Stephanie had gotten the anonymous phone tip to rush to the Farley rental in Queens the night of the U.N. attack, she had wondered about the coincidence of Barrington's first meeting with her, essentially ordering her to investigate the evangelical Christian movement and this headline-making discovery. Considering she herself had barely picked up a Bible since she was twelve, religious talk was now filling her days.

The competitive reporter in her was more than a little envious about not getting to follow up some of the links resulting from the U.N. window painting. That seemed like hard news, or, more appropriately, hard lack-of-news, because no further evidence had been uncovered to connect Farley either to a known evangelical group or to any additional physical evidence of a U.N. bombing plot. But her revelations of that night still stuck in people's memories.

Now she was following a direct tip from Shane Barrington himself. When he called to congratulate her—first time ever—on her scoop, he let slip that high-level people in Washington had told him that the FBI had questioned none other than Professor Michael Murphy in connection with the U.N. attack. Stephanie had suggested that they were probably talking to Murphy as an expert on the Bible to get clues about the painted message, much like the networks all had talking-head experts for every crisis.

But Barrington suggested she should go to Preston University and snoop around about Murphy. After all, he was a TV personality, and TV people like nothing better than a whiff of scandal about another TV star, even if he was only the star of some dusty archaeology specials on cable.

Which was how she found herself listening to Dean Archer Fallworth drone on and on about the university grade-point average and student community service initiatives. She did not want to tip her hand about her interest in Murphy until she had gotten a sense of how hc fit into university life, but now it was time to cut to the chase.

"Dean, how about the evangelical Christians? Are they active on campus?"

Fallworth's eyes narrowed. "Evangelicals? Well, yes, we do have some very"—he waved his hand, searching for the right word—"*energetic* members of that particular religious group at Preston. Only a handful, really, but they tend to make rather a lot of noise." He flashed a smile he wanted to appear to be conspiratorial. "What exactly is your interest?"

"Let's just say there's a lot of concern among ordinary citizens that these evangelical groups are getting too big, too scary. I want to find out how a fine liberal arts university like Preston is affected. Institutions like yours as the front line in the battle against bigotry. Our viewers would be interested in that."

Fallworth's smile became a Cheshire cat's grin. "I like to think we do our best. Fighting the good fight against ignorance and intolerance." He clasped his hands together and leaned forward over the desk. "But it isn't always easy. They're *very* well organized, you know. And some of their leaders are tremendously cunning."

Here we go, thought Stephanie. "Anyone in particular?"

Fallworth pursed his lips. "I don't want to speak ill of any faculty members, of course. . . ."

"Unless it's in the public interest."

"Quite so. Well, there is one professor here who makes it his business to stir up trouble, filling impressionable young minds with the worst kinds of spiritualistic nonsense. His name's Murphy." He winced, as if Stephanie had forced an unpleasant confession out of him. "Professor Michael Murphy."

Bingo. That was the name Barrington had given her when he'd called two nights earlier. Just a little follow-up, he'd said. To focus the investigation. She had no idea why he was so keen to nail him, but there was no doubting the strength of his feelings. In his icy way, he was practically breathing fire into the phone. And Murphy seemed to be just as unpopular with Fallworth.

He must be quite a character, she thought.

"So, what does this Murphy teach?"

"Biblical archaeology, if you will. His mission is to authenticate the Bible by digging up artifacts that confirm Bible stories.

The very opposite of science, in my opinion."

"And has he found any?"

"So he would claim."

"And his classes are well attended?"

"I'm afraid so. Students tend to find him . . . charismatic. He's something of a cult figure on campus, and I mean that in the worst sense. Perhaps it's because he's an outdoors type." *Unlike real scholars such as yourself,* thought Stephanie, noting Fallworth's paunch and pasty complexion. "Rock-climbing, archery, all very gung-ho."

Stephanie stood and gathered her briefcase. "How intriguing. If I'm going to go after these evangelicals, it looks like Murphy's the place to start. So, where can I find him?"

THIRTY-THREE

THE MAN KNOWN as Talon entered the house and let the screen door shut in Chuck Nelson's face behind him.

As he scrambled to pull open the screen door to this place where Talon said he was living, Chuck was really puzzled. The guy had plenty of cash, whipping out a large roll of small bills at every store, yet he was living in this house Chuck figured was two grades below a dump. It was about twenty miles outside of Preston, so it was not even close to anything except back roads and forest. The porch was sunken to the point of near collapse, there was a leak in the roof

over two of the bedrooms, and the bathroom sink had only one faucet knob, and it
was crusted with a muddy mix of years of
rust and dirt.

Chuck's reflexes were a little slow because
he was tired from having driven Talon
around for four hours. There were stops in
three different megastores—each in a different county, miles apart from one another.
None of what they bought made sense to
Chuck, and it especially did not make sense
that they couldn't just buy it all in one place,
but Talon made it clear early on that questions of any kind were not part of his
routine.

"Start hauling the bags and boxes out of
the car," Talon ordered.

"I'm beat. Can't it wait until morning?"

"Haul. Now. School's in session."

Chuck scowled. "What school?"

"Shut up and learn, genius. I'm going to
teach you how to shake things up but good
in this hick town of yours."

Within an hour, the card table in what
once might have passed for a living room

was spilling over with torn bags and ripped-open boxes. As Talon showed Chuck how he wanted the crude ingredients mixed, he surprised Chuck by being in a more talkative mood than before.

"That sister of yours, she got a thing for that Professor Murphy?"

"I told you, I haven't spoken to her pretty much since I was in the joint. I'm just living there because I can't afford to be on my own yet, and it's clean, a lot cleaner than this place. But I doubt it. She's just a goody-goody girl, always was."

"What do you know about Murphy, or his wife?"

"Don't make me laugh. You expect me to know something about a teacher and his stupid wife? My sister knew him from church, before she went to college, I know that much. Why are you so curious about Murphy?"

"A warrior always studies the enemy."

After Talon sent Chuck home for the night, letting him drive the rental car and telling him to be back in the morning to pick him up for a full day of errands, he grabbed his secure satellite-link phone and dialed a New York number.

It took a while for Shane Barrington to answer. "You're not a religious man, I know, Barrington, but get out your sackcloth and your funeral suit. In two days, you're going to announce the tragic death of your only son, Arthur."

Barrington had now come to dread Talon's calls. The only consolations were that they were brief and that the calls were better than visits. "You know you killed my son days ago. Whatever you did with the body, how can I just announce that he died?"

Talon pulled out his checklist, to make sure he did not forget any detail. "It's rather simple. First off, you're rich and powerful, which in this country means you can do whatever you want, pretty much. Why, a rich creep like you can even buy the sympathy of the American public. And that's exactly what you're going to do."

THIRTY-FOUR

"DO WE NOW find ourselves in the best of times or the worst of times? Show of hands." Murphy stood in front of the lectern. "First, you doomsayers. Who thinks we are living in the worst of times?"

A few students' hands shot up right away, but most looked hesitant to commit. "Come on, folks, your answer will not count toward your final grade. At least not in this course. So, worst of times?" About half of the students raised their hands.

"Okay, now for you more optimistic folks. How many of you feel that you are alive during the best of times?" A little less than half of the students raised their hands. "I'm going to give the rest of you who didn't raise your hand the benefit of the doubt that you are not unsure about whether you're alive at all."

"So, what's the right answer?" a student in the last row shouted.

"Well, I'm not here to tell you my opinion, despite Dean Fallworth's fears, but I can tell you that going right back to Eve's fall from the Garden of Eden, many people in each generation have believed the human race's best times are in the past, that civilization as they know it, or perhaps as they nostalgically prefer to remember it, is declining, and that even darker times are coming."

A voice rang out, "The end is near!"

"Yes, many of you have probably seen the cliché cartoon figure, the madman storming through the streets carrying the sign REPENT! THE END IS NEAR.

"Well, lots of people consider such belief so extreme that it's to be laughed at.

"But in most societies throughout history, people sought out signs, gods, idols, superstitions, science—yes, science—to try to get some predictive leg up on exactly what the future held, especially about any dark times on the horizon. In most of those societies, the men and women who could convincingly make interpretations and predictions held a place of honor, at least until they were proven to be frauds or, sometimes, when their unpopular predictions came true.

"The more formal practitioners of this predictive knowledge are called prophets.

"You probably have never met any prophets, but you might be surprised to know that today, many of your family, friends, and neighbors, millions of people of all ages, in all walks of life, in all parts of the country, all believe in prophecy. These people especially believe that the end is near, and they believe that the end is near not because of reading the entrails of a goat they have sacrificed in their yard, nor by calling the Psychic Hotline, nor by how their bunions feel in the rain, or secret signals from little green Martians, but because of this book."

Murphy held up his Bible. "That's right, the Bible is not just a history of what hap-

pened back in ancient times and a compila-
tion of lessons for how we should live our
lives. The Bible also is filled with many
prophecies that have *already* come true and
many more prophecies that a huge number
of people believe *will* come true. People
who are not crackpots, I daresay. People
like me.

"Now, one day, I hope that the university
will allow me to teach a course in Biblical
prophecy, because I believe it is both a fascinating and an important intellectual discipline, separate from the issue of belief in
what the prophecies lay out for us. However, here in good old Biblical Archaeology,
I am going to focus instead on showing you
how one archaeological discovery, which I
hope I am very close to digging up, could
help to authenticate the historical facts behind the prophecy that many believe is the
most important one in the Bible, the
prophecy of Daniel based on the dream of
King Nebuchadnezzar.

"Nebuchadnezzar was the greatest ruler
in the great empire of Babylon and had at
his beck and call the best prophets and high

priests of his pagan world. None of them could interpret his dream of a statue, but one of the Hebrew slaves, Daniel, was able to tell him in no uncertain terms that his dream was a vision given him by the one true God.

"Daniel explained that the huge image in the dream was a statue of Nebuchadnezzar himself, built in four levels. Each of the four levels represented one of the only absolute world empires: first was the Golden Head, representing Babylon; next the silver chest and arms, representing the Medo-Persian empire, which consisted of the two countries that conquered Babylon; then came the belly of brass, which represented the Greeks; and they were followed by the iron legs of the Romans. The closer you get to the present, the weaker those empires became, as you can see by the declining quality of the materials used to render their portion of the statue.

"Prophecy, which is history written in advance, is one of God's ways of proving that He exists. For example, the fact that God twenty-five hundred years ago revealed to Nebuchadnezzar that there would be only four world empires until 'the time of the end' is a miracle in and of itself.

"For, as all students of history know, there have been only four world empires since the days of the Babylonian empire. The most amazing thing is that many ruthless leaders have tried to rule the world, such as Genghis Khan, Napoleon, Hitler, Stalin, Mao, and others. But they all failed. Why? Because the God of heaven said there would be only four world empires until the Latter days.

"Not a bad piece of prophecy, you have to admit, considering it was written five hundred years before Christ.

"And the real reason so many millions study Daniel's prophecy is that based on the accuracy of his account of the *past,* there is every reason to believe his account of what will happen in our *future.*

"Again, time and our course work will keep me from going into greater detail now, but feel free to stop by my office anytime and I will be happy to explain why this generation has more reason to believe that when you study Daniel's prophecies and others, there are more Biblical reasons to believe that Christ will return to set up His kingdom in our lifetime than in any generation before us.

"But back to where archaeology fits into all of this. I bet it's safe to assume there are some skeptics among you who figure Daniel never lived and his prophecies have no basis in fact. Well, remember in my last lecture I told you about the Brazen Serpent made by Moses at God's instruction, and I showed you a piece of the actual bronze Serpent as proof of its truth as the Bible told it? And remember, I went through the incredible journey of that Brazen Serpent over so many decades and so many different ancient societies, finally ending up, based on where and how I found it, to have been right there in Babylon, in the time of Daniel's prophecies for Nebuchadnezzar.

"Well, while I've called in a much smarter scientist than myself to try to interpret the next clues for me, which will lead to the finding of the rest of the Serpent, I hope, I went back to study the scroll that got me started on all of this, the new interpretation of the life and times of the Brazen Serpent. A much longer life and much more interesting time than we knew about that Serpent up to now."

Murphy brought a slide up onto the screen behind him. "I'm sorry that once again, for you lazybones in the class, the underlying message here is not a religious one; it is: When in doubt about what you're doing, study, study, study, and study some more. I still could not figure out what the connection was between my source for this scroll telling me that it had something to do with Daniel and what we had known about the Brazen Serpent.

"Now that I have found the tail of the bronze Brazen Serpent, thanks to a scroll dated from the time of Daniel in Babylon, a scroll seemingly written by King Nebuchadnezzar's most trusted high priest, Dakkuri, I believe that we can place the Serpent in Daniel's time even though the Old Testament never mentions the Serpent after Hezekiah had it destroyed in the Second Book of Kings.

"However, even I would not claim that this is absolute proof of Daniel's historical existence or that it unequivocally helps to authenticate his prophecies.

"Then, as I pored over the scroll, it hit

me. Actually, it was when I was taking a break in the lounge, when I passed the NO SMOKING sign I've passed a thousand times before, that it hit me. You know the international slash-through sign for taking all the joys out of everybody's life?

"Well, I thought this mark here over the symbol for the king—that would be Nebuchadnezzar—this line aiming at his head, was just a decay line or some dirt on the scroll. But I realized it was the writer of the scroll doing his version of a NO SMOKING symbol, except he was saying 'no king.' That wouldn't make sense though, for a high priest to be making a sign against his king. After all, what if the scroll fell into his enemies' hands? One look at the 'no king' line there and you can bet there would quickly be no high priest's head instead. Unless, I realized, King Nebuchadnezzar had said it was okay to do away with his own head."

"You mean King Nebuchadnezzar committed suicide?" someone asked.

"Not suicide as we know it, no, but he did have himself destroyed. Again in the

Book of Daniel, we learn that Nebuchadnezzar let the news of his supreme empire,
the Golden Head of his dream statue, go to
his own head.

"Nebuchadnezzar had the dream statue
built and then went mad worshiping himself. After seven whole years, he recovered
from being crazy and made amends to God
by having the statue destroyed, broken into
pieces, much the way Hezekiah had the
Brazen Serpent broken into three pieces.

"That's right, Nebuchadnezzar went on a
tear—literally—when he stopped being a
madman and was returned to power. He
pledged his renewed loyalty to God by ordering all idols and graven images destroyed—including the Brazen Serpent,
which he had broken into three pieces
again—and his own giant statue of himself.
What this symbol of the line coming down
toward the king's head has to mean is that
Nebuchadnezzar himself ordered the statue
destroyed.

"And this is the amazingly exciting conclusion I have realized, ladies and gentlemen. Because I think there is a big fat clue

here to a discovery that will absolutely prove that the events in Daniel really took place.

"What the scroll shows us, and what my finding of the tail of the Serpent by following the scroll seems to prove, is that whoever wrote this scroll had secretly gone against King Nebuchadnezzar's orders. He had somehow *rescued* the pieces of the Brazen Serpent from the royal trash heap.

"And why would Nebuchadnezzar's high priest, Dakkuri, save the pieces of the Brazen Serpent? So that one day they could be rediscovered by some worthy person who would put the Serpent back whole, just as Dakkuri did after Hezekiah had destroyed it.

"And because the high priest Dakkuri was going against the direct orders of his king, who had just renewed his faith in God, it seems most likely that Dakkuri did not believe in the God of heaven. He was holding on to some idol. Or I think it's possible that he felt he was getting some special powers, most likely some dark powers, from the Brazen Serpent.

"And I think he's telling us right in the

scroll that whoever finds the Serpent pieces and puts them together will be able to plug into the very same powers that Dakkuri believed in and that Nebuchadnezzar wanted destroyed.

"But that's not all. He's showing us something else here in the scroll. That in addition to the special powers of the Serpent, you get an even bigger prize, according to the high priest Dakkuri, a bigger prize that Nebuchadnezzar was trying to keep from the world. Somehow, the whole Serpent put back together will lead you to the *other* object that this Dakkuri saved and hid away against Nebuchadnezzar's wishes.

"I think he's promising a prize the Bible tells us is gigantic in size. I think he wants someone to use the Serpent to find and dig up the Golden Head of the statue of Nebuchadnezzar."

THIRTY-FIVE

LAURA SAT ON the bench at the top of the little hill overlooking the campus. It was a beautiful day, a warm breeze blowing leaves across the grass while starlings chattered in the little stand of birch trees behind her. The kind of day when you'd catch yourself smiling for no reason. She was meeting Shari after Murph's class to go for a quick lunch.

The tranquillity was shattered by a car she did not recognize screeching to a loud and sudden stop in front of her bench. She involuntarily frowned when she saw Chuck Nelson in the driver's seat, though she knew it could not be his car. It must belong to the pale, thin man with dark glasses and dressed all in black who sat in the front passenger seat. Neither man looked very happy to have given a ride to Shari, who was getting out of the backseat.

"Thanks, Chuck. Will you be home for dinner?"

Without answering, in fact without even waiting for the back door to click closed, Chuck sped away. Despite his dark glasses, Laura had the uneasy feeling that the stranger had been staring at her the whole time it took to dislodge Shari. Laura was glad he was wearing the sunglasses, because even shielded, there was something about the stranger's face and manner that gave her chills despite the warmth of the sun.

She was not alone in this discomfort. As Shari came and sat beside her, Laura could almost see the dark clouds hovering over her head. Without saying anything, she reached across and wrapped Shari in a tight hug. When she gently pulled back, Shari had tears in her eyes.

Laura felt her own tears coming and willed herself to be strong. But it was so hard. She thought back to the long sessions they'd spent in her office talking about the pain Shari still felt years after her mom and dad had died in a five-car pileup on the interstate, her dad at the wheel with half a pint of Wild Turkey inside him. How she'd tried to help Shari make sense of it all. Help her work through the anger she felt toward her dad and try to reconnect with the love that had once been there. Help her find a way of giving thanks for everything her mother had been and would always be.

And hardest of all, Laura had tried to give her the strength to reach out to her brother. Chuck had been getting into mischief from the day he could walk, and by the time he was sixteen, the neighbors were no longer taking bets on how long it would be before he found himself in jail. Throughout his troubled adolescence, he'd treated both parents with everything from sullen indifference to outright contempt—and Shari was sure her father's drinking was his way of numbing the hurt, while her mother's heart quietly broke behind her ever-loving smile.

But when Chuck found out that his parents were gone forever, he seemed to go into some kind of shock. As if he suddenly realized there was no chance now of making amends. For a brief period Shari dared to hope that their parents' tragic death would be a kind of terrible wake-up call for him.

Unfortunately, as soon as the shock wore off, Chuck cranked up the bad behavior to an all-new high—drinking, fighting, dealing drugs. It was hard to figure out who he was really trying to punish, his parents or himself, but there was no doubt he was set on a path of self-destruction now and it would be only a matter of time before he achieved his end.

For a sister still dealing with her own grief, seeing Chuck do his best to destroy himself was just too much. So when Judge Johnson handed him some jail time after the police stopped him in a stolen car filled with drugs, it gave Shari some much-needed breathing space. She could sleep at night knowing he wasn't getting into any harm, and maybe her daily prayers for her brother would have a chance to work at last.

But the Chuck who'd turned up on her doorstep was meaner than ever.

And now there was an added concern, this new friend. Laura knew the stranger was the main reason Shari had asked her to lunch.

"I just met him for the first time in the car. I couldn't even see his face with those creepy dark glasses and his cap pulled down. The way Chuck talks about him it's like he's some sort of godfather. He says he's giving him *important jobs* to do."

"What kind of jobs?"

"He won't say. He just grins like it's some big joke on the rest of us. But whatever they're doing, I don't think it's just stealing cars." She squeezed Laura's hand. "I'm worried. Really worried, Laura. I don't want him getting himself killed."

Laura squeezed back. "Don't worry, Shari. We're not going to let that happen." She didn't have the first idea *how,* but it was important to seem confident and determined. Shari needed to know her friends were strong enough to help her deal with just about anything.

Laura thought for a moment. "If this guy's a criminal, do you think Chuck met him in prison? Maybe we could find out who he is that way."

"I don't think so. Chuck says he met him in town. Said he was having some trouble making a cash withdrawal, and this guy helped him out." She frowned. "But he won't tell me anything else about him."

"Well, that's not much to go on, but why don't I ask Chief Rawley if he can keep an eye out for Chuck and this friend and maybe he can get a better sense of what's going on with the two of them."

"Laura, I don't want to get Chuck angry with me by making him think I'm getting him spied on by the police."

"Oh, Shari, we both know that Chuck is likely to be angry whether you try to help him or not. You're a caring sister, but you can take it only so far. Eventually, he will have to make the decision to help himself."

"I know. I was lucky I had my friend's mother, who started taking me to church for the first time after my parents died. And you and Murph have been so wonderful looking out for me."

"Yes, and speaking of looking out for

yourself, how about you, Shari? When was the last time you went out with a friend—a boyfriend?"

"Well, since you brought it up, I had somebody over recently, a transfer student, Paul Wallach, who's in Professor Murphy's class with me."

"Nice. So?"

"So, nothing. I'm just getting to know him. He's got major issues, as in issues with his major, still wrestling with the business course his father forced him into, even though his father died months ago."

"Why don't you tell him to come see me?"

"Oh, I already did, Laura, especially since the course that is really exciting him the most is Professor Murphy's."

"Whew, that's some leap, from the gold mine of business administration to choking on dust, looking for bones in old mines."

"Well, you of all people should know that. I hope you don't mind, I suggested that he should go talk things over with you."

"Mind? That's what I'm here for. Otherwise, I'd have to spend more time in the field with *my* dreamboat archaeologist."

"And isn't that him coming right now?" Murphy circled his Dodge in front of the bench and stuck his head out of the window.

"Ladies, can I interest either of you in a walk in the North Woods, where I will be winging a few dozen arrows into unsuspecting trees just to keep sharp?"

"I don't think Shari's ever caught your Robin Hood act, but we're going to lunch. Murph, are you skipping off because I asked you to round up the clothes you want to give to the church clothing drive?"

"Busted. I'll do it later." He floored the accelerator before he could hear Laura yelling at him.

Laura shook her head and looked at Shari. "See what I have to deal with? We once figured out that Murphy can say 'later' in twelve languages, most of which are as ancient as his promises to do any chores."

"Oh, I twisted Paul's arm to come to our Wednesday church meeting and told him he should get in the swing of things by helping sort the clothing in the basement."

"Great. But we'd better eat so we can keep our strength up, because if we rely on the men, we'll probably be left doing all the lifting and sorting ourselves."

Talon scowled over at Chuck. "I told you to slow down. I don't want to get stopped in any speed traps down here."

"Okay, okay. It's just that I haven't been behind the wheel for a while. Tell me why we're going all the way up to Raleigh for shopping like yesterday. There's lots of stores closer."

"I don't want anybody to remember what we're buying."

"What did you want to give my sister a lift for? Man, I can tell she doesn't like you."

"Yeah, the feeling's mutual. That's why you can't tell her anything. She'd rat you out to the cops in a heartbeat. So don't tell her anything about what we're doing."

Chuck's bored eyes brightened. "I don't know anything, so what could I tell her? Hey, man, when are you going to tell me what you're planning for? Whatever it is, count me in."

Talon shook his head. "Of course you're in, you fool. Now, just shut up and get us to the mall. We're buying clothes. Lots of clothes."

"Clothes. That's cool. I could use some new duds."

"They're not for you. We're giving them away."

"I don't get it. Why are we buying clothes to give them away? What's the scam?"

"Didn't you listen to your sister natter on in the backseat about that Preston Community Church clothing drive?"

"So? Don't tell me you're making me go to church!" Chuck braked to a stop in the middle of the highway. "What kind of junk are you pulling here, anyway?"

Talon smacked Chuck's head just once, but once was enough. "I told you to shut up and drive. Relax. We're just going to be making a special donation to the church this week."

THIRTY-SIX

"DESPITE MY GRIEF and shock, I had to come forward to warn the American people." Shane Barrington was speaking in front of dozens of reporters. Though he did not usually make media appearances, he found himself warming to his assignment.

The assignment had been the latest from Talon, to go public with the death of Arthur Barrington, his son. Of course, the story he was now telling was far from the truth. No mention was made of the horrible way in which Talon had murdered his only child. Instead, Barrington had embellished Talon's curt instructions and devised a completely fictitious account of Arthur's death.

Barrington stared into the cameras, calculating whether he should try to manufacture a tear as he told his tale. "Three days ago, my office was contacted with a ransom note informing me that my only son, Arthur, had been kidnapped in broad daylight from the streets of New York. The kidnappers demanded five million dollars for Arthur's safe return—as long as I did not contact any authorities. Like any parent, I was distraught, and my only thought was to do whatever it would take to save my son."

Trying not to distract himself with the true image of how he had actually stood by and watched Talon kill Arthur, Barrington stared straight at the media cameras. "Out of no disrespect to our fine law enforcement officers, in order to do what I felt was necessary to save my son, I instructed my private security team to make contact and arrange the payment of the ransom. Yesterday morning, instead of welcoming my son home alive, my security team uncovered his dead body, horribly mutilated by these heinous criminals."

Even the usually cynical press corps gasped at this terrible revelation by Barrington. "If my son is not safe in this country, your children are not safe either. As I mourn the loss of Arthur, I am setting aside my grief to pledge my personal energies and personal resources to marshal public action for the end to the unchecked and alarming spread of criminal violence in our society. Thank you."

Questions burst forth from the press. "Mr. Barrington." He acknowledged his own network's reporter. "Can you elaborate on what kind of efforts you will mount in your campaign to fight back, as it were, against the violent elements out there?"

Barrington gave a smooth delivery of Talon's answer to the natural question. "There are many actions I plan to lead in the coming months in the fight back by the citizens against the out-of-control violence in our country. Like so many of you, I am fed up with the politicians who do not do enough."

Another question was called out: "Mr.

Barrington, are you indicating that you are planning to run for office yourself?"

"To the people of this country"— Barrington fixed his gaze coolly on the cameras—"I will make this pledge: If the politicians do not protect us, then I will set aside my work running Barrington Communications and will lead this country back to citizen safety."

"My colleagues at the Seven are most pleased with our Mr. Barrington." Talon was listening by satellite-link phone to John Bartholomew of the Seven. "You prepped him well, Talon. Over time, we will exploit that gruesome murder of yours into a whole new political power if Barrington can continue to follow orders."

Talon sneered. "If he doesn't, he will meet his own unfortunate, untimely death."

"Now, we have been reviewing your latest update about your Preston progress, Talon. Something you noted in passing actually connected with one of my diabolical colleagues, and it can fit very nicely in this new phase with Barrington."

"What do you want me to do?"

"That young man you mentioned, the Wallach lad who is warming up to Murphy and the sister of your stooge. We have a little change of plan for him."

THIRTY-SEVEN

ON WEDNESDAY EVENING, Paul Wallach parked in front of the Preston Community Church. In the fading light, its whitewashed clapboard facade gleamed invitingly. His heart skipped a beat and he was not sure if it was because he was about to see Shari or because he was about to *choose* to enter a church for the first time.

The door was open but he didn't go in. He wanted to go right to the basement to show Shari he was sincere about helping out with the clothing sorting. He walked to the side of the building to the steel door that led to the basement. He pushed it open and climbed down the narrow wooden stairs.

As his eyes adjusted to the gloom, Paul could make out a bare concrete floor with neatly stacked piles of wooden planks and some cardboard boxes at the far end. He felt along the wall for a switch, and a single bare bulb flooded the basement with light. He could see more boxes, and piles of clothing spilling out of garbage sacks.

"Hello, I'm here to volunteer," he called. "Where is everybody?"

Over in the corner was what looked like an old boiler and an archway leading to another part of the basement. Ducking under the low ceiling, he stepped in—and nearly fell over a sack of clothes. Except that it wasn't a sack of clothes.

It was a body.

Paul knelt down, and the face of a young man with long blond hair stared sightlessly back up at him, one arm flung out at a strange angle. He did not recognize the man, but Paul instinctively stepped back, bumping his head painfully against the wall, his mouth open in shock. Taking a deep breath, he knelt back down and put a trembling hand to the young man's carotid artery. Nothing. He tried to think what to do next, but his brain wouldn't function. He'd never seen a dead body before. Then a single thought came to him with piercing clarity.

"Shari!"

He stumbled to his feet and looked desperately around the basement. There was a steel table with what looked like a laptop and a tangle of wires, more boxes—and under the table . . .

He ran over. A girl. But not Shari. He felt his throat tighten. The pretty, oval face framed with a mass of auburn hair was familiar. Where had he seen her? On campus? Somewhere in town? What did it matter—*Check for a pulse, you idiot.* It was there, very faint but definitely there. *Okay, remember your CPR.* Breathing first. He put his ear close to her mouth, hoping for a whisper of air.

"Hello, Paul."

He gasped. Chuck Nelson, in a loose-fitting tracksuit, was grinning down at him.

"Who's your friend? I thought you had the hots for my little sister. She's going to be real upset when she hears about this." Chuck shook his head. "And in church, too, you dog."

"Chuck, what are you doing here? And where is Shari?"

The grin disappeared. Chuck shrugged. "Who knows? Who cares?"

Paul was torn between making sense of the situation and trying to help the girl. "Look, Shari said to meet her here. Chuck, what's going on?" He put his ear back to the girl's face. "We need help. Have you got a cell phone? We need to call 911."

"Gee, I think I left it at home." Chuck was really enjoying this. "What a shame. Guess it's up to you to wake Sleeping Beauty here. Better hurry. I think she's fading fast."

Paul leaped to his feet and grabbed Chuck by the front of his tracksuit. "Look, this isn't a game. This girl is seriously hurt. Go get help while I try to get her breathing."

Chuck shrugged him off. "She's had all the help she's going to get." He took a step forward, letting something dark slide out of his sleeve and into his palm. "And I'm getting a little tired of your whining."

Paul took a step back, a hand raised defensively in front of him. At least his brain seemed to be working again. If he could distract Chuck for a second or two, maybe he could make it to the stairs. He half turned, looking for something he could throw in Chuck's face—then there was a flash of movement as something very hard punched him off his feet and his head slammed into the floor.

Then his world went black.

THIRTY-EIGHT

THE PARKING LOT in front of the church was filling up as Murphy pulled his beat-up Dodge into a spot. He went around to the passenger side to help Laura out, but she waved him away. "Save it, Murph. You don't want to set a bad example for the community."

Standing by the door of the church with a welcoming smile, Reverend Wagoner held his arms out. "Laura, Michael. Good to see you both."

Murphy looked around the almost-full lot. "Likewise, Pastor Bob. Looks like a full house tonight. The free hot dogs seem to be working."

Wagoner laughed. He was dressed in comfortable slacks and a sport jacket over a green polo shirt that showed a hint of a paunch. With his tanned features and thinning white hair, he looked as if he'd just come off the golf course. Which he probably had. "I need something to give me an edge. Actually, I think you two are responsible for the big turnout. Folks are pretty excited about your discovery of this Serpent piece, Murphy."

"As long as you don't want me up at the pulpit, talking about it in front of everybody, Bob. You know I come here for a break from all that. But don't you put me to sleep, okay?"

Laura nudged him in the ribs. "Don't listen to him, Bob. He's just jealous. He knows a really inspirational speaker when he hears one."

"Well, thank you, my dear. Now you're making me nervous."

"Come on, Laura, let's see if we can get a front row seat. What do the kids call it— the mosh pit?"

Inside, an expectant buzz was already building amid the simple wooden pews. They spotted Shari sitting near the front, looking for someone, and made their way over.

Laura gave her a hug, then noticed her worried look. "What's up?"

"It's Paul. I challenged him to come tonight and said he should come early and help with the sorting for the clothing drive downstairs, but then I got stuck in the library and came right here. His cell phone doesn't seem to be working."

"It looks like we're starting. Let's save a seat for him. If he's like Murphy, he'll probably make a dramatic late entrance, especially if there was work to be done earlier. I'm sure he'll be here any minute."

Shari smiled, but there was still worry in her eyes. "I'll sit with you, but I hope I didn't scare Paul off."

Talon's natural instinct was to slam Chuck's body against the wall to focus his thick-skulled brain on the task at hand. But he had a use for Chuck tonight and not a lot of time. He could not afford to have this slug of a human being curl up and sulk. So he tried a more moderate action. He slapped Chuck's face hard, twice in succession.

"Hey! Ow, what—!"

"Shut up and pay attention. We've dumped your sister's boyfriend here in the church basement, we've spread out all the pamphlets I brought, what's left to do?"

Chuck was breathing hard and rubbing his cheek, paying no attention. Just aching from that head slam, Talon thought. "The backpack, remember? Take it off so I can load it up."

"Okay, okay. It's a little tight over my jacket." Chuck struggled to get the straps of the backpack off but could not get them over his Preston High jacket.

"Then unzip your jacket." Talon rolled his eyes in exasperation.

"I can't. It's stuck. The zipper gets caught a lot."

"How did you ever get out of kindergarten?" Talon grabbed the jacket in both hands and pulled with no success at the zipper. He tried to tear the zipper from its setting. In total exasperation, Talon's right arm flashed up and across the front of Chuck's jacket, cutting it neatly in two halves. He pulled the backpack from Chuck's shoulders.

"Hey, that was the only jacket I have. It's cold tonight."

Talon slashed his sharpened index finger once more, this time across Chuck's throat, nimbly stepping aside to allow the heavy body to fall to the basement floor.

"Not to worry, Chucky. It's warm where you're going."

THIRTY-NINE

THIS WAS A good night for the Preston Community Church, Reverend Wagoner thought as he stood surveying the faces in the pews. The crowd could be described as hushed and expectant, but what made this such a gratifying event was that almost all of these people could be called a community. He grasped the pulpit firmly and cleared his throat.

"Welcome, friends. It's truly wonderful to see so many of you here this evening. I'd like to give thanks to God for bringing us all together on a day that isn't Sunday. Many of you will have heard about the amazing archaeological find our dear friends Michael and Laura Murphy have brought back from the Holy Land.

"And if you haven't, let me tell you the good news. They've found a piece of Moses' Brazen Serpent. The one King Hezekiah destroyed in Second Kings, Chapter Eighteen, Verse Twenty-three." There were a few gasps. Clearly some people hadn't heard the news. "Now, I'm not going to talk about the archaeological significance of this discovery. I'll leave that to the professionals.

"However, this week, when so much puzzling and disturbing news has been reported at the United Nations and so many shameful things are being said in the media about Christianity, it does make me want to talk a little tonight about some of the significance I think we can still draw from what the Bible tells us about the Brazen Serpent."

Reverend Wagoner paused, and his gaze seemed to fall on each person sitting in the hall.

"You'll recall that the Hebrews who fled out of Egypt in search of the Promised Land didn't have an easy time of it. Sometimes when the going got tough, they began to question, began to doubt God's plan for them. In short, they lost their faith—"

There was a flash, and Murphy had time to wonder why Reverend Wagoner was flying through the air toward them before the thunder of the explosion hit, and then Murphy himself was lifted out of his pew by the blast-wave, his arm instinctively reaching out for Laura as he was flung sideways into the aisle.

After that, everything seemed to happen in slow motion.

The stained-glass windows imploded in a shower of red and gold, and the floor seemed to heave upward, toppling pews and spilling their occupants into the rubble. The chandeliers began swinging violently, the lights flickered once and went out, and then there was just smoke and darkness and the moans of the injured, a faint undertone behind the buzzing in his ears.

Murphy was on his feet and without thinking staggered toward the flames beginning to shoot up from the gaping hole behind the shattered pulpit. For a moment, he felt as if he were looking directly into the depths of hell itself. Then he stopped, and it seemed to take him forever to turn his head back toward the spot where he'd landed. Lungs seared by the acrid smoke pouring into the interior of the church, he felt his way through the debris until he found Laura. He grasped her arm, and he felt her fingers clinging to him and he knew she was alive.

Out. We have to get out, he thought, slipping his arms around Laura and hauling her to her feet. Murphy wasn't sure he had the strength to carry her in a fireman's lift, but then he felt her take a step and together they staggered through the haze, over broken pews and huge chunks of plaster, toward the door.

Air, he thought. *Air and light.* As they stepped through the doorway, the night air hit them in a wash of blessed relief and they both drew in huge lungfuls. Murphy placed Laura on the ground as gently as he could.

Murphy knelt beside her, blowing bits of wood from around her closed eyes and brushing blackened particles from her cheeks and hair. Laura coughed and opened her eyes, which showed fright and were rimmed by smoky tears.

"I'm okay, Murphy," she said between gasps. "Was it an explosion?"

"It must have been, but I don't think it was the boiler blowing up. Does anything feel broken?"

"My knees are grazed and my elbow hurts a little. . . . Are you okay?"

"I must look worse than I feel. If you promise to lie still here and get your breath, I can get back in there and see if I can help."

"Murph, I'll be fine here, but do you think you should? We don't know what caused all this. It looks like there's real damage to the church. You don't know what could happen still. Please."

"We don't know what happened already, and if anybody's hurt in there I've got to find a way in." He turned back to the church. Black smoke was billowing out of the doors. A dozen other people had walked out unscathed and were sitting or lying on the grass. That left how many?

He watched as a petite figure covered in plaster dust walked unsteadily toward them. Shari.

Murphy went to her, ready to catch her if she fell, but she shook her head and pushed him away. "Paul," she said in a croaky voice. "We have to find Paul."

She's in shock, Murphy thought. "It's okay, Shari. Paul isn't here. He wasn't in the church."

She took his arm in a fierce grip. "His car. It's in the lot. He must have gotten here early. He's here."

"But where? We would have seen him."

Her eyes went wide. "The basement!"

Murphy gently took her hands and squeezed them between his. "Okay. Stay here with Laura. Don't worry, I'll find him."

He pulled out a handkerchief and held it to his nose and mouth as he stepped back into the inferno. The smoke was thinning now, and in the dim glow of the emergency lights he could see people stumbling toward the doors while others tended to the injured. Over the crackle of the flames and the sound of wooden beams splintering like rapid gunshots, he could hear someone moaning.

He saw Wagoner bent over a prostrate figure and clambered over an upturned pew to reach him.

"Bob. Thank God. Are you okay?"

"I think my arm's broken, and my head

feels like it's been knocked around a little, but I'm in one piece. I'm not so sure about Jenny," he said, looking down at a middle-aged woman in a tattered white dress streaked with black. Her eyes were closed and she wasn't moving. Murphy put his ear to her mouth while he felt for a pulse.

"I think she's dead."

Wagoner closed his eyes. "Dear God."

Murphy clutched his shoulder. "We need to get help here, Bob."

"I called. They're on their way."

"Good. Can you make it to the door?"

"I'm not going anywhere. There may be other people—"

"The emergency guys will be here any minute. It's not safe. The roof beams could start coming down."

Wagoner got to his feet and started reluctantly for the front of the church. He turned. "What are you doing, Michael?"

Murphy was already heading toward the ruined pulpit. "I'll be right there. Something I've got to do first." And then Wagoner lost him in the smoke.

The explosion had ripped a huge hole in the floor behind the altar, and through the flames Murphy could see shreds of clothing floating amid a jumble of twisted metal and broken timber. He had no idea how hot it was down there or whether there was any air to breathe, but he could see a spot on the concrete floor that seemed to be clear of debris, so he took a deep breath and jumped.

He landed in a crouch, his hands sinking into a pile of clothing that hadn't yet caught fire, and then he was up, handkerchief to his face, shouting above the roar of collapsing timbers. "Paul! Can you hear me? Paul!"

He thought he heard a noise—something faint but human—coming from the back of the basement, the farthest point from the seat of the blast. Skirting piles of blackened paint tins and upturned filing cabinets, he made his way along the wall until he could see a hand sticking out from under a pile of boxes. He hefted them aside, and there was Paul, curled up with one hand under his chin as if he were asleep. There was no time to examine him properly, to see if any major bones were broken, and he just had to hope there was no damage to his neck or spine. He went down on one knee, got both arms under him, and staggered upright.

Through there, he thought, turning toward the narrow archway. *Let's just hope there's a way out.*

There was a loud crash behind him, and he felt a rush of heat against the back of his neck. He lurched forward and his knee struck something hard. He almost went down, but he was in the main part of the basement now and he could see the concrete steps. Grimacing with the effort, he shifted his grip to get a better position under Paul's shoulder and put one foot on the bottom step.

"Just one..." He put a foot on the next step and pushed upward, straining like a weight lifter. "And...uh...another," he grunted.

He had his eyes closed and realized he was at the top only when his foot hit the bottom of the door with a clang. Maneuvering around so he could grasp the handle while still keeping hold of Paul, he gave it a firm tug. Nothing. He paused to get a good lungful of air and gave it everything he had. It wouldn't budge. Either it was locked or the explosion had somehow jammed it shut.

He pulled back, mind racing. No point in

wasting his last reserves of energy pounding on the door. He'd have to go back the way he'd come and hope the fire hadn't cut them off and they could somehow get through the hole in the floor before the whole structure collapsed on top of them.

He turned to go back down the steps, and suddenly there was a roar of screaming metal, and then a rush of cool air as the door was torn off its hinges and he found he was looking into the face of a young firefighter.

"All right, Mr. Murphy," he said, arms outstretched toward Paul. "Let's get you the heck out of there."

Two paramedics took Paul's weight and carefully laid him down on a stretcher. Murphy's arms suddenly felt as if they were floating upward and all his muscles seemed to relax at once. He sank to his knees, closed his eyes, and was about to give thanks that he'd managed to get Paul out, when the thought struck him like a sudden blow to the temple.

Paul looked like he was dead.

FORTY

BY THE TIME dawn broke over Preston, the fire trucks and the paramedic vans had gone, leaving only a cluster of police cruisers at the front of the church.

FBI Agent Burton Welsh pulled up the collar of his raincoat against the morning chill and breathed in the sickly smell of wet ashes. The wood-frame structure was still intact, the spire standing proud against the rose-tinted sky, but he guessed it would be a while before the sound of hymns came from the blackened husk.

Because of the unknown nature of the explosion, a bomb was suspected, which led to the FBI's being called in. Hank Baines had been the first agent sent to the scene, making the return trip from Charlotte to Preston. Then, when his preliminary search of the church basement yielded some suspicious material, Welsh got an emergency summons from his U.N. investigation.

Chief Rawley of the Preston police force was waiting when Welsh arrived. "Your man's down in the basement."

"Body count change in the last hour?"

"Yeah, one more. Don't know who yet, he must have been practically right on top of the blast. Then two more downstairs and two upstairs. Those are the dead. By some miracle, even though there was a pretty good crowd attending church tonight, there were not too many others really badly wounded. Except for the kid they pulled out of the basement, Paul Wallach."

"How's he doing?"

"Last I heard, he still hadn't regained consciousness."

"Well, let's get to it." Welsh followed Rawley down the steps into the basement. They had pumped most of the water out, but the retreating tide had left a scum of sodden ashes under their feet as they made their way to the site of the explosion.

They stopped by the scorched and twisted remains of a steel table that had been blown off its legs. Folding chairs that had fused together in the blast like modernistic sculptures lay around it, along with a scattering of broken power tools.

Welsh leaned closer until his face was just inches from the tabletop. The scorch marks etched deeply into its surface were unmistakable. Baines was studying the marks as well. "Baines. Good work on your phone report."

"Agent Welsh. It's good to see you again, sir. Quantico seems like a lot of cases ago. What do you think? Was I right?"

The chief wrinkled his brow. "Right about what? Explosive?"

Welsh snorted. "Chief, you don't get these from a gas leak."

Rawley was keen to show he was no hick. "You mean C-four?"

"Ten. Makes these green striations." Welsh started to examine the floor around the table. "Let's see what else we've got here."

to give our isolated Vermont young people some contact with natures that have good points different from their own."

But no, try as he might, he could never bring out an opinion as the successful Wall Street operator did, with the authentic ring of finality. In years past, thinking that if he could learn to use it he might turn it back on its practitioner, he had tried to analyze the Wheaton intonation which announced with bluff, manly plainness that when he had set forth his opinion of a matter, it was a woman-ish waste of time to discuss it further. But T.C. had long ago realized that the authority in that voice, whether it was laying down the law about education, painting, politics, the position of women, or sexual morality, was unshakeably based on successful speculating with profits made in manufacturing and selling carpets. Of course it was something no mere schoolteacher could acquire.

"Howdoyoumean—civilized?" Mr. Wheaton challenged him. "One of those precocious, smart-aleck, Jewish bookworms, I sup-pose."

"Here's where I get his goat!" thought the schoolteacher, yield-ing to a cheap temptation, and aloud, with a poker face, said seri-ously, "I wouldn't say he was bookish. I was referring to a certain sensitive fineness of personality—he was gentler to a tiresome mother than any Yankee boy would be—and he has a living per-ception of musical values. To come in contact with these qualities would be very wholesome for the esthetic ignorance and blunt roughness of most of our Vermont students."

This was a success. Not having made money and not being always surrounded by yes-people, he could not, it was true, present an opinion of his as all there was to say; but he knew which ideas could be counted on to make the lion's den resound. He sat back, smiling inwardly, listening to the roars, looking up at the broad blunt nose of the portrait, adroitly flattered but still recognizable, at the hard blue eyes, larger and bluer than in life but faithful to the stony coldness of the original. To push one of the buttons which made Mr. Wheaton go into the air gave Timothy Hulme a malicious pleasure he was not proud of, but could not resist—the pleasure of contempt. For when the successful speculator was aroused to indignation, the veneer of semi-civilized catchwords over his ordinary conversation cracked and showed a Yahoo, Black

149

Legion savagery, the baseness of which made up to the teacher for his own economic inferiority.

"Let me tell you, T.C., LET—ME—TELL—YOU, that we want no effeteEuropeanartyideas corrupting our American he-boys into—"

"Well, well, you wouldn't believe it if you didn't hear it with your own ears," thought the schoolteacher, wallowing richly in his scorn. "Really Sinclair Lewis is a phonograph record! When you read him, you think he's laying it on too thick. Not at all. He doesn't exaggerate a hair." The roars began to die away for lack of breath. Mr. Hulme looked down at his memorandum and prepared to take up the next item on his list.

But the trouble with making Mr. Wheaton roar was that the sound of his voice, no matter what it said, always tuned to a higher pitch his certainty of being right. What he was shouting about the value of plain old-American-stock characterbyGod compared to the slippery Oriental superfluities of the arts, pleased him so much that by the time he stopped to pour himself out a glass of water from the silver-mounted thermos bottle he felt a mellow man-of-the-world compassion for the poor teacher from the backwoods. Without help from a sensible man he would be lost, poor simp, in the rough-and-tumble of the world of men, and the Academy with him.

"Well, let all that go for this time, T.C.," he said. "Did you and old Dewey knock together some kind of a budget after Van and Swettinger blew up if I'd had my way we'd-have-sold-those-bonds-long-ago."

They talked figures for a while, Timothy Hulme trying to force himself to an expression of what he felt at such times, a wistful admiration for Mr. Wheaton's grasp on the complications of investment and finance. He knew that not to recognize this superiority openly, put him on a level with Mr. Wheaton's monstrous ignorance of what magnanimity is. But apparently he could not claim to live on a higher level, for he could never bring over his lips a single word of appreciation for what was invaluable help. He hoped this was because he knew the air about the financier to be so poisoned by adulation that in it the plainest sincerity turned into flattery. He feared it was because he was not man enough to acknowledge ability and power of any kind in a man he personally disliked.

On this occasion, when the time came for the usual hand-to-hand

He bent down by a paper supermarket bag in the corner and pulled a wire that was hanging over its top. "My, my." He sifted through spools of telephone wire, then held up a pair of detonators. He mimicked pushing the spiked probes into a block of plastic explosive.

Rawley stood with his mouth open as Welsh rummaged some more and came up with a charred circuit board and the half-melted cases of two high-tech cell phones.

He took a plastic evidence bag out of his jacket pocket and slipped the remains of the phones inside. "Baines, get the lab working on these right away. I'm not a technician, but either folks around here leave some very strange items in the pockets of their old suits or this is no ordinary clothing drive."

Rawley looked sickened. "I know what I'm looking at, but I'm telling you, it just can't be."

"Chief, so far every sign I'm seeing down here is pointing one way. Somebody was using the church as a bomb factory. At least for tonight."

"Welsh, that's impossible. These people

are my neighbors. They're no more bombers than I am."

Agent Welsh eyed the chief as if to say that was a less than convincing argument. "This was not some penny-ante operation either. They weren't making cherry bombs."

"So, what, you think this C-ten stuff went off accidentally?"

"Sure. Terrorists are always blowing themselves up. Comes with the territory."

"*Terrorists.* I can't believe I'm even saying the word. Not in this place."

"Rawley, terrorists can be anywhere these days. From just a quick look down here, you got yourself a flea market of stuff that can go boom. With a few different kinds of ways to blow people up, it doesn't look like a terrorist bombed this place. Or maybe I should say that some of the neighbors you're swearing by were playing the terrorist home game and blew up the basement by mistake. Happens often enough, especially when you have rank amateurs messing with this stuff."

Agent Welsh picked up a charred flyer

battle over salaries and wages, he was glad that he had not wasted any appreciation. The fight was hot, hotter even than usual, the second dip of the depression and troubles with investments serving as plain proofs of the rightness of Mr. Wheaton's ideas of thrift.

One of his first suggestions was that the French teacher could be cut from nine hundred dollars to eight hundred.

The Principal made his harsh voice harsher, "It's starvation pay, already, Mr. Wheaton."

The Trustee brought out one of his favorite axioms, "Why, T.C., we could cut the salaries down fifty per cent, and still get plenty of teachers, you know we could."

"What kind of teachers?"

"Oh, a teacher's a teacher. Anybody can teach Latin grammar about as well as anybody else. There's no competition in Latin. It's not like football."

The Principal swallowed, drew a deep breath, and suggested dryly that all they could do at this time was to make a tentative budget on which the other two Trustees would need to pass. Mr. Wheaton disliked being reminded that there were two other Trustees, frowned, left Latin and French and turned to the three hundred and fifty dollars which were the Academy's share of the salary of the part-time music teacher. "Now look here—there's a modern frill for you! We never had a high-salaried music teacher when *I* went to school. You're always talking, you modern teachers, about encouraging initiative. Here's your chance. Don't have'm bossed about their singing. Just let'm sing! Or—why, you could take that on, T.C. I've heard you play the piano. You're a whiz! You could give'm all they need. Three hundred and fifty dollars is worth saving. The pennies count. The pennies count. All the big men know that!"

The Principal thought, "Oh, Lord, here comes the story about John D. and the solder on the oilcans," for it usually was brought out at about this point. But he was spared. Mr. Wheaton, intent on his own economy, asked, "Well, suppose you try taking on the music, yourself. How about it?"

The Principal folded his lips, took off his pince-nez, put it back on, and said, "All right." He would reserve his powers of resistance for more vital needs, later.

151

Not later. Immediately. Mr. Wheaton, running his eye down the faculty names, frowned, cried, "All that money for a teacher of *Domestic Science*" (he made the words a sneer). "That's just poppycock, T.C. The place for girls to learn homemaking is at their mother's knee. How much does a desiccated spinster know about making a home?"

T.C. jumped at the chance (he tried never to miss such a chance) to expound once again those ideas of his which he considered of prime importance to Clifford students, about making the best use, both as to food and house-furnishings, of what was readily available in Clifford, and also about making the best use of modern buying opportunities. One involved, he rapidly explained, skillful shaping of raw materials, the other, skillful and informed buying, which in turn involved learning something about the principles of modern co-operative action. And neither of these arts could be learned from their parents, since—

But Mr. Wheaton had no more interest than ever in other people's ideas, and, raising his voice, drowned out the teacher with one of his visions of the Academy as he would have it. "Now cut out those two salaries for that fool Manual Training, and Domestic Science and there'd be enough to pay a *real* salary to a crackerjack athletic coach that'd put my dear old school on the map."

Timothy said, through his teeth, "There is nothing we offer our country young people more valuable to them than those two courses. I'd rather cut out Latin and higher Algebra."

Mr. Wheaton brought his wrinkled old hand down on the table, "You're crazy, man! You couldn't prepare for college with those gone."

"A good many of our Clifford young people don't go to college."

"That's just the point, T.C., that is—just—the—pointI'malways-making. I keep *telling* you and Dewey that our budget troubles come from using so much of that miserable little endowment to provide education for young people who don't need it and can't use it. Sherwin Dewey and that red-headed pudding-stick of a district nurse—they all but ruined the school, setting up Dewey House to grease the way into the Academy for back-roads ragamuffins. It was bad enough before! Kids that will never be anything but mill-hands or farmers—they're better off with no schooling beyond the

from the floor and read out loud. "'Will you be left behind?!?!'"

"For what it's worth, the reverend of the church says he never saw that flyer before, nor any of these others." Baines pointed to some bundles of now-drenched flyers and brochures on the floor.

"Yeah? I was beginning to think I was the only man in America not on the subscription list for this religious hooey. But it looks like the reverend needed to check down in his basement a little more frequently. Were the dead and wounded all locals?"

"As far as I know. Except for the kid, Paul Wallach. He was from the university, but I don't know where he comes from."

"Chief, does a small-town college like this get a lot of weirdos, freaks, and troublemakers hanging around campus? I mean, you don't know this kid Wallach, I bet. What's to say he's not some out-of-towner down here to shake things up?"

"Well, all I know about him is he's a friend of Shari Nelson, a coed who works for Michael Murphy. She's a great kid, and I couldn't imagine her getting caught up with anything fringe."

"Fringe. That's a quaint term. She a good member of this good church?"

"Yeah. Welsh, you can't be serious that somebody like Shari Nelson or any of these people could actually have been making bombs down here."

"Chief, until we can trace every step of every bit of this stuff and solve this bombing, the only person who's not a suspect is me—and that's only because this is the first church I've set foot in since I was fifteen."

FORTY-ONE

TALON PREFERRED BEING close in, looking at his victims face-to-face. It was neater, riskier, and always more memorable to look at their fear just before he slashed them. Of course, he also derived extreme pleasure from the deadly precision of the falcons he had trained for so many years.

Explosions were so messy, even with these new thin, ultra-high-powered bombs.

But tonight's was effective. He admired the scene from the shadows of the parking lot. There was enough explosive force in that backpack to bring down half the building, and it had been packed into a plastic sheet that looked like a laminated pocket protector. There were also other explosive materials packed in the bags he and Chuck had planted around the basement, but it would not take the FBI long to determine that those were just window dressing.

It did satisfy him to be perpetrating an act of major mayhem, with a real body count, as opposed to all his work up in New York.

Too bad the oaf Chuck could not have lived to see the results of their setup. Once he had killed Chuck in the basement, he had packed the C-10 explosive sheet into the backpack, since he hadn't wanted Chuck walking around with it, then put the wired backpack back on Chuck and left him in the basement. Talon had checked to make sure that Chuck had left Paul Wallach far from the explosion so that he would survive.

Chaos and fear, those would be the legacies of tonight. Terror coming to a small town, not a big city, and to a church, no less. Making it look like the accidental explosion of a basement bomb factory run by evangelical Christian extremists would not hold up for long under the scrutiny of the

grades! Teach'm to read and write, give'm a job and leave'm alone
—that's the American way. You tell *me* what a Searles Shelf boy
wants of any more education than the three R's!" But he did not
wait to be told. Leaning back, he launched out on Oration No. 2:—
"What I could do with the Academy if those damned hayseeds
would only give me a free hand! There's a lay-out there that no
new school could duplicate. Why, I love that school! It's got
atmosphere, genuine atmosphere! It's got history! It's got American-
ism! I could make it into one of the places with a waiting list years
long, every name on it from a *good* family. And I'll tell you how!"

He had told T.C. how on many another occasion. The Principal
could have recited the oration with him.

"Cut out the girls of course. You'll never get gentlemen's sons to
go to the same school with girls. Make your curriculum over—cut
out everything but athletics and what's needed for college entrance
—tighten up on the entrance requirements, exclude Jews and foreigners, raise the fees, make it hard as the dickens to get into. EX-
CLUSIVENESS! That's the secret of prestige, T.C., *exclusiveness!* Keep
people out and everybody wants to get in! If the Academy could
just cash in on its assets—it's got wonderful assets—old-American
New England tradition, a hundred and forty years of experience. . . ."

Timothy closed his lips over the correcting "hundred and seventeen"—and let it go. The real business of the interview was over.
He had what he came for, advice about investments, a statement of
finances. He needed only to pay for it by a little more listening
and he could escape. He sat sadly thinking about his failure to do
more than to resist the further paring down of meager salaries.
He had again given up his hope for at least a tiny pension for
weary Miss Benson, who had spent most of her vitality and all of
her tiny salary in keeping alive an ancient mother, and who now
after forty years of service to the Academy faced old age without a
penny. Nor had he spoken of the plight of Melville Griffith, the
janitor, who, on fourteen dollars a week, had somehow not been
able to keep a wife alive and bring up children and also save
money. The Principal held his tongue on these two topics partly
because he knew it would do no good to speak, and partly because
he felt that the limit of his endurance was almost reached, and that

153

FBI. Just like the vapor-thin trail he had left behind with his New York stunt to make it look like extremists were plotting to blow up the U.N.

There would be days of hysterical news reports following the connections of the church members, of Murphy, and of Shari once they found enough of her brother to make an identification, and her connection to her transfer-student friend, Wallach, who would be cast as an out-of-town trouble-maker. And that mystery man who had been seen with Chuck. By the time the FBI saw that the bomb factory "evidence" was just window dressing, the media would have moved. In its wake would be a time of noise and confusion, and people would re-call mainly a bunch of crazy evangelicals to be afraid of. Not a bad night's work.

Then it hit Talon. Hard. Chuck, that miserable loser, had managed to screw up things even after he was dead! His stupid jacket that he got stuck in, so Talon had to cut him out of it. It had fallen to the floor, and with all he had had to do by himself to finish off the ground-zero site in the church basement, he had forgotten to grab it. And he literally could not, just then, endure Oration No. 3, which a mention of old-age pensions would bring out:—that was the lecture about the blasphemy of putting any check on the workings of sacred competition. "Competition in a free market—that's what made America what it is, and don't you forget it. That's the old America for which Vermont, God bless her, still stands."

As it was, the Principal paid for help in handling Academy finances no higher a price than listening to Oration No. 7—on what Vermont meant to George Henry Wheaton, the cradle of the ideals of my boyhood, the sanctuary where they are now preserved. Year by year this speech grew more colorful as Mr. Wheaton's boyhood in a South Dakota small town and his years as a salesman in the carpet department of a Chicago store receded into the past. He no longer prefaced it with an explanatory, "Although part of my youth was spent out of our dear old state . . ." (One of his grandmothers had been a Clifford girl and he had spent a summer vacation or two with her in his youth.) Mr. Hulme was as usual sardonically amused by the tender Wheaton reminiscences of old times in Vermont and the strong sinews they gave a boy for the great enterprise of wresting money from the world outside of Vermont, but he winced when Mr. Wheaton branched off to brag about a recent addition to his collection of Vermontiana, for rare items of which he was willing to pay anything, be the item a piece of Bennington pottery or an eighteen-century deed to land in Caledonia County. The price he mentioned as having been paid by his buying agent for a copy (with flyleaf intact!) of the history of a now-abandoned over-the-mountain town was, Mr. Hulme thought sourly, more than the salary of the drawing teacher who, to everyone's sorrow, had been dropped last year because of the diminished rate of interest on the Academy endowment investment; or it would have lighted Miss Benson's dark future; or placed on the Academy shelves some of the much-needed reference books. "And I was one of those who voted for him because I thought the Academy would get some of his money!" he reflected gloomily.

But his own eloquence had had its usual effect as a catharsis for Mr. Wheaton. He made no more proposals to reduce salaries. He dismissed from his mind the folly of paying more to an English teacher than to a basketball coach. At the end of this talk he even drew a check for four hundred dollars and handed it over to pay for the realization of a pet idea of his—a handsome bronze tablet bearing the names of all those students at the Academy who had served in one of the four wars waged since its foundation. Some years before, he had offered to present to the Academy a machine gun still bedizened with the war-paint of its camouflage, to set up beside the tennis courts as a souvenir of the amenities of the World War. Timothy had flown into one of his quick rages over this and had refused it with a bellow of wrath. He now looked unsmilingly at the check, noted with exasperation that the u was left out of Coulton, and the l out of Hulme, and said stiffly, "I'll see that your wishes are carried out."

The interview was over! The secretary-acolyte, her skirts wafting incense, showed him out. The Gothic elevator dropped him twenty-four stories to the entrance hall. He stood downstairs in this narthex of the temple, marble inlays to his right, gilded bas-reliefs to his left, and felt like flinging his hat up to the Renaissance coffered ceiling. Not till the June Trustee meeting would he need to hear Mr. Wheaton's voice again.

As he sat, waiting to be served, in the inexpensive restaurant where he ate his lunch, he noted with an ironic eye the frieze of urgently worded notices on the walls, warning patrons that any belongings left for a moment unguarded might be whisked away by nimbly thieving big-city fingers. "Oh, yes," he told himself, "I must not forget that I am at the hub of twentieth-century civilization," and thinking of the never-locked Clifford house-doors, he moved his hat and coat from a hook just behind him, to one in plain sight and in reach of his arm.

He was hungry. But he ate very little. The combative hatred always aroused in him by personal contact with that old-American, George Wheaton, had fallen. Now he did not so much hate him as fear what such a man could do to make life intolerable for those who believed in the standards Timothy Hulme tried to impart to his students. Yet—he had this thought after every talk with the rich man—old Wheaton himself was no better, no worse than any other ordinary coarse-fibered old man with an undistinguished mind and plenty of energy. There were men like that in every collection of

155

human beings anywhere. Clifford had its share of them. Timothy could name three or four, no better, made of the same stuff. Yet he neither hated nor feared them. On the contrary he often thought that one of life's sure-fire comic effects was the combination of their utter ignorance of anything but a few material processes, and the massive weightiness with which such men pronounced judgment on questions civilized people knew to be so complex as to be insoluble. To hear one of them talking about books or music was as good entertainment as reading a Horatian satire. But although he realized that Mr. Wheaton provided the same farce-stuff, he never found him laughable. Sometimes he shuddered at the old man's coarse insensitiveness to human values and his wallowing like a great hog in self-admiration; sometimes he hated everything about him to the buttons on his superbly tailored clothes. Why should he take with such painful seriousness a man who was (outside the world of money) only a grotesquerie of pretentious ignorance? Why did he waste hatred on what was no more than despicable?

Crumbling his bread and looking down moodily at his cooling plate of stew, the schoolteacher from the country sent his mind searching for the answer to this question. It lay of course on the surface. That a man totally ignorant of civilized standards and values should fancy himself an arbiter of those values was the same absurdity in Mr. Wheaton's case as in that of many another man with a thick, Stone-Age skull. Yet Mr. Wheaton was not absurd, he was a terrible and awful power for evil, and what made him so was his money, was the mountain of dollars from which he ruled people, institutions, human endeavors he was proud of not being able to understand. Hospitals, colleges, universities, museums of fine arts, laboratories for research—he was on the Directing Board of all these. There was no counting the number of noble enterprises put in Mr. Wheaton's power by money, like a club in his fist to beat down fineness and delicacy of feeling whenever he caught sight of it. There was no comedy in that. The swaggering boor who fancies himself a cultivated man of honor is traditionally a figure of fun— his mind roamed from Terence to Molière—yes, but hardly when his forefinger with its dirty nail is crooked around the trigger of a loaded machine gun.

At this point his mind, deploring heat of feeling in the weighing

in the pocket were the car keys, which also had Talon's prints, plus he had seen Chuck stuff the last shopping list in his jacket pocket. The chances of the jacket surviving the blast, and of the FBI tracing him from what was left in the pockets, were minute.

But that was enough to make Talon uneasy. He would have to go back, which shouldn't be too hard with all the rescue teams going in and out.

Talon slipped into the church through what had once been the basement door.

As he did so, Laura Murphy circled the side of the building on her way to the Dodge, in which she always had a trunk full of drinks, a first-aid kit, blankets, and other supplies in case she and Murphy decided on a whim to go off exploring. She got a good look at the figure entering the basement, and he did not look like one of the rescue workers, and he certainly was not a church member. Nor did he look like anyone she knew from Preston, but she was positive that she did recognize him as a face that had been hanging around.

The creep who had been hanging around with Shari's brother.

Laura forgot about going for the supplies and decided to follow Chuck's companion and see why he would be going into the bomb site.

Could it be? She was horrified at the thought that struck her. Could this stranger and poor, angry, lost Chuck have been involved in this bombing?

She walked down the basement steps, wincing as her wounded knees felt the impact. There was a sound in the darkness ahead, and she limped toward it. The pain in her legs was going to stick with her for a while, it seemed.

But she instantly forgot that pain, because an intense, far greater pain rippled through her as a pair of incredibly strong hands grabbed her arm and throat in the darkness.

"Hello, Mrs. Murphy. It must be bingo night at church, because I've just got the big prize." The voice was hoarse. "I can't do anything to that husband of yours while he's still useful to us. But nobody said anything about needing you. And without you, maybe your husband will have more time to work a little quicker."

Laura did not know what this madman was talking about, but she could not speak, so powerful was the pressure of his hand on her throat. It began crushing her windpipe.

Talon kept pressing, deciding not to use his razor again. The result would be the same.

Laura Murphy looked into the face of Talon, refusing to give him the satisfaction of averting her eyes even though she was shocked by what pure evil could look like.

She started to pray in her silence and she showed him no fear.

FORTY-TWO

CHIEF RAWLEY USHERED them into the interview room and indicated three chairs on one side of the steel table bolted to the bare floor.

"I'm sorry we couldn't use my office. I don't think I could have fit you all in comfortably. Not with all this . . ." He indicated the two large carboard boxes in the center of the table without looking at them. On the other side of the table, Baines stood up and offered his hand with a neutral expression.

"Reverend Wagoner. Professor Murphy."

of evidence, bade him beware of falling into the vulgar error of generalizing from one case, reminded him that money in the possession of a man of decent standards is as great a power for good as Mr. Wheaton's for evil, and pointed out that it was unfair to hold Mr. Wheaton responsible for the fact that other men, because of his ability to get and keep money, gave a damnable weight to his opinions on art, on education, on the care of the sick, on—of all things!—matters of taste. He personally would have been harmless enough if he had been subjected in normal human relations to the ordinary give-and-take checks on egotism. What was to blame was the fawning yes-yes on all subjects which was society's reaction to his many dollars. What had turned him into a monster had been the long years of unmerited, unquestioned authority in matters he knew nothing about. "Good heavens!" thought Timothy with passionate unreason. "Is there a millhand, a back-roads farmer in Clifford who has so little respect for things too fine for him to understand, who has so little sense of human dignity—*that* man to talk about the harm Jews might do to his America!"

With a gesture of anger he did not know he was making, he swept his glass of water from the table and gave his ironic bark of laughter to see it roll along the floor unbroken. "A brave, big-city glass!" he apostrophized it, picking it up. "A thoroughly hard-boiled, urban glass guaranteed to have no instincts delicate enough to be breakable." He ordered apple pie for his dessert (misguidedly remembering Miss Peck's pie) but when it came, crouching withered and clammy on its plate, he picked up his hat and went to pay his check.

His next appointment was with a Mr. and Mrs. McCann, parents of a prospective student. The address was in the upper East Eighties, probably an old brownstone house made into an apartment. He wondered why people with an adolescent daughter were not in the suburbs. Well, how should he, this time, manage this recurrent big-city business of getting himself from where he was to somewhere else? He had had enough of the subway for one day, and marched off across town towards the Madison Avenue bus line, passing great plate-glass show-windows filled with handsome objects for sale, being passed by towering trucks loaded with things for sale, turn-

157

He shook hands solemnly with each of them before sitting down again, and his gaze returned to the boxes.

Rawley seated them like an attentive maître d'. "How's the arm, Bob? You know, folks are saying it's a miracle you're alive."

Wagoner winced as he eased into the chair and adjusted the cast on his arm. "I can't feel a whole lot, to be honest, Ed. And that goes for my head too." He tapped the bandage around his forehead. "Alma says it just goes to show that the Lord knew what He was doing when He made it out of solid maple."

"And how about you, Murphy?"

"Oh, I'm fine, Ed. Just a few cuts and bruises. I guess I've got some maple in me too."

With a tight smile Rawley went and stood awkwardly to one side of Welsh. He seemed reluctant to occupy the empty chair next to him, as if he wanted to distance himself from what was about to happen.

"We were the lucky ones," said Wagoner. "Four dear friends died, plus one body has yet to be identified in the basement. That

ing and veering on the crowded sidewalks to avoid collision with the men hurrying to sell, the women hurrying to buy.

Mr. McCann, the father of Jane, turned out to be a public high-school teacher, and Mrs. McCann to be a librarian in a branch of the public library. They were a pleasant, tired couple with a pleasant gawky daughter of fifteen whose front teeth were being straightened. Their apartment was, as he had expected, the second floor of an old brownstone house. From one look at the long, narrow front-room where they received him, he knew, anyone would have known, just what quarters they had:—this room, another like it in the back, between them a kitchenette made out of the old wash-room, and across the hall something or other for the little girl's bed-room. Or perhaps she slept on the couch where she and her mother now sat. And when she was sick—he remembered the cluttered, dirty, hall bedroom where he and Downer had slept and eaten and washed and cooked and been sick.

He was rather surprised to see that the child did not look sickly. The usual reason for sending a student to a country school was health. The father said, "No, Jane's not a delicate child. Not at all. But you know—or *do* you?—what a New York public high school is like."

The Vermont teacher said he had taught for a while in one, many years ago, but had not seen one for some time. So the city teacher told him:—six thousand students in one building, the cor-ridors between classes as jammed, pushing, and dangerous as the subway in rush hour, the lunchroom a yelling mob snatching at platefuls of hastily slammed-down food, the long lines waiting for a chance at the drinking fountain, the constant need to keep your possessions in sight or locked up because of incessant thieving, one of Jane's teachers a paranoiac, kept in her place by political influ-ence: all of the teachers, even the best of them, sunk by numbers. "Do you know how often Jane recites? Two minutes, twice a week. Do you know how the teachers correct English compositions? Well, you teach English: just think for yourself what would happen if you had two hundred and fifty in your classes, writing composi-tions. How many would you throw away unread and uncorrected? And do you know what happens sometimes in the toilet rooms when the crowd is so thick that . . ."

158

"I see," said Timothy Hulme. "But, listen, you're a colleague of mine—do *you* know what a beggarly country school in a poor mountain town is like?"

"We've read your catalogue from cover to cover," said McCann, and his wife added earnestly, "We *like* your ideas about discussion groups and assignments by the week, and Domestic Science that teaches young people to use what they have."

Jane's father said, "We can hardly believe there's a school within our means where Jane'll have somebody really trying to teach her something, not just trying to keep hell from breaking loose. She won't know how to act!"

The Principal of Clifford Academy laughed ironically. "Didn't you ever read any other school catalogues? Don't you know what is left out of a catalogue—by intention? I'll just tell you some of the things left out of ours. Our gymnasium is an old barn, heated by a wood stove. And we'll probably never have anything else. Some of the seats in our classrooms were there during the Civil War. I mean literally. Our heating plant is forty years old. The woodwork hasn't been painted since—since the American Revolution! Our edition of the Britannica is the 1911 one. Our teachers are frightfully underpaid—and not very well trained. One of them is worn out and only hanging on because there's no provision for pensions. Many of our students come clumping in straight from the farm and lots of them use the double negative when they first appear at the Academy. We haven't had a new . . ."

"How many in your classes?"

"From twelve to twenty."

The McCanns looked at each other, exulting. "Do the students have a chance to see anything of the teachers outside the classrooms? Would Jane, for instance, be in personal touch with you?"

"Oh, as to that, yes. Everybody in a small school and a small town sees everybody else all the time. The house where I live is at one end of the Main Building."

"Let me tell you a story, Mr. Hulme," said the father of Jane, "to give you some idea of the size of our building, and the kind of life the children have. At the beginning of our last term, a teacher in our department reported one of the Freshman boys absent from her class four days in succession, where he was by her list due to

159

be present. We looked up his record and found he'd been at school those days, so I sent for him to come to the office. He turned out to be an anxious little kid, twelve or thirteen years old, whose family had just moved in from up-state somewhere. And he said the trouble was he couldn't *find* his English section. 'I have a gym period just before my English,' he told me, 'and when I leave that to go to my English class, I can't find the way. The first day I came out on the roof. And the next day in the basement. After I'd been miles up and down the halls every direction I could, I thought, "Well, I know how to get to that English class from the front door. If I went out and came in from outside I could get to it." So I went out a side door but when I tried to come in the front door the big boys wouldn't let me. . . .' "

Mrs. McCann broke in to explain, "That's the squad of Seniors stationed there to keep the tardy students from slipping into their classes without reporting."

Her husband went on, "The kid ended up, 'If I could only find Benny he could take me to that class. Benny knows the way. But he's got a different gym period from mine, and I never see him any more.' "

"Poor child!" said Mrs. McCann compassionately.

"Well, yes, I get your point," admitted Timothy, "but I'm afraid you'll only find it like St. Lawrence asking to be turned over on his griddle."

"That edition of the Britannica is really better than the latest one," said the librarian mother, evidently presenting this fact as a symbol.

"Let's see Jane's report cards," said Timothy.

They were all right. Jane was all right. She was, in fact, it seemed to the Principal, like any one of hundreds of nice little girls with gold bands on their teeth who had passed through his classes. The question of tuition came up. The McCanns did not ask for a reduction of tuition, but they laid their family budget before him and inquired if there was any fair way in which Jane's living-expenses might be lessened. Mr. McCann's salary was considerably more than that of the Principal of Clifford Academy: and in addition there was the pay of Mrs. McCann—although T.C. was shocked by the meager salary given librarians by the great and rich city. Their combined income came to more than half as much again as his own.

160

poor Wallach boy in a coma..." His voice trailed off. "But we're going to start rebuilding just as soon as we can. And then we'll be back in that lovely church, praising the Lord again."

"Don't go do any rebuilding yet, Reverend," Welsh said coldly. "Right now your church is still a crime scene."

"A crime scene? I don't understand."

"That explosion wasn't an accident. That old boiler in the basement is one of the few things that wasn't damaged in the blast."

"Then, what did cause it?"

Welsh looked at him steadily. "I was kind of hoping you could tell me that."

Murphy was on his feet, leaning over the table. "Just what are you suggesting? Bob was nearly killed in there."

Welsh didn't blink. He waited until Murphy sat down again, then lifted the flap of one of the boxes.

"The explosion was caused by a bomb. Plastic explosive. And we found detonators and other equipment for making more bombs. The basement of your church was being used as a bomb factory, Reverend. Your parishioners were making bombs."

He let that sink in, watching as Wagoner went pale.

"That's absurd," Murphy said. "Why would members of this church be making bombs?"

Welsh scratched his chin as if he were asking himself that question for the first time. "How about to blow up the U.N.?"

"The U.N.? What are you talking about?"

"This kid, Paul Wallach, they pulled out of the basement, he wasn't from around here, was he? I know he's a student, supposedly, but my information is that he only recently started attending, is that correct?"

"What are you suggesting? That Paul Wallach was somehow responsible for this explosion? That's crazy. He's just a kid."

Welsh smiled sourly. "In my experience, kids do the funniest things. Especially when they come under the influence of fanatics." He said the last word as if he were spitting out something unpleasant.

Murphy jumped up. "Fanatics? What are you, the Joe McCarthy of G-men, Welsh? Conspiracies everywhere. Fanatics like who?"

"Like the sort of people who believe the U.N. is evil. Evangelical Christians, for instance."

"We don't believe the U.N. is evil," Wagoner interjected. "We believe it does some good work. Peacekeeping in certain third world countries where there is chaos, humanitarian aid, health programs, and so on. But we are suspicious about their efforts to promote globalism by uniting all religions regardless of their beliefs, and by uniting the world's governments under a single entity. In particular, I'm very concerned about turning the sovereignty of the United States government over to a world court."

"Are you saying you oppose striving for world peace through global unity?"

"Every single attempt to secure a one-world religion or a one-world government in the past has resulted in a totalitarian regime, inevitably causing the deaths of countless numbers of innocent citizens. We must learn from history. Man is incapable of bringing peace to this planet on his own. This world will never enjoy world peace until Christ Himself comes to set up His kingdom. His kingdom will last for a thousand years, and the Bible is very clear regarding this prophecy."

"Then maybe some of your people thought a few bombs might hurry it along."

Wagoner was stunned. "*Our* people? Evangelical Christians don't set off bombs, Agent Welsh."

Welsh jabbed a finger at him. "How about the people who bomb family-planning clinics? Who kill doctors who perform abortions? They're Christians, aren't they?"

"Not in my book," Wagoner said fiercely. "Yes, it's a terrible thing to take the lives of the unborn, but more murder is definitely not the answer. The Christian community universally opposes killing, even to save the unborn from being killed."

Agent Baines had been quiet while Agent Welsh had carried on with his arguments, but he could contain himself no longer. "Sir, I know I'm out of line, but I have to speak up. I certainly don't pretend to know the facts of this bombing, and there is certainly circumstantial evidence that makes it look pretty bad that something crazy was going on in that basement. Except I know

Yes. But the rent they paid for the two light and the one dark room they lived in! The hours of Mrs. McCann's work, they explained, obliged them to live there, instead of moving to the suburbs. The price of milk, butter, and eggs! The bill from the New York dentist (also paying New York rents) who was straightening Jane's teeth! They had not yet caught up on the doctor's bill from last winter's flu. They always had a good many doctor's bills. They had not been to a theatre in four years. Mrs. McCann's winter coat was in its fifth year. They never bought books. They had no savings account. There was an ancient aunt, back up-state, to whose support they felt obliged to contribute their share.

T.C. explained the co-operative basis of Dewey House, and asked if Jane would be willing to do her share of the house and garden work. There was one room still vacant, he told them, a very small one on the third floor. With a sloping ceiling. But its two dormer windows looked west into the sunsets in the Gap, and under them an old pear tree bloomed white every May. Jane's eyes brightened, looked imploringly at her parents. They needed no persuasion. It was soon settled, Mrs. McCann went into the alcove which was the kitchen and made them tea, over which they sat comparing notes on their professional life.

Mrs. McCann did not listen. In a pause, she said, "I was brought up in the country too, Mr. Hulme. Tell me, do country children—still go out in the woods in May to pick wildflowers?" She put this question hesitatingly, as though she knew it to be mawkish.

Timothy answered her without conviction. "Oh, yes, Vermont land isn't much good for wheat, but it can grow arbutus and hepaticas all right."

The wildflower names sounded as unreal to him as to the McCanns. It was five in the afternoon. Since eight that morning he had been up to his neck in the city. What were hepaticas and arbutus? Nothing real, surely, like merchandise for sale. He could not remember how they looked.

A truck carrying iron rails clattered by the house. It aroused him to remember that he must get back to his hotel, where he was to meet two country girls and do something to entertain them. He found he could not remember exactly how they looked—except that there was something the matter with their hats.

161

these people. Not these people specifically, I don't mean that, I mean I know churchgoing folks in a community like this, because that's who I am. I know their hearts, and they could never be terrorists, bombers, or murderers for any cause, no matter how righteous.

"Look, something terrible has happened here in Preston. People have died, more are in the hospital. And everyone wants to know why. *We* want to know why. Professor Murphy risked his life to save someone. Is that the action of a wanton murderer? Reverend Wagoner was lucky not to be killed himself. These are not the people we should be hunting down. I know that's gut talking, not forensics, sir, but sometimes we have to listen to bigger evidence than what our eyes tell us, don't we?"

Welsh just gave a sour, angry stare to Baines, and never got a chance to answer him, because Laura Murphy stumbled through the doorway looking wild-eyed and in pain.

She stared straight ahead for a moment, as if trying to think of the right word, then Murphy watched in horror as her eyes rolled back in her head and her whole body went limp like a puppet whose strings had suddenly been cut. She put a hand out to steady herself, and the chair crashed to the floor as Murphy caught her in his arms.

"Get an ambulance," he screamed at Baines. "Now!"

On the stoop of the brownstone house he stood to try to think how to get himself back downtown. "If I had any sense I'd take the subway again." But he had no sense and took the Third Avenue Elevated.

At once he regretted that he had not walked. He had forgotten the screaming rattle of the elevated trains, and the ugliness of the brick tenement houses through which they passed. But at least some of those ignobly mean houses were empty. The "For Rent" signs in many windows proved, didn't they, that there were really some things in the city so hideous that even very poor people would not endure them. Or was it only that very poor people had now not enough money to pay rent?

His head ached with the barrage of din laid down by the train as it advanced. He took off his hat and put it on his knee—but, remembering the warning signs in the restaurant, kept one hand tightly closed on its brim; buttoned up his coat over his watch, put his other hand in his pocket on his purse—what was the Horatian tag his father used to quote about a great city of another era?— *surgunt de nocte latrones*—and ventured to close his eyes. The ancient car had a flat wheel. He was soon listening, his teeth nervously clenched for its inexorably recurrent banging. And he was obliged to open his eyes at every station to cope with the people who pushed their way in, crowding the aisles, stepping on his feet, pushing against his knees. Because it was a poor quarter, they were working-men and women, dressed in dreary imitations of the clothes of those who do not work; because this was at the end of a day's work, they sagged limply on the straps, undone with fatigue; and because they were city people, they ignored each other's presence and let their haggard faces disintegrate in nerveless vacuity as though they had already sunk down on their beds in the solitude of their hall bedrooms. "I must try to manage so that I won't need to come to the city so often!" cried the country schoolteacher to himself. "It's impossible to remember how awful it is."

At this, his faithful mind aroused itself to its responsibility to keep an intelligent man from unreasonableness. "Bigot! Crotchety fanatic! Just because you've run into a few disagreeable incidents! To take one noisy Elevated train for the city! How about fine concerts?" his intelligence asked him pointedly. "How about good plays? And the society of quick-witted, informed, and lively companions? And museums full of finished beauty—where but in the metropolis do you find them? And the joy of doing whatever you please with nobody to criticize it because nobody knows what it is? And something gay to do at one in the morning? And how about these rivers of electric lights, as stimulating as the shout of bugles?"

But reasonableness was nowhere to be found in that aching head. The hour with Mr. Wheaton cast the shadow of money across all that the city had to give. To give? To sell! Cash was the stuff of which city pleasures were made. They rustled dryly in his ears with the papery thinness of the green bills which could buy anything the city had to offer. How much did that city teacher and his under-paid librarian wife have of the civilized pleasures of the metropolis? Bang! Bang! Bang! The flat wheel pounded its way across his nerves. The pale, seedy working-man now lurching against his knees gave off an exhalation of old sour sweat. "So this is the sum total of humanity's struggle through all the ages!" thought Timothy with a groan. "Laboriously and expensively to build up hell."

His mind cast a swift glance at the possibility that this sudden city-phobia, quite new to him, might be connected with a certain young country woman, not with a certain elderly city man. But there was evidently nothing to be done with the idea—with any mere idea. His black mood, soaring through wider zones, began to shadow with its careening bulk far more than city life. His mind recognized this as one of the danger-times when brains are of no use to a man, and turned to summon to the rescue the all-powerful vitality of the senses. What visual memories of beauty could be called up to stand against this sick exaggeration of ugliness? "Snow!" it suggested tentatively to Timothy. "Diamond-gleaming, up-tilted, clean fields of snow with dark tapering hemlocks, lapis-lazuli shadows at their feet."

With its bang! clatter! bang! the train riposted insolently that snow was what lay below on the dirty, dimly-lighted, poor-man's street. Snow was something scraped together into grimy hillocks, with chewed-up cigar butts frozen into it.

Well, then, persisted his mind, patient as a mother with a fretful child, sumac with its crimson fanions—maple trees with pools of fallen scarlet leaves, bracken turned from green to gold lace. But he incautiously opened his eyes. Lavender asters faded before the lithographed battle between contending brands of cigarettes: the golden filigree of frost-touched ferns vanished behind the bosom of a bathing girl expensively printed in three colors, her Chinese-red lips drawn back to show carnivorous ivory. Timothy closed his eyes again, his brains knocking against his skull in the throb-throb of a hard headache.

His mind brought out its trump card—the high-water mark of beauty of each year, the June night when the Principal and old Mr. Dewey and the boys of the Senior class went up to sleep under the open sky on the great rock over the Crandall Pitch. Look back, Timothy, look through all this, back at the luminous blue of those distant mountains, at the silver wheeling of the constellations, let your heart sink into the magnificent silence of the moment just before night dies, when the morning star . . .

"FOURTEENTH STREET!" yelled the guard. That was reality. Fourteenth Street was actual. What was the morning star?

He clapped his hat back on and reeled with other passengers in the stampede to the door.

Like one diving from a mild patter of summer rain into mid-ocean waves he came down from the puny soprano scream of the train into the many-voiced pandemonium of Fourteenth Street under the Elevated at six o'clock of a winter evening. He felt a nervous impulse to react to the noise by screaming at the top of his voice, but his mind, still gallantly battling for good sense, told him severely, "You take it hard because you've got out of the habit of it. When you lived here, you got used to it. You never felt this hysteria. Everybody gets used to it. You know they do."

"Why in the name of hell should anybody *have* to get used to it?" he shouted angrily. An elevated train crashed along the rails over his head at that moment and his shout was as inaudible as a whisper. He pushed his hands into his overcoat pockets and stepped off into the shuffling mass on the sidewalk, jostling and being jostled with ferocious unconcern. After the right number of street crossings he mechanically made the turn at the right corner, but striding gloomily ahead, hypnotized by the dark chaos around him, he passed the entrance to his hotel without seeing it. When he saw

164

FORTY-THREE

FOR THE SECOND time in a matter of weeks, Stephanie Kovacs thought, the gods of media good fortune were smiling down on her. She had decided to spend the evening in the hotel poring over more of her research before snooping around Preston the next day to get more background about Professor Michael Murphy.

She heard the church bomb ignite from her hotel room and was already beeping her cameraman when the BNN national bureau chief called her. Within an hour of the blast she had gone live with her first report. Even as more reporters swarmed over the site, she stayed ahead of the pack with a combination of her own drive and some additional tips being fed her by the New York and Atlanta bureaus. Now, the day after, she was ready for her next exclusive.

"Stephanie Kovacs, BNN, live from the horrific bombing of the Preston Community Church in Preston, North Carolina. Even while the search for victims and assessment of the damage continues desperately, there are ugly realities beginning to come to light at the scene.

"Most shocking of all is the report that we are talking not about a terrorist attack upon the innocent churchgoers, but rather a far greater nightmare for the citizens of our country. There is now evidence that, contrary to earlier reports that suggested the church was the *target* of a terrorist bomb, the truth could be something even more deadly and cowardly.

"Sources have revealed to BNN that the cause of the explosion was in fact a bomb *factory* in the basement—a bomb factory that went tragically, horribly wrong for four members of this tightly knit congregation. And these same sources have further sug

his mistake he turned back in a temper, pushed open the swinging door and stepped into the small dingy lobby.

A girl was sitting there. She was rather pale and looked a little anxious, and she wore a last year's hat. But although she was evidently tired she did not lean back in the threadbare, overstuffed armchair, she sat nervously far forward, and kept her eyes fixed on the door. When she saw him come in, she sprang up and went quickly to meet him, saying his name on a deep, shaken note, "Oh, Mr. *Hulme!*" she cried, as though she were astonished to know that he still lived.

He whipped off his new hat and, crushing it under his arm, took both her hands in his, looking down at her in relief and astonishment as great as hers. "Susan!" he cried. "Why, *Susan!*" He could not let her hands go, he could not take his eyes from her, from all that sprang to life around her. It was real then. He had not dreamed it. Back of the girl with the beautiful gray eyes and the tender mouth, stretched fields of immaculate snow shadowed by tapering hemlocks, under her feet lay a glowing Persian rug of fallen October leaves, around her floated the fragrance of arbutus, beside her stood old Sherwin Dewey, grizzled, powerful, calm, his feet firm set on integrity—dawn and the morning star were in her eyes.

He could not speak. He stood holding fast to her hands.

She gave him that deep melting look of hers that came from very far within, that came from her heart, that told him what was in her heart. And it was love. Her face was not—not yet, he told himself hastily—the face of a woman in love. But it was the face of a woman who loved him.

She smiled at him then, she poured her full heart into a Clifford phrase, and turned it to untarnishable gold. "Oh, Mr. Hulme, you don't *know* how good you look to me!"

He loosened his hold on her hands gently, let them go. "Well, you look rather good to me, Susan."

They drew breath. They remembered where they were and looked away from each other for a moment.

Delia, short, broad-shouldered, sturdy-legged, appeared from a door at the side, her hat in her hand, her curly dark hair freshly

165

gested that evidence found in the debris here at Preston points to a connection with another recent terrorist attack."

She paused dramatically, as if she needed to compose herself before making her biggest revelation. "Though authorities are making no public statements yet, we are told that there are indications that members of this church terror group were connected to Farley the Fanatic, yes, the suspect who is still at large and wanted for questioning for his role in the recent attack on a United Nations building in New York.

"We're told that there were disturbingly similar materials found at the two investigative scenes, the basement of the Preston Community Church, just a few feet from where I'm standing right now, and the house of Farley the Fanatic, where, you may recall, I was standing reporting to you just a few days ago. I am told these materials include religious publications and pamphlets of the evangelical variety and evidence that the bombing of the U.N. was a very chilling possibility. And still could be, perhaps by surviving members of the terror cell whose plot went so horribly wrong here tonight in this church."

Reluctantly, she broke eye contact with her viewers for a moment and turned to a tall, balding man in a black polo shirt and brown sport jacket.

"I have with me Dr. Archer Fallworth, dean of the School of Arts and Science at Preston University, many of whose students and faculty worship at this church." She smiled sincerely, regretfully. "Thank you so much for taking a few minutes to be with us at this tragic time, Dean Fallworth."

Fallworth looked as if he just managed to stop himself from saying *My pleasure.* He nodded, pursing his lips.

"Dean, I think we're all in a state of shock about these revelations. I mean, members of a church congregation making bombs? And possibly connected to those plotting to commit terrorist attacks in our major cities? Can you throw any kind of light on what's been going on? Can you make any sense of this for us?"

Dean Fallworth looked up with a serious expression. "I'm not sure I *can* explain what appears to have happened here in Preston, Stephanie. I don't know if anyone can. When fanatics maim and kill innocent people, I think we all . . . I . . ." He shook his head, apparently overcome with emotion.

Stephanie decided to help him out. "When you say fanatics, Dean Fallworth, what exactly do you mean? Who are these people? What's their agenda?"

Fallworth cleared his throat. "Well, I've been at this university a good number of years, and I have to say I've witnessed some disturbing changes in recent times."

Stephanie's brow was furrowed with concern. "What kind of changes?"

"We've always had a strong evangelical presence here. Nothing wrong with that, of course. But I believe more extreme elements—fundamentalist evangelicals, if you will—are gradually taking control. And I believe these elements may be behind the terrible tragedy we witnessed here yesterday."

"You're obviously well acquainted with this group. What exactly do they believe? And if what we're being told is true—and I'm sure like a lot of our viewers I'm find-

combed, her brown eyes snapping. "Hello there, Mr. Hulme. Are you as nearly dead with tiredness as Susan? Not me! I'm crazy about this town. Didn't you use to live here? Gosh, how do you ever *stand* Clifford? It's got Boston beaten a mile. Here's where I'm going to live, you watch me! What are we going to do this evening?"

"Let's look at the paper and see," he said gaily. They put their heads together over the list of movies and places to eat. (He could not have afforded three good seats at a theatre and was not willing to take poor ones.) They went to a restaurant with mirrors all around the walls, and foreign-speaking waiters in black clothes, and ate fish in a white gravy with oysters and—what are these pink things, Mr. Hulme? Oh, shrimps. I never saw any—and for dessert had thin, thin pancakes but not with maple syrup, with another kind of syrup that the waiter touched a match to and it actually burned for a while. There was a fat woman across the room from them who wore such a comical hat that they couldn't stop laughing about it and her air of being sure she looked a beauty. The waiter's reverently solemn ways with the food set them off, as soon as his back was turned, into wild fits of fun. They laughed over everything. After the movie, Timothy took them for blocks up Broadway, its myriad electric lights, just as his mind had told him, resonant as bugles. Everything he saw reminded him of some story of his life in New York as a boy, so amusing that the girls were in gales of mirth. But he was in such high spirits, he could have made anything sound funny.

Chapter Thirteen

THEY were good months, January and February of that winter. Everything went well. There were no epidemics, only the usual colds; the minx from New Jersey could not stand the rube school another minute and to everyone's relief, her parents took her out of the Academy; the two new students from the city, the little McCann girl and Jules, fitted easily into Academy life, and Professor Hulme's queer old aunt began to make a fuss over Jules because he played the 'cello; Mr. Bowen provided diversion by starting what he called a riding club with the three or four boys whose parents had money enough for this sport of aristocrats, and strode about in riding trousers and boots to the amusement of Clifford wags and the admiration of some of the girls. None of them, of course, were invited to belong to the club. Mr. Bowen did not approve of girls, either in his classes or on athletic teams. They had, he said, a higher destiny than being educated or winning games. The skating continued excellent, the perfidious January thaw which usually ruined the ice, lasting only a few hours. The hockey team had its fair share of successes, and the basketball teams, both the boys' and the girls', an unusual series of victories. Perhaps the most unexpected event of the winter was the solving of the old problem of how to get the basketball teams and their supporters transported to the towns up and down the valley where their out-of-Clifford matches were played. It was Eli Kemp who invented a way to manage that. Of all people!

Yet when you heard how it happened, it was natural enough. Selling that gadget for carburetors, Eli had learned a good deal about cars (from his poverty-darkened childhood he had had the yearning passion for automobiles of the boy brought up without one) and he had come to know several of the mechanics in various garages. One of them was Bill Peck, a rough-spoken older workingman employed in a garage in Ashley. Peck had a brother working in St. Johnsbury who happened to write him that the old bus line there was about to replace its two battered ancient busses with new ones.

When Eli heard this news he was awed to feel, blowing from it as from the Delphian pit, the authentic wind of inspiration. Dizzy, but agonizingly in earnest, he told Peck that if those two old cars could be had at a bargain he was sure something could be made out of them at the Academy. There is no resisting those who have breathed in the divine afflatus. Peck was a pool-playing old bachelor with no wife to restrain him from follies; he withdrew a few hundred dollars from his savings account, borrowed a little more for insurance, and went into the bus business, he driving one and Eli the other. This did not interfere with his job at the garage, since that was daytime work, and since Eli, after school hours and on Saturdays, did all the repair and up-keep for the two venerable vehicles.

The engines were still in fair shape, but the bodies and seats were disreputable. The older man was willing to put the first profits into paint and denim, and Eli got up eagerly at dawn, day after day, to scrape, mend, paint and patch. Even at their worst, the two rickety busses were more comfortable, enclosed as they were, than the open pulpwood trucks in which, standing up on zero nights, the teams and a few hardy backers had formerly ridden to out-of-town games. With Professor Hulme to help him, although really, Timothy thought, he did nothing but sit by watching with astonishment the energetic play of the boy's awakened mind, Eli worked out a season ticket plan. Two weeks later he was back in the Principal's office.

"Say, Perfessor Hulme . . ."

"Yes, Eli."

"Perfessor Hulme, I want you should let me put some money in the savings bank, and have the book in your name."

"What's the matter with *your* name?"

"My father'd take it. I ain't of age."

Mr. Hulme looked at him.

"I'm not of age," the boy corrected himself.

"Well, all right. But we must put something in writing to show it is yours."

168

ing it hard to take all this on board—why are they targeting institutions such as the U.N.?"

"Stephanie, I think the most important thing to say is that whatever they believe—whether it's that the end of the world is approaching or the Second Coming or whatever—they just don't accept that you or I might take a different view, that we might have different beliefs—even different *Christian* beliefs."

"So what are they trying to do—bomb us into belief?"

Fallworth gave her a patronizing half smile that would have been familiar to his students. "I think that's very well put, Stephanie. Yes, that's exactly it."

And I've just written tomorrow's headline, Stephanie thought.

"Stephanie, the welfare of our students is my topmost priority, and we have to be aware of anybody who may be trying to influence them in a negative or dangerous way."

"Would you say Paul Wallach, who is now in a coma, was influenced in the way you describe?"

He hung his head. "Tragically, I believe so."

"And do you know who is responsible for turning such a promising student into what could be a fanatical killer?"

He flinched a little. Maybe she was laying it on a bit thick. But he couldn't turn back now. *Come on,* she thought, *you know what you have to do. And you really want to do it too.*

"It hurts me deeply to have to say this, but I believe one of our own faculty is the leading voice behind this pernicious movement." He winced to show just how deeply it hurt him.

Stephanie moved the microphone closer, almost as if it were a cattle prod.

"Professor Michael Murphy."

She affected horrified surprise. "And what subject does Professor Murphy teach?"

"Biblical archaeology," he said, making it sound like a disease. "At least that's what he was doing until today." He turned and looked directly into the camera. "In the interest of the students, I will be recommending to the university board that we suspend Professor Murphy until we conduct a proper internal inquiry."

FORTY-FOUR

MURPHY CROUCHED ON the floor
of the ambulance and held Laura's hand
while one of the paramedics got an IV into
her arm and the other wrapped thermal
blankets around her. "She just collapsed?"

The last few hours were a blur. Murphy
could hardly think. "Yes. She was in the
church when the bomb went off. We both
were. But they said she was okay. Just
bruises, nothing serious."

As the ambulance sped down Route 147,
the paramedic briefed the waiting trauma
team. By the time he'd finished, they'd already turned off the highway and onto the

"Naw, I don't want nothin' written down."

"Now, *Eli*—! . . . 'don't want nothing . . .'"

"I mean I don't want anything written down. My father'd get hold of the money somehow."

"Oh. . . . But, Eli, suppose I should die? How could you make anybody believe it was your money?"

"Oh, Perfessor, you ain't agoin' to die, you know you ain't! I mean you're not agoin' to die. Now, Perfessor, *please*. . . ."

The first entry was of four dollars and twenty-one cents. And then there was one of one dollar and two cents. And after that, six dollars and eighty-four cents. Presently the bank book showed twenty-three dollars and a half—more than any Kemp had ever owned at one time. Eli's long, melancholy face was calm and bright as he watched the other boys and girls stream in, cheering and yelling, "You gotta win! You gotta win! You *gotta* WIN!" to the Town Hall or gymnasium or made-over barn where a match was to be played, while he stayed outside in the sub-zero night to nurse and tend and warm up and listen to the valiant old engines. And test the brakes. Making sure of the brakes was Eli's daily joy. His busses might be overcrowded, but there were to be no accidents with them. He drove slowly and with impassioned care. His elderly partner always disappeared in the direction of the village pool parlor till the game was over and the Clifford rooters came out yelling,

> "Slingulation!
> Jingulation!
> One! Two! Three!
> Clifford Academy
> And old T.C.!"

It was in style, therefore, or relatively in style, that the Academy team and its rooters went off to games on Friday and Saturday nights. Some of the older Clifford basketball and hockey fans joined in, those who formerly had not been willing to take their own cars out to wait for hours in Arctic temperatures. Some of the younger teachers in the Primary School—ex-Academy girls themselves, mostly—often came along too, as much for the fun of the trip as

main campus roadway leading to the hospital, sirens blaring. Murphy pressed a cold hand to her cheek. "Hang in there, sweetheart."

They stopped with a jolt and the paramedics pulled the gurney out onto the tarmac and started barreling toward the trauma center like a bobsled team trying to gain momentum. The automatic doors slid open and closed like a greedy mouth, and they were in the receiving area, where the waiting trauma team instantly surrounded the gurney, brushed-steel equipment carts at the ready.

More IV needles went in. A vital-signs monitor was hooked up. A nurse started calling out pulse rate and blood pressure. All while the gurney accelerated toward a set of doors marked TRAUMA STAFF ONLY.

Murphy was sucked along in its wake, trying to keep Laura's face in sight as the trauma team worked furiously around her. Then the gurney was bumping through the doors and a hand gently held him back from following.

"I'm sorry. You'll have to wait out here.

We'll update you on your wife's condition as soon as we have more information." He mumbled a thank-you and the nurse disappeared after the gurney. He could hear the urgent back-and-forth of the trauma team for a moment, then the doors thumped shut and he was alone.

"Professor Murphy, what's going on? What are you doing here?" Shari's eyes were red-rimmed from crying.

"It's Laura. She just collapsed. They don't know what's wrong with her. I . . ." His voice trailed off.

She slumped in a seat and put her hand to her mouth. "Oh, no. Oh, no. Not Laura too."

Murphy pulled his seat closer and put his arm around her shoulders. He looked toward the double doors. "Paul's through there, too, isn't he?"

She nodded, sobbing quietly. They stayed like that, Shari's head on his shoulder, not knowing what else to do except silently pray. The minutes passed and then Murphy

for any interest in basketball. That forty-five to fifty were jammed into space meant for thirty only added to the hilarity.

T.C. used sometimes surreptitiously to put cotton in his ears, to give them a little rest from the barbaric hullabaloo of the yelling and cheering, but he never closed his eyes to rest them from what they saw. Sitting at the end, his legs stretched across the not-very-reliable door to make sure that none of the younger children fell out in the course of their rough-housing fun, he gazed and gazed (very well aware of the wealth the show to him had brought) at the contrast between the raw adolescent faces—chubby lumpish girls all the more touchingly childish because of their absurdly adult coiffures, raw-boned, uncouth lads, none the less little boys because of the gawky Adam's apple in their long necks—and Susan's face hanging in their midst like a star. It was young too, yes—but shapely with the subtly modeled ripeness of womanhood. The mild gray eyes were mature enough to meet his, often, with the smile of one indulgent adult to another in a crowd of lovable but preposterous children. The extravagance of youth all around her was like a complementary color, bringing out the fact which made T.C.'s wakeful nights happy ones, that she was not so young—not so young—not too young!

He never missed one of these expeditions. Many times that winter, Clifford parents, settling, relieved, to quiet evenings after their boisterous, disorderly boys and girls had gone out, gave a moment's grateful thought to teachers in general, and said how faithful Professor Hulme was to go around with those crazy kids and keep them in order the way he did; they expected he got pretty sick of it sometimes.

The late Sunday afternoons in the living-room of the Principal's house turned out better that winter too, or so it seemed to Timothy. He had invented them, long ago, as a substitute for the traditional entertaining required from a Principal, impossible for him because of Aunt Lavinia's housekeeping. But he had lived through many years of their ups and downs and had no illusions about them. In his mind his only claim to real success with them came from the fact that they had been the occasion of one of the few of his many battles with old Mr. Wheaton in which he had come off absolute victor. With the keen eye for commercial publicity which had been

170

the basis of his first success in selling carpets, Mr. Wheaton had first proposed and then insisted on a paragraph in the Academy catalogue, along the lines of . . ."delightful hospitality from Mr. Hume assures intimate personal relations with students—gathering around the century-old hearth where their fathers and grandfathers sat, the young people munch apples and under the old Hume family motto of 'Noblesse oblige,' listen to the Headmaster, famed for his reading aloud of the classics . . . townspeople are also welcome, which affords an opportunity to the students for contact with fine old-American . . ."

"But, Mr. Wheaton, that's not the hearth where their fathers and grandfathers . . . ! It had been closed up from about 1840 when stoves were first brought to town, till I came here and had it opened. And I'm *never* called the Headmaster—Clifford hasn't enough money to go in for that imitation-English business. I'm just the Principal. And 'noblesse oblige' is *not* the Hulme family motto —*with an l* if you please—the only reason it hangs on my wall is because it is a piece of needlework done by some grandmother or other that my aunt has an old-woman's notion for keeping. And very few older Clifford people ever appear—except Mr. Dewey of course. I wish they did, but I never can get them to. Most of them frankly find it an awful bore. And I do not by any means always read aloud. Sometimes the young people can't bear the thought of being read aloud to, any more, and they start to sing. . . ."

Mr. Wheaton's soft, wrinkled, manicured old hand reached for a pad. He began to write, reading his words aloud as he did, "Gathering around the piano in the twilight to the accompaniment of the Principal's accomplished playing, they . . ." Timothy broke in with some violence, "*Howl*, I should have said. It's frightful. They have *no* ear for music! My aunt can't endure it. Let them start, 'Jingle Bells,' she beats a retreat that makes her forget her stiff knees." Fixing Mr. Wheaton with his coldest eye, he laid down the law, "To put anything at all in our catalogue about those afternoons would be an overstatement. When I've been especially dull for a while, or when the skating's good, or in spring when there's a full moon, why, the only students who come are the kind who think I'll give them better marks if they do. Sometimes there's nobody at all."

Yet the very Sunday after this protest, Mr. Wheaton had sent a photographer all the way from the city to get a flashlight picture of the younger generation gathered at the Principal's knee as he read the classics. Timothy had always valued the Sunday afternoon gatherings more highly after the day when he had shut the door in that photographer's face.

As a matter of literal fact, in spite of the wormwood he had hastily distilled into Mr. Wheaton's synthetic syrup, there were often a good many people in the house on late Sunday afternoons, and they showed, in the astringent Vermont way, that they rather enjoyed themselves. These events were always managed, year after year, with exactly the same inexpensive and labor-saving system, because, what with his lack of extra money and the odd housekeeping of his aunt, that was the only one possible for the Principal. The house was open all the afternoon, but till along about five, most people—students, teachers, occasional townsfolks—took naps, went skating, sat in a corner holding hands, wrote letters home, read the Sunday newspapers. Professor Hulme was due to appear in his living-room at five. He brought with him apples from the cellar, and from the kitchen, doughnuts, popcorn, salt, and a small pitcher of melted butter. Those who were thirsty went out to the dipper at the kitchen sink. There were two corn poppers, the fireplace being a broad old-fashioned one for long firewood, and they and the flat-irons on which the butternuts were cracked, were kept going to the accompaniment of an incredible din of chatter and shrieking laughter till everybody had had all he could eat.

Then—well, in the old Vermont phrase which always amused Timothy—they "did what they felt to." Sometimes they wanted him to sit down at the piano and bang out the accompaniment for the songs so afflicting to Aunt Lavinia, from "The Bull Frog on the Bank" to "I Was Seeing Nellie Ho-o-ome." Once in a while a chance question started a quite interesting discussion like the time when a Senior boy asked if Professor Hulme really thought it would be a good thing to have everybody finger-printed, the way that piece in the Sunday paper said, and before they were through with this subject an ink pad had been brought down from his study and the collection of Academy finger-prints begun which later helped a graduate to a good job. Aunt Lavinia said frankly

172

lost all sense of time and he was arguing with Laura about something and then she started laughing and his heart leaped because she was all right and then he realized he must be dreaming and woke up with a start.

Dr. Keller was standing at his elbow. He nodded to Shari. "There's no change in Paul's condition. But we weren't expecting anything just yet." He turned to Murphy. "Laura's stable, but I'm afraid we still don't know why she collapsed. The signs look like someone of enormous strength tried to crush her windpipe.

"We're doing everything possible. And we will continue to do so. But at the moment I have to tell you she's losing ground."

Shari gasped and Murphy instinctively tightened his arm around her shoulders even though he was the one desperately in need of comfort. Then he stood and held a firm hand out to Keller. "Thank you, Doctor. I know you're doing all you can. And we'll do everything we can."

Keller shook his hand and nodded solemnly before walking back through the trauma center doors. Unusually for him, he'd run out of words.

Murphy saw the fatigue drawing dark circles under Shari's eyes. "Come on, I'm sure we could both use some water or a cup of coffee. We've got a lot of praying to do."

FORTY-FIVE

SEVERAL HOURS LATER, Murphy went to Laura's bed to give her hand a squeeze. Despite the respirator and the IVs and the machines that surrounded her, he thought she looked like a princess from a fairy tale. Her skin was almost porcelain white, her lips impossibly pale. The pill that was making her sleep was a powerful one, but her eyelids fluttered as he watched, showing she was still there, struggling to get out of her prison.

He thought he heard something above the hiss of the respirator—a whimper of protest, as if she were saying, *Please, someone,*

(what her nephew often thought most adults feel) that young people bored and fatigued her; but once in a while a flicker of her old charm flared up as she took the center of the stage to recite a poem of Robert Burns in her broadest Scotch, which, she always told them impressively, was *not* a dialect but more truly a language of its own than their meager Yankeeisms. Mr. Dewey, whose great stooped frame was always there in the background, had been known to tell one of the old Clifford stories—what his grandfather had told him about the battle of Hubbardton, or the time his great-grandmother killed the bear with the pitchfork.

The one rule which Timothy laid down about these gatherings—a rule born of desperation as he looked forward to an uninterrupted succession of them in his future—was that the Stern Daughter of the Voice of God was not to be let into the house on Sunday afternoons. Nobody was to come, the Principal wanted that clearly understood, if there was something else he'd rather do; nobody need stay if he'd rather go or if he felt like using rougher language and making more noise than was the custom in a living-room; nobody was to talk if he'd prefer not to; everybody was to say anything that came into his head as far as decency permitted. He insisted on the same privilege of spontaneity for himself. They could go elsewhere to be dutiful, he told his guests; and if they wanted him to be dutiful, they could just look him up in office hours. All that he had to offer them in his home on these Sundays was a two-hour chance to do collectively what they enjoyed doing: a vacation from what somebody thought might be good for them. That's what he expected from them, he said, and that was all they might expect from him.

There was, of course, he knew, a good deal of pretense in this invitation to sincerity, as in everything human. He by no means always read aloud what he would have preferred, and it was all too often necessary to put on for decency's sake a look of interest in the proceedings that was far from expressing the clock-watching resignation into which he fell when he was in a mood of juiceless school-teacherism. But that winter there was much less of this necessary pretense—the Sunday afternoons seemed distinctly agreeable. The new boy, Jules, had found an old 'cello in the corner of Miss Peck's attic, strung it and brought it along with him Sundays, to

173

get me out of here, but he wasn't sure he could trust his senses anymore.

He bent over and kissed her gently on the forehead. "Hey, baby, I'm here. Don't worry. Everything's going to be okay."

He looked down and was surprised to see he was clutching something in his hand. Dr. Keller must have given it to him. It was a small Ziploc bag with Laura's personal effects. A thin gold wedding band, wristwatch, pearl earrings, keys. And the little wooden cross on its cord.

He imagined walking out of the hospital still holding the bag, and tears suddenly blurred his vision. "Don't leave me, sweetheart. Please don't leave me." He heard the door open and felt a flash of self-consciousness and then thought, *Don't be so dumb—she's seen it all before.*

But it wasn't the nurse.

Standing by the door, looking past him at Laura with an expression of infinite sadness, was a red-haired woman in a long black coat that looked too big for her. "Mr. Murphy?" she said in a trembling voice. Her accent was lilting and familiar, but for the moment Murphy couldn't place it. "I'm

Isis McDonald." She locked eyes briefly with Murphy, then her gaze went back to Laura. "I'm so, so sorry."

He looked perplexed, as if she were a character from a dream and he couldn't understand what she was doing standing there, apparently solid, talking to him like a real person.

"You must forgive me," she said. "I shouldn't have just come like this. I didn't want to intrude on your . . . I didn't want to interfere. We don't even know each other. It's just that I . . ."

Murphy breathed out and tried to relax his shoulders. He indicated the chair. "I'm sorry. Please, sit down. You've come a long way."

She sat down, clutching a battered-looking briefcase tightly in her lap. She didn't seem to know what to say or do next.

The awkward silence was broken when the nurse returned with a container of coffee. She took in Isis, nodded hello, and handed the cup to Murphy with a sympathetic smile.

"I don't really want this," he said as the

door closed behind her. "Would you like it? No cream or sugar, I'm afraid."

She took the cup, grateful for the distraction. "Thank you. That's fine."

They were silent for what seemed a long time, just looking at Laura and listening to the soft hiss of the respirator.

"Look, it's good of you to be concerned," he said. "But it's not as if you knew Laura. I don't mean to be rude, but what are you doing here?"

Isis put the coffee on the window ledge and settled her hands on top of the briefcase.

"I brought you something." She undid the clasp and pulled a padded manila envelope out of the briefcase. Reaching inside, she tipped the envelope up and something fell out.

The tail of the Serpent lay on the top of the briefcase, gleaming dully.

"I don't understand."

She picked it up and held it out toward him. "I thought you might want it. I thought it might help."

"Help? How is that going to help?"

She couldn't look at him. "Isn't it sup-

resort to in case of singing. It was astonishing how his playing the air with long sweeping arrogant bow strokes herded back to the proximity of the key even the worst of the waverers. Susan Barney's voice began to show the effects of Aunt Lavinia's bullying lessons. With Susan at one end of the piano, always in the middle of the note, her eyes fixed on the pianist to keep in time with him, and Jules sawing professionally away at the other, there were times when Aunt Lavinia sat through even "Nita, Jua-ha-nita," and "Aca-ádemee! The years with thee, will ever he-elp and strengthen me!"

It turned out to be a good year for reading aloud too. Letting his young audience make their own selections, Timothy roamed from Wodehouse, W. W. Jacobs, and Howard Pyle to Stevenson, Mark Twain, Booth Tarkington—even, one afternoon, preposterous as this was, some of the Uncle Remus stories. He was so tickled by the thought of how supremely funny his Scotch-New-York-Vermont Negro accent must be, that he joined wildly in the screams of laughter from his young audience, obliged to lay down the book often, take off his pince-nez and wipe his streaming eyes. Ponce de León should have read Uncle Remus aloud, he thought that day, his eyes on Susan's lighted-up face, her mouth stretched wide in the hilarious grimace of the mask of comedy.

There was even, that winter, an occasional successful half-hour of poetry, although poems usually drugged the young Vermonters into the trancelike inattention, broken by unrebellious yawns, of those who listen to Commencement addresses. Possibly they liked poetry better that winter because the reader found his own ears suddenly open to it. He had loved poetry from his boyhood; his earliest recollection of his parents was hearing them recite Meredith sonnets; he had never stopped reading verse, both professionally as a teacher of English and as a matter of personal habit and taste; there were so many poems in his memory that his very thoughts often presented themselves to him in quotations. Yet it occurred to Timothy, startled by the freshness of this winter's new delight, that perhaps he had been for years, without realizing it, slowly sinking from the quickening awareness of poetry into the sleepy prose of middle age. He had been growing dull not only to poetry but to the vibrant stuff of poetry in life, to love and sorrow and beauty, to the harmonious

174

flowing loveliness of the valley where he lived, to the wonder of dawn, the splendor of sunsets, and to snow announced by all the trumpets of the sky.

If he had been half asleep, he was now aroused. Poems he had always known by heart burst upon him with as fresh a revelation of deep, unearthly meaning as though—he thought—this were the first poetry he had ever seen. How could he have read tamely such lines as "How soon hath Time, the subtle thief of youth . . ." and "Scatter as from an unextinguished hearth . . ." and "The wreckful siege of battering days . . ." and "Into my heart an air that kills . . ." and "The woods are lovely, dark and deep," and "And they saw neither sun or moon, But they heard the roaring of the seas." Several times that winter he turned over the pages of an anthology for a half hour at a time, reading what struck his eye and heart, almost forgetting that he had listeners. They were quiet enough to be forgotten, the few older people sagging in their chairs, the boys and girls sprawled on the floor, supple as panthers, their absent eyes fixed on the dozing wood fire; or on the sky darkening beyond the windows; or on the fiercely blazing pin-point of the evening star, blood brother to the sleepy hearth flames; or on the photograph of the group from Chartres over the mantel—God bending his grave, benevolent, puzzled face down over man, sparkling in simian malice.

Even when they could not follow, they were shaken and held because he was shaken and held to rediscover what he had forgotten —the power of poetry. Sometimes he plucked, unaware, a secret string which gave off a cry, as for the Milton sonnet on his dead wife. "I woke: she fled, and day gave back my night," he read, and was startled to hear the gangling fourteen-year-old Jules choke back a sudden sob. Timothy looked down at him surprised. The father-less boy whispered piteously, as if they were alone in the room, "Last night I dreamt Papa was alive, and when I woke up . . ." In the hushed room, Timothy could hear, like the rustling of wings, the stirrings of sympathy in those poetry-quickened hearts. And once, "Yet, Freedom, yet thy banner torn but flying, Streams like the thunderstorm *against* the wind," struck out a cry of admiration from old Mr. Dewey. He himself, Timothy, looking away from his book one day to where Susan, her head on Aunt Lavinia's knee, fixed dreaming eyes on him, found himself reading, "She was a

175

phantom of delight . . ." in so deeply moved a voice that—he thought that night in bed—it must have been like the child's chalked scrawl, "Timothy loves Susan."

It was a scrawl he would now gladly have chalked up on any wall. He would have been enchanted to have her, to have them all, hear what was in his voice as he read, "Sweet records, promises as sweet . . ." Why not? Why not?

And yet he was in no hurry to cut short this period of waiting for the ripening of his golden apple gleaming through its fresh young verdure. He was happy, he who had almost forgotten what it is to be happy—had quite entirely forgotten (had he ever known?) how happiness, greatest of creative artists, laughs at the limitations of its medium, can catch up any moment, the most ordinary, and make it sing like a seraph, or glow like welcoming home-windows, or ring with the lost laughter of childhood.

Aunt Lavinia had been impatient with Susan's progress in music; Mrs. Washburn had been disagreeable about the uninteresting scales coming from Susan's attic room at Miss Peck's—"For heaven's sake, come here to my room in the evening for your hour's practice, where I can keep you from making such idiotic mistakes," said one cross-grained old lady, and, "A great relief to have some quiet in the house," said the other.

Timothy now refused, on one pretext or another, the usual winter round of invitations to supper, always was at home in the evening, and sat upstairs in his study no more. When Susan came downstairs after her wrestle with Aunt Lavinia, he was there, sometimes with his newspaper in the sheltered corner under the stairs, sometimes sitting smoking in the living-room before the fire, sometimes with an artfully disposed bait to keep her with him, like the photographs he sent away for in January, to add to his collection of famous paintings, statues, and buildings, sometimes shown to the Sunday evening group. The two spent a long evening over the new photographs, looking at them, talking about them—at least Timothy talked about them, told stories of vacation experiences here and there among the originals. "When I can rent this house furnished to a summer person, it just makes enough for a vacation in Europe," he explained. "You can do it for very little, you see, if you

176

posed to . . . Don't you believe it has healing powers?"

Suddenly he understood why she'd come. "No! Absolutely not. It's just a piece of bronze."

She seemed bewildered. "Just a piece of bronze? But you risked your life to get it. I thought it was supposed to have healed the Israelites when they were bitten by poisonous snakes. I thought that's what you believed."

"That is not what I believe. It was God who healed them because of their faith. The power was in their faith, not in the Serpent. When they started worshiping it as if it had magic powers, that's when God told Hezekiah to destroy it."

She still held it out, willing him to take it. "But how do you know? How do you know that it doesn't have any power? How do you know it won't help Laura?"

Murphy cleared his throat. "Because I know that's not how God works. There are no magic tricks."

"What about faith healers? That seems like a magic trick to me."

"No. We don't know why God some-

go on a slow old ship or third-class on a fast one. And of course, walk or bicycle mostly, once you're in Europe." Susan listened creatively. When she stood up to go, "Haven't you a favorite picture or statue?" he asked her. "I'd like so much to give you one of these photographs for your room, to live with. If there's one you like."

She made a little cry of pleasure out of his name—Timothy's delight in hearing her say his name was fatuous—and leaned over the spread-out photographs to make a choice. He wondered which one she would take, but forgot to notice, delighted by the perspective in which he saw her, the cross-lighting from fire and lamp correcting the ever-so-little concave silhouette of her face. She looked, he thought, like a soft-eyed Correggio angel leaning with clasped hands over the Cradle. From that evening on, it was thus—no matter what the lighting—that he saw her face.

He varied his bait. "Susan, I wonder if you'd have time to do something for this tear in my overcoat? I can sew on buttons, but it's terrible work I make of mending. And Aunt Lavinia's worse."

This was always a success. It was sweet to see how she snatched it from his hand, how she sat stitching, proud of her skill, showing it off to him. "There! How's that?"

"Perfect! I'd never know where it was!"

As time went on he offered no bait, simply drew up a chair for her near his when she came down the stairs, as if it were the natural thing to do. Sometimes he, sometimes Susan, then brought out laughingly an absurd formula which had once been inadvertently let fall by one of them, they could never agree which one. It ran, all on one breath, "Come on, let's have a talk what shall we talk about?" The grouse in the gunroom, thought Timothy, smiling, had no more immortal life than this small foolish joke that was their own. He was enchanted that he could see how silly it was, and yet join with all his heart in Susan's young laughter over it.

What they talked about was mostly what had been going on that day in Timothy's inner world where his mind, if it liked, ran after its tail frivolously, or if it liked better, bayed questions about the nature of things at the unanswering moon. They laughed together about his mind—how sometimes it was like a faithful servile dog, sometimes like a mischievous unruly monkey, or a playful non-

times heals people. Just like we don't know why . . . why sometimes He lets them get sick." He couldn't help glancing at Laura. "Even good people. Even the best. The very best."

She was standing now, and Murphy thought she was going to press the thing into his hands, like a person desperate to make a sale. "But why not try? Maybe it won't work, but it couldn't do any harm, could it? Isn't it worth trying?"

He put his hands on her thin arms and looked at her, imploring her to understand. "It would be wrong. It would be like saying to God, 'I have more faith in this piece of metal than I do in You.' It would be sinful."

"What does it matter? So what if you commit a sin if it saves Laura's life? You're just being selfish, worrying about the cleanliness of your soul when she could be dead." She flushed again and put a hand to her mouth. "I'm sorry. I shouldn't have said that."

He didn't say anything. Just took the tail of the Serpent and put it back in the envelope and then into the briefcase. He snapped it closed and held it out to her.

"Take this back to the museum. Lock it up in the vaults. Then, if you want to say a prayer for Laura..."

She took the briefcase, not looking at him. "Yes. Yes, all right. I'm sorry." He thought she looked like a little girl who'd been caught doing something naughty. "Look, there's something else. I've finished translating the inscription. I know this isn't the right time, but I brought it with me. It's...rather extraordinary. I thought I ought to give it to you as soon as possible."

He looked at her blankly. "I'll call you. When this is...when this is over." She nodded and walked out, gripping the briefcase tightly to her chest.

He took Laura's hand and laid his cheek against it. "I wish you could talk to me, sweetheart. You always know what to do."

Exhaustion finally claimed Murphy, and he slipped into a troubled rest. When he awoke twenty minutes later, it was to the sound of an urgent alarm buzzer from the respirator.

Something in the room had changed. He looked up, confused for a moment, and then he understood what it was. The regular beep-beep-beep of the vital-signs monitor had turned into a single urgent note of alarm. He leaped out of the chair and was halfway to the door when it burst open and Dr. Keller ran in, followed by another doctor and a nurse pushing a trolley.

He watched as they bent over her. The nurse was holding the electric pads in her hands, waiting for Dr. Keller's okay, and then strong hands took hold of him and he closed his eyes.

FORTY-SIX

THE CRIME SCENE investigators had finally left, the last piece of police tape had been removed, and Preston Community Church was once again what it had always been, a place of worship.

Restoring the physical damage, however, would take longer. Though the structure had been secured with steel props under the weakened floor, a section of scaffolding supporting the east wall, and plastic sheeting covering most of the shattered windows, the charred and smoke-blackened door frame was a reminder that days earlier the

chalant cat, and then again leaned into the collar and pulled its
load like a hard-working cart-horse.

"Does it ever," Susan asked him a little shyly, "seem to you like
a bird—just springing up and soaring off to the sky, because of some
sudden happiness? Once in a while mine does that."

"Yes, sometimes," answered Timothy gravely, his eyes on hers.

"But mine can't do figures of eight all over the ice like yours,"
she said. "That's *terribly* interesting to me! Ever since that time you
told me about Mrs. Washburn I've thought how a person simply
can't be bored if his mind will only . . ."

"Oh, yes, he can too!" protested Timothy. "Today when the Reverend Mr. Randall was here—he's the third Trustee you know—I
thought I'd die of boredom. He's such an old sheep!"

"Oh, tell me about it!"

So he told her about it. His hand was always on the latch to open
when she knocked.

Sometimes they talked about their profession, tried to see more
clearly into the complex problems of the art in the practice of which
they both spent so much of every day. Timothy had not realized
that any of his colleagues, especially any of the younger ones, felt
so devoted an interest in teaching. Sometimes they shamelessly talked
personalities, discussing people they knew and taking them to pieces
—was it possible, Timothy asked himself, that he could be so light-
heartedly dancing on the ruins of the triple walls of his Scotch-
Vermont, professional, and celibate reticence?

He even did what he had never done before with anyone, he
talked over with her some of the "case-histories" of students: that
sex-crazy Marylyn Forbes from New Jersey; the nice McCann child,
so subdued, on her guard and watchful when she came, now beginning to stretch out and open up and gather confidence in herself
and others; and poor Jules (for he now knew Jules' story), fine,
sensitive, naturally civilized son of an honorable and distinguished
father, left by that father's death helplessly in the power of a coarse-
fibered materialistic mother.

"How do you suppose Mr. Bernstein, Jules' father, ever happened
to marry such an ordinary woman?" asked Susan wonderingly.

"Oh, alas! there's no use trying to figure out why sensitive, fine,
and superior people so often marry ordinary ones."

178

Jules' situation reminded Susan of something her grandfather had told her about a man who had lived on the next farm to his, and she passed that story along to Timothy, who listened as though he had never rebelled against old-time Clifford stories.

Once or twice Susan, half-bold, half-shy, let him in to some of the traditional Academy jokes about him, like his saying, *"Ha!"* when he was amused or scornful—she was astonished that he had never overheard the students putting each other down with an explosive imitation of that "Ha!" And didn't he know that when he took off his eye-glasses in a certain special way and put them on again before speaking, everybody recognized it as a storm-signal of his displeasure? And was it possible, she ventured further, that he had never heard the story, told each Freshman class by their elders, about the dumb girl who said she guessed Wordsworth's poetry was all right, only it was cram full of quotations from Professor Hulme's talk?

No, Timothy had not realized, he said in all naive seriousness, that he said, "Ha!" It sounded rather silly and affected, he feared. "Oh, we like it!" Susan reassured him. "We wouldn't know you, if you didn't." Nor had he any idea, he told her, that his habit of thinking in quotations had reached his everyday talk, and when Susan, overcome with mirth at his not knowing what everybody else knew so well, burst into laughter, he joined her, enchanted to be laughing with her. Sometimes in a single hour their talk wandered from the reasons for Delia's liking mathematics to religion, to skating, to "what is morbid," to hats (Susan now asked his opinion seriously about hats), to architecture, to the refinishing of antique furniture. "But this is the real companionship that's supposed not to be possible between men and women," thought Timothy fondly, as surprised to find himself discussing whether Aunt Lavinia looked better in gray or lavender as to see a blooming girl passionately attentive when, one evening, flinging down in a rage the newspaper with its daily poison-news of Nazi anti-Semitic torture and hatred of civilization, he opened his heart and in a long excited tirade poured out some of the horror and despair felt by decent men of his time. "What does it mean, this triumphant Fascist reversion to Apache savagery? What can it *mean?*" he ended his outburst by shouting to the ignorant country-girl the question to

179

which he knew no answer. And then, perhaps because he had given an emotional expression to one of his deepest emotions, his mind cleared and brought out, as a definite and tragic answer, a theory that had long been hovering in the background: "The only thing it can possibly mean is that the human race has completely gone to pieces from the strain of trying to be civilized—trying to keep down the old grab and kill instincts. We're done for! Yes, we're done for. On the way back to the jungle!"

Susan caught the implication. "Of course! That's so with children too. . . . If they're kept in the classroom being 'good' and quiet more than just so long—why, you can't do a thing with them. They act like little devils." She looked at him hard till she had his attention, and added earnestly, pressingly, "But, Mr. Hulme, they really are *not* little devils." Yes, she knew what he was talking about, she always did. She knew that it was despair he felt, that he was urging her to feel. And, strong vital spirit, she would have none of it, nor let him drink from its narcotic cup. "They're just human, only little boys and girls."

He drew his brows together and looked at her hard, unused to opposition in Clifford, astonished to have her oppose an intuition of hers to an opinion of his.

She met his challenging gaze steadily. She said with spirit, "Seems to me it's up to their teacher to have more sense than they do. They may think they're really little devils. He ought to know better. He ought not to lose his head. They'll act decent again tomorrow—if their teacher's any good."

"You mean—that the Fascist idiocy may be only a temporary hysteric attack—like—well, like what happened in Salem over the . . ."

"Oh, Mr. Hulme!" cried Susan. "That's a *won*derful idea! You *do* have such good ideas! Why don't you take it for one of your morning Assembly talks? Why, even my little third graders in their American History lessons could understand that. The witchcraft craze is in our course of study. I could teach it that way. The children could understand, I know they could, how ashamed the Salem people were when they got over being crazy, and how proud we all are now of the few Salem folks who kept their heads and acted decent. And how proud we'll all be if our country can keep its head

interior of the church had been like a vision of hell. Only the steeple, a finger of pristine whiteness pointing to heaven, remained untouched by the blast, and as the church members started to file inside, it was hard not to see it as a symbol of hope and endurance.

Wagoner stood at the entrance, as he had done on the night of the blast, welcoming the faithful. With one arm still in a sling, he couldn't administer the bear hugs he felt were sometimes needed, but his handshake was as firm and strong as ever. One by one the parishioners filed inside, settling into the dozen or so pews that had remained undamaged and turning their eyes toward the makeshift podium standing in place of the shattered pulpit.

Murphy sat in the front row, Shari at his side, her hand clasped in his. From the east window, now empty of stained glass, a shaft of sunlight angled down, catching the edge of the casket positioned crossways at the foot of the altar, and making the floral arrangements around it blaze with color. Sitting to Murphy's right, Laura's father stared straight ahead, focusing on some distant place that only he could see. His wife clutched his arm, sobbing quietly.

Looking at Laura's face as she lay in the open casket, it was hard to believe she was dead. Her ivory dress seemed luminescent, lending her pale features a vibrant glow that almost matched the flowers framing the coffin and the daisies threaded through her hair. Through the empty window, Murphy could hear birds singing and wondered if they, too, had been fooled by Laura's lifelike appearance. *Someone should tell them,* he thought. *I ought to speak to Pastor Bob.* He started to get up, and felt Shari's hand anchoring him. He settled into the pew again. Perhaps it would be okay to let the birds continue singing for now. They would surely stop when they saw her being put into the ground.

Wagoner slowly climbed the steps to the podium, keeping his eyes on Laura all the way, then looked out over the congregation.

"This is a very difficult time for all of us," he began. "Sometimes it seems like a lifetime ago, sometimes, I know, it seems like just a few moments, that we were last gathered here. Some of us lost loved ones or

now and act decent. Do you think it would be all right to do that? A teacher's not supposed to talk politics, of course. May I?"

"A teacher is supposed to be a civilizing influence on her students," cried Timothy warmly. "You certainly may!"

"Oh, listen!" she cried, lifting her hand. "What's that Aunt Lavinia is playing?"

It was a movement from one of the Brandenburg Concertos, he told her. They sat in silence till its end when Susan asked, hesitatingly, "I never heard any Bach till this winter. But now I do—it's queer how—it's so—he sort of knows where he's going. It makes a person feel—"

Timothy thought he knew what she wanted to say and said it for her. "He makes you feel safe."

"Yes, yes, that's it exactly. Oh, Mr. Hulme, how beautifully you put things!"

"Well, don't tell Aunt Lavinia I said so. She'd skin me alive for being literary about music."

Every joint in him, stiffened by loneliness, every sluggish vein chilled by his solitude, was quickened to life by these evening talks. They were not by any means always serious. Susan was often in a merry mood, brought him the amusing sayings of the day from her classroom—the little boy, sitting on his foot till it went to sleep, who told his teacher wonderingly, "It feels like ginger-ale." Or she exploded in laughter over a new funny story, "Do you know this one, about the Southerner who was driving North for the first time and how his little boy looked out of the window and said, 'Daddy! *I* see a Yankee!' and the father said—"

Or it might be about cooking they would talk with respect, Susan being awed by the religious care shown by Miss Peck in the preparation of food. "Why, Professor Hulme, if it's no more than *hash,* she prays over it."

It was so free, so natural between them that sometimes Timothy thought, "Why, some evening when she stands up to go, her lovely face all alight with fun, I shall not be able to keep myself from taking her hand, pulling her roughly down to me, saying, 'Don't go, Susan! Don't go, *ever!* Stay!'"

181

family members, all of us lost friends. And all of us bear the scars from that terrible day—and I don't mean the physical scars. I mean the pain of loss that will remain with us forever."

He coughed into his hand, and for a moment it seemed as if the church were full of smoke again. Then he continued, his voice strong, and the air was clear. "If you're like me, some parts of that night will be a little hazy for a while," he said with a wry smile. "But I do remember what I was planning to talk about. I was going to talk about having faith in God's plan for us. About keeping faith even when it might seem as if He's forgotten us." He paused. "And I guess right now might seem like such a time. How could such a terrible thing have happened? And now, adding insult to injury, the very people who have suffered the most in this tragedy are being accused of terrible crimes. On the TV and in the newspapers we are being talked of as murderers and terrorists. How can this be?"

He shifted his arm a little in its sling before continuing. "The truth is, I don't know. God hasn't revealed to me what exactly He has in mind for all of us. But I do know He *has* a plan for us. And I know He's watching to see how we cope with these trials and tribulations." He gripped the edge of the podium with his good hand. "And what does God see when He looks down on us? Well, I'll tell you what I see. I see people beginning to rebuild what's been destroyed. I see people returning to a place that was desecrated by a terrible act of violence and making it holy again with their worship. I see people keeping the faith. Because ultimately God's plan *will* be revealed to us. It's going to take a lot of hard work—it's going to take all the skills and energy and application we have to restore this church to what it was. And it's going to take every ounce of our faith in God to get us through the turmoil that now surrounds it. But together, with God's help, we will do it."

He took a deep breath and wiped his brow with a handkerchief. He hoped he'd managed to raise the congregation's spirits just a little. They would need all their strength for what was to follow.

All eyes were now on Laura's coffin. The light had moved on, and her face was now

And that would be all. That would be enough. They were so close a word would bridge the gap. The cup had brimmed slowly up till one more drop would make it overflow.

Yes, every hour was brighter than the one before it. It made him think of nights when in a silvery premonition of the rising moon, the black sky above the Wall turned by imperceptible gradations to flooding light.

Yet there were still times—hours—instants—when in an anguish of sudden panic he doubted it all.

One of these came on the last evening of February, came as a cold reaction from one of the most glowing of the good hours.

It was just before the beginning of the mid-winter vacation, which that year was the first week of March. Susan was to spend it with Delia who had come on from Boston to join her. They were to visit some of their father's over-the-mountain, Barney kinsfolk. Aunt Lavinia had asked the girls to spend the evening before they left at the Principal's house and had stayed downstairs till they arrived, warming her knees before the fire. She was amused by Delia's cool sub-acid comments on life, although she considered her a climber— "not a social climber, she's far too keen to waste time on nonsense, but a climber all the same. She jumps at every littlest thing you do that's better than what she's seen, and makes a round for her ladder out of it."

"Well, what's the matter with that?" Timothy had asked, although he did not like Delia very well himself.

"Oh, anybody of my age knows that all that ever happens to a ladder is to get kicked down. You just wait. But I don't deny an occasional drop of the gir-r-rl's salt and lemon juice is tasty."

Timothy had waited in the hall corner for the callers, his day-old New York newspaper in his hand, but at the sound of the knocker on the front door he had flung his paper to the floor.

"Come on in here by the fire, Delia," called Aunt Lavinia.

Timothy hastened to draw near him a chair for Susan. Pulling off her knit cap and shaking out her hair, she sat down to unbuckle her overshoes and open her windbreaker jacket. They began to talk, but because they were not alone and because they both knew that Aunt

182

Lavinia was likely to tire suddenly of Delia and to summon Delia's sister, no wandering speculation was started. Susan began to give a decorous account of where they were to go during the week of their absence. He did not listen. Watching the play of light on the Correggio-soft young face, delighting in certain tricks of her expression, and in the foreshortening of her face when hesitating for a word she lifted her eyes toward the ceiling, he did not hear a word she was saying. Apparently she herself did not take her account of her Barney kin very seriously, for after a time she broke it off to say in a more intimate tone, glancing over her shoulder towards the living-room, "Do you know, I positively hate to go away—even for a week! Why should I? Isn't it silly? What could happen in a week? But I've had such a wonderful winter—I never knew anybody could have such a wonderful time. It's been—you've been . . ." She hesitated for a word.

To make her go farther, he protested provocatively, "Oh, I haven't. . . ."

She went farther with a generous rush. "Yes, yes, *you!* You can't imagine what you've done for me."

From the room beyond them, "Susan!" called Aunt Lavinia imperiously. "Come here a minute!"

She went when Aunt Lavinia called—what else could anyone do?—but, sheltered from other eyes in the angle of the hall-corner, she gave Timothy, with shrugging shoulders and a fond smiling grimace, the assurance she left him unwillingly, that here with him was where she fain would be.

Glowing and confident, Timothy held up his newspaper to hide the broadness of his answering smile—and felt a chilling inner wind blowing, as from Arctic ice-fields. Horrifying. Inexplicable. Where, in the safe security built around him in the last two months, was there a chink left through which this icy self-doubt could blow? With one disdainful puff it put out the beautiful clear fire burning on his inner hearth, and whirled the ashes away to darkness. He saw that he was a fatuous fool to assume that the frankly loving ardor in the gray eyes, the fond confident intimacy of voice and manner, meant that Susan was a woman opening her heart to the man she was falling in love with. Wasn't it rather the simple-hearted open affection of a very young girl, talking to a man who seemed to her so old, so far from her in experience and years that she needed no caution?

He sickened. He was terrified. "Help!" he called faintly to his mind, holding the newspaper up before his stricken face.

"The India shawl on that table belonged to my grandmother," came Aunt Lavinia's voice. "It was brought to her from India by her brother, Major-General Keith."

His mind rushed to the rescue, doing the poor reasonable best which is all a mind has at command, "Quiet now! Take it easy! Can't it mean that she is simply so young, so inexperienced, that she doesn't know what is happening to her? Yet, for all that, it may be—it must be—it is happening. Even if she doesn't realize what she is saying to you with that free warm open look, she really is saying it!"

"The Gibbon was part of Timothy's Hulme grandfather's library. The set was sent to the States when Timothy's Aunt Cornelia died. In her will . . ."

Yes, that would do, Timothy told his mind, that would do. For the present.

Although his pulse was still hammering in the after-effects of shock, his face was composed enough to make it safe for him to lay down the shield of his newspaper, light a cigarette, and sit listening to the dialogue in the next room, once in a while glancing up at the mirror. It showed a reflected Delia, absorbed in a book (as glad to stop talking to Aunt Lavinia, apparently, as Aunt Lavinia to have her) and Aunt Lavinia sitting weightily before the fire, her skirts folded back to expose her knobby wool-stockinged knees to the heat, occasionally answering over her shoulder a question asked by Susan, who was wandering here and there in the room. Sometimes her reflection, slim in her dark blue woolen dress, passed across the mirror, sometimes she was an invisible voice.

"Where did this three-cornered armchair come from?"

"What does *noblesse oblige* really mean?"

"Well, how *would* you translate it?" wondered Aunt Lavinia. "The idea is that the very fact of being a superior makes it your duty to be responsible for the welfare of people who are your inferiors."

184

in shadow. The flowers had faded to a muted glow.

Wagoner cleared his throat and began. "You don't need me to tell you that Laura Murphy was a beautiful person, inside and out. Anyone who saw her smile, heard her laugh, the way she would make others laugh"—he smiled—"sometimes with a joke at their own expense—and I speak from experience here—will know what a joyful and joy-giving woman she was. She was also a very talented archaeologist who could have had a glittering career—but she chose instead to devote herself to helping others, helping students to achieve the very best that they could. There are a lot of people in this town who owe her a debt of gratitude for setting them on the right path or helping them off the wrong one, and I'm sure there are a few of them here today. If any of you are wondering how such a wonderful person could be struck down when she still had so much to give, I want you to try to think about everything that Laura *has* given us. How many people give so much during their whole lives?"

He heard a few sobs and sniffles from

around the church and gave people a moment to collect themselves. Or was it to collect himself? How many times had he done this—dispensing comforting words to the bereaved? And how many times had he secretly needed someone to give him comfort too? But this was the task God had given him, and thankfully He had provided the strength to carry it out.

"Laura loved life and she loved God—and she loved her husband, Michael." He looked down at Murphy, whose eyes were fixed on Laura with a strange half-smile, and he wondered if he really understood that she was gone. "Only those who have lost a loved one know what Michael is feeling today. Our hearts truly go out to him. We pray that God will give him the strength to bear the terrible pain he's feeling."

He drew himself up as straight as he could on the podium. An old leather-bound Bible was open in front of him, but he didn't need to look at it. "Early on in Christianity, when believers died, the living were a bit confused about what would happen to them when Christ returned for them in the rapture. The apostle Paul wrote in 1 Thessalonians 4:14 to 18 that when Jesus comes from heaven He will descend...with a shout...and the dead in Christ will rise first. Then we who are alive *and* remain shall be caught up in the clouds, to meet the Lord in the air. And we shall always be with the Lord.

"The Bible says that we should comfort one another with these words. And what greater comfort could there be? Laura is now with Jesus. She isn't sad or in pain, as we are. Her body may be broken, but her soul, her perfect soul, is in heaven. And it is God's promise to us that if we believe in His Son's death on the cross for our sins, and that God raised Him from the dead, we shall see her and all fellow believers and 'ever be with the Lord.' No wonder the apostle could say to us in our sorrow, 'Therefore, comfort one another with these words,' for you will see Laura again."

The last words were spoken slowly, and he looked directly at Murphy as he said them.

Then Wagoner picked up his hymnbook.

Murphy rose to his feet and soon the sweet sound of voices joined in sorrow and thankfulness rose up from the battered pews.

Murphy walked over to the casket for one final look at Laura. As he looked down, it took him a moment to notice it, and he thought the tears in his eyes were distorting his vision. But as he reached over with his hand, his fingers confirmed the shocking sight. Someone had snuck in and taken the wooden cross Murphy had laid around Laura's neck and partially snapped it so that its three pieces now dangled from the necklace.

"But how ever do you know which you are?" asked the young Yankee.

Timothy chuckled to himself at the simple, declarative, non-ironic seriousness of Aunt Lavinia's, "No Coulton ever had any doubts about that." He looked quickly up into the mirror to see if Susan too was amused. But he saw only her back, her straight, supple, young back, and his memory quoted joyfully. "Earth in her heart laughs, looking at the heavens, thinking of the harvest: I look and think of mine."

The girl he saw in the mirror, turned to one side, lifted her head and glanced at a faded photograph in an oval frame. Timothy had forgotten that photograph hung there. He started. Good heavens! Suppose she asked about that! What a way for her to learn—how could he not have told her himself long ago about Ellie?—the little there was to tell? If she asked now, what careless wounding bluntness might Aunt Lavinia put into her answer, which he could not spring to correct, separated from Susan as he was by those alien presences in the room.

But perhaps she would not ask. She had dropped her eyes, she was looking admiringly at something on the table. Relieved, he leaned back in his chair. She was saying, "What is this . . . well, it's like a stone saucedish with pretty little white birds on the edge?"

"From Rome," said Aunt Lavinia promptly. "A silly late-Roman trinket all commonplace people buy in Rome. It was my nephew, Downer, brought it to me. He hasn't an atom of taste. Nobody would ever believe Downer and Timothy are brothers. Canby Hunter told me once his Uncle Downer had brought back five of the foolish things, all sizes. I think he had the inspired idea to use the smallest one for his salt cellar. You remember, don't you, that Downer is not really Canby's uncle. It's his wife who is Canby's aunt."

Susan, unaware that she could be seen, continued to look down at the small object in her hand, and Timothy, peering at her reflection in the mirror, laughed inwardly to see that she looked stubborn. "That's my honest Susan," he thought approvingly. "Nobody's going to bully her into not liking what she does like."

185

FORTY-SEVEN

MURPHY HEARD THE last shovelful of earth being laid on the top of the grave and finally understood that Laura was gone. The body in the coffin, although it was still beautiful, was not her. She was somewhere else, somewhere he had thought about a good deal over the years but now couldn't quite imagine. He knew she would never grow old there; she would always be as he had seen her last. Perfect.

Laura's parents were clinging to each other by the grave, and he tried to think of something he could do for them, but when he reached inside himself, there was just a huge emptiness and he knew that if he tried to comfort them, the right words wouldn't come.

Shari walked over. "I'm going to take Kurt and Susan back to the hotel. She needs to rest and I can stay there for a while if they want me to." He nodded, grateful for the openheartedness that allowed her to read his mind.

Wagoner was standing by the church door, shaking hands with the departing mourners and offering final words of consolation from his seemingly inexhaustible store. Murphy realized there was nothing more for him to do there.

He got in the car and sat for a moment, then started the engine and drove slowly out of the parking lot. He couldn't go home. Not yet. Her presence there would be too strong, and just seeing a hairbrush or a coffee cup lying where she had left it would paralyze him with grief. He drove aimlessly for a while until he found he was on a road leading to the university. That was no good either. He made a right turn, wishing he could find a place that held no memories, a place Laura had never known and that wouldn't cry out her name as he got near. He decided to keep driving until he was on an unfamiliar road and then he'd keep going until...until what? He didn't know. Until something changed, perhaps. He passed a gas station and a row of body shops, and when he saw a sign that said fifty miles to somewhere, he made the turn and put his foot down. The wheel seemed to grow lighter in his hands and the world began to stream behind him. He lost all sense of time.

He heard a horn blaring and wrenched the wheel to the right, narrowly missing a truck coming the other way. He pulled over sharply and rested his head on the wheel, waiting for the hammering in his chest to still.

It was no good. There was no point trying to escape. He knew where he had to go. He eased into the traffic and headed back the way he'd come.

Half an hour later he came to a halt in front of the church and got out of the car. He was glad to see the parking lot was empty except for Wagoner's old pickup.

He walked back to the grave and stood

over it, looking at the pale headstone with its simple inscription. *One day I'll be bringing flowers here and it'll be worn smooth,* he thought. *Moss will be growing in the cracks.*

He looked up and Bob Wagoner was standing on the other side of the grave, hands clasped in front of him. "I thought you'd come back," he said.

Murphy felt something stir inside him and realized that this was what he had come for. "I keep thinking about what you said, about God's plan, and I . . . I just can't accept it. How could He have done this? How could He have let it happen? If I'd been killed in Samaria, or in the fire . . . but Laura. She was such a woman of faith. She didn't have a bad thought in her head. She was . . . like an angel."

Wagoner came and put an arm around his shoulder. "God understands your grief, Michael. He's not offended by your questioning either. Remember, His own Son questioned Him." He noticed Murphy was holding the little wooden cross. He recognized it as the cross Laura had worn around her neck. "You have the answer in the palm of your hand, Michael. When Jesus was dy-

Following their own mysterious laws, the inner currents of his mood began to flow in another direction. He thought easily, confidently, perhaps this is as good a way as any for her to learn about Ellie. It may not make any special impression on her. (Oh, if it only would!) If she *does* seem—well, put out, or vexed that I haven't told her, of course with Aunt Lavinia and Delia lagging superfluous, I couldn't explain here and now, but the very day she gets back from her vacation—Delia won't be hanging around then—I can get her by herself to tell her. It will be easy to speak of it then because it'll have been mentioned. It's nothing, anyhow. We are so close now, I can set right anything that even Aunt Lavinia can say.

He saw Susan set the marble paperweight back on the table, lift her head again and look straight into Ellie's eyes.

He was astonished to have the sight agitate him as though he had but that instant realized whose photograph it was. His hands began to shake.

Light, casual, airy, the young voice asked, "Who's the invalid-looking girl in the oval frame?"

"That's Ellie. She *was* an invalid. She was Timothy's wife."

Wild scarlet flooded over the girl's face—a burning reflection of it instantly on that of the man who watched her. His very eyes were suffused with heat. His heart did not beat, clenched its fist and stood still while he suffocated.

"His . . . *wife* . . . ?" Susan's startled voice faltered self-consciously over the word, was struck into silence by it. She put a hand up to her flaming cheek, and hung her head.

With a plunge Timothy's released pulse hammered gloriously at his temples, brought him up standing. He must have more air. He must be by himself. He could not stay here *now*—separated from her by the other two, by the convention which kept him from rushing to take her, netted in her blushes, like a dove alighting in his arms.

He was at the door. He had flung it open. Till he could see her alone . . . till he could tell her. . . .

The sword-thrust of the zero night made him reach mechanically for a coat, a cap.

Aunt Lavinia was saying, "Ellie was a connection on his father's

186

side. An orphan, she was, brought up by one of the clerical cousins. Very frail in health. I, myself, always thought that the Hulmes didn't . . ."

The door to the Principal's house fell shut behind a young man who plunged down the steps and off at random, anywhere his feet took him.

Chapter Fourteen

HE had rushed out of the house and gone tearing off, not knowing where, because the prosy presence of those others suffocated him. But even outside, all the tremendous vacancy of the winter night was not wide enough to contain the greatness that burst his heart.

He could have shouted full-voiced, have leaped and run, without matching the rush through his mind of hurrying exquisite pictures, memories of the past, and—as literally real—previsions of the future. They poured upon him as from a vast Horn of Plenty, so many that he could catch but a glimpse of one before another flashed before his eyes. He looked back at the months behind him and saw all his doubts brighten to rosy certainties in the reflection from that young blush—how could he have been so torpid as not to see, not to be sure long ago! He looked away from the past to that moment in the future—near, near, near to him now—the first instant after her return when he could see her alone!—when, sure of himself, sure of her, he would take her into his arms. As if he had hurled himself against something palpable he was halted by his astonishment to find that his arms, that all of him from head to foot, had already a fore-knowledge of that firm, yielding, pulsing young body. He stood stock-still for an instant, there in the snowy deserted road, clasped in her arms, and she in his. "Why, I am in love!" he cried exultantly. In love! He was astounded at what it is to be in love— Susan! Susan! Susan! Susan! To say her name loudly in the dark was life-giving, like breathing deeply, like eating, like drinking.

He plunged forward again, as if trying with long strides to keep pace with a fresh explosion of images bursting like rockets, burning bright against the dark—Susan's head on the pillow by his—Susan combing her cloudlike hair before his mirror—now they sat together in front of the hearth in her old home, his home, their home—and she was leaning not against Aunt Lavinia's knee, but his. He put out his hand gropingly in the dark and touched—at last!—the spun-silk softness of her hair, staggered, caught his breath with a loud indrawn a-a-ah!, and rushed forward faster yet, to fit action to his beating downpour of felicity—Susan—Susan—Susan—

All one man he was now, no longer a jangle of conscience-judge, acid self-satirist, and over-burdened mind trying to make the pinched heart and flesh forget their hunger. He was one now, complete, whole, ten times what he had ever been—a man. A man with his head above the stars—Susan—Susan—Susan—

As his hurrying feet pounded hard on the frozen earth, he was looking down on the stars, pitying them, scorning them for the poverty of their barren glitter compared to the vitality running like rivers of warm light all through him. He looked away from the stars, saw young brown hands that he loved, caught them, kissed them. He saw Susan, warm, alive, blushing, hanging her head, murmuring piteously, "His—*wife!*" and heard the other words in her heart, "Why, I thought I was to be his wife!" and cried aloud to her, "You are, darling. You are!" He looked forward from that Susan of but a moment ago and yet already of the past to the Susan of the future, saw her with a child, saw Susan smiling down at his child—and burst into a gloating shout of laughter to remember that he was the fool who had thought a teacher's students can take the place of children of his own. Then, startled to hear his voice loudly laughing and talking, and to feel himself swept with recurrent fits of trembling exaltation, he folded his lips shut and leaned hard to the steepness his feet were now climbing with so wild a haste that his laboring lungs all but gave way.

Yet around the turn at the top, his breath came back, sweetly, softly, for Susan was there, calm, sunny, wifelike, waiting for him, slipping her hand into his, swinging along beside him, her every step a promise that he need never walk alone again. The hurricane in his mind and heart quieted to peace. After those jagged flashes of physical excitement piercing darkly to his body's core, it was a benediction to come out into blithe early-morning thoughts, singing and soaring above the future, no longer bleak but lying before him like a fertile sunlit plain, its happy highways open to him because there trod beside him, close and dear— He tightened his hold on

ing on the cross, He asked His father, 'Why have you forsaken me?' He felt abandoned, just as you do. But God didn't abandon Him. Just as He hasn't abandoned you. You must trust Him, Michael. It's hard, I know. But it's now, when we're at our lowest ebb, that we need to hold fast to our faith. We'll pray together, Michael, and God will hear us."

"Will He hear us, Bob? Was He listening when we all cried out in pain and terror the night of the bombing, when, it seems clear to me now, whoever blew up our church didn't feel they had done enough evil for one night? So they had to go and attack Laura in the basement and in a way that made sure it would take time for her to die. And they didn't even stop with that."

Murphy held up the wooden cross in his hand. "The final outrage. Whoever was responsible for all this dared to sneak in at some point the day of the funeral and break her cross into three pieces. It's like it's connected to the three pieces of the Serpent search, though I can't begin to think of what the evil connection of all this can be. But most of all Bob, I cannot see what the point of all this suffering is. I've lost the most important thing in my life. What can God do for me now?"

Pastor Wagoner sighed. "It's natural for you to ask that question at this terrible moment, Michael. All I can tell you is that I have seen it many times before. What God can do for you now is that in the face of the greatest tragedy, the most profound heartache, He gives us what I call coping grace. He gives us the strength we need to get through it. The strength to carry on through our sorrow and fulfill His plans for us."

Murphy snorted. "You think God still has plans for me?"

"I know He does," Wagoner said firmly.

"Well, I'm not too sure I care."

"Look, Michael. Laura was a special person. But so are you. You have a special courage, you're not afraid to go head-to-head with evil. And right now I believe very strongly we need you to do that."

Murphy looked at him quizzically. "What are you talking about?"

"Look around you, Michael. You started to say this yourself. Somebody tried to destroy this church. Literally *and* metaphorically. I'm sure you haven't turned on the TV or read a newspaper since Laura died, but if you had, you would have seen headlines about 'evangelical terrorists' and 'Christian bomb conspiracies.' Someone is trying very hard to discredit us—and so far they're doing a pretty good job, judging by the way the media are jumping on the bandwagon."

Murphy thought for a moment. "But what can I do? I'm just an archaeologist."

"I'm not sure, Michael. But I believe God has a special task for you. And I believe if you let Him, He'll tell you what it is."

"I'll try, Bob. But I think right now I'm too angry about Laura to hear what He has to say."

Wagoner clapped him on the shoulder. "I'm going home now, Michael. But I'll be here tomorrow. There's still plenty of work to do getting the church back into shape. We have to show that evil can't win."

Murphy looked down at the pile of earth in front of them. "Maybe it already has, Bob."

"Nonsense, Michael. Laura is with her

Lord in heaven, remember that. Maybe you should go home too. Go home and pray. He'll give you what you need."

Murphy stood by the grave and listened to Wagoner's retreating footsteps. The shadows of the tombstones lengthened on the grass and the sun began to dip behind the trees. After a while a white dove settled on top of Laura's tombstone, seemingly oblivious of his presence, cooing gently as it preened its perfect white wings. He found himself smiling.

"Bless you, sweetheart," Murphy said softly. He put her cross around his neck.

The dove cocked its head to look at him, then suddenly took off and swooped across the tombstones and behind the church.

He looked up to see what had spooked it. High in the branches of a tree a large bird of prey was picking at its talons with a great curved beak. It gave a single piercing shriek, then launched itself lazily into the air, slow wing beats taking it back toward the darkness of the woods. Murphy watched it disappear from sight, then trudged back toward the church. He'd chosen to stay at the church because he knew he'd be alone

the young hand, and forgot that there was anything in the world but its staunch loyal clasp on his.

Dimly aware of a barrier to his lunging forward swing, he slackened his frantic pace, floated slowly down from where he had been striding from star to star, and halted to look around, astonished to find his feet on the earth, to see above his head the lacy fretwork of winter branches.

He had been stopped on a country lane, just beyond a small low stone house. Close before him were wooden bars across the road. He had come to an ending. He knew that barway. His hands had set that barrier in place. He was standing before the old house where Susan had lived as a child, as a girl. His house now, her house, their home. His faithful knowing feet had brought him home. The five old maples spread between him and the stars the tracery of their myriad twigs. The little house, stout in the strength of the great stones in its walls, ignored the ferocity of the cold. Its small windowpanes smiled in the starlight.

He had come back to the spot where he had stood with Susan, watching the first fire on his hearth, on their hearth, flickering in the twilight. Here was where he had the first of those senseless, self-tormenting fits of despair. He gloated over his vanished misery. He thought, "I will bring Susan out to this very spot and tell her 'here is where you told me—and I thought you meant—yet all the time'—" He turned to put an arm fondly around her shoulder.

But the Susan who had walked beside him, warm and dear, had slipped away and was back in the valley, looking up daunted at the picture in the oval frame, saying falteringly, "But I had thought *I* was to be his wife." He came to his senses now, enough to think that perhaps she might still be waiting there in the valley for him to come back—why, what must Aunt Lavinia and the two girls have thought of his silent disappearance?

He felt for a match, found that his hands, bare to the Arctic cold, were almost too stiff to bend, struck a match, looked at his watch and saw that it was long past ten. He could not believe his eyes. It was not possible! Why, five minutes ago he had been holding his breath in suspense while a young voice asked lightly, "And who is this in the oval frame?" He struck another match, looked at his

190

watch again, shook it, held it to his ear, and heard its hard-headed realistic ticks, oblivious of stars, telling him to step back into prose, and to remember that he was five miles at least from the picture in the oval frame. He could not have walked it in less than an hour. It would take him at least an hour to return.

Only five miles! he thought wonderingly, putting the watch back in his pocket. He had been away on another planet. Only an hour ago? He had left time behind.

But, if an hour has passed, of course she has now gone home, she and the little sister to whom she so touchingly tries to play young mother. She must be in her bed by now—sweeter unposses'd, have I said of her my sweetest? Not while she sleeps—

A crack like a revolver shot from one of the great maples startled him back to where he stood shuddering with cold. It was mad for any flesh-and-blood creature to stand still an instant on a night like this, when the very trees were being frozen to the heart. Blowing on his hands, he started back down the road at his fastest walk. It was not for Aunt Lavinia's sake that he was hurrying; she had never sat up for him, she would have gone to bed long before he could reach the house. Yet he walked fast and faster and presently broke into a swinging trot, striking his numbed feet with all his might on the hard-beaten snow of the road to whip up his blood, almost congealed by that unwitting stand under the maples. How long had he been there dreaming? Too long. But he knew what to do; as he ran he beat his arms across his chest and breathed deeply although the thousands of frost-crystals in the air cut his lungs like little knives. The stars, very high above the tiny black figure running heavily down the winding white thread of the road, threw off malignantly from every frosty ray an unhuman killing cold.

But his body for all its soft vulnerability was too much for them. By the time he ran, panting hard, out on the highway of the valley, and, turning south, settled into a fast walk, every cell was glowing in a victory of self-created warmth that made a mock of the ice on the defeated frozen brook beside the road. His lungs, drawing in the dry, savagely cold air, turned it triumphantly into the moist jungle heat in which alone his body could survive, and sent it back to the winter outside in disdainful wreaths of steam.

But he was tired! His legs ached. Not for years had he run so far. He would gladly have slackened to a saunter, loosening those taut tendons and muscles to ease, but he dared not. His only protection against the cold was rapid motion. Oh, well, he had not far to go now, not very far. He settled down to a plod. His mind, no longer needing to whip his body into speed, began to wander self-indulgently in dreams. Sober ones; he had run clean through those fires blazing in the night and had come out into the daylight. His thoughts now were of how they might rearrange the house after Susan was in it, giving Aunt Lavinia the two rooms on the south side of the second floor, taking down the partitions on the west side to make one large room out of the three; he thought of what they might do next summer, he would ask Downer to—no! he would not ask Downer anything, he would tell him that he must invite Aunt Lavinia to spend the summer at the seashore while he and Susan lived on the mountainside in the little stone house—walked knapsack on back through English lanes—bicycled in Normandy—camped out in the Rockies—drove through the painted desert—learned Spanish together in Mexico City. He thought, making an effort to keep his heavy feet from dragging, of how he must now change his will and leave the few poor thousands of his savings to Susan. His mind warned him, "But she will spend them all in pushing her Delia up," and he thought in utter fondness, "Let her! Let her do what she will with me and all that I am and have."

Like a revelation it came to him, "Why, when I open my closet door, her dresses will be hanging there!" Tears came in his eyes, the eyes which, wild with the glory of awakened senses, had looked in pitying scorn on the cold infertility of the stars, ". . . her young plain dear and darling country dresses, pink and blue and gray, every thread perfumed with Susan-sweetness." It did not occur to him as he dashed the tears away, grateful for them, that he need rejoice because he no longer cringed before the imp of self-mockery taunting him with "Sentimentality!" He had forgotten that he had ever so cringed. He was a free man, no slave to irony, free to bury his face in those clean young cotton dresses and kiss them one by one.

But he was, in literal fact, extravagantly tired. How could he,

there, and because he couldn't yet bear to go home. And also because he thought if God wanted to speak to him, communication might be easier in a place of worship. He was tired and confused about so many things. If God wanted him to understand His plan, He'd have to speak loud and clear to get His message across.

without knowing it, have fled over all these mile-long miles? His feet had been wing-shod. They were weighted now with lead. Every mile was two. A knot in the muscles of his thighs began to pull together more tightly. One knee was stiffening, the knee which, twenty-two years ago, he had twisted in a fall on a tennis-court and which had always been weaker than the other one. His mind, wandering vacantly at random in its fatigue, idly picked up "twenty-two," and set it beside the bright center of all his life. ". . . twenty-two years ago—Susan twenty-two years ago—but she had been a very small child then, only beginning to talk and walk. When Timothy had been a grown man, almost married, Susan was . . ." His mind was in a panic, perceived that this was of all things just what it must never do, and hastily bade him think only of his exhaustion.

It was easy to make him forget that slip, to make him forget everything except the left! right! left! right! of his dragging feet. He was in Clifford now, on the back street next to the mountain, along which he must have raced out to the country road. The few houses were black and closed. The creaking of the snow under his feet, as he stumbled along, was the only sound in the frost-paralyzed world. A recurrent whitening of the sky above him made him think that probably the Northern Lights were streaming up behind him, beyond Hemlock Mountain. But he was too tired, too cold, too stiff, too absorbed on pushing his way through his thick fatigue, like a diver pushing his way through the pressure of mid-ocean depths. He would not turn his head to see the aurora. He had seen it before. He would look at it another time. He must concentrate now on reaching the refuge of his own house, dark and sleeping like the others, but warm. It was not far now. One more stretch of the pound, pound of his aching feet and he would be in sight of it.

But it was not dark. Every window of the two lower stories gleamed yellow, and flung out foreshortened squares of gold on the heaped-up snow. What could have happened? Was Aunt Lavinia ill? He had thought the last few days she looked a little as though she might be drifting into one of her bad periods.

His conscience darted a suspicious look at a door the lock of which could not be trusted, saw it swinging open ever so little, and

FORTY-EIGHT

HAD IT BEEN a face-to-face conversation, one of the most powerful men in the world would have been lying dead within a minute. Instead, Talon had to listen to the intense screaming of John Bartholomew of the Seven without reacting, except to scrape his sharpened index finger across the motel desk, back and forth, back and forth. If the conversation had lasted longer than two minutes, it is possible the desk might have been cut in half, so vicious were his slashes.

"Talon, I explicity told you nothing was to harm Murphy."

"What are you talking about? I didn't touch him, I killed his wife."

"And if there was any sort of normal gene in your makeup, you would realize that if someone loses a loved one, it can have devastating consequences. We don't care that she's dead, but if it distracts him from getting those last two pieces of the Serpent, you will have failed us. And even you must fear those consequences."

"Look, I made a judgment call. She was in the way and could have exposed me. It was only a matter of time. Besides, I was going stir-crazy just hanging around with only an archaeologist to watch, of all things, and a bombing to plan that had no . . . personal satisfaction."

"I am going to trust that we understand each other and that this type of conversation will not need to be had ever again, Talon."

Try saying this to my face and see how long the next conversation goes, thought Talon. "That woman from the Parchments for Freedom Foundation visited Murphy in the hospital and I heard her say she got the tail decoded."

"You see, that's all the more reason to get Murphy back on the case. Then that piece can be ours. I do believe that he will snap back quickly. Once he does, you can get back in action. Still not, I repeat not, by harming Murphy. But it is time we claimed that first piece of the Serpent."

"Back in action, that's what I like to hear."

Murphy shot his fiftieth arrow as he had shot each of the previous arrows that afternoon. Aimlessly, just pulling the bowstring taut and launching it into the trees.

Normally, Murphy focused on his archery with precise discipline. Since he was a teenager, he had been a serious bow marksman. He hunted occasionally, but it was target archery that really stimulated Murphy's natural competitive drive.

Even in the distracted fog of his anger, Murphy went through all the motions of a skilled bow shooter. He adjusted the plastic protector around his left forearm before picking an arrow from the quiver hanging at his waist. Slowly, he drew back the

leaped up in frantic haste to slam it tight. The rush, the slamming of the door—they were gone before Timothy knew what they had been, aware only of a faintly sickening flutter in his heart, quickly stilled.

Anxious and remorseful that he had left her when she might need him, he walked as rapidly as the knotted muscles of his thighs would let him along the side of the tennis-court rinks and came up before the house, close enough to see through an uncurtained window in the living-room that Aunt Lavinia sat there, in a dressing-gown, her night cap on, leaning back in her chair, laughing, a glass in her hand. She was not ill then. He drew a long breath.

A car stood on the curve of the driveway, he saw now. Who in Clifford would leave an automobile out with the thermometer at twenty below zero? No one in Clifford; the license was a Wisconsin one. *Wisconsin!* He stood gaping. The car was small and battered. Its canvas top was patched, one mudguard gone.

His shoulders, his back, his lungs, the exhausted muscles of his legs—none of them acknowledging any responsibility for keeping him alive—were enchanted to have him stand still, and began deliciously to relax, cold or no cold.

The door of his house was flung open, a man's figure stood in the oblong of light, a voice cried, "Well, Uncle Tim, welcome to our city."

Timothy started stiffly up the steps. A tall, loose-jointed man ran down to meet him. His cold hand was taken into warm flexible muscular fingers, a gay voice began facetiously, "Aunt Lavinia and I were thinking of starting the Fire Department and the Sheriff out after you. . . ." The grip on his fingers tightened, the light voice deepened to affection—incredulous, astonished at itself—"You haven't changed a hair! Why, *gosh,* Uncle Tim! *You look just the same!*"

His hand was being shaken interminably. They were standing in the hall now, the light fell on a familiar, blunt-nosed, big-jawed face topped by tousled hair, one lock sticking up at the back. Brown eyes shone behind glasses; the broad smile showed irregular teeth, the two in front crossed slightly, like a schoolboy's.

Before he himself knew who was there, his hand recognized the

194

new-comer. It suddenly came to life and began returning with astonished warmth the absurd pumping Anglo-Saxon up-and-down substitute for a caress. "Why, Can!" he cried, his eyes searching the ugly, attractive, bulldog face. "Why, Canby Hunter, how in the Lord's world did you ever get *here!*"

bowstring on his laminated carbon-fiber-compound bow. At full draw, the system of cables and eccentric pulleys mounted at the limb tips put an awesome power at Murphy's fingertips. He just needed to breathe out, let go, and his arrow would be speeding toward its target at up to 330 feet per second like a laser-guided missile.

However, this afternoon the tears that streamed from his eyes without warning, the anger that buzzed through his mind, and the residual pain in his shoulder combined to make the arrows speed through the trees in erratic but still deadly fashion.

Murphy did not seem to care. The release from his muscles with each shot of an arrow seemed as natural yet as uncontrolled as his tears.

Unnoticed by Murphy, the man known as Talon had tracked him and was watching from several hundred yards away through binoculars. With the Seven's warnings about Murphy still being off-limits to him, he knew he could not take Murphy that afternoon. Without being able to channel his killing skills into immediate action, Talon was quite surprised to find himself admiring

Chapter Fifteen

"WELL, Uncle Tim, where in heck have you been? Here, let me take your coat."

"Oh, I . . . why, I . . . just stepped out for a walk. Didn't you notice the Northern Lights? Oh, yes, Aunt Lavinia, sure I'll take a glass of toddy. A double dose of whiskey in it, please. It's colder than I thought. And I forgot to take my gloves. Well, Canby—it really *is* Canby, isn't it? How in the world—? Just poke up that fire, will you? When did you begin to wear glasses? But see here, you can't leave your car out all night with the thermometer where it is."

"I've got anti-freeze in the radiator. It tests down to 25 below."

"But your grease would freeze so solid you couldn't get it started from now to June. You take it right around to the—*put your coat on!*—don't go without your gloves!—back of the Academy next to the furnace room, there's a . . ."

"What the hell, Uncle Tim! You don't need to tell *me* where to put a car for the night here. I'll be back in a jiff."

Bent over the fire, sipping the whiskey and hot water in quick gulps, warming his hands around the steaming glass, still once in a while shivering in the remnants of his chill, Timothy listened to an explanation of Canby's appearance from Aunt Lavinia. But facts always bored her. When required to cope with them in any way she took refuge in an impatient elliptic shorthand that was not very intelligible.

"I'd gone to bed—well, not to bed, my light was on. That was why he knocked. If he hadn't seen a light he'd have gone on down to the Tavern at the Depot. He hasn't any heater in his car, and he was all but frozen. I made him some toddy, this is the second pitcher, and now I think he's had too much. He sounds decidedly mixed-up. He never was an especially bright boy. But he didn't use to be incoherent. Or did he?"

196

Murphy's clear strength. His physical strength, the arm muscles and coordination needed even to work the bow to shoot wide of any mark, not Murphy's strength of character, because Talon had zero gift for empathy so he could not appreciate how racked with grief Murphy was.

Talon stirred himself from staring when there was a sound approaching Murphy from the opposite side. In another moment he heard a man's voice but still did not see a figure other than Murphy's. For a second he thought the deeply disturbed Murphy was shouting at himself.

"Ach! You call that shooting, Murphy? I have seen blind men come closer to their targets." Levi Abrams came crashing through the trees on the other side of Murphy.

"Levi, go away. Please."

"I can't. I've been sent by your Smokey the Bear to protect the trees. With all of your anger shooting all these arrows into the trees, you could kill more trees than a forest fire."

"Levi, I'm warning you, I'm in no mood. Leave me alone."

"No can do, Murphy. I'm going to go

"How do you mean, mixed-up?"

"Well, he says he's left Wisconsin and the bank—for good—because of the girl he was engaged to. And he said it was by an accident that he came here at all. He just happened to think of us on his way to New York to take his ship."

"His *ship!*"

"For one of those round-the-world cruises. I asked him if he had money enough for anything so expensive and he laughed and said he certainly had not. But if he hasn't, how can he?"

Timothy set his empty glass down rather hard, and made an attempt to untangle this skein. "Did you gather that Canby had got fired from his job?"

"No, no. Not at all. He was getting along all right in the bank. I told you it was because of the girl he was engaged to."

"Did his girl take the position away from him?"

"Don't be an idiot, Tim! It was *because* of her. He resigned of his own accord."

"Oh, she threw him over."

"No, he threw her."

Timothy stooped, suppressing a groan at the pain in his back-muscles, and began unlacing his shoes. "Well, it doesn't make sense. But it's his affair. Hello, Can, did you find the place?"

"Good grief! Uncle Tim, think of anybody's being hardy enough to take a *walk* on a night like this! Here, let me get to that fire. I bet I've frozen my hands."

"I told you to take your gloves. Aunt Lavinia, anything more in that pitcher?"

Aunt Lavinia pushed the pitcher towards them, yawned, went to bed, leaving them to stretch stockinged feet to the fire and to finish up the toddy. From the top of the stairs she called down, "I've put the sheets for Canby's bed on the banisters."

"*Make it blankets!*" Canby implored her loudly. They heard her chuckle. Her door closed. Her slow step shuffled across the room above, and then magnificent basses and altos, tenors and sopranos began sturdily to proclaim that *pleni sunt coeli.*

"Same old girl, I see. What's that she's playing?"

"Something by Bach. 'The heavens are full of the glory of God.'"

197

out on a limb here, while there is actually a limb left on a tree in this entire forest. I will not mince words, Murphy. What happened to Laura was horrible. I can only imagine your pain right now."

Murphy did not stop his automation-like shooting into the trees. He had only a few arrows left.

"Actually, Murphy, I can do better than imagine what you're going through. When my first wife and daughter were blown up in a bus bombing in Tel Aviv five years ago, I didn't think I could go on. For me it wasn't a bow and arrow. It was two hundred and ten rounds of ammunition on the firing range while I put away a quart of whiskey in record time. That was just the first night. It took me six months to get a grip. And you know what?"

Murphy let loose his last arrow. For the first time all afternoon it landed dead center in the trunk of a tree, the tree closest to where Levi was standing. Murphy threw down his bow and faced Levi with a wild-eyed stare. "What?"

"Those were six wasted months. I was letting those Arab dogs win. I was letting them take in their dirty, bloody murderers' hands the sweet, sweet memories I had of my wife and daughter and twist them into victims. You don't want that for Laura. She was too fine for that. And so are you, my friend."

Murphy turned away. The tears stopped. "Levi, I can't make sense of it."

Levi reached an arm around his friend. "I can't either, Murphy. I am no expert, but I did seek out two people who are experts and I know they can help you get going again, as you must. I spoke to your Pastor Bob. As a Christian, you believe in a resurrection, a life after death, when you will forever be with Laura again. Look forward by faith to that event, and in the meantime, get back to work! You know that is what Laura would want you to do. I don't pretend to understand that part of your faith, but I know you do, and it is time you put it into action.

"Second, Murphy, I spoke to that Isis McDonald. She's ready to go over the translation of your Serpent's tail with you. I've got you a plane to take you to Washington, D.C., this afternoon."

Murphy picked up his bow. He grabbed Levi around the neck. "Levi, thank you, my friend. You would make a good Christian if you ever decide to come on over. You know I'm praying that you will. I will take you up on your plane, but first I've got a stop to make."

Talon watched the two men walk off through the woods. Good, he thought. Now he could also look forward to getting back into action. On to Washington.

FORTY-NINE

LAURA WOULD HAVE been mortified but not surprised to see the unshaven, dirt-smeared, exhausted Michael Murphy walk slowly but purposefully up to the church pulpit.

Reverend Wagoner reached out a hand of welcome.

"Pastor, may I say a few words to the church?"

"Of course, Michael."

"Friends—many of you are my friends, and I guess that's a concept that becomes more important only when you're grieving,

"I never knew she was religious."

"She's not."

"What makes her play *that,* then?"

"What makes her do anything?"

Canby laughed. "I get you. Still doing just what she feels like. I'll never forget that day when a bunch of us students had been up in your study and as we came down she was walking across the landing with a chamber-pot in her hand! Did she step back into her room? Not Aunt Lavinia! She carried it right through the blushing lot of us, girls and all, to empty it in the bathroom, nodding to us and saying, 'Just excuse me, please,' and, '*How* do you do, Matthew?' and, 'I hope your mother's better, Louise.'"

"That's now one of the legends," said Timothy.

"And do you remember what you had to eat the time you had the Trustees to lunch and she'd forgotten to tell Lottie? And the time she took that tipsy old—what was his name?—Myron something-or-other—to the Church-doings Christmas time, and she'd had a spot too much herself. . . ." He began to laugh boisterously.

"Now, Canby, that's enough about Aunt Lavinia. I remember more about her than you ever heard of, and a very different sort of thing."

Canby stopped laughing. "Oh, sure! I remember some other things. She's a perfect whiz at music, of course." He thought for a moment, and brought out, "And that time that Polish girl at the Depot got into trouble, it was Aunt Lavinia backed her up against her family not to marry the fellow if she didn't want to. I thought that was pretty swell. If she didn't do it just out of cussedness." He took a lengthy drink of his toddy, turned his head, looked hard at Timothy and went on, "All the same, she forgets to wash, and she does what she darn pleases, no matter how much trouble she makes you, and she's a holy terror generally. She certainly has skimmed the cream off *your* life, for lo! these many years. It makes me sick to see how Uncle Downer pushes it all off on you."

Timothy was passably startled by this comment. He had thought that family arrangement wrapped in decent obscurity. Who, he naively wondered, had been talking to Canby about it? He himself had never said anything, except to Susan—and Downer was the last person to acknowledge, by mentioning it, the existence of their

198

Aunt Lavinia-problem. Could it be more visible to outsiders than he had thought? He was annoyed to have it spoken of, and for a moment put on his cold forbidding look. But he was exquisitely warm after having been half-frozen, and the alcohol had had time to break down some inhibitions. He remembered that Canby had grown up since he had seen him last and now perhaps could claim the right of any adult member of the family connection to comment as he pleased on the way the clan ran its affairs. And he had always liked Canby.

There was a peaceable silence. The clock struck a half hour—half past eleven.

"Want anything to eat before you go to bed?" he asked his guest.

"Had something. When Aunt Lavinia was brewing the drink, I went out in the kitchen with her and there stood the cookie-jar as though I'd never been away. And when I took the lid off, there were those same sugar cookies, looking as though I were still seventeen years old. It all but made this strong man weep. I ate a dozen. I gather that Lottie still survives?"

Timothy nodded.

"You and she still ships that pass in the night? She come in the morning after you leave, and go away before you get back?"

"I don't think I've laid eyes on her since you were here last." They had found the bantering tone which had been their habit with each other.

Canby chuckled, lifted the pitcher to fill the two glasses again, said, "Aunt Lavinia's Scotch comes out strong on toddy, I see. She's made it strong enough to float an ax. I've lost track of how many I've had. If we finish it we'll have to help each other upstairs. Let's finish it. I suppose you must be wondering what brings me here?"

"Aunt Lavinia told me."

"The hell she did! What did she tell you?"

"She told me you'd given up your job in the bank because you had broken your engagement. I failed to see the connection."

Canby nodded seriously. "There was a connection. That's no joke. That's the way it was. God! It was terrible. See here, Uncle Tim, since it's you, I'd kind of like to have you know the straight of it."

But he did not go on. He stared into the fire, bringing his lower

199

but I haven't felt much like being among people since Laura's death.

"I guess because it's clear to me that some sorry excuse for a person, some walking evil, struck her down.

"And I couldn't stop it. Which is why I haven't felt much like being around myself either.

"And worst of all, I haven't felt much like being around God, because I've been angry and I've been blaming Him, and I've been just so unable to go on, so let down by Him and confused. But I realize that God has a plan for me, no matter how painful this portion of it has been.

"I guess I started to realize it when a well-meaning colleague of mine brought me the piece of Moses' Brazen Serpent in the hospital. The piece that Laura and I found on our last great adventure together. For a moment I was almost tempted to forsake my God as this colleague suggested and place my faith instead in this false icon.

"I realized this morning that the Serpent is a sign to me not to give up my faith but to renew it. I believe this was what Pastor

lip up over the other as if in thought, a mannerism of his boyhood. Timothy noticed with an inward smile that he still kept another of his boy habits—how vainly the older generation had labored to break him of it!—the habit of sprawling and leaning against whatever was near him. He had collapsed in his armchair till he looked like a random disconnected collection of arms and legs and body. Timothy was amused to find the exhortation, "Sit *up,* can't you?" still near the surface of his mind. But he said nothing. He was quite tired enough to collapse in his own armchair, wondering how he was ever going to bend that stiffening knee to get upstairs to bed; but pervasively happy in a dreamy way, warmed all through, at last, by the fire and the hot toddy. He forgot Canby. Putting up his arms, he clasped his hands behind his head and sat smiling to himself, looking forward contentedly to what he would see in the dark after he had put his light out and lay in peace. He would watch Susan taking off her knit cap to shake out her hair, he would see her looking down with stubborn admiration at the trinket Aunt Lavinia had told her was silly, he would hear her telling him ardently, "It's been wonderful here. You've been . . ."

Canby stirred in his chair, reached for the matches, lighted his pipe and began his story. "Well, I guess there's no doubt about it I gave Mildred a raw deal, and I'm sorry for that."

Timothy, recalled from his dreams, asked himself blankly, "Mildred?" and then, "Oh, yes." He turned his head to look at Canby as he listened.

Canby heaved a long sigh and shook his head, "But God! am I glad I'm out of it! Night before last in Cleveland I dreamed we were still engaged, and the hotel clerk had to come and pound on the door to make me stop groaning and hollering in my sleep."

"What ever was the matter with her?"

"That was the point. There wasn't anything the matter with her. She was the world's nicest! What's called a 'perfectly lovely girl!' Say, Uncle Tim, did you ever know a 'perfectly lovely girl,' and if you did, God help you, how *did* you escape spending the rest of your life giving her and her children your life-blood to drink?"

Far in the back of Timothy's mind a long-shut door opened, and to his honest astonishment a far-away inner voice said matter-of-factly in his ear, "She died."

200

Bob here was getting ready to talk about the other night when the bomb went off. I was helped to focus on it by, of all people, my Israeli friend, Levi Abrams, which I guess shows us that guidance and inspiration come from all sorts of places if we open ourselves.

"Here, in the face of the greatest pain and most unknowable mystery of my life, the loss of my soul mate, just like Moses with the Serpent, my faith is being tested, but I will not turn away. Just like Moses with the Serpent, I have a responsibility to fulfill, my duties, my service, in the face of all the evil and the fear and the turmoil of the world around me.

"So today, I wish to announce to you, my Christian friends, that I am going to trust our Lord for the future and believe that He still has a plan for my life, even while I am grieving. And with His strength and hope, I can put my life's worst tragedy behind me and get back to work. So, thank you for your prayers and for letting me get this off my chest. Now I'm off to find the other two pieces of the Brazen Serpent. I am confident that is what both God and Laura would want me to do."

"For God's sake!" he exclaimed aloud, shocked at his thought, pushing away the half-full glass which he held responsible.

"I know—I bet it sounds crazy," said Canby apologetically. "I know I can't make anybody understand. I'm no hand to describe things. I never could get it over to you, not if I talked all night." But he went on talking. His alcohol-loosened tongue went on explaining what he could not explain. "I don't say I was right. I wasn't right. I was wrong. But take it from me, *any*thing that could happen to Mildred would be better than being married to this particular wild Indian here. Somebody else would do just as well for her. Anybody would. It didn't even have to be a man. All she wanted out of anybody was a peg to hang a home on—what *she* called a home, doilies the right shape, and the curtains and bedspreads, whatever the advertisements in a booby-trap like the *New Yorker* say are the kind you gotta have."

He lifted the pitcher, shook it, looked into it, shook his head forebodingly, poured out what was left into his glass. "Well, let somebody else pay for her curtains and her doilies. Maybe some men would like to. You hear about men who are just looking for a sweet wife like that—in the books you hear about them, anyhow. Not for this baby! She's lucky to be rid of me, if she did but know it. Maybe I wouldn't ha' wrung her neck *every* day, after she'd asked me forty times whether the rug looked better that way than the other way, and did I like her hair the way she had it yesterday—but I'd have taken to drink and beat her up, that's one sure thing. That's the kind of brute I am." He took what was in his glass in one long shuddering swallow. "Golly, it makes me take to drink just to think about it. You see, on top of everything she's one of those damn *serious* women. You know the kind, Uncle Tim, you must have had girls like that in your classes. I don't only mean she couldn't take a joke—she couldn't, not for her life—but you couldn't ever say *any*thing except just facts, or you'd have her asking you what in the world you meant. You'd hear somebody's tire blow out with a bang, maybe, and you'd say, 'Oh, an air-raid. Just hand me my gas mask, will you?' and she'd say, so earnest, 'What *do* you mean, Canby?' and look at you the solemn way a cat does, you know how a cat's face never cracks a smile—you know how a cat'll stare at you, so sherious—I mean serious. I guess that last glass was

FIFTY

IT WAS A day of wrenching opposite emotions. As Shari kept her vigil with Paul in his unconscious state, he began to stir, and then without any warning opened his eyes. He was very weak, but he was able to speak, and seemed to be showing few effects of his temporary unconsciousness. He even managed to smile at her. The doctors and nurses rushed in and wanted to begin testing Paul, so Shari was asked to step out.

FBI Agent Baines was waiting for her in the hallway of the hospital. His news was horrible, one of her worst nightmares made true, but it brought with it a sense of relief for Shari. Tests had finally revealed the identity of the remaining victim from the church basement. The body had been completely destroyed, so DNA testing had been a challenge. However, they were now convinced that it was her brother, Chuck. And the FBI believed that Chuck had actually been the one to detonate the bomb that had been some form of a pack worn on his back.

Shari had not seen Chuck since the Wednesday morning of the bombing, and, of course, she had worried where he had gone off to, even allowing for the possibility that he could be involved in the bombing in some way, though he was both the most unreligious and unpolitical person she knew. Strangely, she had been rooting for his just having run off on some spree with his new friend.

Now the seeming truth was settled and she felt the hot tears running down her checks. What could he possibly want with bombing the church? It had to be his strange friend putting him up to it. Shari braced herself for Agent Baines's likely barrage of questions. To her surprise, he was very kind.

"Miss Nelson, I am sorry for your loss. There are a lot of questions you could help us with about how and why your brother would have bombed the church. But if you need time to deal with this, I understand."

Shari looked at the medical team attending Paul, her happy story, and realized she would probably not get to see him for hours. She turned to Agent Baines. "No, let's deal with Chuck now and start putting this tragedy to rest."

It became clear pretty quickly that Chuck was likely more victim than evil mastermind of the church bombing. Based on his criminal record, the FBI could see he had neither the experience nor the brains to have worked with the explosives, and Shari stressed his complete lack of interest in being part of any religious group, even if there had been a bomb factory of religious zealots in that basement—which the FBI was not inclined to believe once they sifted through the rubble and conducted their interviews.

Agent Baines drove Shari back to the hospital after an hour. "Bizarre as it sounds,

one too many. Here, let me have what's left of yours. Honest, Uncle Tim, it scares me to death—I'm no more of a coward than most, but it just scares me to *death* to think I might have gone on with it. Every time I'd get off a wisecrack—the littlest, measliest wisecrack —'What *do* you mean, Canby dear? What *do* you mean?'"

"But, Canby, how did you ever get engaged to a girl that didn't suit you any better than that? Did she grab you?"

Canby groaned and slid farther down on his spine, "No, I did the grabbing, such as 'twas. Nobody was to blame but me. She's too much of a lady to grab anything, let alone a man. Why, *you* know how young folks get engaged, Uncle Tim? You start going around with a gang to the country club, and the movies and swimming and whatever, and then they kind of pair off, and you get to taking the same girl around and people begin to kid her, and she acts embarrassed and you feel kind of responsible, see? Then you get a raise in your salary, and you're awfully sick of eating in restaurants, and she'd got one of these rosebud mouths, and you think it'd be kind of fun to kiss it, and you do, and then you do it again, and the others in the gang start getting married and you go to the weddings, and there's a lot of joshing that sort of gets you going, and your girl's as pretty as any of them, and when you touch her, oh, hell, the ads are right, it's the touching skins that *really* gets you going of course! And then one of the other girls tells you about a high-class little apartment for rent she's heard of, cheap, with a south exposure, frigidaire and radio included—and then one evening you take a drink or two to make you forget how fierce her talk bores you and to make you remember how smooth and soft she feels, and you think, well, now, maybe you can fix it so there'll be a lot of that and not such a lot of talking—and oh, *you* know! Don't tell me you don't know. Crazy's the word! The real word!"

He shot up in his chair, sitting tall and straight, pulled his tie off, loosened his collar and reached around with his handkerchief to mop the back of his neck. "Good grief! I never want to look at a girl again. Anyhow not another nice girl. Not one of the sweet homemakers! They're awful! And breaking away from them is awfuller. That was *terrible!* I'm going to get along by myself from now on. You've known how to turn that trick all right, Uncle Tim. I bet I can. Why not? But if I can't, I'm going to hunt me up a poisonous gold-digger, with 'steep hill, narrow bridge, dangerously slippery when wet, proceed at your own risk' posted all over her. But I don't want *any* of them. Not any. Once is the last time for *me!* I'm never going to take my hands off the steering wheel again, never!"

Timothy looked down from the lighted window of his warm safety, and said patronizingly, "All this means no more, Canby, than that you weren't in love with her."

"That's what *you* think," said Canby, looking inside the empty pitcher sadly.

"We ought to get started for bed," said Timothy, not moving.

"We sure ought," said Canby, disassociating his members again and letting them fall back into the chair.

"What's all this about a trip around the world? Did Aunt Lavinia dream that?"

"No, I told her. Why, the point is, I'm off the banking business too. I don't like it. From the worm's-eye view I got of it, I'd just as soon for my own taste never step into a bank again. I never had liked it, so when I got up my nerve to wave good-by to Mildred, why, while I was about it, I kissed my hand to the bank too. That was swell. I told 'em just what I thought. I brought up a deal or two I'd helped them manage and a thing or two I'd helped them hush up. The Banking Commissioner was there. I called him a name. Gosh, that did me good. There's one swell half-hour nobody'll ever get away from me. Well, before that, I'd realized on everything I had, and put it into travelers' checks. So here I am, free, male, white, and twenty-seven, with the world before me as long as five thousand six hundred and seventy-four dollars and sixty-one cents will last me. That's my total capital, and some of that made out of inside information I oughtn't to've had. You don't work in a bank for nothing. Well, what can you do with a capital of five thousand six hundred and seventy-four dollars? I ask you. All that came into my head was one of these world cruises—there was a folder about it on the counter in the place where I got my travelers' checks. Maybe I'll find me a job in Indo-China. Or Constantinople —Istambul now, isn't it? Maybe I'll go and beat the hell out of Hitler. I want to get in some ski-ing somewhere too, I've never yet had enough. Maybe I'll go to Norway."

203

I almost wish you all were a bunch of religious fanatics, as the press is making out. This just looks like some nasty attempt to implicate evangelical Christians, as with the U.N. message. To what end, beyond troublemaking, we don't know. But we will figure it out and catch them."

"I hope you do, Agent Baines. We'll all be relieved to be out of this disturbing spotlight someone is shining on our faith, seemingly to hurt innocent people and embarrass us."

When Shari got back to Paul's room at the hospital, she was glad to see that the doctors had left, but he was not alone. A very distinguished-looking man in a handsomely tailored suit was leaning in very close to where Paul lay, talking very seriously.

"Hi, Paul."

Paul smiled as she entered the room. "Oh, Shari, great, you're back. This is Shane Barrington, *the* Shane Barrington. He came here to visit me, can you imagine?"

"How do you do, Miss Nelson. Paul here

"Well, anyhow, we've got to get to bed tonight," said Timothy, standing up by a great effort of the will.

Canby connected his limbs and his head with his body, and stood up too, leaning at once, lop-sidedly against the mantelpiece. Timothy restrained the avuncular, "Stand *up,* can't you?" which rose to his lips, and said, "I've got to go down and bank the furnace."

"I did it," said Canby. "Aunt Lavinia told me to. I used to do it, once in a while, when I was here. Golly, it seemed good to be going down those old cellar stairs again. I went into the fruit cellar and got me an apple. I thought, 'I'll just see now, is the fruit cellar in the same place?' I didn't think it could be."

"Why ever would it be moved?"

Canby picked up his suitcase and followed him towards the stairs. "You don't get me. That's the very point. That's the point of Clifford. That's the point of you. By God! Clifford's the only place I ever struck in all my earthly pilgrimage that stayed put, see? You're the only person that ever—say, Uncle Tim, where are you going to put me to sleep?"

They were climbing the stairs slowly. Timothy's stiffened knee had set hard. He was limping and pulling himself up by the banisters.

"Why, Uncle Tim, have you got a misery in the joints too, like Aunt Lavinia? Don't you want to put an arm over my shoulder?"

"No, I don't!" said Timothy shortly. "Thanks just the same of course. This is nothing. No, no, I never have the slightest trace of arthritis, not the slightest. I got a game knee falling on a tennis-court years ago—still goes back on me once in a while."

"Oh, tennis . . . !" Canby stopped to look back at the memories evoked by the word. Then continuing to talk volubly to the other's back, he followed on to the landing where the sheets were waiting. "Have you still got that mighty backhand of yours in working order? Your backhand has been the inspiration of my life, do you know it? It's stood by me in lots of tight places where prayers and fasting wouldn't have done a thing. Many's the time I've said to myself, 'Now, Canby, live up to your Uncle Tim's example. What was it he taught you to do?' And then I'd turn my back to the net,

204

has been saying what a good friend you have been to him. What a tragedy for a young man to have to struggle with the year he has had, and that was before this."

There was something about Barrington that made Shari stand back and be wary. "Yes, Mr. Barrington. But, forgive me, why would a rich, powerful man like yourself care about what's going on in Paul's life?"

Weak as he was, Shari's question made Paul pale even more. "Shari, there's no reason to be rude to Mr. Barrington."

"Oh, I don't take that as rudeness, Paul. I have recently suffered some terrible violence in my family that took my only son from me. When I heard about this bombing and what happened to Professor Murphy and to you, I felt I wanted to come and offer my support. This is exactly what I talked about in my press conference. I want to help victims and fight criminals of every kind."

Paul smiled. "Well, it sure is good of you to come, sir."

Barrington patted Paul's shoulder. "I'm not here just to be sociable, Paul. My staff looked into your story and it made me think of my son, of the chances he'll never have now, and, I'm sorry to say, of the missed opportunities I had to be there for him when he was growing up and having some problems." He pulled an envelope from his pocket. "So, I have taken the liberty of drawing up a special Barrington Communications scholarship for you to Preston. Now you have no financial worries as long as you stay in school."

Paul's eyes welled up with grateful tears. Shari became even more suspicious of this Mr. Barrington and his sudden interest in Paul. This was turning into quite a day.

and remember not to run up on the ball—Uncle Tim, you're the only person in the world that ever taught me *any*thing! Here, let me take those sheets. What do you bet one's torn and the other one's been slept in? Not that I care. It tickles me to get back to Aunt Lavinia's housekeeping. I like it. I've learned better than not to like it. From now on, you bet I'm going to like it when things are dirty and torn and in a mess. Daintiness comes too high. *Daintiness!*"

They were climbing the steep stairs to the third story now, Timothy plodding ahead, amused by Canby's flow of talk. Over his shoulder he said now with a laugh, "How much had you had of Aunt Lavinia's Scotch welcome before I came in? It's hung your tongue in the middle."

"Don't you think it's just the whiskey. Not all of it anyhow. A whole lot is upliftedness at getting back here. Would you believe it that I only just happened to remember there was such a place? Maybe there was something in what you used to tell us kids about Socrates' devil, or whatever it was that always told him what to do."

"Daemon."

"Well, be that as it may, whatever its name is, it certainly sailed down from the firmament on high at the Schenectady viaduct, and grabbed the steering wheel, and said, 'Hey there, idiot! What'll you do with yourself for three days in New York? Just get into more trouble, you know you will. Fix your eye on the North Star and step on the gas.' And when I saw you—just the same as ever—coming up the steps I knew Mr. Daemon had hit it right. Well, may I be damned if here isn't my own room waiting for me!"

"Can you stand up in it now?"

"Oh, in the middle, the way I always could. Do you know why I always was crazy about this room? Because I could lean up against the ceiling, see?" He performed this feat now, leaning his long person at a broken scarecrow angle against the steeply sloping ceiling. The suitcase slid from his hand to the floor, the sheets on top of it. "Seriously now, Uncle Tim, seriously speaking, those four school years here—that was the only time all the while I was being brought up that I ever was in the same place more'n a week.

FIFTY-ONE

NEBUCHADNEZZAR STOOD on the highest part of the palace ramparts as a spring breeze from the river gently stirred his robe and filled his nostrils with the smells of new life. How strange are the workings of the mind, he mused. Just a few months earlier he had been tormented by the dream of the great statue, reduced to an impotent wreck by his inability to remember a single detail of it. Then the Hebrew slave, Daniel, had restored it to him, and since that day he had dreamed of the statue every night, intense, almost unbearably vivid reveries that left him not drained and confused as before, but eager and invigorated when he awoke.

Ever since Daniel had explained the dream's meaning, that there would be no greater empire in the history of the world than Babylon, no greater ruler than he, Nebuchadnezzar, king of kings, he had felt a new energy surging in his veins, a heady, intoxicating feeling of almost superhuman power. Surely none could resist him now; surely every tribe, every nation, from the far mountains where the sun rises to the unknown shores where it sinks back into the underworld, must acknowledge his mastery, must bow down before his imperial might and feel his foot upon their necks.

Looking out over the plain, he could already see many of his subject peoples toiling in the spring heat. Hundreds, thousands of men, pulling ropes, lifting great beams, swarming like ants on the arid ground. Even at this distance he could faintly hear the crack of the whips, feel the sting of leather biting into naked flesh as his foremen drove them on beyond the point of exhaustion.

Was it just his imagination, or did he smell the sweat of their labors on the breeze? His wife, Amytis, had filled her gardens with every kind of blossom and shrub to remind her of the lush sanctuaries of her native Persia, and he often walked

Not literally I don't mean. But pretty close to it, at that. Morally anyhow."

He picked up the sheets and began to shake them out. Timothy tumbled off on the floor an accumulation of pamphlets and books that had been piled on the bed. One on each side, the two men spread on the sheets, pulled the blankets back, got the pillow into a pillowcase. Canby dropped heavily down on the bed, looking around him, nodding his head as if in recognition of one and another memory he found waiting for him. "All the time I been runnin' around, and runnin' around . . ." he murmured, and sat silent, pulling his under lip up over the other one thoughtfully.

"Well, good night, Canby. It's fine to have a glimpse of you!" Timothy spoke warmly. To see the long-legged fellow sprawling on the bed brought back memories of the four winters he had spent in that room. They were among the best of the many boy-memories the teacher had. "Breakfast any time you want it. If you need another blanket, they're in the closet. How long is it you can stay? Make it as long as you can."

"Oh, one day's all I've got. The steamer sails day after tomorrow. I'd have to start tomorrow night. Or at dawn the day after. Don't shut the door . . ." Still sitting on the bed, Canby turned his head, and looked across the narrow hall into Timothy's study. "Yep, your desk in the same place too. Everything in the same place. D'you know, I didn't think *anything* could be—after all that's happened, all over, everywhere else. I remember how I'd lie here after I'd put my light out and watch you over there correcting papers. You'd light a cigarette and forget to smoke it—hold it, absent-minded, in your left hand, and when it burned down to your fingers you'd yell, 'Damn*nation*!' and fling it on the floor and then have to get up and stamp it out. It used to tickle me. I'd bet myself a nickel that'd happen every time I saw you light one. Most generally I'd win." He let himself fall back, his head on the pillow, his eyes closed, and went on in a dreaming murmur, "And then I'd drop off and wake up, and drop off and wake up, and every time, there you'd still be; but after a while, when it got late you'd have got through with your work and be reading a book—something you *wanted* to read, I could tell that. I'd watch you for a while, kind of

206

half-asleep myself. All I could see was your side-face with the light on it, bent down towards the book. I could almost tell what you were reading because you looked like what you were reading, if you get me."

He opened his eyes, looked at the slant ceiling close over his head and put his great square hand up against it. "When it rains hard on the other side of one of these attic ceilings, it sounds like a drum rolling, doesn't it?" He sat up, leaned forward, said earnestly, "Let me tell you something, Uncle Tim—*it wasn't only tennis!*"

"Why, Canby!" exclaimed Timothy, touched and astonished.

They shook hands heartily and said good night.

Timothy was halfway down to his room at the other end of the hall when he heard a few long strides taken hastily, Canby's door opened and Canby's voice whispered hoarsely, "Blankets in the closet nothing! What's in the closet is some dirty underwear and a frying pan!"

Timothy was still trying to stifle his laughter when he stepped into his own room. But Canby was forgotten before he had closed the door behind him and put on the light. He was thinking with elation, "Why, I don't need to wait a week! I could write her. I could sit down and write her this instant."

He pulled a chair up to his table, fumbled for paper in a drawer, took out his fountain pen and began in the large square handwriting familiar to two decades of Academy students, "My darling Susan: I am just back from your old home—yes, I went all the way up to the old house on foot—and the reason I did was because . . ."

He wrote four pages at top speed, and then in the middle of the fifth stopped abruptly. It had occurred to him that his handwriting must, to Susan's eye, be colored with a thousand prosaic and impersonal teacher-and-school-superintendent associations of marginal corrections on English themes and revisions of classroom programs. He pushed this idea away from him with a startled "Ha!" but after a moment's hesitation tore up what he had written, thinking as he pushed away from the table, "If there is one thing a man wants to say with his own voice and his own arms, and one thing a woman wants to hear and feel, not read off a piece of paper . . ."

there, filling his lungs with their rich scents. But even the most exotic of her blooms did not smell as sweet as this, the sweat of men who would die for no other reason than to glorify his name.

As the sun rose higher and the air began to tremble with the coming heat, his eyes lifted from the teeming crowds of workers to the massive object in the center of the plain. It lay like a prostrate giant bound with a massive spider's web of ropes. But the ropes were not to keep it in place. They were there to raise it. And as he heard the shouts of his foremen and the cruel lashing of whips grow in intensity, he knew that the statue was about to take its appointed place at last. That his dream was finally becoming a reality.

For a time the huge figure didn't move, and for one terrible moment he wondered if his engineers had miscalculated, that it was simply impossible to raise such a massive weight from the ground no matter how many slaves you had at your command. For surely such an ambitious feat had never been tried, never even been imagined before.

But then the groaning of thousands of feet of twisted hemp mingled with the agonized cries of muscles straining beyond endurance gave way to a deeper, wrenching sound as the statue seemed to

His bent knee had ossified. He was barely able to straighten it enough to hobble to the medicine shelf in the hall. After he had undressed, he sat for some time on the edge of the bed rubbing the aching joint with liniment. But he was not thinking about liniment. He was smiling. Even after the light was out, he lay, still smiling, in the dark.

raise itself out of the dust and started to float upward. The king opened his mouth in awe, unable to shake the conviction that the statue was somehow alive, pushing itself toward him.

Cries of horror and pain suddenly cut through the air as several ropes attached to the statue's huge torso snapped, and dozens of workers were flung to the ground in the vicious recoil. The figure seemed to hesitate; then, as Nebuchadnezzar willed it forward through clenched teeth, it seemed to regain its momentum and with one last mighty effort its great feet thudded into place, sending up a huge cloud of yellow dust.

Nebuchadnezzar didn't hear the sounds of thousands of men crying out either from the pain of torn muscles and snapped tendons or simply relief that their torment was over. All he could hear was the frenzied beating of his heart and the rasping of his breath as he clutched the wall and gulped great lungfuls of air. Slowly, agonizingly slowly, the dust enveloping the statue began to disperse on the wind and his vision gradually shimmered into life before him.

As if someone had touched a flame to a cauldron of oil in a night-dark room, the sun suddenly caught the broad expanse of forehead and at once the great head burst into golden light.

Shielding his eyes from the dazzling visage, Neb-uchadnezzar heaved great sobs of exaltation as the rest of the statue revealed itself. First the chest and arms of silver, then the belly and thighs of bronze, and finally the legs of iron straddling the heaps of broken scaffolding and bloodied corpses.

Standing fully ninety cubits high, its muscular frame etched in hard, metallic lines, the statue loomed over Babylon like a great, cruel god.

As the king's eyes adjusted to the glare, he could at last make out the features of the golden face. The broad lips were curved downward in a vengeful sneer, the empty eyes blazing with ferocity.

With a roar of laughter that rang out over the plain, he recognized the face as his own.

Chapter Sixteen

AT the breakfast table the next morning, Canby, freshly shaved and with his hair combed, looked like any other young business-man who had been for some days driving long and hard, and who had taken on rather too much whiskey the night before—a little pale, a little glum, a little older than his age, the lines from his nose to the corners of his mouth deepened. "How's your knee?" he said to Timothy instead of good morning. Timothy swung it back and forth to show it was better. "I told you it was nothing serious."

They ate in silence till Aunt Lavinia said, "Take that last piece of bacon, Canby. It's not so bad as most American bacon. Comes from the Rollins farm."

Canby fell into thought and came out of it with, "Rollins house, story and a half, big maple trees, Churchman's Road, half a mile before the hairpin turn for Searles Shelf." He asked Timothy, "Will the Professor of Psychology please explain how I remember that, me that's lived in every State in the Union since I was here?" He added, "How come there's still a farmer smokes his own bacon? Out in the packing-house country where I've been, they say they can't afford to."

"Well, they can't here, of course," said Timothy.

"I wish you'd tell me how they afford to live at all?" asked Canby, lighting a cigarette. "Driving along yesterday and looking at the country—why, good God, Uncle Tim, there's *no* farming land! No business either. I kept thinking, 'How does anybody make a living!' "

"They don't. Not really. A lot of them think they're using up their last reserves. When one of the abandoned settlements is men-tioned—you know, like the one that used to be on the Crandall Pitch—you can see that they're wondering when their town will go."

"But how'd they ever do it? That's what I'd like to know."

FIFTY-TWO

ISIS TOOK A last look at the tail of the Serpent, its bronze scales shimmering under the halogen lights, and dropped it into a nylon bag. She took a card key from around her neck and inserted it into a heavy steel door that swung open with a soft hiss. Inside, the gray metal shelving was mostly empty. Just a strongbox she knew contained a priceless necklace from the site of Troy, and two steel tubes stuffed with papyri from the recently excavated tomb of an Egyptian princess of the Third Dynasty. She placed the bag between the tubes and pushed the door firmly shut.

"This place is like Fort Knox," she said. "I can't imagine how anyone unauthorized could get down here. And if they did get past the alarms and the security guards and what have you, they'd have to get through here." She rapped the door with her knuckles. "Let's just say I sometimes have nightmares about being shut in here by mistake. When they finally opened the door, they'd just find a dried-up old mummy," she said with a shudder.

"I guess that'd be poetic justice, wouldn't it?" said Murphy.

"I'm sorry?"

"You know, to be turned into an ancient artifact."

She sniffed. "If I were an archaeologist, maybe. I think you're the one who needs to be careful." She winced and put her hand to her forehead. "Look, I'm sorry. . . ."

Murphy put a hand on her arm. "Let's get something straight. You don't need to walk on eggshells. You don't need to worry you're going to accidentally mention death and I'll go to pieces. You can even talk about Laura if you want."

She breathed a sigh of relief. "Good. I'd like to. Talk about Laura, I mean."

It was a subject on which Timothy had thought a good deal. He launched forth:—"Well, general farming used to pay here—just about as it did anywhere. No money in it, but people brought up their families on it, and got their children educated." He looked back into the past. "There were some paying specialties too. There are still a few. In some towns they used to make money out of sheep. Real money. Most of the first pure-bred Merinos came from Vermont. The biggest part of the Academy endowment, what there is of it, was a bequest from one of those old sheep raisers. Twenty years ago, when I first came here, you'd often meet one of the older men who'd been to Australia in charge of a cargo of Merino stock. But of course when it comes to *big* flocks—big the way all modern business has got to be, to survive—why, Australian plains can beat Vermont hill-pastures. And now that all have got the seed, why, all can raise the flower. So sheep have gone. Granite and marble are being driven out of the market by concrete and steel. Things that used to be made in the small woodenware mills are made of metal now, somewhere else. The woolen mills have almost disappeared. Of course there's still dairying. Didn't you ever hear it said that there are more cows than people in Vermont? But dairying's like everything else. It's only the big combinations that can hold their own. The individual farmer hasn't a look-in. The twentieth-century knife is out for anything that's not on a huge scale. Still, there's something rather interesting in the air, there, the co-operative movement."

Still full of his subject, he paused for breath and to finish his coffee. Canby, lounging loose-jointed in his chair, had been fiddling absently with his fork. He now turned his hand over and looked attentively at his fingernails.

"I'm boring him!" thought Timothy, astonished, nettled and resentful, yet remembering how, when he was Canby's age, he had suffered under the tendency of older people to take a simple question as excuse for a lecture.

He said no more about dairy co-operatives, but setting down his empty coffee cup, kept a rather grim silence. In it, a whispering murmur from Aunt Lavinia became audible, *"Wo die weis-sen Wass-er plät-schern,"* she hummed, indicating the accented notes with her knotted hand. Her face was rapt and absent. Canby heard

210

She walked to a door in the floor-to-ceiling wire-cage wall and opened it with her card key. As it shut automatically behind them, Murphy glanced at the metal plaque, which read: SECURE STORAGE AREA—NO UNAUTHORIZED PERSONNEL BEYOND THIS POINT. He saw Isis disappear around a corner and hurried to keep up. He realized that he would never be able to find his way through this subterranean labyrinth on his own.

"Was this place designed by the same guy who built Annacherib's pyramid?"

"The one with all the dead ends and false corridors? What do they call it—the Maze of Forgetting?" She laughed. "I wouldn't be surprised."

At last she led him up a staircase to a door that, to Murphy's surprise, opened directly onto the employee parking lot. Isis noticed Murphy was looking at the security booth off to one side. "There's one at each entrance," she said. "The security guards are in radio contact with the central security station in the main building. That's where all the electronic surveillance systems are monitored."

her too and grinned. "Nobody can bore *her,* talking business," he said cheerfully.

Timothy was not especially amused. He stood up and tried his knee again. "We'd better move on. There'll be trouble if Lottie finds us still at the table when she comes." They began to move towards the hall.

Canby said, "Well, I guess I'll go out and bat around the old town, and see if I'd know anybody."

"Why, you'll know everybody. You talk as if you'd been away for fifty years."

"I feel as though I had!"

"You'll find quite a lot of your own classmates here. Herbert Crane has gone into the store with his father. Ed Randall is in the bank. Do you remember that lame Margaret Parr? Mr. Dewey has taken her into his sawmill to keep his books. Some of them are married. Ed Randall has a boy and a—"

"Thank *you!* It'd give me the jitters to see anybody that was married."

He picked up his felt hat, rather broader of brim than Clifford hats, and put his hands on the doorknob. "Well, so long. Shall I get your mail when I'm out?"

"Hold on! For heaven's sake, hold *on!*" said Timothy, pulling him away from the door. "You haven't looked at the thermometer. You don't know what to wear yet. Where do you think you are? Florida? Maybe it *is* fifty years since you were here!"

They went to a window together and looked out at the tube of mercury. Canby whistled. "Twelve below, with the sun shining like that!" He tossed his hat over his head in a long curve which landed it on the piano. "What's anybody got to offer me in the way of parkas?" His eye slid past the thermometer, caught the feathery tip of a snowy hemlock above the rim of Lundy Brook Hollow (they were looking from a south window) and passed on to the long reach of the valley, its rolling fields white, the shadow of every tree and bush long and sapphire-blue, the dark, moving waters of the river like polished onyx under the filigree silver of the frosted alders over-hanging it. Timothy, startled by the change in the young man's face, followed the direction of his eyes and saw with him the familiar miracle of the winter contrast between

He seemed satisfied. "Okay, where are we going?"

"I'm no expert on local restaurants, I'm afraid. I don't eat out an awful lot. Usually I just have a pizza at my desk."

"What about in the evening?"

She looked embarrassed. "Same thing."

"And always pizza?"

"Why not? Pure carbohydrate. Minimal nutrition. It could be the Scottish national dish."

"Pizza it is, then."

She pursed her lips. "I think we can do better than that. How about Scotland's second favorite national dish: curry?"

"Anything hot sounds good."

"You may come to regret that," she said, taking his arm.

A cab took them down the 12th Street Expressway, one of several tunnels that cut through the Mall, the three-mile-long expanse of greenery, monuments, and government buildings at the heart of the city. They emerged onto E Street and were soon headed for Chinatown.

The Star of India, nestled improbably between Yip's Noodle House and the Jade

the gleaming, indomitably living water and the frozen world, its earthen body lying rigid in death under the snow's shroud, dead, invisible, forgotten, while its airy soul hovered in crystalline glory above.

He saw his companion's eyes lift to the mountains across the valley, and looked with him at old Hemlock, resplendent in hoarfrost against the clear gold of the on-coming sun, the shadows of its hollows like no other shadows, not the opposite of light but another kind of light, throbbing in an ineffable intensity of blue. The two men gazed in silence. It was the moment when the late winter sun finally rose above The Wall. The brightness behind the mountains was at the summit now, struck a long ray of gold across the valley to the glittering top of Hemlock, and as the sun climbed into the sky, flowed down its slopes, lightening to a higher key the already angelically pure blues and silvers and mauves of the valley, till their heavenly soprano voices sang together.

The sight was a familiar one to Timothy. How many thousand winter sunrises had he seen turn the Necronsett Valley to a street in Paradise! He looked away from it to the face so near his own. It astonished him. He would, he thought, hardly have recognized it. He had never thought Canby a boy capable of any esthetic emotions at all, certainly not of this amazed rapture. His lips, usually firmly closed, were open a little and quivering. His eyes—why, behind his glasses, the boy still had those very nice eyes, Timothy saw, their peat-water brown as clear as when he was sixteen.

The young man felt this scrutiny, looked away, blinked, took off his glasses, rubbed his eyes and asked very simply, evidently wishing to be answered, "Was it always like this?" He put his glasses on. He looked like any other young American.

"Why, how could it have changed?"

Canby drew a long breath. "Aren't boys the brute beasts that perish?" he said, turning away from the window. "I don't see how anybody stands them long enough to let them grow up. I don't see how you ever stood me for four years, damned if I do."

Timothy was touched. He put his arm around Canby's shoulder and gave him an affectionate reassuring shake, saying in the dry cool local vernacular but with a warm accent of liking, "You

212

Palace, was dark and virtually empty. Over tea and popadums, they scanned the menu while the latest Hindi show tunes played in the background, Isis settling for a shrimp vindaloo while Murphy acknowledged defeat before the contest had even begun by ordering a chicken bhuna.

"So, tell me about the inscription."

"I thought you'd never ask," she said, clearing a space on the table. She pulled a crumpled piece of paper from her bag and smoothed out the edges. "It took forever. Really quite the trickiest bit of Chaldean I've come across. But after your call, I think I finally cracked it—at least the important bits. I think your theory is right, that the high priest Dakkuri wrote this puzzle with two minds. He wanted the reader to understand how to find the rest of the Serpent, but on the other hand, he's keen that the wrong people not get their hands on it. So he wraps it all up in metaphorical language that's quite tough to penetrate. Like a sort of shell around his message."

"Who are the wrong people?"

"Hard to say. We know that Dakkuri was told by Nebuchadnezzar to get rid of the

weren't hard to stand, Canby. You were a nice boy. As nice as any I ever saw. And I've seen lots."

The young man gave him a look he never forgot: the clear brown eyes, very close to his now, softened into an expression almost appealing. He breathed deeply, he said with feeling, "Oh, Uncle Tim . . . !" made a grimace with his lips, shook his head and turned away, silent.

They walked together out to the hall closet where the wraps were kept. Timothy was thinking sympathetically, "Well, of course, to have thought you were settled in life, with a home and a wife and a steady job—to break away from all that, no matter how loudly he talks about being glad of it—it must be something of a jolt."

Canby got down on his knees and began to rummage on the floor of the closet among the overshoes, rubbers, and skates.

"And yet," thought Timothy, much experience and many misunderstandings having forced him to recognize the total opacity of human beings, "there may be something else he hasn't told me. There may have been another woman he wanted and couldn't get." Or he might find himself moved by no more than the emotion— Timothy had never decided whether it was egotism or poetry— which he often saw in former students returning after an experience of active life to the scenes which reminded them that they had once been young.

"Jesus Christ!" cried Canby from the closet, irascibly, sitting back on his heels to pull a sliver out of his finger.

"See here, Can," said Timothy, "you might as well soft-pedal the profanity while you're out talking to Clifford people today. They usually leave it to the lumberjacks to use swear-words as ingredients, not as condiments." He feared he had sounded too uncle-like, and added, "Don't bother if it seems a nuisance to you. After all, since you're here for only one day . . ."

"Oh, it's no matter of principle with me, if that's what you mean. I've grown up a *little!*" He drew out a pair of overshoes, tried to pull one on, gave it up, and flung them back into the pile, talking over his shoulder, "Really, you know, Uncle Tim, that was one swell show, that sunrise. Think of that happening every morning— all the mornings I been rolling out of bed to look at a rain of soot falling through a soft-coal smokescreen."

Serpent, along with all the other idols. Presumably, if someone loyal to the king found where Dakkuri had hidden it, he'd destroy it—and Dakkuri himself wouldn't fare much better."

"That makes sense. So who are the *right* people? Who does Dakkuri want to find the Serpent?"

"Good question." Her finger ran down the lines until she found what she wanted. "Here. There's a formal incantation. It's quite common. You see it on all sorts of inscriptions. Something like 'only the pure of heart shall find what they seek.'"

"Sounds like the good guys."

"I said it was *something like* that. In fact, he substitutes another word for 'pure.' It doesn't quite make sense, but the nearest I can get is 'only the dark of heart' or 'only those with darkness in their hearts.'" She smiled. "So I'm afraid that rather scuppers your chances, doesn't it?"

"You'd be surprised," Murphy said. "There's quite a lot of darkness in my heart right now." She looked at him and bit her lip. He nodded at the paper. "Go on. What clse does the man say?"

"Well, there are some more incantations to a few of the lesser-known Babylonian gods—and then we get down to it." She pointed to a paragraph. *"The pieces of the sacred snake are scattered far, yet still are joined. He who is wise enough*—actually 'wily' is probably a better word—*to find the first already holds the second in his hand. Find the third, and the mystery shall return.'* That last bit really had me stumped for a while. I'm still not sure I've got it right. But 'mystery' is the only way I can see of translating it."

"Mystery," Murphy repeated. "Okay. What he's saying is that each piece of the Serpent has an inscription telling you where to find the next one."

"I think so."

He smiled. "So...where's the second piece?"

She turned the paper over. "Right at the end. I suppose he assumed that if you'd made it this far, you were definitely his sort of person. Here we are. *'Look to the desert and Erigal's master will take your left hand....'"*

"What does that mean?"

"Well, Erigal is a very minor Babylonian

demon. Some experts don't even include him in the textbooks. But my father was a bit more thorough than most," she said proudly. "I looked him up in one of his old notebooks. Anyway, Erigal's function was doing odd jobs for Shamash, the chief Babylonian god. Like Zeus or Odin. Chief male one, anyway. I couldn't figure out what Dakkuri was on about until I realized Shamash was originally a sun god."

"So?"

"So, Erigal's master—Shamash—taking your hand could mean the sun rising."

"And if he takes your left hand, you'd be facing south."

"Exactly."

"And if you stood near Babylon and looked south, you'd be looking toward... Saudi Arabia."

"*The desert.*"

Isis snatched the piece of paper off the table as a waiter in a dazzling white shirt and black bow tie put their plates in front of them. Breathing in the aromatic fumes, Murphy suddenly realized how hungry he was. But he couldn't eat until he had the answer.

"You mustn't think it happens here every morning," said Timothy reasonably. "When it's cloudy or dark—you know we have a good deal of detestable weather in December."

"Don't talk such damned pure Vermontese," said Canby, backing away from the closet with a pair of long felt socks in his hand. "I mean darned pure." He stood up. "Can I have these?"

Wearing Timothy's red and black windbreaker with the sheepskin collar turned up, and Timothy's cap with the ear flaps pulled down, and mittens and lumberman's socks and pacs, and wishing plaintively that Aunt Lavinia would loan him a shawl, he went out as Timothy started up to his study to answer the personal letters which in term-time always piled up on his desk waiting till a so-called vacation allowed him to turn from one kind of work to another.

He took the cover off his typewriter, looked at the keys, decided to clean them, decided it would take too long, and began to write. He wrote Jim Nye of the class of 1922, now building a bridge in Brazil, that he strongly advised keeping the children there and having their mother teach them. Myra (she was of 1923) was a bright girl, she could do it all right, he would send down some notes and materials from the Primary School. Anything would be better, he wrote as always, than separating young children from their parents. He wrote the textbook publishers in New York to keep that high-pressure salesman from coming again or the Academy would never buy another book of the company, didn't they know better than to send an effusive how-are-you-boys man like that to Vermont? He wrote Lucy Merrill and Pete Donaldson congratulations on their engagement and what would they like for a wedding present, please? He wrote Harry Merrill (of 1927) that perhaps the trouble was not that he hated his job but that he needed a vacation—a person did get worn out by too much of the same thing (especially Harry, he thought, remembering his erratic course in the Academy). He wrote a dull letter to dull Eliza Pond, of last year's class, now in college, advising her to take as many courses as she could under Professor Kimball, he being the best man on that faculty. (He meant he was the only man with vitality exuberant enough perhaps to light a fire under Eliza.) Aching over the bald futility of words, he wrote the parents of Jim Hard a letter

214

of condolence about Jim's sudden death. He was called downstairs by a telephone from the janitor who asked if Professor Hulme wanted he should turn the water off from the Domestic Science room. "For Heaven's sake, yes, Melville. You always do in a winter vacation. That should have been done the minute the fire went out in the range."

He went back up the two flights of stairs and wrote Molly Dean (of 1920) that her letter sounded to him as though she was bearing down too hard on her daughter. Bella was fifteen, wasn't she? She sounded to him about like most adolescent girls, he said, and took occasion to put in a discreet reminder to Molly of the time when he had had to drive off in a hurry after her and that worthless Moore boy and bring them back by the back road so that nobody would know. He re-read with lively interest and answered at some length Malcolm Craig's account of the psychological experiments going on in the laboratory where he was assistant, to see how many stimuli sheep could respond to without going to pieces nervously. "Neurotic sheep!" he smiled as he wrote, at the incongruity of the phrase. The telephone rang again. He toiled down to answer the call, thinking that he really must scrape up enough money to have an extension phone put into his third-story study. It was one of the Four H children asking if he would buy tickets to their play.

Yet today the long climb back was sweet, for it gave him time to summon Susan to walk beside him. When he reached his study he did not go at once back to work. He went to the window and looked out unseeingly at the splendor of the sunlit valley, thinking with thanksgiving of his dear love. But the clock struck eleven and he hurried back to his desk. What, he wondered, reading over Myron Rudd's letter, was there to say to a bright idealistic kid who knew there was one answer to all questions, and that answer Communism? As he considered this, he noticed that Aunt Lavinia's music-machine below him was playing "The Sunken Cathedral." He stopped the weary tap-tap of his own machine for an instant to listen to the deep bells giving tongue through the surge of the ocean swell, and thought how at every sight or thought of Susan all the bells in his heart that had hung voiceless so long—

He would never get through that pile if he stopped to dream. He finished the letter to Myron, he replied to the Reverend Mr.

"That's a big desert," he said. "Easy to lose an army in there, let alone a foot-long piece of bronze."

"He is a little more specific than that," she said testily, as if Murphy were criticizing her personally. "He goes on to say that *'twenty days hence, the seeker shall slake his thirst. And beneath his feet it shall be found.'*"

Murphy looked at her blankly.

"Don't you see? He must be talking about an oasis. Twenty days south of Babylon." She folded her arms in triumph.

Murphy grinned. "Does this place have a name?"

"Ah," she said, her face falling. "That's the problem. It has a name, all right. And a population of about a million people. If the second piece of the Serpent is under Tar-Qasir, you're going to have to dig through an entire modern city to find it."

Randall's protest about the girls wearing ski-pants, that he thought it a great mistake to lay as much stress on a mere matter of changing fashion as on a question of real moral significance like the students forming cliques that excluded the less well-to-do. (Mr. Randall was the Trustee who rather favored fraternities.)

He heard someone knocking on the front door, limped down to open it, found Mrs. Foote there to tell him about a complaint the Parents' Association had to make about the sliding hill used by the Primary School children. He disposed of her, went back to his typewriter and wrote the president of the Alumni Association that he was delighted to hear of the fund being raised but he would rather have a set of large modern maps for the Academy library than a new rug for the boys' sitting-room. Boys didn't appreciate good-looking things around them, didn't, as a fact, really like them, and the Academy needed modern maps terribly. He pulled another letter to him, read it, thought for a moment, put a sheet in the machine and began, "Dear Bud: I believe if I were you I would tell that girl . . ." when two stories below him the lunch bell rang. He sprang up so eagerly as to tip his chair over, and went downstairs as fast as his lame knee would let him, feeling himself nothing, all his personality shredded to the bits he had sealed up in one envelope after another.

Canby was there, his face reddened by the cold. "Nice restful beginning of the vacation?" he asked ironically.

Timothy thought of the morning back of him and looked grim.

"You're the only man in the round world that still writes his own letters, Uncle Tim. For heck's sake, why don't you have a stenog?"

"You know why!" cried Timothy, exasperated.

"Aw, go on! Stenographers don't cost much."

"They cost something."

"Well, anyhow," said Canby, falling sharp-toothed on his hash, "you'll be glad to know I stopped at the Post Office and brought you a nice big sheaf of letters."

"We are not amused," said Timothy, coldly.

Canby laughed. "Don't try to pull the martyr act on me. I know you always take time to read something you want to read before you go to bed. I've seen you at it!"

216

FIFTY-THREE

"LOOK, I'M GRATEFUL for everything you've done." Murphy was sitting in Isis's disaster-area-passing-as-an-office and feeling quite at home. "I wish there were some way I could repay you. But there's no way you're coming to Tar-Qasir. I'm going to leave the Serpent's tail here at the foundation for the time being for safekeeping, then I'm going to arrange for a trip to the Mideast to find the the rest of it. By myself."

"But what if you do find the second piece in Tar-Qasir?" Isis insisted. "You'll need me to translate whatever's inscribed on it. I'm the only one who can do it." She was

He said this nonchalantly, but with it went a warm glance from his brown eyes that was a reminder of his affectionate reminiscences of the night before. Timothy thought, surprised and pleased, "He really meant some of that, then."

The transformation—as once in a while you saw it—of a heedless, self-centered adolescent into a complete human being aware of help given him in youth and grateful for it—that was a miracle school-teachers forgot, especially in those withering moments of self-doubt when their profession seems rather a bad joke. Perhaps, Timothy thought for the first time, all during his queer disjointed boyhood, Canby had been troubled by the rootless instability of his home life, more than his elders realized.

"Well, Canby, how did Clifford look to you?"

"Didn't look too bad," said Canby, deprecatingly, with a guarded flat intonation. He laughed then, his big irregular teeth glistening. "Just wanted to show you that you're not the only one that can talk Vermontese," he explained. "In New Yorkese, I like Clifford fine. Californianly speaking, I'm mad about it—absolutely mad." He fluttered his fingers at an invisible person and said, "Never mind, Mildred, now never mind."

"What in the world . . . ?" demanded Aunt Lavinia.

"Somebody I used to know," explained Canby, "would have asked me, 'What *do* you mean by Californianly speaking, Canby dear?'"

"Who'd you see this morning?" asked Timothy.

By the time Canby had named the people he had seen—it took him some time—three Academy Seniors had clumped into the hall in their ski boots, and were silently waiting in the living-room. "I'm going to show'm the wood-road over to Henley Pond," said Canby, wiping his mouth hurriedly and standing up from the table. "The poor fish've never been there."

"Where did you get skis?" called Timothy after him.

Canby put his head through the door. "I bought'm!" he said luxuriously. "I just went and bought'm down at Harvey and Sackett's Emporium. And boots. And poles. And a windbreaker of my own. And mittens. And a cap. And some red woolen underwear. I've got all the money in the world and nothing to do with it."

aware that her voice was becoming more shrill as her anger flared, but she didn't care.

"You've walked me through the inscription on the tail. I think I've got a feel for it now. I'll call you if I get stuck."

She snorted in derision. "Hah! You wouldn't know where to start. I don't think you'd know this kind of cuneiform from a hole in the ground—which, considering that *you're* an archaeologist and *I'm* a philologist, makes a certain amount of sense, don't you think?"

He sighed. "Look, I don't understand why you're making such a big deal out of this. It's not like you're a field researcher."

Actually, she didn't really understand either. Up until a few days ago, the closest she came to field research was trying to unearth some books or papers from the dusty piles in her office. Now she was volunteering to travel halfway around the world on a bizarre quest for an artifact that, if not actually cursed, certainly seemed to have a distinctly unpleasant aura around it.

She took a deep breath and tried to get a fix on the mix of emotions swirling around inside her. "I'm sure you're trying to be chivalrous and all that nonsense, but I wish you would just admit that if you're serious about finding all the pieces, you're going to need me."

Murphy stayed tight-lipped.

"I know you think I'm just some weak-kneed woman who's spent her life with her head stuck in old books." She caught the beginnings of a smile on Murphy's face. "And maybe you're right. But maybe I've decided it's time to blow away the cobwebs a little. Maybe I've decided it's time to show the world my father wasn't the only Dr. McDonald who was willing to take a few risks to get what he wanted."

Murphy stopped himself from saying *And look what happened to him.* "You're a very stubborn woman, you know that?"

"Yes. Stubborn—and resourceful. I took the liberty of talking with our PFF chairman yesterday. He has agreed that the Parchments of Freedom Foundation will provide their plane and support funding for your expedition—for *our* expedition—in return for being able to exhibit the Serpent here at the PFF Museum. That is, assuming there is a body and head to this Serpent, and we find them, and we can bring them home."

"Isis, you know you were way out of line going for the funding before I agreed you were going." Murphy gave a long sigh. "But thank you, because I don't think I would be getting to Tar-Qasir without the generosity of the foundation."

Isis watched him with nervous anticipation. "All right." Murphy smiled. "*We* go to Tar-Qasir. But if things get out of hand, and I say so, you're on the first plane back. Deal?"

Aunt Lavinia cried, shocked, "But, Canby, how silly to buy all that gear just for one day! You could have borrowed it."

"Scotch my Scotch!" said Canby impudently, thumbed his nose at her and vanished.

Aunt Lavinia laughed. Timothy did not. For an instant he felt a slight discomfort, almost like a sensory impression. He sent his mind scurrying to look into this, but it faded as suddenly as it had come.

The heavy front door was shut.

"Do ye hear that? He didn't slam it! He's really grown up," remarked Aunt Lavinia, "and ver-r-y much improved too. Who'd ha' believed that gawky green-apple of a lad would have made such an attractive man?"

Timothy, lighting a cigarette, said nothing.

Aunt Lavinia went on, speculating objectively, "Would anybody think now that there'd be a woman-feeling left in a person of my antiquity? But d'ye know, I quite feel Canby's vigorous masculinity."

Timothy took his cigarette out of his mouth and looked at her.

Amused by his expression, she explained, "Well, 'quite feel' is claiming too much, of course. What I really feel is that he's just another young American barbarian. I mean I can understand how he'd make a young woman flutter."

Timothy drew on his cigarette thoughtfully, considering this. "Well, I like Canby," he said. "I always did like him. Better than you did, when he was a boy here. I agree with you that he's turning out rather well. But I shouldn't say he was good-looking at all. Rather commonplace and ordinary, with that undershot jaw and that nose. And spectacles!"

"Don't talk like an idiot," said Aunt Lavinia. "I never said he was good-looking. I said he is probably attractive to women. What have his looks got to do with that?" She explained, "I suppose what I mean is—why be an old woman if you can't tell the truth even if it's coarse?—that he's a full-grown vigorous male *dans la fleur de l'âge,* and any woman within ten years of his age couldn't but feel that. You mark my words, he'll come back from this round-the-world cruise engaged. Married, perhaps."

"You don't know what you're talking about," said Timothy.

218

"You ought to have heard him going on against women last night—when he was telling me about breaking off his engagement. It's made him sick of the very sight of girls, he says."

Aunt Lavinia laughed, old age's insulting laugh at naïveté. Someone banged the knocker on the front door, and because it was very cold for anyone to wait, Timothy stepped quickly to open it. Jules stood there, muffled to the eyes, his tall 'cello box beside him.

"Oh, come in, Jules!" called Aunt Lavinia. She pushed Timothy to one side and, taking possession of the young guest, began to bully him with animation about the tempo of some minuet or other. Unwinding his many-layered wraps, the boy answered with spirit. When his ugly, fine, and sensitive face became visible, Timothy was struck by the change in its expression. The shy melancholy dignity was gone. As he argued laughingly with the queer old lady, and peeled off his galoshes, he looked like any boy of almost fifteen. "It is not either!" he cried, cramming his mittens into his pocket. "What's a person going to do with that run if you start as fast as that?"

"You just come in here where the metronome is!" she said threateningly. Both of them ignored Timothy as though he were invisible.

Lonely and aimless, he stood for a moment, exiled from the eager caring of the other two, and thought, How the meaning goes out of life again when Susan isn't here! This is how I felt about things before she came. But even to say her name in his thoughts brought her back to him. Smiling, well content, he took her hand in his as he limped up the stairs to his study to go on with his letters.

FIFTY-FOUR

ON THE AFTERNOON of the day Isis McDonald and Michael Murphy flew to the Mideast, the guard in the security booth of the PFF entrance did not notice the pair of peregrines emerging from the roof of a black van in the parking lot. But his job required him to concentrate for long periods with little in the way of stimulation, and it's possible that as dusk fell at the end of a long day, he was beginning to glaze over from the stultifying routine of watching the monitors and checking the hourly logs.

If he had noticed the falcons, he would have seen the slim, dark shapes powering

Chapter Seventeen

FROM where he lay, sprawled on the couch, as much at ease after twenty-four hours of Clifford as if he had been with them all the winter, Canby asked idly, "Say, Uncle Tim, how'd you ever happen to come up here in the first place? You and Uncle Downer were New York boys, weren't you?"

"New York and Edinburgh!" said Aunt Lavinia firmly.

"Oh, yes, I'd forgotten your folks were English."

"Scottish!"

"Were you born in the old country?" asked Canby.

"No, no. On West Twelfth Street."

"But only th-r-ee months after his parents landed."

"Conceived in the Old World, born in the New—like democracy," commented Canby.

The old woman ruffled her feathers. "No Coulton was ever a democrat!" she said tartly.

The two men laughed. "You're a pippin, Aunt Lavinia," Canby told her, "a museum piece. But, Uncle Tim, from Edinburgh to Clifford is queerer yet. How'd it happen?"

"D'ye know," said Aunt Lavinia, "I never heard Tim say how, myself!"

But she did not listen. It was late. In honor of Canby's last evening with them they were sitting up indefinitely and she had been having restless nights of late. It was one of her low periods. She now dropped off to sleep between one word and the next, her long bony figure collapsed in a corner of the armchair, her gray head tipped back, her mouth a little open. Her knotted hands, stiff even in sleep, were gray, the fingernails black. Timothy's eye was caught by them. His face grew grave. He sighed and shook his head.

Canby thought he feared their talk would disturb her and asked, with lifted eyebrows and a sidelong look towards her, if they

220

their way skyward in a classic spiral ascent, using the warm updrafts from the sun-beaten asphalt below to augment the regular beats of their muscular wings. Had he been a birder, their elegant silhouettes would have been instantly recognizable and he might well have smiled to himself as he watched, his spirits lifted by the unlooked-for sight.

Peregrines were in some way the epitome of wild, untamed beauty, and it was no surprise that the greed and rapacity of man had driven them from many of their natural habitats. And yet, they were surprisingly well adapted to living in the heart of the most modern and densely populated cities. In the wild, they were happiest nesting on tall cliffs and preying on other birds; in cities, skyscrapers and pigeons provided for their needs in almost supernatural abundance.

Perhaps, had he been of a spiritual turn of mind, the guard might have reflected that a time would come when many cities were abandoned as the world was plunged into conflict and chaos, and the falcons would inherit the empty skyscrapers as if they had belonged to them all along.

What he would not have imagined was that in a matter of minutes, one of the birds was going to kill him.

His colleague, stationed in front of the door from which Murphy and Isis had exited the building, was equally unaware. At the moment the two birds reached their pitch, approximately a thousand feet above the ground, his mind was chewing over a familiar puzzle. His meager salary was not enough to cover his gambling debts, let alone support a wife who seemed to blame him for the way time was ravaging her face and figure and took her revenge out on his credit cards.

And yet here was the guard, literally sitting on a gold mine. A gold mine to which he had the key—or at least some of the many keys—in his hand. Deep down he knew that it would take someone far smarter and more inventive than he would ever be to parlay his security access into hard cash, but in the same way that some people chew tobacco or whittle away at sticks, he found the seemingly pointless process relaxing.

He was very relaxed when the larger of the birds, the female, steadied herself in the

would better leave her to sleep. But Timothy shook his head. "If she woke up alone, she—she might be startled, you know," he spoke guardedly. "When you were with us as a boy, didn't she ever . . ."

"Why, no," said Canby, surprised that he might be supposed to know how an old woman woke up from a nap. He glanced over at the time-ravaged sleeping face, its defenses down, looked away, shocked, and asked, "How old *is* she?"

"I didn't exactly mean that this was a good time to talk about *her!*"

"Oh . . ." said Canby, abashed. "I see. No, of course not." He pushed another pillow under his head. "Well, let's hear your story. I begin to think you came up to the sticks to keep something dark."

"There's nothing interesting to tell." Timothy waited.

"Come on!" said Canby. "Let's have a house-party. I've told *you* everything. Come clean!"

Timothy smiled at the quip. "All right. Let's see. The first year after I graduated from Columbia I taught in a public high school. A big one. About six thousand boys."

Canby rose on his elbow. "Did you say *thousand?*"

"That wasn't the worst. The trouble was there were hundreds who couldn't be squeezed into the building."

"Where'd you have classes for them? On the street corners?"

"Just about. Factory lofts, furnace cellars, attics, empty stores. Too hot, too cold, no blackboards, no books, you never knew where you were going to be sent, from one day to—oh, well, never mind. That wasn't the point." He stopped, lighted a cigarette, held it in his hand as he went on, "Towards the end of the year I was assigned—one of the grand shifts all around—to keep order in a newly-improvised study hall. The seats had those contraptions under them to hold hats, and you'd better believe it didn't take the boys five minutes to find out they could get a twang out of the wire they were made of. It sounds funny. But it was my tail the can was tied to, so it wasn't very funny to me. Those kids had themselves a wonderful time. I couldn't hear myself think. I'd dash over where the noise was loudest, but the boys there would look innocent and stick their noses in their books. Then the boys back of me would start it up—

air with a flick of her wings and turned her piercing tunnel vision on the tall figure standing in the parking lot a thousand feet below. He was dressed from head to toe in black, and to anyone looking across the lot, he might easily have merged into the lengthening shadows. But to the falcon, he stood out like a beacon. Partly because of her extraordinarily acute vision—and partly because she knew him so well.

She also knew what he expected of her.

The man was holding a falconry glove high over his head. To anyone passing, he would have looked like a man hailing a cab. A strange thing for someone to be doing in the middle of a parking lot, no doubt. But he was in fact doing something much stranger.

He was calling death down from the air.

Talon looked up and saw the speck of black against the delicate pink of the early-evening sky. She seemed to be perched weightlessly in the upper air, and he could almost feel her impatience. She wanted him to cut the invisible thread that held her fast and set her free.

Bringing the glove down sharply to his

side, he did just that. Seeing his gesture, she swiveled once to set herself, fixed her eyes on her target, and tucked her wings under her. Gravity did the rest.

A falcon descending from such a height can accelerate to speeds of almost two hundred miles an hour. Too fast for the human eye to follow, the best guide to her progress is the sound of the air being sliced apart by this speeding bullet of muscle, feather, and bone. Talon preferred to watch her target and simply wait for the inevitable.

As his mind wandered through familiar get-rich-quick fantasies, the security guard noticed that a dark-clad man standing between two rows of cars was looking directly at him. Was it his imagination or a trick of the fading light, or was there a look of amused expectation on the man's face? A look that seemed to say *I know something you don't.*

He instinctively turned to his right as a blur of movement registered at the edge of his vision, and then the razors attached to the peregrine's talons tore through his throat with blinding speed. Carotid arteries draining, he staggered a couple of steps, a

and then they'd all laugh, the whole two hundred of them! They certainly had me on the run." He looked back at the scene, and said more seriously, "You see, none of them had ever been in my classes. Not one of them had ever laid eyes on me before. Nor I on them."

"How old were you?"

"About twenty-one." He paused, regretting having started this, wishing he had put Canby off with an evasion.

"Well, then what . . . ?"

"Well, the end of that first period came. I had five minutes before the next bunch was due. But that's all the good it did me. I was in a cold sweat. Literally. Were you ever in a real cold sweat?"

"I'll say I was!" cried Canby, wincing. "The day I went to tell Mildred that I was breaking the engagement. It makes me sick to think of it. Go on! Go on!"

"Well, you know then what it feels like. I was just in a panic, not an idea in my head. I couldn't imagine what anybody *could* do—single-handed against so many. Before I knew it, the first of the boys in the second period began to straggle in. They were grinning at me. I could see the word had been passed around. The minute they sat down, the twanging began."

After a silence, "I said 'Go on!' " urged Canby.

"Well, I lost my head. I saw the Assistant Principal going by the door. He was a man I despised. Anybody would. But I've got a yellow streak, always had, and it came out then. I ran out and appealed to him. He said, 'I'll show you how to fix that.' The boys were crowding in now. It was almost time for the next period to begin. He stood by the door for a minute or two, looked them over as they shuffled by, picked out a little fellow in short pants, and knocked him down."

"What!" cried Canby.

"Stepped in like a prize fighter, with a short hook to the corner of the jaw and sent the kid to the floor as if he'd been hit with an ax. When he was down, he kicked him. Hard. The kid screamed. The Principal said between his teeth, 'Get up!' and kicked him again. Harder. The little boy got up and stumbled along to his seat, his arm over his eyes, crying. The other boys hung their heads, took their places in perfect order, got out their books and began to

222

study quietly. He stood there, sticking out his jaw, and looking them over. The only thing you could hear was the kid sobbing. Then the Principal said, plenty loud enough to be heard, 'Now, Hulme, you won't have any more trouble. If you do, just try that.'"

"You're making this up!" said Canby incredulously.

Timothy smiled coldly. "He knew what he was talking about. I didn't have any trouble from that time on. That word was passed around too. And then I was fool enough to go to that man and ask him, 'But the boy you . . . *that* boy hadn't done a thing! Why did you . . . ?' He laughed at me, 'Of course any nitwit would know you have to pick out one that won't fight back.'"

The narrator made no comment. Canby needed none. "I see," he said, and then, "That kind of thing wouldn't be allowed nowadays. It'd be against the law."

"You don't suppose it was 'allowed' then, do you?" cried Timothy. "But it would happen again."

"I get you," said Canby. He reached for more pillows and propped himself up to a sitting position. "So you got out. I should think so!"

"Yes, my simple-hearted, magnanimous idea of what to do in that situation was to go somewhere else." His forgotten cigarette burned down to the end, now scorched his fingers. "Damnation!" he cried and flung it into the fire.

"Hell, Uncle Tim, you couldn't have done anything if you stayed."

Timothy thought, "What's got into me to go back over all this?" He told himself, "Oh, well, Canby'll be gone tomorrow. I may never see him again," and went on. The fact was that having begun he could not stop. "How many boys have been knocked down since I turned my back on them, I wonder?"

"Go on! You talk like a woman! What'd be the sense of staying where you wouldn't do anything?"

"Well, anyhow, I didn't. I had one good look at what needs to be done in the century I live in—and walked away."

"How do you mean—'what needs to be done'?"

"Managing large numbers without affronting human dignity."

Canby began argumentatively, "But I don't call that the real problem. I should say that the real . . ."

hand clutched to his shattered larynx, then collapsed in a heap of twitching limbs.

Talon waited until it was over, then walked over and examined the corpse, careful to avoid the spreading pool of blood. Sliding his hand inside the jacket, he removed a set of keys and started feeling for the shape he wanted. Behind him he could hear footsteps coming from the direction of the security booth, slow and deliberate at first, then accelarating into a trot as they came closer. He put the keys in a pocket and waited.

"Okay, buddy. Stand up slowly and turn around. Keep your hands where I can see them."

Talon raised his hands and gave him his best *Who, me?* smile. The guard held him at the end of his revolver and sneaked a look at the body on the ground. Realizing he couldn't help his colleague and keep watch on Talon, he reached for the radio at his belt. Talon let one of his arms drop sharply to his side.

"I said keep your hands—" But the words died in his throat as the second peregrine slammed into the back of his neck, severing his spinal cord with a single punch of its talons. Talon stepped aside as the guard dropped heavily onto the tarmac. Opening a plastic Ziploc bag, he took out a couple of dead mourning doves and held them at arm's length. After a few seconds, both peregrines swooped out of the shadows and settled on his wrists, chewing happily on the unexpected treat as their talons dug into the leather armbands he wore under his jacket.

He walked back to the van and settled the female onto her perch. She hissed angrily as he slipped the hood over her head, then instantly quieted, soothed by the cocoon of darkness that suddenly enveloped her. He held the smaller male by his jesses and turned toward the booth, clucking softly. "You still have work to do, little one." Inside, he quickly found what he was looking for.

The door to the museum at the Parchments of Freedom Foundation opened with a satisfying click, and Talon slipped inside.

———

It was Saturday, but Fiona Carter had decided to take advantage of Dr. McDonald's absence to try to organize the office. She did treat herself to lunch out at an actual restaurant, something she rarely got to do when she was keeping tabs on Dr. McDonald. Fiona wondered how her boss and Professor Murphy were faring out in the field and wondered which of them was in for the greater shock.

Her mouth dropped open at her own discovery. The bodies of the two security guards were horribly mutilated and tangled together as if they'd been doing a gruesome tango when the killer had struck. Fiona bent down and tried to make sense of their wounds, but could not, and it was all she could do to keep from screaming and fleeing. Instead, she forced herself to enter the building to call 911.

Inside, the corridors were eerily quiet. There was no reason to expect anyone else to be working at this hour on a weekend, but the silence was somehow too thick, as if the whole building had stopped breathing.

Instinct made Fiona head for the secure storage area. Turning the corner, she could

"Well, you're wrong. That's what's the matter with us. The minute your group gets so big you don't know anybody in it and they don't know you—there's hell to pay. And most groups nowadays are that big. The older decent ways of organizing life just crumple up under the weight of modern crowds."

Yes, Canby's nod showed that he followed him, as far as that.

Timothy's voice rose a note or two, as he went on, "But when modern trucks get too heavy for bridges made of wood, did we just let them fall down? And give up bridges altogether? And go back to fording and swimming—and drowning? We did not. Our collective gray-matter thought of using steel. But do you see anybody seriously trying to invent new and decent ways to keep order in crowds? You do not. They accept indecent ones. They turn tail—like me up here. Or they holler for Fascism, like me down there."

"What's Fascism got to do with it?"

"What was that sock on the jaw but Fascism? Wasn't it the jaw of somebody who couldn't fight back? Knocking down enough people and kicking them when they're down, to scare the rest into letting you get away with murder—the minute Mussolini began to stick out his jaw, I knew what he was up to. When Hitler knocked down the Jews and began to kick them, I recognized the gesture."

He said to himself, "Now this is enough. I'm ranting. What does Canby care?" But his impetus carried him on, "But I honestly didn't intend to stay up here in safety all my life. At least I think I didn't intend to. But maybe my yellow streak got me there too. I meant it for a respite, till I could think what else to do. At least I think I meant it for a respite. But the first summer when I went back to England for a vacation I met Ellie and got married. And Ellie died. And right after that Aunt Lavinia came back from Australia."

They looked over at her. She had slid lower in her chair, her jaw had dropped, a thread of saliva trickled from her mouth.

Canby sat up, said with energy, "You can talk all you want to about turning tail, but, by God! Uncle Tim, you've done your full share. The way Uncle Downer never . . ."

Timothy cut him short with a displeased gesture. "Did you ever see a slacker without a plausible alibi?" he asked.

Canby said nothing. Sitting on the edge of the couch he filled

224

his pipe, tamped the tobacco down thoughtfully, lighted it, and began to smoke. In the silence Aunt Lavinia's occasional droning snore could be heard.

Timothy was annoyed to have let himself go. He lifted his arms and clasped his hands back of his head. Through some memory-association, this position often loosed his taut nerves, often brought him a memory of his boyhood. Sometimes, after he was quite relaxed, he caught a distant echo of his mother's voice, singing. The voice he heard now was Susan's, "It's been so wonderful here this winter. *You*'ve been so . . ." He closed his eyes and saw her face, Correggio-sweet, cross-lighted between the fire and the lamp. He smiled—and perceived that Canby had asked him a question. "I beg your pardon, Can, I missed the first part of that," he said.

Canby began over again, "I was just wondering, Uncle Tim, if you'd ever thought about how the Academy could be developed? Old New England Academies done over new are all the style. Lots of them are being turned into the peppiest kind of prep schools. You could do it here, easy. Clifford's an awfully pretty old place. Now, if you had some young fellow as assistant principal or manager, somebody with business experience—I bet it wouldn't be five years before you would work up a clientèle of middle-western and city families that'd bring as much prosperity to the town as a shoe factory."

Timothy opened his mouth to speak, closed it, and after an instant, said patiently, "Let's hear your idea."

"Well, I haven't really figured it out yet—not the details. I only thought of it today. But I can see right off that you'd have to start by jacking up the tuition fees. Any American parent in the income bracket you'd want would be scared off by your low fees, see? And that'd work both ways. Give you scads more money. Just think what you could do with some real cash. Wouldn't I like to see some live-wire, crackerjack teachers at the old school!"

"Who'd be crackerjack athletic coaches, I suppose?" suggested Timothy smoothly.

"That's the eye! And scholarships offered to boys that show football promise. Or basketball."

Timothy gave up the pretense that the idea was new, and said, not quite so patiently, "Well, Canby, of course with that sort of

225

see the wire mesh door was open. When she got to the vault, the heavy door was open. Fiona looked inside, knowing what she would find. Or, more accurately, not find.

The tail of the Serpent was gone.

In its place, cut with deep, fresh slashes into the metal shelf of the storage room, was a quickly carved rendering of a snake. The snake was cut into thirds—head, middle, and tail. Next to it was an even more disturbing symbol. She was going to have to page PFF chairman Compton. And then she was going to have to try to track down Professor Murphy and Dr. McDonald. She hoped it was not too late for them to turn back.

FIFTY-FIVE

THE FIRST LEG of the flight had taken them from Washington to London Heathrow, where the plane was refueled and the crew was changed. Murphy and Isis quickened their pace toward their departure gate. Her slim frame weighed down by a voluminous leather briefcase stuffed with books—rare editions she simply couldn't bear to check—she was struggling to keep up. But repeated offers to carry it for her had met with stiff resistance. "I can manage quite well, thank you. And anyway, you have your own precious cargo to contend with." It was true, the competition bow in its

thing being done all over the map, I've thought of it myself. One of our Trustees is always harping on that idea. But . . ." He was overcome at the memory of his struggles with old Mr. Wheaton.

"Well . . ."

"Well . . ." said Timothy resignedly, "a slick snappy prep school wouldn't fit Clifford needs very accurately, would it? Our tuition fees that you think are funny they're so low, they're so high that Town Meeting never can be got to vote to pay all of them. And a lot of our parents, back-roads farmers, factory hands at the Depot, find it hard to scratch together enough to pay the rest. Why did you suppose M'Sanna Craft got Dewey House started? It's so they can bring the firewood and food from the home-farms and not have to pay cash for board. They haven't got the cash."

Canby moved from the sofa to a chair and, for a moment, sat up almost straight, as, pipe in hand, he gave his attention. He looked puzzled. "I don't get you, Uncle Tim. Do you mean you are *keeping* the school as poor as poverty on purpose?"

Timothy gave a groaning laugh, "Lord no! When I'm in the room with moneyed people—it doesn't happen often of course—and think what a gift from them would mean, even a little gift, I tremble all over like a dog that sees a piece of meat."

"Well, for heck's sake then! What'd be the matter with moneyed parents?"

"Oh, Canby, use your wits. What comes in from the fees of parents to a snappy up-to-date prep school isn't money the school can use for what it thinks best. Every penny is earmarked for what well-to-do people think best. They don't give cash, they give a promise to pay for a background that will fix in their children the habits and traditions and standards that go with good incomes. How well do you think our Clifford boys and girls would thrive in that background?"

Canby opened his mouth to speak. Timothy said hastily, "I know what you're going to say—scholarships. But they're no go."

"What makes you so sure you know what I was going to say? I never thought of scholarships!"

Timothy apologized, "I thought you were, because that's what usually gets trotted out about this point of this conversation."

226

Somewhat nettled still, Canby asked, "But now you've mentioned them, what's the matter with them?"

Timothy explained his impatience, "You see, Canby, today may be the first time *you've* thought of this idea, but it's not exactly a brand-new one."

Canby doggedly repeated, "What's the matter with scholarships?"

"Oh, it would take too long to tell you. If you'd ever actually seen how they work, you'd know. They never do what they're supposed to. They turn out to be only a talking point—a kind of smokescreen to cover up what the school is really not doing for poorer young people."

"Smokescreen?" cried Canby, outraged. "If I ever saw a smokescreen being thrown up . . . !"

"Yes, I know I'm not being very clear. But you know how hard it is to make anybody understand when he hasn't had the least experience of what you're talking about. What kind of work would you make out of getting me to understand the difference between banking laws in different States? Just take it from me, I'm not theorizing. I've seen your plan tried in plenty of New England Academies. If you'll excuse my saying so, it's a perfectly obvious idea. And exactly the same thing always happens, right away. The local students vanish. You see, about scholarships, there never are enough—nor large enough. Nobody with money enough to be interested in that kind of smart school can possibly imagine how little cash the poorer families up here live on. There'd have to be ten times as many scholarships, ten times bigger, and even then, the general atmosphere . . ."

Canby was looking oddly at him, he thought. Was he perhaps boring as well as bored? Was he once more penalizing a casual young question with a verbose older-generation lecture?

He made a short-cut to an end, "Now, Canby, just think—you know what our plain young people from the farm and factory are—their clothes, their table-manners, their fingernails, their way of speaking. Don't tell me you think they'd be welcome and at home in what's called a 'good' prep school. Neither welcomed, nor respected —not really. And not being welcome nor respected, would they thrive, no matter how many bronze memorial gates you had, nor how many cups your basketball team won? The Academy is no

impact-resistant case wasn't exactly heavy, but it was awkward to carry, and she was determined she wasn't going to add to Murphy's burdens.

At least he had stopped arguing about her coming with him. While she thought of herself as a professional equal of Murphy's, and while she could not match his most recent personal loss, when she thought back to the death of her father, she felt she could empathize with him personally as well.

Murphy and Isis didn't talk much during the long journey to Tar-Qasir. Murphy slept for most of the flight to London, unconsciousness unexpectedly settling on him like a blessing almost as soon as he was buckled in. While they waited for their plane to refuel, he paced Heathrow's cavernous corridors and malls in silence, like a man trying out a new pair of shoes. He wasn't thinking about anything. He was just getting used to his new life, his new existence: the one without Laura.

Isis had a sense that she should leave him be, that he needed time to gather his strength for what was to come, and was happy enough to bury herself in her books. Although she wouldn't admit it, she was worried that she was going to slow Murphy down and consequently was determined that at least her linguistic skills would be honed to razor sharpness. If they did manage to find the second piece of the Serpent, she wanted to make sure she could unlock its secrets.

In particular, she was revisiting an old volume that had belonged to her father. Bishop Henry Merton's *Lesser Chaldean Apocrypha.* She had read it before, of course, but not, she was beginning to realize, with quite her full attention. Or perhaps it was simply that Merton's study of some of the more obscure corners of ancient Mesopotamian religious belief had never seemed terribly relevant. Now, however, his exhaustive analyses of Babylonian idol worship seemed tailor-made to her needs.

Of course, he hadn't been "Bishop" Merton when he'd written the book. Just a young country vicar in a half-forgotten parish in Dorset, England's sleepy southwest. That was where her father had first come across him. As he told the story, they had both been reaching for the same first edition of Frazer's *The Golden Bough* in a secondhand bookstore in Dorchester. After a protracted argument, during which they each insisted the other had first claim on the book, her father had finally prevailed (steely Scots self-denial winning out over English politeness), practically herding the young cleric to the counter with his prize.

After that, of course, Merton could do no other than invite his benefactor to tea and scones at the little shop around the corner. It was there, amid the chintz and china, that his interest in the dark rituals of the world's forgotten religions was revealed. An interest, her father recalled, bordering on obsession. Not that there was necessarily anything wrong or even strange about that, given her father's own proclivities—except that Merton was wearing the black shirt and collar of an ordained Church of England vicar. "It just seemed rather odd," he'd recalled, "to listen to this young man, who by rights ought to be spending his time harvesting souls for Jesus, speak with such passionate intensity about the demons in-

great shakes of a school, but it does need and respect the students it was founded for. Since it's about the only door open to them, wouldn't it be sort of a pity to push it shut?"

"So *that's* really why you . . ." began Canby with a rush. He did not finish. Instead, after a pause, he said cautiously, "You seem to have thought a good deal about this."

"I take it you have given some thought to banking."

"I sure have." He relighted his pipe. "I suppose you know, Uncle Tim, that there are some funny-looking implications wrapped up in all that."

"About what?"

"American ideals."

Timothy laughed once, harshly.

Canby said, "O.K. I get you," shoved the pillows from behind him and sprawled again at full length on the couch. Timothy stepped to the window to look at the thermometer outside, glanced at the clock, kicked the fire together, and sat down.

"God! How still it is!" murmured Canby. "Nobody'd believe any place inhabited by humans could be so quiet."

"It's rather late at night, by this time," said Timothy pointedly. Canby did not stir. Timothy leaned back in his chair and clasped his hands behind his head again, in his memory-position, hoping to hear Susan's voice. But instead of anything imagined, he heard from above an actual and present sound, very familiar in winter in the old house with its steep, slate-smooth roof—the whispering rustle of piled-up snow, starting to slide. Knowing what was coming, he listened unconcernedly to the scraping of the huge snow-wave, gathering weight and momentum as it slipped faster and faster, and to its heavy, unresonant plunge from the eaves into the snowbanks below the window. The two masses of snow met each other with a sound so deep as to be almost below audibility; but the suddenly displaced air rattled the loose old window frames and shook the eardrums.

At the first slipping noise, while the tons of snow were rushing down the steep slope of the roof—it sounded rather as though the house were being torn in two—Canby sprang up from his prostrate sprawl, in one powerful reflex, crying, "What's that? What's

228

that?" But at once, as the windows rattled, he recognized the sound, said sheepishly, "Oh, yes, I remember," and sat down.

A small, shocking, animal-like noise from Aunt Lavinia, instantly strangled, brought him to his feet again. Both men turned towards her. What they saw froze Canby. But Timothy was at her side instantly, saying urgently, "Aunt Lavinia! Lavvy dear! it's all right. You're *safe,* Lavinia!"

She could not at once find her way out from the terror which made her cower low, shrinking back in her chair, turning her head to glare up from under her eyebrows at him like a trapped animal. Timothy put his hand on her arm and shook her gently, "Wake up, Lavinia. It's Tim." She slowly drew her gaze away from his face to look down at his hand, and quailed away from it. She looked as though she might die of fright.

"The whiskey, Canby. On the sideboard."

Canby raced into the dining-room, snatched the bottle and a glass and returned on the run. The old woman had made herself small and smaller. Her hands were pressed hard over her eyes. Timothy, his hand steady, his face sad and unsurprised, poured half a glass, got down a little stiffly, on one knee, put his arm around her and said in a peremptory voice, "Lavinia! See here! You must drink this." He took her hands down forcibly from her gray face and held the glass to her lips.

The raw liquor burned her lips, burned her throat, burned away the horror from her eyes. She shuddered. The color of her face changed fom a ghastly ash-yellow to her usual paleness. She took the glass into her own hands and drank again. The ignoble terror in her eyes dissolved, her face blurred, changed back into her own. She looked down at the glass and said crossly, "Tim! What's got into ye, giving it to me this way? Ye know I hate it raw."

"Well, that's so. I forgot," said Timothy, hauling himself to his feet. "Canby, go see if the kettle is boiling. We'll all have a nightcap before we go to bed."

He took the glass from her hand—it was almost empty—and carried it into the kitchen where the kettle sang on the back of the stove. Canby, looking sick, leaned against the wall. "For God's sake, what's she so afraid of?" he asked in a whisper. Timothy with shrugged shoulders said wordlessly that he hadn't the least

habiting the gloomier reaches of the Sumerian underworld."

Despite the elder archaeologist's instinctive qualms, a lively correspondence had ensued after they parted. The lure of Merton's vast erudition was simply too much to resist. But after a few months, her father had stopped replying to Merton's letters, and it was clear to the adolescent Isis that something had deeply disturbed him.

She never discovered what it was. But now, as she slowly turned the pages of *Lesser Chaldean Apocrypha,* she remembered that this was the very volume her father had been clutching when they found him.

She shuddered, and her fingers went instinctively to the amulet around her neck. It was the head of the Babylonian goddess Ishtar, a gift from her father, and it was a constant comfort in times of stress.

With a little shake of her head, she returned to the book. Whatever the truth about Bishop Merton, he knew his Chaldean rituals. If anyone was going to provide an insight into the mind of Dakkuri, it was him.

On the flight from London to Riyadh,

Murphy hadn't interrupted her reading. It seemed to have the effect of recharging her batteries—something she surely needed after the trauma of the last few days. Certainly by the time they'd made the long taxi ride through the desert to Tar-Qasir itself and settled into a large modern hotel called, appropriately enough, the Oasis, she seemed positively bursting with energy. Murphy had passed out again as soon as he lay down on the cool white sheets before he'd had time to wonder what their next step would be. And now, some hours later, the crisp rat-tat-tat on his door that jolted him out of a dreamless sleep seemed to have all the hallmarks of her restless spirit.

Showered, changed, and newly focused, Murphy met her in the spacious lobby. "I think they should rename this hotel the Empty Quarter," he joked. "Are we the only guests, do you think?"

"Tar-Qasir isn't exactly a tourist destination," she admitted. "But that's not to say it doesn't have its points of interest."

"Such as?"

"I've been doing a little research while you were catching up on your sleep," she

idea, and with a vague wave of the hand intimated that it was nothing of any consequence anyhow, an old woman's notion. "Where are the lemons?" he asked, reaching for the sugar.

She looked quite herself again when they went back, her chin wiped dry of saliva, a corner of soiled underwear that had been showing at her neck, pushed out of sight, a light in her eyes. They drank together cheerfully. Aunt Lavinia drained her glass quickly and held it up empty to show Canby. It was a stirrup-cup to his going around the world, she told him with an unusual mellowness and just a faint thickening of the tongue. He made no answer, drinking down his steaming toddy absent-mindedly. Timothy tried to keep the talk brisk with questions about Canby's singularly complex family circle. "Did Ruth go into teaching? Was young Herb ever able to get a patent on the invention he made?" Ruth was the daughter of Canby's stepfather's second wife. Herbert was her half-brother by an earlier marriage. Canby's step-relatives were a standing joke.

Canby did not seem to find the subject as humorous as usual. After he had finished his toddy he sat heavily, his big hands dropped between his knees. "I don't know about Ruth. I never heard whether Herb got his patent," he said. But he looked up with a start when Aunt Lavinia said, "Come on. Let's go to bed. If I go now while I'm half-seas over with that horrid raw drink you made me take, I'll surely not lie awake. And Canby's got to leave early."

"I'm not so sure," said Canby. "I'm not so sure about that."

They looked at him, astonished. "I'm not so sure I want to go on that cruise at all," he explained. "Just batting around don't look so hot to me now. I never was really crazy about it. I just didn't know what else to do with myself."

"What else would you rather do?" asked Aunt Lavinia.

"I don't know, Aunt Lavvy," Canby told her uncertainly. "I really don't know. Maybe stay here a little longer. If you and Uncle Tim will lodge me and Miss Peck board me. Seems kind of good to be back, see? Maybe if I stick around for a while I might find something to do in these parts." He turned to Timothy. "That was really what I was thinking about, Uncle Tim, just now. Maybe you guessed it. I was the young businessman who might pep up the

Academy. But I get your point." He ran his fingers through his rumpled hair thoughtfully. "Anyhow, what I'd rather do, is to make something with my hands. Well, something might turn up. A person coming in from the outside sees an opening, sometimes, that nobody else thought of. It sort of came to me today that I'd like to give the old place the once-over before I tried anything else. If I wouldn't be in your way."

Aunt Lavinia's considerable dose of alcohol predisposed her to any idea presented. "Well, well, why not? We never use that extra third-story room. I like to have a man around that's young enough to feel his oats. A kinsman too."

"Oh, kinsman!" Canby thought this was claiming too much.

"In the clan! In the clan!" insisted Aunt Lavinia genially.

"Now understand, this is no go, unless you'll let me pay for my —unless it's a regular business arrangement," said Canby awkwardly. "It's all off if you don't."

"You can have it anyway you like, of course, Canby. Can't he, Tim?"

"Oh, of course," said Timothy. "Anything he likes."

Aunt Lavinia had a qualm. "But look here, Canby, all the young people here are mad to get away. And all the clever ones do. Are you sure you want to stay? Clifford is the deadest little hole in creation."

"Gosh, no, Aunt Lavinia. I'm not sure! I'm not the least bit sure of anything. Maybe when I wake up tomorrow I'll feel like studying law. Or going to Hollywood. Damned 'f I know *what* I want. But I know a thing or two I don't want. And that cruise is one of them, see? I got to thinking about it today, and I could hear the women cackle."

Aunt Lavinia said derisively, "If you think there's no cackling here . . ."

"But a person doesn't have to stay on the same deck with it. A man can get on his old clothes and beat it off to the woods."

"Well, that's settled then," said Aunt Lavinia, losing interest. She stirred weakly in her chair. "Canby, I feel more than usually like an ancient foundered horse. Take your turn at heaving me up to my feet, will you, and give your Uncle Tim a rest?"

"That's one of the things I thought maybe I could do if I stayed,"

231

said with a twinkle. It sounded as if sleep was something she indulged in only rarely, like the occasional drink. "As we know, it began as an oasis. A convenient crossing point of various trade routes through the desert. Gradually it grew into a proper market town as merchants began to settle here instead of just using it as a watering hole. And by the Middle Ages, it had become a genuine city. Actually, rather a unique and unusual one."

She was clearly enjoying herself, and Murphy was pleased to see it. "Unique *and* unusual? Let me guess, they had ice-cream parlors? No—baseball was invented here!"

She shook her head. "Rather more interesting than that. They had *underground sewers.* You see, the spring that fed the original oasis provided enough water for a remarkably efficient system. Probably the first of its kind."

Murphy scratched his chin. "And it's still in operation?"

"Heavens, no. But the original tunnels may well be intact. They built things to last in those days. If we want to find out what lies beneath the surface of downtown Tar-Qasir, maybe the sewers are the answer."

"That's a lot of maybes," said Murphy. "How do we get in? And how do we find our way around when we're down there?"

Isis hefted her backpack and stood up. She was dressed in combat shorts and hiking boots, but somehow still managed to look like a philologist rather than a mountaineer. "I suggest we pay a visit to Tar-Qasir's municipal library and see if we can find out."

Murphy sighed. A library. Of course. Where else would Isis suggest they go?

Out in the street the heat hit them like a solid wall, and they were relieved when an air-conditioned cab pulled up a minute later. But it was long enough for the sweat to have already soaked though Murphy's shirt. Isis, on the other hand, looked as cool and pale as if they'd been hiking in her native Highlands. *Maybe being an ice maiden does have certain advantages,* Murphy thought.

From the outside, Tar-Qasir's library didn't promise much. The Victorian facade of the modest three-story building boasted more character than the washed-out concrete blocks that seemed to make up most of the downtown area, but its broken windows and dusty entrance hall suggested that its best days were long gone. An impression that was confirmed by the man who appeared to be its only inhabitant.

"We are in need of some refurbishment, it is true," Salim Omar admitted, stroking his trim beard. "Tar-Qasir is a modern city that looks to the future, not the past, and all this"—he gestured to the shelves—or in some cases piles—of books that filled the room—"is considered irrelevant and unworthy of study." He sighed. "It is a shame. For myself, I believe that it is only by looking deeply into the past that we can understand what the future holds for us."

Murphy sipped from his glass of steaming mint tea and nodded. "I'm with you there, Mr. Omar." He felt a surge of fellow feeling for the quiet-spoken librarian who appeared to have been stranded on an outcrop of the past as the tidal wave of modernity swept past him, and would have liked to spend more time drinking tea and learning his story. But Isis was all business.

remarked Canby. Stooping, he picked her up and carried her briskly to the top of the stairs. Timothy looked after them. The powerful young back was as straight as if he were carrying a child. "There," he said, setting her on her feet at the top. The effort had not so much as quickened his pulse. His chest rose and fell slowly and regularly as he smiled at the old woman. A little color had come into her pale face. She smiled back at him. "The very riband upon the cap of youth," she told him, and gave his cheek a pat.

Timothy turned away and opened the door to the cellar stairs.

"Hey, Uncle Tim!" shouted Canby from the upper landing. "Leave that furnace alone! That's my job!" He came racing down the stairs four at a stride.

Timothy stood back to let him pass, saying, "Thanks. That's very good of you, Canby. Better not close the draughts too tightly. When I looked at the thermometer just now I saw it stands at seventeen below."

He felt nothing. Almost nothing, that is. No more than the inconsiderable prick from the point of a hypodermic needle as it slides under the skin.

Up through the register came the rattle of grate-bars in the cellar, the swish of coal shoveled with energy on the fire. The furnace door clanged shut. Canby was doing the job with his usual vehemence.

Timothy was annoyed by the clatter. "What's the matter with the boy? There's no need to knock things around like that," he thought disapprovingly. "If he'd put some of that slam-bang energy of his into sticking at what he undertakes . . ."

Without waiting for Canby to re-appear, he called down the register, "Well, good night. I'm off to bed," and went upstairs rather rapidly.

232

Chapter Eighteen

AFTER he was in his own room with the door closed, he found that he was desperately tired. Odd that he should be so much more tired tonight after a quiet day indoors, than last night after that wild expedition in the cold and snow. Was that only *last* night? Had only one single day gone by since he had seen Susan? It was not to be believed! The twenty-four hours without her seemed longer than the two happy months that had slid so quickly between his fingers. He undressed quickly, opened the window, turned out the light, went to bed. But he was too tired now to see her in the darkness. Or was he still too much stirred up by the memories and ideas he had been talking about? What had possessed him to say all that—to talk so intimately about the Academy with Canby? It was because he had thought he would never see the boy again. And after all, he was staying on. A foolish notion that was! There was nothing in Clifford for him. But he was so fitful that by tomorrow morning he would probably have another notion.

Turning restlessly in bed, Timothy kept thinking of points he had meant to make, of objections latent in Canby's mind that he could have raised and met, of phrases that would have expressed his ideas more accurately. His ideas! They were probably no more than his personal dislike for crowds—and that was probably a form of vanity. Were "ideas" ever anything but dressed-up personal likes and dislikes, and vanity? He thought again of the anonymous mass in that hellish din on Fourteenth Street—he thought of the brutally crowded and bewildered children in the big-city school as he had seen it, years ago, as that New York teacher of today had described it to him—but was there anything better in the desperate economies by which alone the lame pinched life of the Academy could be kept going? Or in the irrevocable poverty barring the way of the factory workers' children at the Depot, or among the back-roads farmers? Wasn't it watery Longfellow sentimentality to claim that

"Sewers, Mr. Omar. We're interested in sewers."

Omar gave her a quizzical look, and she wasn't sure if he was simply surprised that anyone wanted to know about such things or if he was particularly shocked to hear a woman express an interest. "Dr. McDonald, it is rare enough that anyone comes here seeking a book. Now two people arrive on my doorstep all the way from America and they want to know about sewers. This is most strange, I must say."

"I'm amazed," said Isis with, as far as Murphy could tell, a straight face. "Surely everyone knows about the sewers of Tar-Qasir."

He looked at her as if she were slightly demented. "Perhaps. But very few make the effort to come and see what is left of them."

"And what *is* left of them?" Murphy asked.

Omar spread his hands. "Who can say? No one has been down there for many years."

"What if someone wanted to go down there? Are there any maps, any records of the construction? Any way of navigating?"

Omar glanced at the dust-covered telephone on the desk, and Murphy thought for a moment he was going to call the police to come and arrest these suspicious foreigners with their highly dubious interest in sewers. He was certainly beginning to look extremely nervous. "It is not good. Tunnels falling down and suchlike. I cannot help you."

Murphy started to get up, but Isis put a pale hand on his arm. "Mr. Omar," she began, giving him her warmest smile. "We would be delighted to make a contribution to assist with the restoration of your fine library if you were able to help us."

He narrowed his eyes. "Some additional shelving would be very welcome. Perhaps some assistance in cataloguing . . ."

Isis kept smiling. "How much?"

He made a sour face as if to say such things were beneath him. "Shall we say one thousand dollars?"

"Five hundred," Isis shot back.

"Some of the shelves are actually quite dangerous. I had a nasty fall only last week. Eight hundred."

"Six."

"Seven-fifty."

the mere isolation of their lives gave them dignity? Weren't his theories merely a defense of his own inglorious rôle in life? Were anybody's theories more than self-defense and special pleading? His heart sank as though such doubts were new instead of being dismally familiar. He tried to remind himself that when he felt this universal gloom about the human race it generally came from nothing more elevated than indigestion.

The tall old clock downstairs struck twelve. And then half past. He dropped off, sleeping he did not know how long, till he woke himself up by a loud, "No! Oh, *no!*" The sound of his voice in the dark was startling. What could he have been dreaming? It was still dead black night. He got up and looked out of the open window. Above the long bulk of The Wall, the winter stars sparkled in cold malice. They frightened him. Something frightened him. "Oh, Susan, darling Susan, why did you go away?" he thought longingly, and, his teeth chattering, got back between his chilled sheets in a misery of loneliness and apprehension. "Perhaps I'm not entirely waked up from a bad dream," he thought. He tried his formula for relaxation, put his arms up and clasped his hands behind his head. But his room was now intensely cold. He began to sneeze, took them down and burrowed forlornly under the covers.

In the morning he thought, as he shaved, "What an idiot a person is to let those night-glooms get him down . . . even for an instant. When we know perfectly well they're nothing more than slow circulation of the blood. They always disappear when you get up in the morning and begin to stir around."

It was Sunday. Was it possible that it was only on Friday night that Susan had gone and Canby had come?

Something said at the breakfast table made Canby cry out incredulously, "You're not going to *church!*"

"Don't you remember I always go to church?"

"Tim's a vestryman. So was his father. And his grandfather. We Coultons were Church people too. Would you have had us Dissenters? That ivory-headed cane that Timothy carries, it was given to . . ."

"Oh, an inherited family trait!" scoffed Canby.

Aunt Lavinia did not approve of lack of respect for inherited

234

family ideas. "If it's to stay with me you're not going to church you'd better go," she told him. "I'm not feeling in the least sociable."

"Never fear," said Canby rudely, "with six inches of powder snow on crust and the spring thaw almost here I don't feel any more sociable than you do."

But after breakfast he said wonderingly, watching Timothy get into his overcoat, "Really, Uncle Tim, how can you? Don't tell me you believe in the Articles of Faith and what-not?"

"I won't bother you by telling you anything about it, Canby, except that I like the Service. I like the rector too."

Canby said tolerantly, "Well, of course, religion hasn't enough pep now to hurt anything. I suppose there's no great need to rear back against it any more."

Aunt Lavinia snorted in amusement. Canby looked first surprised at her laugh and then nettled. Ignoring it and her, he asked Timothy, "Is the rector still that man with the big dark-crimson birthmark on his face? I sort of liked him too. Well, under the circumstances I guess I'll let you go."

"Very obliging of you, I'm sure," said Timothy, reaching for his stick and letting himself out of the front door.

Walking soberly to church, he thought of a reason for going he had not told Canby—that church was now the only place left where he sometimes saw his mother, his young mother sitting between her two sons. The murmur of her beautiful voice came and went through the familiar prayers. "Almighty and most merciful Father, we have erred and strayed from thy ways like lost sheep. We have followed too much the devices and desires of our own hearts. . . ." They were not only admirably chosen words, arranged in a magnificent rhythm, for him they were a charm, a spell, a magic formula which sometimes loosed him from the barren complexities and responsibilities of his adult life, and let him breathe once more for an instant the untroubled faith-in-life of his boyhood.

But this was not one of the good Sundays. He did not find his mother in church, only the usual dusty elderly people and wriggling children—and, vaguely disquieting to him, the assiduous young Bowen, who had now taken to very High Church genuflections.

When after the service he went back up Academy Hill, Canby in his new ski-clothes, well powdered now with snow, was showing

"Agreed."

Before Murphy could adjust to this new assertive Isis he didn't quite recognize, she'd reached into her backpack and counted out a neat stack of bills. Omar flipped through them without comment, then stood up, gesturing for them to follow. Squeezing through a tiny door at the end of the room, they entered a chaotic Aladdin's cave of books and manuscripts piled in drifts against the walls. After several minutes of fruitless burrowing, Omar at last emerged with his prize. He blew the dust off a slim morocco-bound volume before handing it over with a flourish.

"A real treasure. An eighteen forty-four first edition of Baron de Tocqueville's *A Curious History of Ancient Arabia*. I think you will find it has excellent illustrations of Tar-Qasir's sewerage system as it existed in the nineteenth century."

Murphy watched Isis leafing through the stiff, yellowing pages. She looked as if she were in philologists' heaven. "A first edition," she breathed. "I didn't know there were *any* editions still in existence. My father would have..."

He guided her back toward the door, worried that if they stayed any longer she'd never be able to tear herself away from this treasure-house of books.

"Thank you for all your help, Mr. Omar. And good luck with the restoration."

Omar nodded. "And the very best of luck to you both," he said solemnly.

After the heavy front door had closed behind them, he sat down at his desk, poured himself another cup of tea, and sipped it thoughtfully. After a while a young man dressed in a white djellaba slid silently out from behind a stack of books. He began riffling through the notes on Omar's desk. "You let them go?"

Omar shrugged. "What could I do? They seemed very determined."

"The woman was beautiful. I have never seen such pale skin. Do you think we will see them again?"

Omar put down his tea. "Are you serious? Knowing what is down there?"

The young man sighed. "What a shame. She really was very pretty."

FIFTY-SIX

TALON PASSED THROUGH the ornately carved archway that led into the great hall and wondered if he was about to die. He had been summoned to the castle rarely during the two years he had been employed by the council, and each time he had been taken to the subterranean vault, his employers sat behind a huge obsidian table, seven anonymous black silhouettes that for all he knew were distorted further to conceal their identities.

Now, for the first time, a sightless footman, who seemed to navigate his way through the castle by some extra sense, was pointing to a seat at the end of a long oak table where the Seven sat in clear daylight, their features unmasked. If they no longer cared that he could identify them, it could mean only one of two things: Either they trusted him completely or they weren't intending to let him leave the castle alive. If it was the latter, he knew there was no point in trying to formulate an escape plan. But he did wonder how they would do it.

He suspected it would be efficient but also a little theatrical. They definitely seemed to enjoy a spectacle. And they had a keen sense of history too. Something medieval, in keeping with the castle's setting? Perhaps a man-at-arms in chain mail was standing behind his seat at this very moment, ready to decapitate him with a razor-sharp halberd. Or something with more of a religious feel to it, perhaps. Could it be he was about to be flayed alive like St. Bartholomew, or broken on a spiked wheel like St. Catherine? That would certainly be spectacular. In fact, in a curious way, he almost looked forward to it.

At the other end of the long table, a gray-

six or seven tall Academy boys how to double-stem, choosing as terrain the steep slope of the Lundy Brook Hollow down which nobody had ever before dreamed of venturing on skis. Timothy stood for a moment watching their long legs, grotesquely knock-kneed in imitation of Canby's, disappearing over the rim for a short run, sidestepping back up to try it again. They were exhilarated by the new triumph. They shouted loudly back and forth, "Hey you, Ed!" and, "Keep your heels *out!*" Their breath was frosty in the still bright air. From time to time they bowed themselves between their poles, yelling with laughter at those who fell.

Canby saw the vestryman standing on the front walk with his Sunday overcoat, hat, gloves, and walking stick, and came poling himself back with a rhythmical sway. "Say, Uncle Tim, we're going across the valley to Hemlock, and up the lumber road to Hawley Pond and see if we can ski back down Dowling Hollow." His ugly face with its undershot jaw was ruddy with the cold, with the winter sun, with the exercise. Vitality blazed in him like a bonfire. To look at him was like hearing a shout.

"How about lunch?"

"We're going to eat on the way. I made myself some sandwiches and took a couple of apples."

He bent his knees, shot up in the air, flexed his body, came down facing the Hollow, and, thrusting his poles in with energy, slid forward with a swoop.

"You'll never do all that and get back before dark!" Timothy called after him warningly.

"Got flashlights!" Canby shouted over his shoulder and was gone.

My part in that exchange, thought Timothy walking up the steps, and opening the front door, was that of an elderly conscientious nursemaid.

"Just let me get you on skates!" he said.

"What's that?" asked Aunt Lavinia, coming down the stairs.

Timothy was taken aback. "I didn't know I said anything!"

"It's a sign of age coming on to be talking to yourself," said Aunt Lavinia helpfully. "I do it all the time lately, I notice." She added, "Melville has just been over to say that the water pipes in the Domestic Science room froze last night."

"The devil you say!" cried Timothy, dashing his hat down on a

236

chair. "That means he didn't turn the water off when I told him to!" He was in a rage, foreseeing a plumber's bill with not a cent in the Academy repair fund to pay it.

"It's quite becoming to you to be angry," remarked Aunt Lavinia with interest. "Your color's better. You should do it oftener." She moved away into the living-room. A faint odor of decay hung in her wake. She had forgotten again to take her bath.

The frozen water-pipes occupied all the rest of the day, for Timothy was determined not to have a plumber called in. He snatched a sandwich, got into some old clothes and with the old janitor, and later with Mr. Dewey, wrestled with hot cloths and a blow-torch, took unions apart painfully, and put them together again, crawled in from the basement under the floor at the back where the trouble usually came, only to find this time it was somewhere else, kept the furnace fire at top heat, all the time pushing and pulling against the dead weight of old Melville's conviction that each attempt could not but be futile. By four o'clock they had by laborious elimination found where the frozen place was; by five o'clock it was thawed; by half past the wet rags, pails, wrenches, blow-torch, gasoline can, and general clutter had been cleared away and Melville set at cleaning the floor. Timothy, drenched in perspiration and shivering with the cold, had just time to rush back to the house, bathe, dress, and take Aunt Lavinia down in the Ford to Miss Peck's for supper, where old Mrs. Washburn took and kept the center of the conversation with reminiscences of what her husband had done when the water pipes froze, or rather a long account of the wise, penetrating, and unanswerably right things she had always said to him on the subject.

No sign of Canby. He did not come back to the house till long after nine, cold, limping, stiff, starving, happy. They *had* skied all the way down Dowling Hollow and from there across the Searles Shelf road, and straight down over the side of that roof-steep slope to the valley, he told them ecstatically, drinking glass after glass of milk and eating bread and butter like an ogre. "It was great! The stars were just coming out when we scooted into that open field at the lower end of the Hollow. And were they blazing by the time we struck the Rollins upper pasture! It was swell! Skating's all

237

haired man with hard eyes and a nose like a hatchet was smiling at him as if he could read his thoughts. "Welcome, Talon." He spoke quietly, but his voice had enough power to fill the hall. "No doubt you are wondering why you are here. Or, more specifically, why you are being allowed to see us without the benefit of . . . technological trickery. Let me assure you, it is not because we have decided to dispense with your services. Quite the opposite. You have proved yourself most efficient and reliable. Indispensable, even." Nods from around the table. "In tune with our objectives of global governance. All done in the name of world peace, of course. If all goes according to plan, there will be much for you to do in the future—a future I doubt you can even begin to imagine. But I promise you will find it extremely fulfilling."

Talon said nothing. He didn't even change expression from the neutral mask he habitually wore. He didn't want them to think he'd cared about dying. And neither did he want them to see his excitement at the prospect of more killing. Though they were prepared to reveal themselves to him, he wasn't sure he was ready to return the favor quite yet.

He noticed a plump, bespectacled man to the speaker's left, who seemed to be in some agitation. "I think now it might be time to see what Mr. Talon has brought us, don't you think?" he said.

The gray-haired man nodded and the sightless footman was suddenly at Talon's elbow. Talon pulled a cotton bag from inside his jacket and handed it over. Holding it out in front of him as if it were made of glass, the footman slowly walked to the other end of the table and laid it down.

There was a moment's silence as all eyes fixed on the bag, and Talon took the time to scrutinize each member of the council. Nearest to him, to his left, an Asian man in a tailored gray suit sat ramrod-straight, his neutral gaze unfathomable. Next to him was a woman, fleshy, Germanic-looking, with her blond hair pulled tightly back from her forehead. She, too, seemed only mildly interested in what Talon had brought. But the next member of the council, a Hispanic

right, but, Uncle Tim, you just ought to ski!" he said, stretching prodigiously and beginning to yawn. "Golly, it was certainly swell up there. That's a swell bunch of kids too. We're going off again tomorrow."

Timothy thought, "The adolescence of the boys has rubbed off on him. He's gone back to talking like a high school freshman." Canby began to yawn as terrifically as he had eaten. He could scarcely hold his eyes open long enough to finish his sixth glass of milk. "It's about *time* I got on a paying basis!" he said, tipping the big pitcher bottom-side up for the last drop.

They were all in bed by ten.

"Why, this is only Sunday night! Only two days gone!" thought Timothy. It seemed two weeks. "That's because I don't feel well." He was shivering and yet hot. He wondered if he were coming down with a cold. As with an on-coming influenza he was oppressed by a low-spirited general apprehension of nothing in particular. "It's having to fight old Melville's defeatism," he thought.

It took half a day more of steady but vague physical discomfort, not to be explained by any physical cause, to make him perceive that from Canby's first mention of his plan to stay on, his body had been desperately trying to give a danger-signal to his stupidly self-important mind, witlessly dependent as it was on logic and evidence and other intellectual playthings.

Monday about noon his blood and nerves reached him with a warning from a sense of reality far older, far surer than any fiddle-faddle of the brain. He was, at the moment, bending over his typewriter to see why the space-bar didn't work. By that time the danger signal was being given with excited violence. It was with a crash that it broke down the barrier of inattention he had been sedulously keeping up. His first startled reaction to it was as simple, natural, and satisfying as though he were not a civilized being. Canby must be sent away, of course, before the return of—before the end of the vacation. It was axiomatic.

His mind, eager to make up for the besotted slowness of its perception, instantly invented a dozen ingenious ways to move him on: "Canby, I'm sorry but a letter just in makes it necessary to have that third-story room for a new student. . . . Canby, you'd better not stay in Clifford. There's absolutely nothing here for a person

238

like you. . . . Canby, don't say anything to her about it, but I find that it tires Aunt Lavinia to have an extra person in the house, especially a lively young person." But no, that might move him no farther than out of the house. Well, then, "Canby, I don't like to speak about this, but I don't think an idle young man hanging around town will do a hard-working community like Clifford a bit of good. I think it would be just as well for you and better for us if you continued on your travels." That would be plain enough, delivered coldly with a forbidding intonation and a certain grimness that Timothy knew very well how to draw over his high-nosed face. It would be easy to get rid of a person wavering as Canby was from one minute to the next about his plans. He had specially asked if he would be in the way. Well, he would be in the way. And Timothy was the man to tell him so. A man has a right to say who he wants in his own house, hasn't he?

His fingers, continuing to work mechanically, had by this time loosened the catch that had held the space-bar and went on automatically striking the keys very hard through the wax mimeograph stencil, "All students who wish to join the special no-credit second-semester class in English poetry, please leave word at the Prin . . ." when without knowing what he was doing, he stood up abruptly and went to find Canby. It would be better to get this off his mind at once. There was no time to lose. This was—why, it was Monday, Susan would be back at the end of the week. Everything fell from him but the illimitably vitalizing power of animal instinct. He ran nimbly down the stairs, his low-spirited sense of frustration gone, his energies released and focused.

The glowing untroubled certainty of this return to the Stone Age lasted only the length of one flight of stairs. He found the air in the hall below him darkened almost to blackness by a menacing shadow. It was the shadow of the traditions and scruples to which he had been bred. "Oh, but I can't do that!" he exclaimed.

The blithely headlong rush of the instinct of self-preservation crashed, as against granite. The shock turned him sick. He came to a standstill in the middle of the landing, his breath shallow and irregular. Because he was standing as he often did when someone asked him a question, a reflex habit, toughened and resilient from repetition, flexed his muscles, bent his eyes to the floor at one side,

239

man in an electric-blue jacket, with a neatly trimmed mustache, was leaning back and grinning. At the head of the table, the gray-haired man maintained his cold stare in Talon's direction.

Judging by outward appearances, nothing seemed to unite these seven starkly different people. And yet Talon knew from experience the strength of their common purpose. Something had brought them together. Something that required huge resources but also cast-iron secrecy. Something that was worth shedding a good deal of blood for. Something that reached back into the Biblical past and made evangelical Christians their mortal enemies.

As he turned it over in his mind, searching for the elusive link, Talon wondered if he should be looking inside himself. After all, they seemed to think he was almost one of them now. So what did he see when he looked inside his heart? He allowed himself a thin smile. The same as always. Just blood and horror and darkness. Talon was driven by a fascination with evil and ruthless acts. His only interest in the Seven's global plans was that they could provide him the means and unlimited resources to fulfill his twisted desires.

Then an angular woman in a striking emerald dress and with a shock of wild red hair put her hand on the moon-faced man's arm and hissed, "Let's see it. We've waited long enough."

Slowly Sir William Merton reached forward and pulled the foot-long piece of bronze from the bag. As he held it up to the light, Talon could see his plump hand was shaking. Then a curious thing happened. The air seemed to thicken, there was an audible crackle of electricity, and Merton's hand steadied. It must have been a trick of the light, Talon thought, but his eyes seemed to change color, from gray to a deep midnight blue. And when he spoke, the English accent was gone, replaced by something deeper and harder to place.

"Soon you shall again be one. As it was in the first days. And sacrifice shall be yours once more." Then he closed his eyes and let out a long breath, and he seemed to deflate, becoming physically smaller. When he opened his eyes, he looked once again like a portly English cleric.

Talon had had plenty of time to examine the tail of the Serpent, but he looked at it now with a new curiosity. If this was what one piece could do, what were they expecting to happen when they had all three?

Merton had taken off his glasses now, and was peering intently at the Serpent's belly. Around the table, a hush of expectation was building. "Yes, yes," Merton said at last. "Yes, I see. Beautiful, beautiful." He set the tail down and folded his hands over his belly with a satisfied smile.

"Well?" John Bartholomew said.

"Murphy is still working with Isis—Dr. McDonald?"

Bartholomew nodded. "They were last seen on their way to Riyadh."

"The Desert Kingdom. Of course, of course. Well, if she's her father's daughter, she should have no trouble deciphering Dakkuri's little puzzle. Perhaps Murphy even has the second piece in his hands as we speak," Merton chuckled.

General Li turned his head a fraction

lifted his hand to his head in the attitude he often took in reflection. And because his body had, unknown to him, fallen into the pose which for years had been associated with the weighing of evidence, his mind misinterpreting the stimuli given it, unwittingly betrayed him, and began to tarnish and corrode by analysis the bold basic instinct that had brought him leaping down the stairs.

He asked himself first, "But what in the world is the matter with me? What possible reason have I to imagine that Susan might—" He cried out upon his instinct, "Have I lost all sense of decent dignity—jealous of a man she has never even seen!" Yet he was aware that he was beside the mark, that he was leaving something out. Deep, deep down, his subconscious was fumbling with traditional catch words. "It's no fair to rig the game." He snatched this out into the light, looked at it hard and threw it away. "Rig the game! Nonsense! There's no game to rig—just the impulse of a crazy man —or a lover," he added tenderly, and, "I'll think no more about it," he ended resolutely.

But he did think a great deal more about it. Instead of returning to his study he continued to stand motionless, while his mind, coming smartly to the salute, began to draw out from the vast storehouse of self-justifying lore always at the command of a clever mind, some of the rationalizations that might be useful, wiping the self-interest from them as much as possible. "There would be no point in allowing a thoroughly selfish young man—he's evidently that from the way he has treated that fiancée of his—with no principles about hurting other people's feelings, to meet and possibly be a bother to a simple, inexperienced country girl. She would not know what to make of him. Why complicate a situation meant to be simple?

"When I come to think of it, I really know nothing about Canby, now, after not seeing him for years. He may be unscrupulous and insensitive, really bad for our young people. Why should I allow a disruptive influence— See the way he took those boys off on Sunday away from church, from their homes! Our young people have plenty of difficulties as it is.

"It is not for Canby's own good to let him idle his time away aimlessly. He can't find anything to do in Clifford. To allow him to stay here in this backwater would be shirking one's duty to him as much as if I definitely had allowed him—when he was a thoughtless boy here in the Academy—to arrange his studies in some foolish whimsical way that would prevent his going forward in life."

Warming to its work, his mind snatched from the dictionary some excellently abstract words with which to drape his instinct in the grave folds of moral dignity. "In Clifford, where human relations are timed to the rhythm of the permanent, there would be a real danger in introducing a fitful personality like Canby's, trained by experience in the modern technique of being casual, of never allowing enough blood to flow into a relationship to cause bleeding when it is cut short."

The sententious phrases delighted him. He hardly knew what they meant, but they gave him a renewed confidence in the power of his mind to protect him in his wish to do what he wanted. The corners of his mouth stopped watering and twitching as in the onset of physical nausea. How fast it worked, his mind, and how expertly, picking away at the mortar in the wall against which he had bruised himself. It asked for a little more time, his mind did, only a little more, and it would have an opening made through which he could step into safety, holding his head high.

The front door on the floor below opened, heavy steps came clumping up the stairs. Canby appeared, his ski-clothes dusted thick with snow, his face red and shining with sweat. He dragged himself up by the railing, stopping every two or three steps to lean over and shake off the melting snow from his tousled hair. He was breathing hard and scowling, the muscles in his bulldog jaw knotted.

Looking up, he saw Timothy standing in the hallway, right hand stroking back his hair, head bent and turned to the left. Canby's bad humor discharged itself in a sardonic comment. "Well, Uncle Tim, you still haven't got that question thought out, I see. Did you ever know the kids at the Academy used to bet on whether one of them could ask you a question that would get you set like that to answer it? They do yet, they tell me. Who's asked you what, now?"

But he was not interested in an answer, coming on up, knocking the toes of his heavy ski-boots morosely against the risers of the

toward Merton. "Then, should we not be taking it out of his hands, *as we speak?*"

Merton seemed unfazed by the general's tone. "No indeed. I think not. She must have time to translate the next part of the riddle. As you know, the second piece leads to the third, and the third leads...well, I don't need to tell you what that leads to." The looks of ravenous expectation around the table confirmed he didn't. "We must be patient. When Murphy has the last piece in his grasp"—he nodded in Talon's direction—"that is the time to strike. And perhaps then," he added with a leer, "Dr. McDonald and I might have an opportunity to reminisce a little."

FIFTY-SEVEN

MURPHY GRIPPED THE iron ring in both hands, braced himself against the wall of the narrow alley, and heaved. He felt the beads of sweat begin to trickle down his forehead as his arms started to shake with the effort, but the stone slab remained firmly in place, exactly where it had been for what he estimated to be several centuries.

"You're sure this is our best way in?" he grunted.

"Definitely. This will take us directly into the main sewer."

"Assuming it still exists."

stairs like a schoolboy in a temper. "Thermometer's up almost to thirty," he announced glumly. "Snow's likely to go any minute! And I still can't make a jump-turn. I been trying to, all the morning and, God! am I dumb at it. One of the kids that'd never seen any kind of a turn before, did better than I before we quit. I like to've killed myself trying—and did worse with every try. The world's perfect dub—at everything—that's me." He collapsed against the wall and began to unbutton his windbreaker. His red face, greasy with sweat, looked dispirited and because its vitality was blotted out by failure, commonplace and unattractive. He pulled off the wet mittens from his big hands and flung them spitefully down on the stairs. "If Aunt Lavinia can be messy, so can I. I wonder if that damn furnace has condescended to heat water enough so I can have a bath. I'm all in a muck."

It was with exquisite relief that Timothy, from an airy height of distinction, good breeding, coolness, professional success, security, and prestige, looked down on the yeasty, hot, raw, young man, with an ugly mug for a face, with no job, no girl, no manners, no future, with no control of his temper, without even muscular good breeding enough to stand up—Canby had shambled on into the bathroom and slumped to his knees beside the tub, reaching across it to try the water.

Poised on the elastic feet of the tennis player, stepping with the skater's elegant accuracy, Timothy Hulme, very light-hearted, went back upstairs to his study. He was smiling ironically over the folly of his fit of nerves. "Did any sane man ever lose his head more like an idiot?" he asked himself cheerfully. Sitting down before his typewriter, he laid on the keys the long fine fingers that were so like his father's, and his grandfather's, and after an appreciative look at them, went on, ". . . cipal's office before six o'clock on Monday afternoon, March 10th."

Chapter Nineteen

WAS there really, in spite of his impatience with mystical notions, something in the fanciful idea that thoughts do not need to be spoken to make themselves felt? Sitting at his typewriter that morning, he had drawn a secret reassurance from the contrast between his hands and Canby's great paws. That evening, after their return from supper at Miss Peck's, they sat down as usual before the fire in the living-room for a smoke, and as Timothy passed the matches, Canby exclaimed, "Just look at the difference between our hands, Uncle Tim! Wouldn't anybody know that you're a born schoolteacher, and I was made to grab hold of saws and hammers and make things?"

Surprised as Timothy was to hear his unspoken idea put into words, he was yet more startled at the change in its aspect made by Canby's way of expressing it. Annoyed as well as startled. He looked hard at the broad short-fingered palm which Canby spread out. It looked common, yes. But mighty.

"What's the sense of putting a man with a hand like that to pushing a pen?" asked Canby, drawing the fingers together till the hand was a fist, square, hard—a paving stone.

"You have a brain too," Timothy reminded him curtly.

"Well, maybe. But it's a brain that'd take a lot more satisfaction telling that hand how to build a house than finding out a hole in the banking laws that'll let a speculator do what the law didn't intend him to do."

Timothy thought this typical half-baked sophomoric self-righteousness. "There are plenty of bankers as honest as you are," he said dryly, "and plenty of cheating carpenters."

"You ought to have lived a hundred years ago," remarked Aunt Lavinia, "when there were still things that needed to be made with men's hands. I've often thought about the old mason who built this house—and the Academy building."

243

"Have a little faith, Murphy. Come on, are you sure you're really trying your absolute hardest?"

Out of the corner of his eye Murphy watched her as she leaned beside him in the moonlight, mouth pursed in concentration. If a bullwhip had been handy, he had no doubt she'd have used it on him. He was about to tell her to try lending a hand when he felt the great slab shift fractionally. He took a deep breath without relaxing his grip and gritted his teeth. The stone slab started to loosen, and he finally managed to drag it aside. Falling to his knees, he peered into the dark, airless hole.

"Give me the flashlight."

She handed it over and he leaned farther in.

"What can you see?"

The darkness sucked the beam greedily into the depths.

"Nothing much. The brickwork seems pretty much intact near the top, but farther down...I don't know. I guess there's only one way to find out."

She was beginning to look a little nervous now. "How do we...?"

"When in doubt, just jump right in. That's my philosophy."

Her enthusiasm was definitely fading. "You can't be serious. It could be a hundred feet to the bottom."

He swung his legs into the hole and gripped the sides. "I seem to recall this was your idea. Come on." He saw the look of panic on her face and relented. "Okay, they built little handholds into the sides. Just take it slow and follow me."

It wasn't quite a hundred feet, and, remarkably, the ceramic rungs were mostly intact. Apart from the few times Isis lost her footing and a boot came thudding into Murphy's shoulder, they descended without incident. They landed at a junction of four tunnels, and Murphy gave Isis a moment to regain her composure.

"So, where to now?"

Her flashlight beam made her pale face float in the darkness like an apparition as she flipped through the pages of de Tocqueville. "Well, the likeliest spot is at the source of the original well. That's what Dakkuri would have been talking about."

Murphy grabbed a handful of dust and let

it trickle through his fingers. "How do we find that? It's dry as a bone down here."

Her frown made her look even more ghostly. "We just need to figure out the direction of flow, then work backward."

Murphy crouched down and played the beam over the floor. "Okay, when the water finally dried up, it should have left some striations in the mud, and with a little luck they could have been preserved, like fossils." He shuffled forward a few steps and focused the beam on what looked like a long, flat stone. "Here. Unless I'm very much mistaken, we need to go this way."

She followed him into the dark, guided by his flashlight as it swept from side to side along the walls. Inching slowly through the narrow brick passage, drawing the dead, centuries-old air into her lungs, she was beginning to remember why she had never wanted to be an archaeologist. The clean, modern hotel somewhere above their heads seemed a hundred miles and a thousand years away.

She bumped into Murphy's back. "Dead end," he said.

They retraced their steps to the junction

and examined the floor for more traces of the water's passage. Murphy pointed down another tunnel.

"Are you sure?" Isis asked.

"I don't know about you, but this is my first time in a medieval sewer. To be honest, I'm just following my nose."

"Sounds like a plan," Isis said. "In a sewer, I mean."

They started down the tunnel with less confidence now, hoping for a sign that would tell them they were on the right track. After several minutes of slow trudging, Murphy stopped. He pointed at the ground with his flashlight.

"What do you think that is?"

It didn't look like anything. Just a shadow. Then she gasped. "A footprint."

"Yeah, that's what I thought. And it looks new. I guess that means we're going the right way."

To Isis it didn't mean anything of the sort. It meant someone else was down there. Perhaps Omar had sent someone after them to get the rest of their money. She wanted desperately to retrace their steps as quickly as possible and get back to light and people

Timothy was just as well pleased to have the talk turn from hands. "That reminds me—I haven't told you yet, have I, that I own one of these old stone houses now, up on the road to the Crandall Pitch?"

"Do you?" said Canby, not much interested.

"Don't you rather like them?"

Canby leaned over the arm of his chair to look around the room, all but lost his balance, and recovered it with a grotesque convulsion of arms and legs.

Aunt Lavinia said, "For goodness' sake, Can, sit up in your chair like a Christian!"

"Well, they're all right, I guess," said Canby doubtfully, "but what the devil do you do with walls two-and-a-half foot thick when you want a new window or door?"

Wormwood lay bitter on Timothy's tongue. Trying to swallow it down he could not at once think of an answer to make to the young man who had asked that young question. Canby answered himself mockingly, "You do without, I suppose."

"Why, that's exactly what Susan Barney said, when we were . . ." began Aunt Lavinia.

Timothy broke in, in a louder voice than he intended, "But you're *safe* in them—as you never can be in one of the flimsy wooden houses." (He had not wanted to say that.)

"Oh—*safe!*" said Canby, scoffing. "Good Lord! Who wants to be safe?" He corrected himself, "Well, yes, of course, they'd be fine for an Old Ladies' Home. Who might Susan Barney be, Aunt Lavinia?"

Aunt Lavinia began to tell him, but Timothy did not hear her. He sat leaning back in his comfortable chair, a lighted cigarette in his left hand, a tightness in his throat cutting off his breath. As he slowly suffocated, his mind, futile fluttering onlooker, kept assuring him foolishly, "You are not feeling anything in particular. Or if you are, there's no reason for it. Nothing whatever has happened. Everything is just as it was before."

But it was not until his cigarette, at its end, pressed its red coal into the flesh of his hand that he sprang up, flung it away with a curse, drew a long breath, and then another, and felt himself wakened from a bad dream.

244

Aunt Lavinia said severely, "You'll set the house afire one of these days, Tim, with that trick. What's come over you? I haven't seen you do it for years as you have just lately."

Canby went on. ". . . one of these sweet good girls, huh? Not for mine. Your hard-as-nails little Delia sounds better. I like'm when they're mean as hell."

"Because you think that lets you be mean when you feel like it?"

"That's the eye."

Aunt Lavinia broke into her sardonically amused laugh.

Canby was nettled. "What's so funny?"

The old woman raised her eyebrows quizzically, tantalizingly, and made no answer, her laughter subsiding into mocking chuckles.

Canby said boorishly, "Oh, you make me tired!" and put out his hand to Timothy. "Did you really burn yourself this time, Uncle Tim? Let's see." His tone was sincerely concerned.

But Timothy thrust his hand into his pocket, said it was nothing, went upstairs to his study and shut the door.

He tried to prepare some examination questions, he got up impatiently to open the window because he was suffocating, he tried to write a long-due letter, he looked blindly at the last *Manchester Guardian*, he went to shut the window because the room was freezing, he told himself this would be a good time to look over the reports of three students who had failed in mid-years, his head began to burn again, he went to open the window. Standing for an instant by it, he saw that the new moon, just risen over The Wall, pale as it was, began to dim the stars, and he saw that Canby Hunter was going down the first steps, off probably to see one of his former schoolmates. He had renewed contacts with people he had known all over town.

Timothy reached to turn off the electric light, and stood in the dark at the open window looking down at the tall figure. Canby was whistling a swing version of a ballad, very popular then on the radio. Timothy detested the musical idiocy of the perverted melody, and Canby was flatting the high notes abominably, but he stood still, listening and watching intently. Beyond the far corner of the tennis-court skating-rink, where the road made its right-angle turn to the left and started down the steep hill, the sidewalk was villainously slippery. For some days, as he had picked a slow careful

and the twenty-first century. But she wasn't going to try it on her own. She gave her amulet a nervous tug, and hurried after Murphy's retreating back.

After a few minutes they saw another footprint. Then another. The footprints were coming in clusters now, blurring together, like the tracks of a herd of animals. She tugged Murphy's sleeve. "Should we really be following, do you think? There seem to be rather a lot of them."

"You got a better idea?"

"Apart from going back, you mean?"

Murphy turned to face her. "Look, this may be a wild-goose chase, but it's the only wild-goose chase in town right now. At least we know we're not heading down another blind alley. These tracks must go *somewhere*." He waved the flashlight in the direction they'd come, and as it passed across her face he saw raw fear etched on her elfin features. "Look, I'm not going to force you to carry on. Do you really want to go back?"

A wave of relief went through her, followed by a curious hollow feeling, as if in that instant her life had suddenly become meaningless. She took a deep breath, then

way down it, especially over the irregular ice-glazed stones of the steps, Timothy had brought to bear all his excellent sense of balance, had really used his father's ivory-headed walking stick, and several times had thought of having a railing put up. Canby, nonchalantly plunging along, his unbuttoned overcoat flapping around his long legs, swung around the slippery corner so heedlessly that he all but fell—and then instead of trying like a sensible adult to recover and keep his balance, he kept on zestfully slipping, tripping, stumbling, sliding, his arms and legs flying, his overcoat flapping, catching himself just before one headlong crash after another. When he struck the steps, his progress—more like a continuous falling-down than a descent—was accelerated to a staccato clip! clip! clip! as he leaped from one stone to the next, never for an instant in equilibrium, only not falling because of his crazy speed. At the bottom, along the level space in front of the Primary School, the sidewalk lay flat and icy. Striking this at an angle, his feet began to slip rapidly from under him. But he leaned far forward, crouching low, whole-heartedly confident that his speed would hold him up. He let himself go boldly, his arms outstretched on each side like a schoolboy on an ice-slide. And he did not fall. He did not even stop his atrocious whistling of that atrocious tune. At the end of the slide he straightened up, put his hands in the pockets of his still unbuttoned overcoat, and swung off down the street, not having lost a single beat of "Loch Lomond."

Timothy stood at the window a long time after this, looking somberly out at the empty road. The moon rose higher, grew brighter, put out more stars. He was soon miserably cold. The small burn from the cigarette on his hand throbbed painfully. The taste in his mouth of verdigris on copper was sickening. His thoughts, intensely distasteful, grew less presentable all the time, until his self-respect going under for the last third time, called out desperately that if it were not to drown altogether, a gesture must be made. Very well. He made one. He closed the window and turned back to his writing-table, saying aloud to the empty room with a casual airy accent, "Oh, well, let him stay or go, just as the notion strikes him. It's of no consequence to me what he does. Why should I care?"

The next day, being the first Tuesday in March, was of course

246

Town Meeting. Nobody in Clifford did anything but stand in the crowd on the floor of the Town Hall, so closely packed together as scarcely to be able to shift from one foot to another, during the usual long, wrangling discussions over whether the Town snowplow could serve yet another year, what share of the taxes was to go to schools and what to roads, whether it was necessary to go on spending money to keep the brambles out of such forgotten old graveyards as the one on the Crandall Pitch. The town wit set off his usual crackers; the town clown was drunker and more Shakespeareanly hilarious than usual; excitable old Give-me-Liberty-or-Give-me-Death Bradford wrought himself as always to fever-heat over nothing; Father Kirby made his yearly rather jerky financial report on Dewey House; Mr. Hulme when "interrogated" as Superintendent, answered questions about teachers' salaries, numbers of pupils, and blackboards in the primary schools. As Principal Hulme, he made his annual detailed statement about the condition of the roofs, walls, and foundations of the Academy. There was a long-drawn-out quarrel about who should be Tree Warden, although nobody cared.

Everybody there found it, as Town Meetings often are, very dull. Everybody, that is, except the presiding officer. For old Mr. Dewey, tall, stooped, serious, the Town Hall was as always a temple dedicated to the ideals of self-government, equal opportunity for all, and fair play. Devoted high priest of those ideals, he was watchfully ready to put down the slightest sign of disrespect for them as he turned his grizzled head to the right and left in answer to the calls from the floor of "Mr. Mawderator! Mr. Mawderator!" Attempts at speeding up the proceedings always drew a rebuke from him. When some merchant or manufacturer had the illusion that since his time was worth cash it was worth more than other people's, and tried to get things put through efficiently and with fewer words, the very boards in the floor of the Town Hall—certainly every man and woman there—knew the formula with which the Moderator replied, "No, no, there's no hurry about this. We're here for *just one thing,* to give time to every citizen to say what he's got to say. Let's get everything talked out—there won't be another chance for a year." Leaning with stately courtesy towards the abashed young farmer who had been protesting about the Town's neglect of the

turned him around and gave him a gentle push forward. "No, no. I just felt a little light-headed for a moment. The dust, probably. I'm fine now."

He grunted, and they set off again. She kept the beam of her flashlight pointed straight ahead, not wanting to see any more traces of their invisible companions.

When they came to another junction, with tunnels branching off to the left and right, she kept her eyes closed and concentrated on keeping her breathing steady.

"It's going to get narrower," Murphy said over his shoulder. "You okay?"

"I'm not claustrophobic, you know," she said with as much indignation as she could summon. It was true, she'd never been frightened of confined spaces. Once, when Miss McTavish had locked her in a storage cupboard for a whole afternoon, she'd felt nothing but a blessed sense of relief to be out of the clutches of her schoolmates for a few hours and able to let her mind wander free among the gods and creatures of mythology who were already thronging her imagination.

But this was different. Not only were they

in a catacomb of dark and increasingly airless tunnels, they were not alone. According to Omar, no one had been down here for generations. So whom did the footprints belong to? Her anxiety was heightened by Murphy's own lack of concern. Clearly his philosophy really was simply to charge blindly forward, trusting some higher power would keep him from falling down a deep, dark hole. Not to mention her.

She had steeled herself for the plunge into the next tunnel, but Murphy was still rooted to the spot. "Do you hear something?"

She cocked her head to one side. "Like what?"

"I don't know. Wind, maybe?"

She held a hand in front of her face and shook her head. "Not a breath. No, it sounds like . . . water."

He nodded. "And the footprints go in the same direction. Look."

He set off down the left-hand tunnel, crouching so he didn't bump his head against the roof. Isis clung to his arm, no longer caring what he thought. As they went farther, the rushing sound got louder, until she was sure she could actually smell the water above the scent of dust and decay.

When they started to hear another sound, they stopped instinctively. This time they both knew what it was. It came in waves, louder, then fainter, then louder again. Isis put a trembling hand to her amulet and waited for Murphy to say something.

"Can you make out what language that is? It doesn't sound like Arabic."

She forced herself to listen. It had an odd singsong quality, a definite rhythm, as if they were chanting. "I . . . I don't know. There's a hint of Aramaic, perhaps. It could be my imagination. What are we going to do?"

"We're going to be careful," Murphy said, pulling her forward.

As she stumbled after him, a crazy mix of thoughts swirled around in her head. Had she locked her filing cabinet, the one where she kept her private diary? Had she remembered to return her copy of Gilroy's commentary on the *Epic of Gilgamesh* to Professor Hitashi? Had she removed *all* the mousetraps Fiona had insisted on putting down in her office?

With a start she realized she wasn't expecting to return to Washington. She had convinced herself she was going to die. Well, if she had to go now, at least she wasn't leaving any family behind. A thought that led her to speculate on who would attend her funeral. Not many, she supposed. But of course they'd never find her body. So there wouldn't be a funeral. She would just be missing, forever. Like a lost soul . . .

Murphy was touching her on the shoulder and pointing up ahead. There was a distinct rushing sound like water moving swiftly over stone, and the chanting now sounded ominously close. And there was light, too, a ghostly flickering against the tunnel walls.

They inched forward, and Isis felt her toe connect with something hard. The floor of the tunnel was littered with bricks. She looked up and saw a ragged hole in the tunnel wall. Her legs carried her toward it, independent of her will. She no longer felt fear. Her mind seemed to have shut down, just a primitive core remaining—enough to keep her body moving. The last thought she

roads on his hill, he would then say, "Kindly proceed, Mr. Purdy. You know more than we do about that. We are all glad to hear you."

At the supper table that night Canby was rather silent, looking wonderingly at old Mr. Dewey's weather-beaten face. Its deep lines were hewn yet more deeply by fatigue. The tall figure still stooped under its burden of responsibility. The deep-set eyes were grave. Driving Timothy and Aunt Lavinia home after supper, the young man said over his shoulder, out of a silence, "He's kind of a swell old guy, do you know it?"

But the next morning—it was Wednesday—after Aunt Lavinia who had apparently slept in her clothes and certainly had not combed her hair since Susan had gone, had returned to her room and Rameau, Canby said casually, stretching and yawning like a young dog at ease, "Say, Uncle Tim, do you know what you ought to do? You can't possibly go on taking care of Aunt Lavinia all by yourself, as she gets crankier and queerer. Which she certainly is. You ought to get married."

Timothy froze, and waited.

Canby struck a match, lighted his pipe, threw his match at the fireplace, missed it, said, "Damn-I-mean-darn," leaned too far forward to pick it up, fell out of his chair, scrambled ungracefully on his hands and knees to where it was, threw it with a better aim, lifted himself back into his chair with one surge of his muscles, and went on, "Now that teacher that takes her meals at Miss Peck's the dietician, Miss Long—"

"Miss Lane," said Timothy.

"Miss Lane. Now she's swell. She'd make a swell wife for anybody—so comfortable and sensible. The kind that'd stand by and keep things going no matter what! She's nice-looking too, I think. If I were old enough to, I wouldn't mind marrying her a bit. And I bet you a nickel she'd know how to manage Aunt Lavinia. She's probably had old folks in her own family. Everybody up here has. She'd make a swell home for anybody. And all the signs are that she'd be tickled to death to make one for you. I been watching her, and if she doesn't think a good deal of you, I miss my . . ." Chanc-

248

ing to catch Timothy's eye, he was stricken speechless by its cold fury, and faltering like a scared schoolboy, looked wildly for a way out, "Of course I know it's none of my— I didn't mean to— Excuse *me,* Uncle Tim—gosh! I certainly do beg your pardon!"

Timothy drew a long breath. He was reassured by Canby's collapse. It would be simple to propel him out of the house when it seemed advisable. A single look would be enough when the time came to do it. He ground out his cigarette stub slowly, took his time about what to say, and getting up to go, demolished what was left of Canby by a cool, "I think I'll leave Miss Lane to you, Canby."

But he was in a rage all the morning, and by lunch time had decided that on all counts the time had come to move Canby on. For Heaven's sake, why not? Why should he take in a crude stub-fingered young man simply because he was the nephew of a sister-in-law? If he didn't want him, why should he have him?

Lunch was rather silent. He could of course neither say the necessary word nor give the propelling look in the presence of Aunt Lavinia. While they were still at the table, Canby asked if the stiff knee were well enough for skating. "It used to turn me green to watch you skate. I've got some extra time now, I wonder if I couldn't learn to do a figure or two? I bet I'm not any dumber than lots of the kids you've taught."

Timothy remaining passive, he went on, "I bought me a pair of rockers this morning," and after a hopeful wait, said feebly, "We probably won't have this ice much longer. The weather report says a thaw."

Timothy went silently to get his skates, meaning to spend half an hour on the ice till Aunt Lavinia had gone to her room, and then to take Canby back to the house. The whole afternoon passed at the rink. He found it interesting to have somebody try as hard as Canby did. And yet what awkward work he made of it! Tall, elegantly slender in his worn, old, well-fitting, dark-blue skating clothes, Timothy laid down circles, brackets, and spirals, while Canby, burly in his new stiff ski-trousers and coat, tried to follow directions, lumbering and clumsy as a bear. Some Clifford people came up to the Academy rink to take advantage of what would certainly be one of the last days before the spring thaw. The girls, palpably longing to have Professor Hulme invite them to skate, were breathless with pride when he took them out one after another, steering them adroitly, supporting them firmly in the spins and dips of the waltz. He took pains to introduce Canby to those who did not know him, to every single one of them. But no sparks flew. Absorbed in his groping struggle with the law of gravity, Canby barely glanced at them. On their side, they scarcely saw the red-faced young man, panting with his violent misdirected efforts. They could not take their eyes from Timothy. "Isn't Professor Hulme *won*-derful?" they said, to which Canby returned a hearty, "You said it!" or, "He sure is!" pushing off again to try his luck on the outer edge. At last Timothy said kindly, "There, Canby! You've almost got it," and skating backwards with perfect poise, drew Canby around a figure of eight.

"Fine! Splendid!" cried the watching girls. Timothy was quite aware that they were calling to him, looking at him, not at Canby.

Aunt Lavinia shouted impatiently from her window that it was time to take her to supper. "What are you thinking about to stay out so long? Haven't you any sense, either of you?"

Like scolded boys, they clumped hastily up the steps into the house on their skates, unlaced and snatched off their shoes in the front hall, rushed upstairs, unbuttoning and flinging off clothes as they went, took turns in the one bathroom under the shower. As they rubbed down hurriedly, Canby cried admiringly, "Gee whiz, Uncle Tim! What a waistline! No wonder you can skate. Were you a track man in college?"

"No. I was on the tennis team."

"Oh, sure. I forgot."

Dressing with identical speed, they emerged from their rooms at the same time, ran down together to where Aunt Lavinia stood waiting. "You know what Miss Peck's like when anybody's late," she reminded them crossly.

There was a new announcement on the bulletin board: "HE HAS A KIND HEART. IF HE CAN GET WHAT HE WANTS WITHOUT WALKING OVER YOU, HE'D JUST AS SOON GO AROUND."

"Whew! Who's that brickbat for?" asked Canby.

"Oh, nobody ever knows who Miss Peck's brickbats are for. Maybe somebody who died years ago."

250

had was that this was what it must feel like to be a zombie.

Murphy was shaking her, jolting her back into full consciousness. In the uncertain light, he was looking at her with a stern expression, a finger to his lips. She nodded and slowly turned her head to look through the hole in the tunnel wall. Her eyes seemed to have closed of their own accord, and she forced them open.

The skulls were the first thing she saw. There were seven of them arranged in a rough semicircle like Halloween pumpkins, eye sockets ablaze with an oily light that spilled greedily over the body arranged on the dirt floor. The body was stiff, but she was clearly a girl who could not have been older than ten. A ragged cotton blanket covered most of her body, and her narrow face looked waxy, but you could see hints of the beauty she would grow to be.

If she wasn't already dead, that is.

The three men were naked to the waist, swaying back and forth, propelled by the rhythmic chanting that filled the shadowy space. Isis gasped as she saw the long

ing to catch Timothy's eye, he was stricken speechless by its cold fury, and faltering like a scared schoolboy, looked wildly for a way out, "Of course I know it's none of my— I didn't mean to— Excuse *me*, Uncle Tim—gosh! I certainly do beg your pardon!"

Timothy drew a long breath. He was reassured by Canby's collapse. It would be simple to propel him out of the house when it seemed advisable. A single look would be enough when the time came to do it. He ground out his cigarette stub slowly, took his time about what to say, and getting up to go, demolished what was left of Canby by a cool, "I think I'll leave Miss Lane to you, Canby."

But he was in a rage all the morning, and by lunch time had decided that on all counts the time had come to move Canby on. For Heaven's sake, why not? Why should he take in a crude stub-fingered young man simply because he was the nephew of a sister-in-law? If he didn't want him, why should he have him?

Lunch was rather silent. He could of course neither say the necessary word nor give the propelling look in the presence of Aunt Lavinia. While they were still at the table, Canby asked if the stiff knee were well enough for skating. "It used to turn me green to watch you skate. I've got some extra time now, I wonder if I couldn't learn to do a figure or two? I bet I'm not any dumber than lots of the kids you've taught."

Timothy remaining passive, he went on, "I bought me a pair of rockers this morning," and after a hopeful wait, said feebly, "We probably won't have this ice much longer. The weather report says a thaw."

Timothy went silently to get his skates, meaning to spend half an hour on the ice till Aunt Lavinia had gone to her room, and then to take Canby back to the house. The whole afternoon passed at the rink. He found it interesting to have somebody try as hard as Canby did. And yet what awkward work he made of it! Tall, elegantly slender in his worn, old, well-fitting, dark-blue skating clothes, Timothy laid down circles, brackets, and spirals, while Canby, burly in his new stiff ski-trousers and coat, tried to follow directions, lumbering and clumsy as a bear. Some Clifford people came up to the Academy rink to take advantage of what would certainly be one of the last days before the spring thaw. The girls,

butcher's knife each clutched in his lap, and Murphy clapped a hand over her mouth.

She took a deep breath and he slowly took his hand away, then pointed beyond the skulls.

On the end of a pole stuck in the dirt was a thick S-shape of gleaming metal.

The middle section of the Brazen Serpent!

As she realized what it was, she felt herself being sucked down through the centuries into a world of primitive darkness. It was like being in Miss McTavish's cupboard, but this time with real gods and demons and no hope of ever being let out. A whimper rose in her throat and she barely managed to choke it off.

Then Murphy was pulling her back into the tunnel and she felt her whole body relax. They were going back. They were going to survive.

FIFTY-EIGHT

MURPHY GRIPPED ISIS by the shoulders and tried to gauge her expression. In the gloom of the tunnel all he could see were her eyes, and they seemed to be pleading silently. "Can you do it?" he asked.

A whisper escaped her throat. Was that a yes? He gripped harder, almost shaking her, and she nodded. That would have to do. There was no time to go through it with her again. He crawled back to the hole in the wall and she watched as he waited for his moment, then slid into the flickering shadows.

Shuffling after him, she crouched at the

entrance, a hand clamped to her mouth to stop herself from crying. She could hardly bear to watch him. But she couldn't tear her eyes away. If she lost sight of him she'd be truly alone. She gripped the flashlight as a drowning man might clutch a life preserver.

Murphy chanced a glance back in her direction as he belly-crawled his way through the bricks and loose rocks on the other side of the tunnel wall. He could feel her eyes on him, but otherwise she was just another shadow blending into the dark.

He was confident the soft dust covering the floor would muffle his approach, but when his knee struck a brick and sent it skittering into the dark, his whole body tensed. He buried his face in the dirt, not daring to look up, hardly daring to breathe. But the chanting of the three executioners maintained its dirgelike rhythm. They seemed to be in some sort of trance, maybe high on something, but he knew at some point the chanting would stop and those vicious-looking knives would come into play.

He blamed himself for leaving his competition bow back at the hotel. Who knew he'd find himself interrupting a human sacrifice

palpably longing to have Professor Hulme invite them to skate, were breathless with pride when he took them out one after another, steering them adroitly, supporting them firmly in the spins and dips of the waltz. He took pains to introduce Canby to those who did not know him, to every single one of them. But no sparks flew. Absorbed in his groping struggle with the law of gravity, Canby barely glanced at them. On their side, they scarcely saw the red-faced young man, panting with his violent misdirected efforts. They could not take their eyes from Timothy. "Isn't Professor Hulme *won*-derful?" they said, to which Canby returned a hearty, "You said it!" or, "He sure is!" pushing off again to try his luck on the outer edge. At last Timothy said kindly, "There, Canby! You've almost got it," and skating backwards with perfect poise, drew Canby around a figure of eight.

"Fine! Splendid!" cried the watching girls. Timothy was quite aware that they were calling to him, looking at him, not at Canby.

Aunt Lavinia shouted impatiently from her window that it was time to take her to supper. "What are you thinking about to stay out so long? Haven't you any sense, either of you?"

Like scolded boys, they clumped hastily up the steps into the house on their skates, unlaced and snatched off their shoes in the front hall, rushed upstairs, unbuttoning and flinging off clothes as they went, took turns in the one bathroom under the shower. As they rubbed down hurriedly, Canby cried admiringly, "Gee whiz, Uncle Tim! What a waistline! No wonder you can skate. Were you a track man in college?"

"No. I was on the tennis team."

"Oh, sure. I forgot."

Dressing with identical speed, they emerged from their rooms at the same time, ran down together to where Aunt Lavinia stood waiting. "You know what Miss Peck's like when anybody's late," she reminded them crossly.

There was a new announcement on the bulletin board: "HE HAS A KIND HEART. IF HE CAN GET WHAT HE WANTS WITHOUT WALKING OVER YOU, HE'D JUST AS SOON GO AROUND."

"Whew! Who's that brickbat for?" asked Canby.

"Oh, nobody ever knows who Miss Peck's brickbats are for. Maybe somebody who died years ago."

250

Supper was a success. There was oyster soup, made as Miss Peck made it with milk that was almost cream, hot, well-peppered, the oysters plump and ruffled. There were small crusty rolls fresh from the oven. "Oh, *boy!*" groaned the always-famished Canby in ecstasy as his teeth met in his first mouthful. There were scalloped potatoes in a sauce golden with butter and savory with onions; there were pickles, jelly, spiced-currant relish, cole-slaw; a browned pot roast; tender young home-canned Golden Bantam corn; coffee as was made only in that home. It was one of Miss Peck's suppers, and they were hungry. Good-natured Miss Lane said as she ate, "Really, Miss Peck, I must admit you have a hand for seasoning."

"I should have canned the corn full sooner. 'Twas ready a week before I began," said Miss Peck austerely.

Nor did Mrs. Washburn get that running start which was necessary as a take-off for one of her flights of gabble. Canby's theory about protection from her was to talk faster than she could and about subjects beyond her ken, and he had worked up a fine ability for chatter. He talked now as steadily as he chewed, occasionally drawing in old Mr. Dewey and Timothy long enough to let him swallow. He talked about politics, a ski-trail he was planning, the future of Vermont, the Republican party, aviation, cheaper electricity, the last hockey game, Fascism, democracy . . .

Something about this last caught the ear of Aunt Lavinia, dreaming over her plate. "What's that? What did you say about a fly-wheel?"

Canby explained readily enough, as willing to run on those conversational rails as any others, "Oh, I'm just blocking the Vermont-ish move Uncle Tim always makes at about this point. He always says the trouble is there are too many people in the world for democracy."

"I never said that," Timothy protested. "All I said was that we haven't learned yet how to manage big crowds decently."

"But it's true," said Mr. Dewey, "that the bigger the crowd you've got to manage, the slower democracy works. That's why it works so well in Vermont."

"Sure it's slow," admitted Canby. "Just give me another spoonful of those potatoes, will you, Miss Peck? The point I'm making is the slower the better. We gotta have some kind of lag to equalize

in a medieval sewer, but by now he should have learned to expect the unexpected. He flashed back to the initial phone call with Methusaleh. If he'd known where it would lead, would he have told the old man what he could do with his artifact, Daniel or no Daniel? The killings, the bombing at the church, Laura—it all seemed to have started somehow with that phone call. But he knew there was no point thinking about it. He was sure now that God had set him on a certain path and there was nothing he could do but follow it to the end.

Whatever the cost.

The image of the girl lying just moments from being a human sacrifice came back to him, his courage rising, and he wondered if Isis would be able to follow through. She'd seemed taut as a bowstring when he'd first met her. Now, having been catapulted out of her academic cocoon, he was afraid she was on the edge of a total emotional collapse.

He prayed her nerve would hold.

He started to move again, keeping as far away from the three swaying bodies as he could. Was it his imagination, or was the rushing sound getting louder? He didn't want to end up as a bonus sacrificial victim, but he didn't want to disappear into an underground stream either. If they turned their heads to the right, he was in their line of sight now. He couldn't rely on their drugged-up state to keep them oblivious of his presence much longer. He turned his wrist, and the luminous dial of his watch told him there was another minute to wait. Too long. He was suddenly convinced the three executioners would finish their prayers any second and then it would be too late.

Keep going, fellas. Just a few more verses. He concentrated on the haunting sound and felt his focus slipping. He willed the hands of his watch to move faster. Then, just as his head began to throb and his grip on the real world began to loosen, he heard a clatter of dust and rocks and craned his neck to look behind him.

What he saw made his heart jam in his throat.

Framed in the hole in the tunnel wall where he had last seen Isis, a ghastly apparition now appeared, as if the heathen chanting had summoned up a demoness. Lit from below by the flashlight, her corpse-white face seemed to be emitting an unnatural glow of its own as it floated unsupported in the darkness.

For a crazy moment he wasn't sure if it really was Isis, then reality took hold again and he sprang forward. As he'd hoped, the three men were now on their feet, gesturing toward Isis in horrified silence. They didn't seem to notice as he stumbled past them toward the pole and the glowing Serpent, but who knew how long they'd buy Isis's circus act? He bent down to grasp the shoulder of the unconscious girl.

She was not restrained in any way and she was as stiff as a stone angel. *Let's hope she's not already playing that role,* Murphy thought. If she was still alive, then they must have drugged her into this unconscious state, and it could be a mistake to try to bring her awake suddenly, but whatever the consequences, Murphy figured they would be better than being slaughtered by the Serpent worshipers.

After two firm shakes of her shoulders, the girl's eyes shot open and she started to

the power-trusts. And we don't get any lag nowadays out of having to take a month to get from anywhere to Washington."

Unlike Mrs. Washburn, who, when men talked on their own subjects, always threw a metaphorical apron over her head and sat quelled and silent, Aunt Lavinia, once she began, kept on till she was satisfied.

"Washington? Lag?" she asked. "What's any of that got to do with fly-wheels?"

"A plenty!" cried Canby. "Now listen. A hundred years ago it took a week for a man in Boston to buy anything off of a man in Philadelphia. There was no way this country could be run too fast. Geography was the fly-wheel. Anything more in that coffee pot, Miss Peck? Now geography's gone to kingdom come. But we gotta have *some* kind, or we'll shake our screws loose and lose off all our nuts. Looks to me as if democracy's not being able to get anything done in a hurry was a good way to keep us in the road and out o' the ditch."

"Hold on there, young man," said Mr. Dewey, laughing. "It's not the fly-wheel that makes a car go slowly enough to steer it."

"Oh, I'm just talking," said Canby easily, buttering another roll. "A person can say what he wants to, can't he, when he's just talking? You know what I mean all right."

"Well, *I* haven't the least idea what you mean," said Aunt Lavinia, "and it's my opinion you haven't said anything yet."

Canby was nonplused. "But what is it you don't get? It's perfectly simple."

"Just say it, then, if it's so simple."

"Well . . . but . . ." began Canby uncertainly.

Mr. Dewey had an idea. "Perhaps, Mrs. Henry, it's slipped your mind what the fly-wheel does for the engine of an automobile."

"A fly-wheel? *In* an automobile? Is there really? Wherever do they put it?"

They caught a glimpse of the huge power-house fly-wheel in her mind and smiled at each other, the young, the middle-aged, the old man, in brotherly indulgence of womankind. But when Timothy, addressing himself seriously to making a mechanical principle clear, explained the equalizing function of a fly-wheel, she proved quite capable of grasping Canby's metaphor.

252

"Oh, yes, I see. Canby means that it's a *dis*advantage instead of an advantage of Fascism for the dictator to be able to get something done in the afternoon that he thought of in the morning. Yes, of course. And the very fact that democracy has to be slow . . . Why, Canby Hunter, that is a very interesting and intelligent idea! Wherever did you hear it?"

"Hear it! I made it up!"

"You did! Not really!"

At the unmitigated astonishment in her voice they fell into helpless laughter, although Canby protested rather warmly, "Good gosh, Aunt Lavinia, don't you think I've got *any* sense?"

"Why, I've just said you made a remark that shows you have a great deal," she reminded him.

Dessert was there. Peaches. Miss Peck's ragged, luscious home-preserved peaches. And fruit-cake. They sighed happily, loosened a button or two, and went on eating, in a glow. Amused as he often was at this table by the idea of food as the power-behind-the-throne of most life-philosophies, Timothy glanced around the circle of faces, usually more or less shadowed by inner perplexities or trouble, now sunny as in a golden reflection from the peaches. One face was a shade too bright to suit him. Canby was smiling to himself as he spooned up the clear syrup, and there was something about that smile—it looked like the secret, self-admiring look of a man who thinks he has put over something slick. What was it Canby had put over? Drawing his brows together, Timothy looked suspiciously at the pleased unconscious young face. Canby passed his dish for more peaches. Perhaps it was no more than the smile of satisfied gluttony.

Miss Lane said, "My! Miss Peck! It takes you for fruit cake."

Miss Peck disclaimed merit. "Susan Barney made this."

The words flowed in at Timothy's outer ear. Before they had penetrated to his inner, he was bathed in a warm light brightness of relief after pain, as though a hard headache had just left him. By the time he knew what it was Miss Peck had said, Mr. Dewey and Canby had each asked a question.

"Is Susan back?" "Who's Susan?" They spoke at the same time, their words clashing.

Then Canby remembered and answered himself, "Oh, yes, she's

scream at the sight of Murphy. He was counting on Isis keeping the men completely distracted, but to be certain he covered her mouth with one hand while he put his other to his own to try to mime *quiet.* The girl's eyes were nearly popping out of her head with fear, with no sign of any drug aftereffects, but she managed to nod that she understood Murphy's gesture for silence.

He rose and turned toward the pole holding the Serpent's body. Its fiery glow in the reflection of the blazing torches was mesmerizing. He reached up and with trembling fingers began untying the hemp cords securing the bronze segment to the pole. Murphy held it in his hands and marveled at the weight of it, which seemed to perfectly match the feel of the tail.

His study was cut short abruptly as a shout arose behind him from the three sacrificers. Their attention had been torn from Isis by the sight of the girl running toward the hole in the wall. They stopped gesturing toward the escaping sacrifice when one of them spied Murphy holding their icon. They dropped their interest in either female and turned toward him with the full fury of their spoiled evening about to explode upon him.

They advanced on Murphy, grunting with rage, knife blades raised, and showing none of the signs of their trancelike sluggishness of a moment before.

Murphy was out of ideas. He couldn't run. That would leave Isis at their mercy. And there was no way he could take on three knife-wielding maniacs and hope to win. He had done his best; there was nothing else he could do. He hoped Isis would have the presence of mind to run back the way they'd come while they were butchering him.

He tried to suppress his fear and began to pray. In a few minutes he would be seeing Laura again.

He was shaken out of his reverie as the chanting started again. But it was different now. Higher-pitched. A woman's voice. He looked over the shoulders of his attackers and realized it was Isis. She was pointing an imperious hand in his direction and pouring out a stream of gibberish in a strangely commanding voice. At least it sounded like gibberish to him. The three men had stopped in

the one with the peppy younger sister. Say, Miss Peck, can you spare me another slice of that cake?"

"Canby! You'll kill yourself!" cried Aunt Lavinia.

"Speak to Miss Peck about the food then."

Miss Peck answered Mr. Dewey's question, "She made it in November."

Miss Lane added the explanation he needed, "Fruit cake has to stand and season before it is fit to eat, you know."

"Oh, *God!*" groaned Timothy to himself in an astounded revulsion from the bland interlude of gratified vanity into which Canby had tricked him. Of course! He had been telling himself that if you just gave old Uncle Tim a chance to show off a little, you could kid him out of his bad temper. How nice and cheerful and pleasant a fellow could make everything—he had been thinking—when you knew which strings to pull with these simple-minded people?— Uncle Tim so ready, was he, to give the bum's rush to anybody who might so much as look at his Susan?—huh! You could make him forget all about her till somebody happened to mention her name—just turn the spotlight on his figure-skating and—but no, no, Timothy thought, distractedly, Canby knows nothing about Susan— I'm making all this up. I'm losing my mind. I *have* lost my mind. But he *did*—and *I* did . . . ! Well, anyhow, this is only Wednesday night. There's still plenty of time.

The meal was over. He stood up, hauled Aunt Lavinia to her feet with a mechanical gesture, said to Canby, "Will you drive her home, please? I've got something to work out in the office this evening. It may take me rather a long time."

"I'll drop you there, as we go by."

"I'd rather walk. Thanks."

He saw Canby, noting the dryness of his tone, give him an inquiring, speculative look, thought fiercely, "No, you don't, young man! Not a second time!" hunched on his overcoat, reached for his hat and was gone.

their tracks and were looking back in her direction, mouths gaping, as if they couldn't believe what they were hearing.

While their attention was diverted, Murphy made his move, but as he rushed past them a hand lashed out and he felt a stabbing pain in his side. He fell to one knee, expecting the next blow to slice through his throat. Then a sound halfway between a scream and a growl cut through the darkness and he heard the three men fall to the ground.

Isis was revving it up now, barking furiously and waving her thin arms in wide circles. Whatever she was saying, they seemed to have gotten the message. Throwing caution to the wind, Murphy scrambled past her and into the tunnel. He grabbed her arm and she turned a furious look on him as if she were outraged that a mere mortal had dared to manhandle a goddess.

"Come on, goddess, snap out of it," he whispered. "We've got to get out of here before your fan club realizes they've been had."

Isis laughed contemptuously but allowed him to steer her back the way they'd come. "I don't think they'll be going anywhere for a while. Not unless they want to end up as food for the scorpion men."

"I thought you didn't speak their lingo," Murphy said as he hustled her down the tunnel.

"It came to me eventually. A dialect of Terammasic. Dead for a thousand years supposedly."

"And you just happen to speak it?"

"I learned it at the university. Just for fun. It's such an oddity, I thought somebody ought to keep it alive."

"And what were you yelling at them? It got their attention all right."

They'd passed the fork and were rapidly approaching the junction where they'd entered the tunnels. Murphy couldn't hear any signs of pursuit.

"I just reminded them they owed their miserable existences to the creation goddess, and if they touched my familiar dog-spirit they'd be sorry."

Murphy boosted her onto the first rung. "Your dog-spirit? That's the best you could think of for me was your dog-spirit?"

"I was going to call you my snake-spirit, but I didn't think you look believably evil."

Chapter Twenty

HE walked rapidly up the hill as if he were due in his office for an appointment. Well, he was. An appointment with sanity, long over-due. Long? Was it possible that these idiotic chills and fevers had been going on only for three days? They had been endless with the uncountable endlessness of a nightmare. Now, he asked himself with as peremptory a summons as any he had ever issued to an excited or unruly boy, now what is the matter with me?

His mind made a hurried, feeble attempt to feint, "Chills and fevers and ups and downs—aren't they traditionally the lot of a man in love?" And more hurriedly yet, "It's only because Susan is away. Wait! Only three days more and she will be here, and then the nightmare will be over. There is nothing in it but longing for her. Nothing else."

That was too palpable a falsehood to stand an instant against the piercing look he gave it, aroused as he was now. Not out of lover's longing could come these deadly black gusts of hatred for a harmless good-natured boy. He gave them their real name—jealousy —and stood still in the snow, in the dark, astounded, incredulous, ashamed, enchanted.

I, Timothy Hulme, jealous! He had always despised jealousy. He despised it now. And was infinitely proud of it, proud of the un-controllable surge of hot blood at the mere sight of a possible rival. He had feared he was too old, too reasonable to love—he who was beside himself with this primitive madness of the blood. For it was a real madness, he recognized it as such, it had all of insanity's raging blindness to fact. The fact was that he was sure of Susan, a thousand times sure of himself, that there was no conceivable reason to pick out Canby to hate, that it was not Canby he hated, insignificant boy that he was, casually appearing for an hour in his life, it was any man who might conceivably stand in his path.

Yet it was against Canby that he felt this furious impulse to lower

255

his horns and like a passion-blinded stag charge an intruder. He was aghast at feeling himself out of hand. He gloried in it.

This is love, he thought, thrusting clenched hands deep into his pockets and rushing on up the hill, breathlessly. This is love that I never knew, never believed in. I accept it. I thank Heaven for it. If the insanity of jealousy is part of it, I accept that too.

He was panting when he reached the darkened Academy building, but he ran up the steps, unlocked the door and walked at top speed through the echoing corridor, with its musty smell of age and rubber overshoes and mice behind the walls. He opened the door to his office and went in. Without turning on a light, he took off his hat, dropped it on his desk, felt for his chair, and still standing, gripped the back of it hard with both hands—Now, he asked himself, I am jealous of Canby, yes. Does that mean I am to send him away before Susan comes back? Does it mean that I am to decide, not Susan, whom she is to see, to know? Does it? Does it?

At first the room was in complete darkness. But he needed no light to see what was there. Two decades had stamped on his visual memory every familiar detail, from the maze of cracks on the dingy ceiling to the scratches and heel-marks on the marred pine floor. He had no gift for the upholstering of life. In those twenty years he had done no more for his office than to hang on one whitewashed wall his father's photograph of the Holbein Erasmus, and—long after—on another, the yearning St. John the Baptist from Chartres. There was no rug, there had never been money to repaint the ugly gray woodwork, no curtains hung at the gaunt windows with their dozens of small greenish panes. An old pine table, a sheet of blotting paper on it was his desk. The four battered chairs were commonplace modern bent wood. Except for these, the big square room stood empty about him in the starlight, which, now that his eyes were widening to the darkness, came sifting thinly in, cold and faint, from the tall windows.

Empty? It was crowded, so full he had scarcely room to stand, full of the adolescents who for twenty years had come there when they were in trouble, bewildered by the hot throbbing of their young blood, able, only after he had shown them, to understand that they were facing for the first time one of life's myriad tempta-

"Thanks, I think."

"Murphy, I can go back and tell them you're a Biblical archaeologist if you'd prefer."

"On second thought, dog-spirit is just fine," Murphy grunted.

She slithered over the top and took the belly of the Serpent from him as he scrambled after her. Together they heaved the stone slab back into place and sat back against the wall, the bizarre world they had just left now banished like a terrifying dream.

"What do you think happened to that poor girl?" Isis said after a while.

Murphy held up a scrap of cloth. "It looks like she made it out. This is a bit of the dress she was wearing that was caught on a jagged edge of the handholds." He stared at Isis. With her eyes closed, her face still looked ghostly in the moonlight. "Nice work down there, Dr. McDonald. Quite a cabaret act you pulled off."

She bolted to her feet and started brushing the dust off her pants. "It was nothing. My father always said I was a reincarnation of some goddess or other. I guess it comes

tions to buy the heart's desire with a stain on honor. Here, in this room, under his leadership, they had taken their first groping steps away from childhood into responsibility, away from hide-and-seek and tag into the battle for untarnished good faith—the battle which had been raging up and down his life these three days that had seemed years. There they were, the tall, rawboned, anxious boys, wringing their big-knuckled hands and sweating, appalled at what it cost to be honorable men; the weeping girls, crying out that it would be like tearing their flesh with their own hands to try to live up to the cold inhuman standard of integrity. "I see what you mean, Professor Hulme. Yes, I suppose I ought to. I can see that's the right thing to do. But I can't, Professor! I just can't!" An echo of anguished young voices, faint and thin as the starlight, murmured quaveringly in his ear, "I can't, Professor Hulme! I just *can't!*"

But of course they could. And he could.

It was harder than he had thought. Harder than he had been able to conceive. But as he stood there in the dark, sweating and shivering, he felt—startled, helpless, frightened—yet with relief—the rising authority within him of the real master of his life. The captain of the ship came on deck at last, brushed aside with melancholy power the rage of passion and instinct, and read off from the old chart, the old course laid out on it, clear. It looked at first like no more than a small prim tag of family lore, ". . . an honorable man keeps his hands clean," but swept on to dignity with the added, "and accepts the consequences."

His mind, traitor and enemy always to what was beyond its grasp, came rushing in with astonished ridicule, "Oh, priggish conscience-complex! Moral coward! Puritan!" whatever insults it could snatch up most barbed and poisoned. "Since there is no danger from Canby, there's no question of ethics. This is a mock battle. The only question is why in the world a chance visitor should be allowed to intrude on the first days of your real life with Susan."

Yes. That was true. Rationally true in fact, that is. But he was groping for something far beyond reason or fact, something as far beyond the traditional code of the Hulmes and the Coultons. He had it. "A man of decency leaves others free to make their own

naturally to me." She seemed embarrassed now, as if Murphy had seen her naked and they could never just be friends again in the same way as before. "Come on, let's get back to the hotel," she said. "I don't know about you, but I could do with a large glass of scotch."

Murphy didn't reply, and Isis wondered if he disapproved. She was about to tell him that she would drink a whole bottle if she felt like it, thank you very much, after what he'd put her through, when she noticed that his eyes were closed. Then, as she watched, he slid slowly down the wall until his head was resting in the dirt.

It was only then that she noticed the blood.

FIFTY-NINE

"MISS KOVACS IS here, sir."

Shane Barrington had been looking forward to her arrival at his office. "Send her in. And I do not wish to be disturbed."

The woman who stood in the doorway seemed subtly different from the Stephanie Kovacs who'd first walked into his office a month earlier. She still dressed in that provocative-but-don't-mess-with-me way, stilettos and a short skirt offset by her buttoned-up jacket and black turtleneck, and her carefully disordered hair and subtly applied makeup reinforced the image of an attractive woman who had more important things to do than look good. Her stride was still confident, assertive, stopping just short of aggressive as she walked to the single chair in front of his desk and sat down.

But her eyes told him she had undergone a dramatic change since they had last met. Instead of shining with that morally superior glow her viewers had come to love, they were dull and vacant, as if something behind them had died. They were the eyes of someone who'd sold her soul.

"Stephanie. Thanks for dropping by. I wanted to thank you personally for the work you've been doing."

She looked at him warily. "I'm sorry the church-bombing story didn't pan out. The FBI were hot for it at first, but now they've gotten all cautious. And Dean Fallworth is just a blowhard. Nothing he gave me was enough to nail Murphy the way you wanted. Believe me, I—"

Barrington waved a hand dismissively. "It's okay, Stephanie. You did well. We just wanted to free up some of Professor Murphy's time, plant some seeds in the public's mind. You'll be uncovering more revelations about our evangelical friends in time."

decisions. Yes, even the woman he loves. Yes, most of all the woman he loves."

Timothy Coulton Hulme relaxed his desperate grip on the back of his chair, reached into his pocket for a handkerchief, wiped his lips—there was blood on the lower one—blew his nose, put on his hat and went back to where he lived.

To his surprise Aunt Lavinia sat before the piano in the living-room, a music album open on the rack, her fingers, gnarled and crooked, stretched over the keys as they had not been in years. Timothy gave a quick glance around the room. She was alone. Canby was nowhere to be seen. She looked over her shoulder, dropped her hands and said, "Oh, Tim, come in here, will ye? Play me that Haydn Sonata your mother loved so much. I keep saying, you know, at the top of me voice, that machine-music's just as good. But comes a day—"

She got up and left the piano stool for him. He made no pretense that he did not remember that Sonata. It had been "Timothy's piece," so thoroughly taught him by his mother that he could, any night of his life, have risen from a sound sleep and found its tripping grace-noted first phrase at his fingers' end. He did not ask why his mother's sister had, this night, thought of that Sonata; he had long ago given up trying to understand why she did anything. Laying his hat on top of the piano, he sat down in his overcoat, and was off.

It was the adagio that reached him. He heard, as no more than a distant familiar tinkle, that light-footed, light-hearted stamping of the first movement. But the adagio—the darkened, troubled chords and groping sequences, yes, that he heard. And he heard his mother's voice, saying again what she had once so gravely said to her schoolboy son about life and the adagio—was it after all to her middle-aged son she had meant to say it?

How short that dense, weighty passage was, with its recognition of sorrow and uncertainty. His fingers had taken him through its shadow already, and had brought him out again into the same flowery meadow beside the same silvery brook—but yes, yes, his mother was right. Here—after the darkness of the adagio—there was a new depth and meaning to what had been but cheerfulness.

258

"That'll do! That'll do!" cried Aunt Lavinia from behind him. "I don't want any more."

He dropped his hands from the keys, turned around, saw that she was struggling to rise from her chair, and sprang to help her. "You sound too much like your mother!" she told him, her voice quavering, her eyes rimmed with the red which is old age's repellent, pathetic, substitute for tears. "You play it just as she did!"

"Well, of course. She taught me."

Leaning heavily on his arm, she began to stumble toward the stairs. "Whatever possessed me to ask you to play that of all things," she questioned herself gloomily, "when every note of it is full of Margaret?"

They started up. She stopped on the second stair. "Tim, you haven't forgotten your mother?"

"No! I haven't forgotten her."

She toiled slowly up, his supporting arm around her. After a time she said under her breath, "It's that I never learned to live with sorrow." They came finally to the door of her room. He opened it, turned on her light with one hand, helped her to a chair, and looked at her intently. Her hands and face were clean, her white hair was almost in order, there was not in her eyes that special expression, the faint disquieting glitter he had come to recognize as a danger signal. It would be safe to leave her. She looked only very old and tired and sad. This was not one of her bad times.

She closed her eyes, leaned her head back and turned it a little from side to side. "Everybody has that to learn," she murmured, "and I never did." She opened her eyes. "Tim, have you learned that?"

"I don't know, Aunt Lavinia."

She closed her eyes again. In a moment, "Would you like me to help you get to bed?" he asked gently.

"Whatever makes you think I'm going to bed?" she said with spirit. "Not at all. I'm going to have—what's the most different from Hadyn there is—Tim, put on that Chopin Nocturne."

"Now, Aunt Lavinia, don't you go listening to Chopin," he pleaded. "Not to a Nocturne anyhow! You'll be so cross there'll be no living in the house with you."

She began trying willfully to claw herself out of her chair to do

259

Stephanie regarded him with the weary indifference of someone who's already lost the most important thing she has. "You said 'we.' I've been wondering who's really behind all this. You don't strike me as the type who gets hot under the collar about religion, Mr. Barrington."

He smiled. "Ever the fearless investigative reporter. I guess that bloodhound's nose of yours never stops sniffing. Even when I've got you chained and muzzled," he added, enjoying the sudden blush that colored her cheeks.

He got up and went to a smoked-glass cabinet. "Let me get you a drink."

She shook her head. "Not while I'm working."

He laughed. "Come on." He took out a dark bottle and began untwisting the wire holding the cork in place. "A glass of champagne."

"Champagne? Are we celebrating something?"

"I hope so, Stephanie. I very much hope so."

He eased the cork into a napkin with a muffled pop and poured two glasses. She accepted hers expressionlessly.

it herself, so he put the record on and left her, breathing hard and looking scornful, as she listened to its moist self-pity.

He went on up to his study. But he did not, when he sat down at his desk, pull towards him the pile of bills and letters and reports that meant work. He leaned back in his chair, put his hands behind his head, and tried to relax. "The thing to do," he told himself, "the only thing to do is to be natural—to act naturally. To take what comes, as it comes. That's always the only sane thing to do—the best for everybody. No matter what the situation is."

It was in vain. The decision taken in his office had tautened his nerves till they sang like plucked fiddle-strings. Well, it might be just as well not to let down. Not yet.

The door across the hall opened, and Canby appeared. So he hadn't gone out as usual to find contemporaries. A book drooped from his hand. He was ready for bed, bare-footed, his hair more tousled than usual, one leg of his pajamas hitched up to the knee. "Say, Uncle Tim, can I talk to you a minute? I see you're not working."

"Yes, Canby, of course." And he had been trying to let himself down!

He swung in his chair to face his visitor, who collapsed on the old cot-bed that served as bench when the Principal had a committee of students in this room. The book dropped from his hand to the floor. He let it lie. A pillow fell off the other end of the couch. He leaned far over, fumbling absently for it, lost his balance and all but fell himself, seized the pillow, slung it under his head, and stretched out on the cot, his bared leg, muscular and hairy, dangling loosely. His sprawling contortions had burst open the top of his pajama shirt which now gaped wide over his chest, broad, strongly arched and, like that brawny leg, covered with dark hair. Timothy, even in the days of his college gymnasium dressing-room, had never much cared for the looks of men with a great deal of hair on their bodies. He sat straight in his chair, a hand gripping each arm of it firmly, and waited.

Canby seemed in no hurry to speak. Finally, "Say, Uncle Tim, I've got the jitters tonight. Do you ever have the jitters?"

"I don't believe I know exactly what they are, Canby."

"You wouldn't," murmured Canby, turning his head sideways

260

"So what's the toast?"

He raised his glass toward her with a dark smile. "To marketplace domination, of course."

They clinked glasses. "I'll always drink to that," she said wryly.

He put his glass down and leaned against the desk. She was uncomfortably aware of his closeness.

"It could soon be a reality, Stephanie. Barrington Communications is the most powerful communications business on the planet, as you know. But that's just the beginning. Soon there could be so much more."

She looked at him skeptically. "What are you going to do, run for president?"

"I'm talking about *real* power, Stephanie. The sort you can only dream about."

She took a sip of her champagne. "Well, here's to you, Mr. Barrington. But I don't understand what this has got to do with me."

"Please, call me Shane." He stood and walked to the window. "Power and wealth can bring you many things, Stephanie. But I'll be honest, it can be lonely at the top. There have been women, of course, since

to look at the erect figure in the chair. "Well, I'll tell you. It's like something putrid in the air—see?—that you smell everywhere you go—and it makes you sick to your stomach—and scares you for fear it's something rotten in you to make the smell—scares you so you don't dare turn your head to see." He shoved and burrowed his head farther back into the pillow, gazing up at the ceiling. "God knows this baby don't have to look far inside him to see something rotten. Say, look-a-here, Uncle Tim, is there something about me that makes you not *want* me to stay around? I've had a kind of a notion lately that you didn't. Wouldn't surprise *me* any. I know I'm no good. Why *should* a person want me around? I wouldn't, if I was anybody else."

Without hesitation, without haste, Timothy said steadily, "I've wondered sometimes whether it was the best thing for you, Canby." He was ashamed of the priggish turn of his phrase.

But Canby apparently did not take it as priggish. "Oh, *that* was it," he said. "Well, I wonder too, you bet. Sometimes I think the best thing I could do would be to go jump off the Crow Rocks, and get it over with." He hitched himself up sideways and surmised, "Maybe what's burning me is that Mildred business. That was the worst goddamned mess! If I got into that, how do I know I got sense enough not to get into something worse, see?" He looked over at the man sitting straight in his armchair by the desk and suggested, "Maybe I was all off about Mildred anyhow. Sometimes, the last few days, I've kind of wondered. Maybe that was all a person can expect out of getting married. Uncle Tim, do you think that is all a person can expect?"

Timothy took time to consider. "No, I don't believe I do, Canby," he said seriously.

"Do you mean that?" Canby was asking for a real answer.

Timothy took a deep breath. "Yes, I do mean it."

Canby wriggled uneasily. "But there was really more to it than I let on when I told you about it. I was bluffing myself along, sort of. You'd have thought to hear me talk, I hadn't *ever* had any use for Mildred. But at the start I guess I was kind of crazy about her. I was . . . I'm . . . You might not think it, Uncle Tim, but damned if I don't miss her—in a way—sometimes. Once in a while I feel sort of like the dog that's been shut out of the house where the

my divorce, but when you have as much money as I do, it's hard to find someone you can really trust. Someone you can really share with. Do you understand what I'm talking about?"

She was beginning to think she understood completely. He'd bought her soul, and now he wanted the rest of her. Her first instinct was to panic, but then she started to think about it. Maybe it wouldn't be such a bad deal. If she was going to sell out, she might as well get the best price. Barrington seemed to think he was going to be king of the world. She could do worse than be his queen.

She walked over to him and together they looked down over the city. After a while an image from her recent bout of Bible study came into her mind. Satan and Jesus on the mountaintop. Hadn't he offered Him the kingdoms of the world if He would just bow down and worship him?

She leaned her head on Barrington's shoulder. Well, she was smarter than that. Mr. Barrington...Shane...wouldn't even have to ask her twice.

SIXTY

ISIS WATCHED DR. AZIZ disappear into the elevator, bulging black bag tucked under his arm, and closed the door behind her. At the last count she spoke a dozen varieties of Arabic as well as another ten distinct Near and Middle Eastern languages, adding up to who knew how many millions of words. But she was beginning to realize that only one really mattered.

Baksheesh.

For a few dollars, the young man at the front desk had been happy to call Dr. Aziz, assuring them he was "very discreet." And the doctor himself, for another reasonable consideration, had been delighted to patch Murphy up. As she ushered him out, he'd given Isis an old roué's gold-toothed grin. "No police, no police!" he said, putting a finger to his lips.

Whether she could trust either of them not to play both ends of the street and bring the cops running, she didn't know. If it came to it, she and Murphy hadn't done anything illegal, had they? As far as she knew, they hadn't killed anybody, and as for taking the belly of the Serpent, it was hard to say whom it really belonged to. She was beginning to think Hezekiah had had the right idea: It would be better if no one had it.

She leaned back against the door, her body suddenly heavy. "You'll live, apparently. He's given me some nasty-looking painkillers which I think are probably for horses, but seeing as you're stubborn as a mule...Murphy?"

His eyes were closed and he looked very pale, but she thought she could see the slow rise and fall of his breathing. She approached the bed and felt an impulse to

folks are, prowling around in the cold by himself, and looking in at the windows, if you see what I mean. Nobody ever told me that a person'd feel the cold more after he'd been in by the fire. Or thought he was. I kind of miss *something* anyhow."

Against the sickening lurch of the deck under his feet the captain of the ship braced himself with his whole strength, his hands rigid on the spokes of the steering wheel. "Canby," said Timothy Hulme, conversationally, "did you ever happen to get interested in the effect on human feelings of change in barometric pressure? I'm always seeing instances of it. Perhaps this is one: the weather report in today's Ashley *Record* says we're in for the first big spring thaw and rain. Now every year, after the long bracing February cold, the first thaw lets everybody's nerves down. I found Aunt Lavinia with—what did you call them—the jitters—when I came in just now. Maybe yours came from that too."

"Is that really so? Well, maybe then . . ." said Canby, with lively twentieth-century relief in a materialistic explanation for an emotion. "Yes, maybe you're right. I hadn't thought of that." He rolled over and got up on his great bare feet, as lacking in distinction and as powerful as his hands. "Sure! I can see just how that would be." But he did not go off to bed. He hung there, propping his head against the sloping ceiling. "All the same, Uncle Tim, all the same, I don't honestly believe you can lay it all on the barometer. I guess the point is I wish I could fix me up some kind of life like yours. Don't get me wrong. Not teaching. I'd be a hell of a teacher and I'd hate it. But a job that'd have some sense to it, that'd move a person on tomorrow a little farther towards where anybody'd want to go than he is today—if you get me." He leaned over to shake loose the pajama-leg that was caught up, murmuring under his breath, "I'm sort of sick of just millin' around and millin' around." He stood up, asked, "What I want to know is why can't I be on my way? You've been, ever since I was a kid. And look where you've got to," and shuffled towards the door.

To his back Timothy said encouragingly, "Why, Canby, you've all the time in the world. You forget I'm fifty years older than you are."

Canby turned around in the door to laugh at this, saw that

Timothy's face was serious, stopped laughing and asked uncertainly, "What d'you mean by that?"

"Mean?"

"*You're* not fifty years older than I am."

"Did I say fifty? That was a slip of the tongue, of course. I meant—I meant twenty."

touch him. *Just to make sure he's really alive,* she told herself.

His skin was cool but she could definitely feel the blood pulsing just above his collarbone. "Good night, Murphy," she whispered. "Pleasant dreams."

Returning to her own room, she lay on the bed and closed her eyes for a few minutes, letting the confusing rush of emotions swirl around her head. Eventually she took a long breath, blew it out slowly, and sat upright. Work. That was the only way to regain her equilibrium.

She poured herself a glass of Famous Grouse, arranged a dozen sharpened pencils next to a stack of yellow legal pads, then placed the belly of the Serpent in the pool of light cast by the desk lamp. It was going to be a long night.

She awoke to the sound of glass breaking. Yellow pages blew around the room in gusts as the wind poured in through the open window. The bedclothes had been blown aside, leaving her shivering. The lamp lay on the floor, flickering on and off with the fizz of frayed circuits.

Someone was hammering on the door and she instinctively reached down to cover herself. Her hand felt the soft cotton of her nightgown. Confused, she reached for the bedside light.

Everything was in its place. The lamp was on the desk. The pages in a neat pile, with the Serpent on top. The window was closed. Apart from her ragged breathing, all was silent.

Laughing with relief, she went to the desk and read what she'd written on the top sheet. At least she hadn't dreamed that. She read it through one more time, trying to fix it in her mind, then climbed between the sheets. She was asleep before she could recite it to herself.

The next morning Murphy showed no signs of his ordeal. As she joined him at the only occupied table in the cavernous restaurant, he was happily feasting on rolls and coffee.

"You seem very chipper," she said.

He winked. "Sleep of the just."

"Well, take it easy. Dr. Aziz said you should stay in bed for a couple of days at least."

Murphy snorted. "He was just hustling you for a few more bucks, making it look like it was life-and-death. It's just a scratch. Anyhow, we have work to do."

She reached into her bag with a look of triumph. "Relax. All done."

He took the wrinkled piece of paper and read it through. "I'm beginning to think your father was right about you. Didn't you sleep at all?"

She studied the tablecloth. "It didn't take long."

"And you're sure you've got it right?"

She tried to snatch the sheet of paper back, but he whisked it out of reach. "Just kidding." He read it through again. "*In the land of the flood, it rests with a queen.* 'The land of the flood.' That could be the Biblical Flood."

She nodded. "Plenty of references to that in Babylonian literature. The question is, where exactly is it?"

"A lot of people think the Ark came to rest on Mount Ararat. Maybe Anatolia, then. Any queens we know of in that neigh-borhood?"

"Not in the right time frame. Too far north."

Chapter Twenty-one

IN the middle of the night Timothy opened his eyes wide on the thought, "I'm an idiot! I don't have to wait till Sunday! She's not five hours' drive from me. I'll go over tomorrow!"

The thought brought him an extraordinary release from the pain and tension of the last few days; he felt his pulses slow down to a regular beat; the jolting chaos of life re-arranged itself for him quietly in the harmonious pattern which always flowed from any thought of Susan; he fell asleep so soundly that he awoke only to the shriek of the morning train at Lathrop's Crossing. Nine o'clock! He stretched, yawned, felt himself infinitely refreshed, and still rocked in that beautiful long Susan-rhythm, rolled slowly out of bed and went to close the window.

In front of it there was a pool of water. It was raining! Pouring. The first time since November. A wild wind was lashing the water against that side of the house. The weather report had been right. The spring thaw was here. Well, let it come, he thought cheerfully, he could drive in the rain as well as any man. His eye took in the fact that the clouds hung low and very dark over The Wall and Hemlock Mountain, but his frivolous mind, never on duty when it was really needed, tossed the observation unheeded upon the pile of mere miscellaneous facts. Nor did it stop trilling and cutting happy capers of anticipation when, on going down to cold coffee and congealed bacon, Timothy found Canby had long since gone out for an all-day skiing expedition with four or five of the boys who had gathered, fascinated, around him.

"Canby's crazy," remarked Timothy casually to Aunt Lavinia. "You can't ski in the rain!"

Aunt Lavinia, who had never troubled herself to acquire even the most obvious Clifford lore, did not say as anyone else would have said, "But this rain may be snow on the mountains." She said

264

instead, "I *wish* I could find a decent accompanist for Jules. You can't imagine the comfort that boy is to me. The first soul with musical sense I've ever seen in this benighted town."

He did not know the name or address of the over-the-mountain Barney kinsfolk Susan and Delia had gone to visit. But this troubled him not at all. Miss Peck must know. He drove to her house to ask, so careless of what anyone might surmise from his wishing to know where to find Susan Barney that his natural easy manner suggested to Miss Peck only the idea that he wished, as Superintendent, to send her as teacher, some notice about her school work. Hence she, like Aunt Lavinia, did not mention the obvious fact that this driving downpour of cold early March rain was probably a snowstorm higher up on the mountain passes.

It was only when he drove his Ford to the garage for gas and oil that someone among the men lounging there on tipped-back chairs called out, "Did I hear you say you were startin' to drive to Averfield, Professor Hulme? I don't figger anybody can git over the mountain today. If it's a-snowin' up there the way it's a-rainin' here and a-blowin' too . . ."

Timothy flung up an instant barrier against the idea, "Why, we're almost through the first week of March!"

With no change of expression, the elderly lounger turned to the man next to him, "Ezry, d'y remember the time they busted the Ashley Town snowplow t'flindereens?"

"Town meeting day?"

"No, tryin' to open the road so folks could git to old Mis' Bassett's funeral."

"Oh, yes, sure. Eighth o' March, wa'n't it?"

"Nope. Tenth. I remember for sure because that was the day my uncle got his arm broke choppin' down to . . ."

"You might phone up to Barton Corners and ask," suggested the proprietor of the garage. "Nelson Ellsworth's house is the last one before you start over the mountain. He's in the phone book."

The voice at the other end of the wire said complacently it should rather think the road over the mountain was closed—the Highway Patrol said the snow was ten feet deep up there—in the drifts,

265

"Okay, maybe he didn't mean *the* Flood, just a place where it floods regularly."

She poured herself a cup of tea and stirred in some milk. "Like where?"

"How about Egypt? The Nile floods every year like clockwork. Without it there would have been no Egyptian civilization. No Sphinx, no pyramids."

"Makes sense. Read the next bit."

"Entombed by stone, it floats in the air." Murphy shook his head. "Beats me."

She put down her cup. "Hold on. If you're right and Dakkuri's talking about Egypt, then entombed by stone, resting with a queen, that must mean it's in a pyramid, right?"

"Right."

"Come on, you're the archaeologist. How many pyramids are there?"

"More than you'd think."

"But this is no ordinary pyramid."

He slapped his hand on the table and a waiter scurried out of the kitchen to see what was wrong. Isis waved him back with a frown.

"Ever heard of the Pyramid of the Winds?"

"Can't say that I have. Are you sure you haven't just made it up?"

He grinned. "It exists all right. On the Giza plateau just west of Cairo, all by its lonesome. Not close enough to the big three—Khufu, Khafre, and Menkure—to get onto the postcards, so no one pays it much attention."

"So how come the fancy name?"

"According to legend, there's supposed to be some sort of updraft in the center of the pyramid, so powerful it could keep a man suspended above the ground forever."

"A man...or the head of a bronze Serpent," she said.

"Why not. If I remember correctly, it's also the last resting place of Queen Hephrat the Second."

"Bingo! *Entombed by stone but floating in air.* So what do we do now?"

"We take a look inside, of course. Come on."

Back in Murphy's room, she watched over his shoulder as he fired up his laptop and logged into a database in the Preston University mainframe. After a few seconds, a complex diagrammatic of the Pyramid of the Winds unfolded across the computer screen, revealing the interior in three dimensions.

Isis pointed at the series of square holes ringing the base of the pyramid. "What are those?"

"Air shafts. Air is drawn into the great chamber—that's the big empty space at the center of the pyramid, above Hephrat's burial chamber—and it comes out here, these smaller holes two-thirds of the way up."

"That's very impressive. Trust the ancient Egyptians to invent air-conditioning three thousand years before the fact."

"Only for royalty," Murphy said. "And even they had to be dead first. Maybe that kind of logic explains why Egyptian civilization didn't last."

Isis gave him a wry smile. "So where does the legend about things floating in midair come from?"

"I barely remember my high school physics, but here's my theory. The air is drawn in through the shafts at the bottom. Inside the great chamber it heats up, rises, and gets compressed as the pyramid narrows. That increases its velocity and sends it

that is—telephone and telegraph wires all down. Snow's wet. They can't do nothin' with it.

"Good Heavens," said Timothy indignantly, slamming the receiver down on its hook, "there must be some way to manage! What do the doctors do?"

"Nobody on that road to git sick," came from the row of tipped-back chairs, "till you're most into Turners Four Corners on the other side, and they gotta doctor."

The garage mechanic, his slicker streaming with water, came in from outside to say, "Man just went by says eight cars stuck in the snow on the road up t' The Gap."

"March snow, now," said the elderly lounger, "it's wet. You can't do nothin' with it."

Professor Hulme turned to stalk out of the garage. "But it don't last long!" called the mechanic consolingly to his back. "Be all right by tomorrow."

He got into his Ford, started the engine, and sat irresolute. What should he do with the day? His heart was already halfway there. He called it back and drove home. His mind ventured timidly, afraid of suggesting the wrong thing, to remind him that after all March storms never did last long, and that by tomorrow the snow-plows would be out, and the roads cleared. It was poor comfort. But there was no other.

Aunt Lavinia's music-machine was playing Brahms when he went in. It reminded him of Susan. Anything would have reminded him of her. He climbed to his study and sat down at his desk, not to work, but to think of Susan. After all, this delay could not last more than a day. And what is a day to a man of forty-five? The certainty that he would see her tomorrow took his imagination in a leap over the mountain to the house that sheltered her. Waiting for her to come down the stairs into his arms, he remembered very faintly, as though it were bad-dream stuff, all that pother about Canby. The future seemed as firmly in his grasp as the past. Leaning back in his chair, basking in the beauty of the music and the irrational peace that comes with a decision taken, he thought of his love and fell into daydreams.

That first note he had had from her, thanking him for something or other—a book, a magazine—he had left with Aunt Lavinia. He

rushing out of the shafts at the top, at the same time sucking in more air from below. Kind of an endless cycle."

"So you think the head of the Serpent is going to be floating in midair in the great chamber?"

"I doubt that. My bet is it's either in the burial chamber or more likely one of the air shafts."

Isis studied the screen with a skeptical expression. "You know I said I wasn't claustrophobic, but those air shafts look rather narrow to me. How are we going to . . . ?"

Murphy tapped some more keys and the Pyramid of the Winds disappeared. In its place a rotating graphic of what looked like some kind of high-tech vacuum cleaner filled the screen.

"Behold the Pyramid Crawler. A remote-controlled robot specifically designed for navigating the air shafts of pyramids."

"You're joking. Somebody actually makes these things?"

"Sure. I don't know if it's the iRobot Corporation's biggest seller, but right now it's just what we need. What color paint-

remembered every one of its stiff rustic little phrases, "I want you should know how much I like it." "I surely appreciate what you . . ." He laughed out to remember that he had been imbecile enough to find something uncouth in them. Why, they were adorable, delicious, fresh with the new angular young grace of a Primitive.

And the day he had given her a box of candy (the first, he guessed that she had ever had for herself), he smiled again, enchanted by the memory of the honest childish gluttony in her face as she leaned in gloating anticipation over the sweets. How thin-blooded he had been before, with his fastidious revulsion from greediness.

He remembered how, during these last momentous weeks, his need for her had risen in a swelling floodtide, carrying him far beyond any watermarks set by reasonableness, till he was, half an hour after he had left her, as famished for the sight and sound of her as he was this instant, after five days of separation. Once in a while she had not come, in the evening, for her music lesson from Aunt Lavinia. Could he, although he had seen her only three hours before at the supper table, go to bed without hearing her voice again? He could not. Yet when he had made an excuse to stop in at Miss Peck's to see her, or to call her on the telephone, what was there in their quiet talk to calm his ache of longing and restlessness? Nothing. Magic was at work. "Well, I'll try that reading book with the children tomorrow, Mr. Hulme, if you say." Or, "I'm sure there's something the matter with the way I'm doing the outside-edge bracket. I fell all over the ice this afternoon whenever I tried it." The most ordinary phrases, because they were said in her voice, sent him to bed comforted and quieted like a hungry man who has been fed.

The turn of that phrase made him, unashamed of his homely male materialism, think of the savory food that Susan had put on his table the day when they celebrated Miss Peck's birthday by giving her at the Principal's house a meal she had neither planned nor prepared. That had been a feast for the eye, the heart, the palate. Aunt Lavinia was in a new dress, a pretty one of lavender wool, without a grease spot on it, her white hair neatly brushed, her whole person exhaling the washed, well-cared-for decency which Susan alone could produce. Susan had been flushed, bright-eyed, anxious,

267

work do you want? I think the choices are dark gray or a slightly darker gray."

Isis was reading the product specifications: a computer-controlled, quadra-tracked vehicle with two sets of tank treads arranged one on top of the other, so one set was pushed against the floor of the shaft and the other against the ceiling, providing stone-gripping traction. An array of sensors, lights, and miniature TV cameras completed the picture.

"Let's say you can get hold of one of these things. I still don't see how we're going to get access to the pyramid. I know you're not a stickler for red tape, but you can't just hire a camel or two and start digging, you know."

He looked offended. "You think I don't have connections? Ever heard of Dr. Boutrous Hawass, the director of the pyramids? Well, my best buddy at grad school was a man called Jassim Amram. Now he's a professor of archaeology at the American University in Cairo and just happens to be Hawass's right-hand guy. If I know Jassim, he's already got one of these Pyramid Crawlers trained to mix a decent martini and bring it to him in front of the TV."

watching Miss Peck as she tasted critically, and elated to naive strutting when Miss Peck admitted, "Not bad. Not what a person would really call *bad* at all." What coffee they had had that day! Timothy had marveled aloud at the miracle which had produced coffee like that in his kitchen.

It occurred to him now, remembering the nectar that Susan's coffee had been, that perhaps it was all part of the astonishingly vivid keenness with which he lived whenever he was with Susan. All his senses were sharpened, accurate, alert; not only to her in every smallest detail, but to that part of the world where she stood. His eyes took in the soft Luini-like *morbidezza* of her fine-textured skin as intimately as if his hands had already stroked it. And the smoke-lightness of her hair—would his mortal hands ever caress that hair, ever untie the knot of ribbon that held it back, and let it float free like a cloud? He knew as if he had kissed them, her lovely eyebrows, sensitive, mobile, expressive as another woman's mouth, her eyes—he always lost his head when he looked into those gray eyes, honest, tender, attentive, miraculously unconscious of their beauty. But it was not only of these infinitely familiar, ever-new aspects of her face that he was newly aware when with her, it was to everything around her. He could close his eyes—he did now, dreamily—and see the steep-sloping hill, its grasses grayed by frost, see the glitter of sun reflected from the ice on which she glided, see the very grain in the wood of the table on which she leaned with both brown young hands, looking down at photographs of Chartres and the Medici Chapel. He passed them in review now, the well-remembered backgrounds of every time when he had seen her, marveling at the heaping up of such wealth in his bare life.

Far behind it, almost invisible, Canby awkwardly lumbered about on the ice, sprawled gracelessly in a chair, leaned against a wall, hot, sweaty, defeated, commonplace, and flinging his wet mittens down on the stairs with the spiteful gesture of a bad-mannered boy.

And with how absurd an alacrity—he laughed aloud at another memory—did the visible world and its meaning transform itself when she looked at it, as on the day when, to please Fred Kirby, he had stepped in to see St. Andrew's being hung with its annual Christmas decorations. He had been in one of his soured, barren moods, and had thought, "They'd better be doing something useful," as he went through the vestibule of the church filled with heaped-up branches of hemlock and spruce, where the women of the parish toiled to shape them into wreaths and ropes. Inside the half-decorated nave, where tall boys stood tip-toe on stepladders to hang the wreaths on the same old nails, he had glowered ungraciously about him, finding the Christmas greens shaggy, formless, depressing. If you were going to decorate in winter, why choose one of the darkest gloomiest colors in nature? What senseless conservatism and slavery to tradition it was, to keep laboriously on with a custom the meaning of which had long since been forgotten by everyone.

Then Susan had come in, rosy from the cold, her eyes shining, and had smiled at him—good heavens! what *could* it be about her smile that threw him into such foolish glowing bliss?—had smiled around her at the decorations, had said they were "just lovely," and what fun it had been to go to the woods for them, and the church looked sweeter every Christmas, didn't it? And his eyes were opened; he saw that the greens were vibrant with vitality, that they alone of all the winter world had held out against the worst that cold could do, that they were—how could he not have seen it before?—a beautiful, time-worn symbol of life enduring, all the more perfect as folk-poetry because its meaning no longer lay on the surface for the literal-minded to see.

A bell was being rung, he heard its clang faintly in the distance. What bell could that be? Not the doorbell. Its clatter quickened, as if it were being rung in impatience. Could it possibly be lunch time! He looked at his watch, and laughing delightedly over his morning, ran downstairs to be scolded by Aunt Lavinia. "You work too hard in vacation time! You've got as good a right as anybody to have a rest. Sitting up there, slaving over their stupid letters! Let them go! What do you care? You fuss too much about the people here, anyhow."

He nodded absently, serving the hash which was Lottie's almost unvarying offering for lunch. There was a silence. Then looking at the rain, clinging in sibilant sheets to the windowpanes, he said, to make a little talk, "I heard at the garage that this storm is snow on the mountain passes."

"All right," Isis said, opening the door. "You fix things up with your friend Professor Amram and I'll track down our pilot and tell him to get us ready to depart for Cairo."

Murphy had closed the laptop and was already throwing clothes into his backpack. "Sounds good."

The phone rang. It was a secretary's voice. "Oh, thank God, Dr. McDonald. Please hold for Chairman Compton of the Parchments of Freedom Foundation."

"Isis." Harvey Compton sounded rather tense, Isis thought. He was probably worried that she had scuffed up the interior of his airplane. She rushed to assure him he was getting his money's worth. "Harvey, we've got the second piece and have our eyes set on the head of the Serpent."

"Yes, well, never mind that. I've been trying to reach you. Two people have been murdered here and the tail of the Serpent has been stolen. Isis, you and Professor Murphy must abandon your trip and come home immediately."

SIXTY-ONE

STRANGE. STRANGE AND horrible. The murders of the two guards had occurred literally a world away, yet, because they were the real lives of men she had worked with, she was devastated.

"Isis, I'm sorry I got you and the foundation into this." Murphy knew it was no consolation. "Chairman Compton is right, of course, we must head back."

Isis sat staring at the wall. "Murphy, we're not going back. Not now. Especially not now. Whoever, whatever force is trying to take over the Serpent must be stopped."

"Isis, you're in shock. You are in greater

danger than we even knew here in Tar-Qasir, and that was no kindergarten outing. Pack up."

"No, Murphy. We're staying the course. Chairman Compton is too far away to shut us down now. Besides, there is something I haven't told you about the scene at the foundation."

"What?"

"Murphy, whoever took the Serpent's tail was pretty brazen himself. He took the time to leave what could only be a taunting message for you. He carved the symbol of a snake into the metal shelf on which the tail had been kept. It was a snake broken into three pieces."

Murphy walked to the window. After a few moments' reflection, he turned and said, "Well, whoever came after the Serpent's tail is well aware of our quest. Of the few people whom we have confided in about the details of what we're seeking, none of them are murderers or thieves."

"At least up to now, you mean. There's obviously something about this Serpent that over the centuries has made lots of people do lots of strange things."

"What is that to me?" asked Aunt Lavinia, who detested chat—except when she herself began it.

He fell back contentedly to his dreams.

Canby had not been expected to lunch. But he had not come back by the time Timothy took Aunt Lavinia down to the Peck house for their evening meal. Nobody at the supper table felt concerned. The storm had been violent, even for March. Probably, the older people drinking their tea thought, the skiers had made slow work of finding their way. Perhaps were lost. That would be no more than an amusing adventure for them, since even on the mountain it could not be really cold. It was barely below freezing here in the valley; just enough to turn the rain into sleet and to make trouble with telephone wires, not enough to be noticed by vigorous, warmly-clad young men. Miss Lane thought that they would have taken the short cut, down the far end of the mountain, into Ashley. They were probably there this minute, she said, unable to telephone home because the storm had broken the wires, unable to get a car to bring them back to Clifford because the road gang had not yet sanded the icy roads.

But Mr. Dewey's opinion was that the young men would not try to get back at all that night, but would make themselves a camp with a big bonfire and take turns sleeping around it. "Why not? 'T'ain't cold. A bunch of boys. Do'm good. At their age." He spoke with open envy.

"Do you think, Mr. Dewey," Timothy reverted to his own plans, "that the Highway Department will have the roads cleared by to-morrow? The road over the mountain, I mean."

"Sure thing," said Mr. Dewey. "March storms don't amount to a row o' pins for all their hollering. I remember one night when I got caught out on old Hemlock late in March, and a big storm of this wet snow came up. I was all alone but I fixed me up a lean-to of pine branches and a fire, and when I woke up at half past two in the morning, the . . ." He stopped, put his hand to his ear, asked in a startled voice, "What was that? Did you hear something? Seems as though I heard the front door open." They all turned their heads towards the hall, and distinctly heard the front door carefully closed.

270

"Maybe that's Canby now," said Aunt Lavinia.

But nobody came in. There was no sound from the hall. They looked at each other with eyes dilated in astonishment, in uncertainty. There was something taut and troubling about the silence.

The owner of the house half rose from her chair. Mr. Dewey called peremptorily, "Who's there? Who opened that door?"

Fact was there—raw elemental fact, not to be ignored by self-control, not to be held at arm's length by reasonableness, stonily hard and actual fact, crashing across that ordered rational world like a landslide sweeping away all traces of a well-kept road. Chance it was that had opened the door, senseless incalculable chance, its great wheel mockingly crushing human logic and forethought down to dust. Quick light steps hurrying with a sinister softness down the hall brought melodrama into decent self-contained lives which always muffled and turned a deaf ear to their drama, and resolutely refused to admit—for them—the possibility of melodrama.

Anson Craft, Dr. Anson, towered over them as they sat at the table, gaping up, stricken to paralysis by his words, by his nervous energetic gesture commanding silence. He leaned over the table, speaking in a low voice. "An accident," he told them. "Car tipped over on the mountain. The girl that works here is hurt. Badly. No getting her to the hospital, the roads are so icy." As he spoke he flung off his glistening wet slicker, let it fall in a heap, dropped his hat beside it, looked towards the hall and said, "This way." Turning back to Miss Peck, "Is that the door to your bedroom? *Don't stir*— leave it just as it is. My wife has come to take charge of the case. She'll do anything that's needed in the room. *Now!*—not a sound out of any of you!"

Mrs. Craft was there, swift, noiseless, slipping out of her wraps as she crossed to the door of Miss Peck's bedroom. She opened it, stepped in and turned on the electric light. "Here," she said in her controlled nurse's voice to the man who came shuffling in from the hall, a woman in his arms, her head resting on his shoulder. It was turbaned with white bandages, crisscrossed over the face. Only the mouth and chin showed below the swathing cheesecloth. They were marble white.

"Yes, you would have to think that it's not some rival archaeologist who would murder and steal for that tail. So, we can assume that whoever is onto us is working the decidedly dark side of the street."

Isis had a worried look in her eyes as she reached for Murphy's hand before she added the final news. "Murphy, there's something else I have to tell you about the scene at the foundation. Remember what you told me about the cross necklace you gave Laura, and how someone had broken it at the funeral when you took your last look into her casket? Well, carved right next to the snake on the PFF shelf, the same maniac carved a cross broken into three pieces."

Murphy sat in shocked silence. Then he walked over to the wall and banged his fist as hard as he could three times. "Worst suspicions confirmed. It's all starting to make a bizarre kind of sense. All of the signs are pointing to one mysterious connecting element to so many of the events we've been going through. The stranger coming to Preston and teaming up with Chuck Nelson for trouble, the bombing at the church, the

At the gasping indrawn breath of horror from those sitting at the table, Dr. Craft motioned again—with savage irritability this time—for silence. Canby, setting one foot before the other with trancelike carefulness, walked slowly across the room, in through the open door, and came out without his burden, his face broken and quivering. Dr. Craft went in, turned to lay a stern finger on his lips. The door closed.

Miss Peck, rising, motioned them away from the table, out through the swinging doors towards the kitchen. They followed her through the big pantry, turned, passed through other swinging doors into the dish-closet, and came out into the kitchen. Miss Peck closed the door after them, and Canby burst out, in a hoarse whisper, "Gimme a drink somebody. For God's sake, I want a drink."

But there was no alcohol in that house. He glared around him as if ready to tear his drink out of them, standing gaping and aghast. Miss Peck turned, ladled up some soup from the kettle on the stove, and pushed him down before a full plate. He flung away the offered spoon, lifted the plate in both hands and drank down the steaming soup in three or four noisy gulps, holding out his plate for more with one hand, pushing his visored skiing cap from his head with the other. His thick hair was matted densely to his head. He had lost his glasses. A dark smear of blood crossed his forehead and ran down one cheek. There were three unshaded high-powered bulbs in the big kitchen. They all went on from one switch and they were all on now, pouring a brutal white glare down on the red-eyed haggard man at the table, and on the set, unnatural, paled faces of the people leaning over him, straining to catch what he told them in that loud insistent whisper, as he tried to eat, snatching at the food offered him as if he were famished, but pushing it away sickly, unable to swallow it—beside himself as if he were as drunk as he would have liked to be.

It did not take long for them to learn what had happened. At about noon Canby and the three Academy Seniors with him had just finished their sandwich lunch. "I guess we were up near the top of Wolf Hollow," he explained to Mr. Dewey. They had a drink all around out of the flask, which had emptied it—"me without any whiskey!" he groaned, striking his hand angrily on the table, "me without the smallest damn drop left in the flask!" They were start-

272

ing the trip back, but in the wild smother of snow they did not keep to their course very well—"just loping along wherever the going was good. It didn't make any real dif *where* we came out, we knew we'd have to cross the over-the-mountain road somewhere, and when we struck that we'd know where we were." It had stopped snowing—when, after a long quiet, gliding along a traverse course through the woods, they saw that, some distance before them, the road crossed their course, and that farther up, half covered with snow, a car lay on its side in the ditch. They called to each other, pointed it out, took for granted it had been abandoned and were about to turn and tack back along the slope they were on, when near it they saw something moving. With a rush they started up the hill, poling themselves as fast as they could, but slowly at that, for the slope was steep. "God! I thought we'd *never* get there!" As they climbed, panting, driving themselves to breathlessness, they could see a recurrent stir near the car, but could not at all make out what it was—a dog? A child? It was low to the ground. A person half-pinned under the car? And then they saw. A woman, her head wrapped around with bloody bandages, was trying to raise the car with the jack. "She'd get up on her knees for a minute, work the lever three or four times, and fall down again in the snow—but keeping at it, by God! half dead herself, but keeping at it! All alone there in the snow—not running away, not looking out for herself, not giving up—just gritting her teeth and doing what she could—a *girl!*" His voice broke on the word.

Then they had raced to reach her. "Like to've killed that Whitcomb kid—he all but passed out," and heard from her that a man was under the car. . . . "I thought then of course it must be her father, or husband, or something—that's all *I* knew!"—snatched her away from the jack and all heaving together lifted the car up enough to pull out from under it—"what do you think? A measly dirty little old French Canuck, with frizzly gray hair. She'd never laid eyes on him before that day. It seemed he was somebody's hired man that lived neighbor to her folks over where she'd been visiting. She'd started over with him from the other side because she wanted to come back from her vacation ahead of time, she'd heard he happened to be going to Ashley, and they hadn't the least idea over in their valley the storm was so bad." He stopped to draw in a great

273

theft of the tail—" His voice cracked as he thought about the final link.

Isis finished the thought. "The fact that Laura wasn't killed as a result of some debris falling on her. That she was definitely murdered."

"Isis, this is beyond archaeology, or even faith and validating the Bible now. It's personal. We're going to find the head of that Serpent if it kills us. And by keeping up our search, it's only a matter of time before we confront this evil stranger face-to-face."

SIXTY-TWO

"SO AFTER WE find the head of the Serpent, what then?"

Murphy was concentrating on the buzzing, dusty, glaring chaos that was Cairo as their taxi inched its way laboriously through the cars, bicycles, pedestrians, and occasional ox thronging the narrow streets. The question caught him off guard.

"I mean," Isis continued, "it's not as if you can put it back together. The man who broke into the foundation has got the tail now. I mean, I understand about authenticating the Biblical account. You could still do that with two pieces. But that's not why we're here, is it?"

She'd caught a little bit of sun since they'd been in the Middle East, and it suited her. She looked more confident, less like a creature of the dark ready to scurry back into her hole at the foundation at the slightest sign the outside world was getting too close. But he wasn't sure he wanted to deal with her new assertiveness just then.

"Proving the Bible is true is what I do. I can't think of anything more important."

She considered him skeptically, then reached for the door handle as the driver swerved to avoid an old man on a swaying bicycle. Regaining her equilibrium, she said, "No? What about prophecy? Biblical prophecy."

"That's part of it. If we can demonstrate that the Old Testament prophets were writing at the time they say they were, then that proves they were genuine."

"I don't follow."

Reluctantly, he turned his gaze away from the buzzing confusion of the streets. "Some of what they predicted has happened. Skeptics say that's because they were actually writing after the event, so they were looking backward, not forward. If we can show they were writing at the time they claimed, then that proves they really could see history in advance."

"And why is that so important?"

"Because of the predictions that *haven't* come true yet. So people can be sure they *will* happen."

She nodded as if he'd confirmed something she already knew. "Then tell me about the part of the Book of Daniel that hasn't come true yet."

"Daniel? I thought you were more interested in Marduk and Ereshkigal and all that crowd."

She looked at him with an intensity he hadn't seen before, and he realized he was being too harsh with her. For the first time, he noticed she wasn't wearing her amulet.

"I'm sorry. Yes, I'll tell you about Daniel if you like. But why now?"

"You told me your search for the Brazen Serpent began with a mysterious message about Daniel. I think that's what this is all about. That's what we're risking our lives

gulp of air and to crush half a slice of bread and butter into his mouth. But he gagged over it, and spit it out, his excitement still at the fury point. His face from having been very pale was now deeply flushed and his eyes bloodshot. Mr. Dewey asked if the man under the car had been killed. No, still breathing, Canby said, but unconscious, internally hurt probably. Well, what could be done there in the heaped-up snow, with two people badly injured? "And me with no whiskey!" Canby hammered on his temples at the thought. Impossible to get the car back in the road, and if they could, it could not have rolled a foot through the drifted snow, so greatly had the storm worsened since the accident.

It was the girl who, wiping out of her eyes the blood that continually trickled from under her improvised bandages, had asked if the skis couldn't be lashed together to make a narrow sled, a cushioned seat from the car tied on it, and the man placed on that and pulled down the hill over the drifts to a house and a telephone. "*She* thought of it—we dumbbells'd have been there till now! I was trying to think of some way to get'm *both* out, of course. And when we got the skis ready, I tried to send her and keep the old Canuck there, but she wouldn't hear of that. She said he was worse hurt than she was." The old man was placed on the improvised litter, two of the boys towed it as best they could, plunging hip-deep in the snow. The one who still had his skis raced on ahead, to start a relief-sled back.

The man and girl left behind had waited there in the snow, for hours, years, ages—he did not know how long—until, first, the boy on skis came back with whiskey and blankets, and then the slow woodsled, the horses wallowing in the drifts, with Dr. Craft poised impatiently on the side. "I kept her warm all the time, anyhow. I had my hatchet, thank the Lord I hadn't left *that* at home. I got out the other cushion from the car and made her lie down on it. I grabbed out the lining of the top of the car and put that over her, and built a fire—lots of fires, all around a circle almost, with her lying down on the cushion in the middle. The wood was soaked and frozen hard, but with the gasoline from the tank it burned all right—when my fires'd get to going good, I'd go inside and sit down there with her and get my breath a little. It was as warm . . . ! It was like a little round room with walls made of fire. There was

274

a basket of eggs in the car—the Canuck had been going to sell them, I suppose, and two three of'm weren't broken, and I cooked those in the ashes, and we ate'm—she hadn't had a thing since early breakfast, but she made me eat my share. God! was she game! And I cleaned out the grease-pan and melted snow in it till I had it boiling, and cleaned it out again and melted more snow and had hot water for her to drink . . ." He shoved his plate violently away and said, grinding his teeth, "And all the time she was bleeding to death! And I too dumb to know it!" Wildly, looking from one to the other, he appealed to his listeners not to condemn him, to put themselves in his place. "I feel as if I'd killed her, see? If I'd known what to do—if I'd—but I never *dreamed* she was hurt so bad, not till she—not till she—she was so quiet and easy. Why, before she fainted, we talked quite a lot. She told me who she was, and I told her who I was and how I happened to be here—we talked about you, Uncle Tim, and the Academy—I saw the blood trickling down over her face once in a while. I *saw* it—and I didn't do a thing. I *saw* she was getting awfully white, but, Christ! I'm the world's worst loss on first aid, I'd have been afraid of my life to touch that bandage, I didn't have any idea *what* the trouble was—and after she fainted, I was worse scared than ever for fear of doing the wrong thing. I'd thought all along maybe I could just carry her out—on my back —never mind how far!—but I was afraid that would start the bleeding up. I just had to sit there, trying to warm her hands, watching her get whiter—God! I'll never see anything else, I tell you, I'll never see anything else, *never,* but her face with the life going out of it—I'd listen to see whether she was still breathing or not—and I'd climb up into the road to see if I could see anybody coming— and I'd go back to rub her hands and listen to her breathing—*any*body but me would have *thought* of something to do!—but I didn't dare touch that bandage—it looked pretty good to me, I mean it wasn't really *soaked* with blood. You see she'd torn up a nightgown or something she got out of her little suitcase—think of the nerve of her, cut up the way she was, crawling out from under the wreck and getting her head tied up somehow, and then trying to g-g-get that d-damn *car* jacked up!" He flung his arms out on the table and dropped his head on them.

His silence broke the spell which had held the others, leaning to

275

for. So I thought I might as well find out what I'm getting into."

She was trying for a flippant tone, but he didn't quite buy it.

"All right. Through Daniel, God was telling Nebuchadnezzar that throughout history there would be four world empires: his own, the Babylonian, represented by the Golden Head of his statue; then the empire of the Medes and Persians; then the Greeks; and finally the Romans. Each one gets progressively weaker, until with the Romans it actually splits in half—like the two legs of the statue."

"Rome and Byzantium."

"Right. So, four world empires. Just four. No one since the Romans—not Napoleon, not Hitler—has managed to set up a fifth."

She looked puzzled. "So what's the prediction that hasn't come true yet?"

"There's one part of Nebuchadnezzar's statue left. The ten toes. Prophecy experts believe the toes—made of clay and iron—represent an unstable form of government that will take over from today's nation-states in the near future. Probably ten kings or rulers of some kind, paving the way for the Antichrist."

She looked away, taking a moment to try to absorb what he was saying. They were cruising comfortably now as they took the Corniche al-Nil, the main thoroughfare that paralleled the east bank of the Nile, and the opulent mansions of the embassy district streamed past the window in a stately procession.

"And you think the secret, the mystery, Dakkuri was talking about might have something to do with that?"

He shrugged. "My gut tells me it has something to do with Daniel's predictions, yes. Something was nagging away at the back of my mind, and it took me a while to figure out what it was. The word you just used: *mystery*. In the Book of Revelation, that means Babylon. Dakkuri said the mystery would return."

"I don't understand. Babylon's going to return?"

He nodded. "The power of Babylon, yes. When the Antichrist sets up his one-world government."

She ran her hands through her hair.

his harshly whispered words, their faces blank white under the glare of the unshaded bulbs. They straightened themselves stiffly, took their eyes from the narrator for the first time, and looked at each other unseeingly.

The door behind them opened, closed, noiselessly. Dr. Craft was there to issue commands:—absolute quiet in the house tonight, his wife would stay with the case till the roads were sanded and he could get another nurse down from the Ashley hospital. "Yes, yes, she has a chance. But it's touch and go. She's lost an awful lot of blood. Shock too. That's probably the worst. Maybe some internal injury. I can't tell about that till I examine her carefully, and I can't do that till her pulse is stronger. Maybe a transfusion tomorrow— Say, *you,* whatever your name is," he said roughly to Canby, sprawled forward in his chair to listen, "you go home and get to bed. You're just about all in yourself. You ought to know better than to heave on that heavy woodsled the way you did, when they turned it around. Didn't you ever hear of such a thing as a rupture? Now remember, all of you, not one sound tonight! Miss Peck, if you try to clear off that table till I tell you you can, I'll strangle you. The rest of you, that don't live here, don't go back in there. Go out the back door." He went out of that door himself, closing it with infinite care behind him.

They stirred, drew breath, stood uncertain. Miss Lane asked, "What's all that blood on your face, Mr. Hunter? Did *you* get cut, too?"

He started wildly up and ran to the mirror over the kitchen sink, stooping to look into it, wetting his fingers at the faucet and rubbing at the red smear. It came away cleanly, leaving no mark behind. "That's *her* blood!" he told himself, in a tense whisper, looking down at the pink stain on his fingers. He drew up his great hand to a knuckled fist and swung it to and fro. "Blood running down all over her poor little face and not a goddam scratch on my hide!" he said with fury, and lunged with all his might at the wall beside him, dashing his fist against the rough plaster as though it were the jaw of an enemy.

The blood came then—spurting out in a scarlet stream from the knuckles, dripping from his thick out-stretched fingers to the floor.

Aunt Lavinia was appalled. "Canby! You're crazy!" she cried.

276

Miss Peck reached for a cloth to stop the bleeding. Mr. Dewey put her to one side. "Leave him alone," he said. " 'Twun't do him a mite of harm."

Back of them, Timothy Hulme leaned faintly against the wall, and then let himself down into a chair because the droning in his ears made him too dizzy to stand up. It was the chair in which Canby had been sitting. Like Canby he laid his arms on the table before him. But he did not bury his face in them. He sat looking down at the long slim distinction of his hands, so like his father's and his grandfather's, and at the perfectly intact, slightly middle-aged skin which covered them.

"Now you've lost me. Let's go back to the Serpent for a moment. If what we saw in the sewers was anything to go by, people have been worshiping it—or at least the middle piece of it—in secret for years, possibly thousands of years. Heaven knows how many innocents have been sacrificed along the way."

"I know. It's incredible. Horrifying."

"But has this cult got anything to do with what you were talking about—the return of Babylon?"

He scratched his jaw. "Let's just say there's a strong underlying connection. The forces of darkness. Evil. In the end it's all the same."

"And you and I are heading straight into the jaws of the dragon, aren't we?"

He struggled for something to say, some way of reassuring her, but at that moment the taxi pulled up at the main building of the American University, and a tall, white-suited man with a broad, brilliant smile was opening the door, ushering them into the blast-furnace heat.

"Murphy, you old dog! Welcome back to Cairo." Ten minutes later Jassim was sitting back in an uncomfortable-looking steel-backed chair that somehow seemed to perfectly accommodate his gangly frame. He sipped appreciatively from his martini glass.

"You're sure you won't?"

"Are you kidding? I know what you put in that stuff. The alcohol is the least of it."

Jassim laughed his rich, mellifluous laugh. "Same old Murphy."

"Same old Jassim." Murphy raised his glass of lemonade.

"Yes, sadly, I am a very bad Muslim."

"I don't know about that, but you're still a very good man in my book. Your letter after Laura died really helped."

Jassim's ebullient expression sobered. "I'm sure it didn't, but I had to tell you what was in my heart."

They drank in silence for a while, lost in memories of Laura.

Eventually Jassim said, "Dr. McDonald is okay? She was very pleasant, but perhaps a little distracted." Isis had made her excuses and gone straight to the lodging Jassim had arranged for them both in the campus complex for visiting professors and their families.

"She's got a lot on her mind," Murphy said.

Jassim didn't pursue it. "Well, I hope she is fit and well tomorrow. We have a big day ahead of us." He shifted in his chair, beaming like a kid on Christmas Eve.

"So, Professor Hawass went for it?"

"In a big way. When they X-rayed the tomb of Queen Hephrat back in the sixties, it was totally empty. The tomb robbers had beaten us once again."

"By a couple of thousand years, probably," said Murphy.

Jassim laughed. "All that was left was a deep, dark, empty hole at the bottom of the pyramid. So the notion that there is something still in there, something the robbers may have missed—something a Chaldean priest from the time of Nebuchadnezzar may have hidden there—the head of Moses' Brazen Serpent, no less! That would be quite an amazing story. Professor Hawass was delighted to put all of our humble resources at your service."

"Could we start by storing the middle section of the Serpent here? Given what happened at Washington, I would understand if you said no."

Jassim waved his hand. "We do not scare

Chapter Twenty-two

HE had known at that moment all that was to be, and he might as well—he thought, leaning forward to drop a dry stick on the sober little June watch-fire—he might as well have yielded at once to the first intimation as to resist for these last three months of misery.

The white-hot core of the fire, tiny but ardently alive, throbbed as it seized with passion on the new food for flames. A column of murky smoke rose into the still night air, and then, as the blaze burned clear, thinned to an airy plume. Timothy sat back on his granite ledge, his eyes fixed on the bowing of the little plume of smoke towards the west, where, long hours ago, the sun had gone down. Often enough he had noticed that smoke-drift in other Junes, up here at night on the Cobble. In those other years, rational years, he and Mr. Dewey and the boys sitting around the fire had sometimes speculated about the reason for this, wondering whether on still nights the warmed lightness of the air around the setting sun created everywhere on the globe this soft almost imperceptible steady breathing towards the west of the night wind. But now he was not thinking of what was before his eyes. He was thinking that he had known, there in the kitchen, throbbing like the core of a fire in the fierceness of Canby's excitement, he had known at that moment what was before him—his every fiber darkly stained with his foreknowing.

At the other end of the Cobble, a shower of sparks, rising in the darkness, showed that old Mr. Dewey too had put fresh wood on his watch-fire. Between the two, stretched rows of dark forms, rolled in blankets. They lay motionless in the trancelike sleep of youth, still as the great rock that was their bed; but just below, where the granite crest of the Cobble softened into upland pasture, the sheep, uneasy at the invasion of their solitude, moved restlessly. Sometimes a bell tinkled. Sometimes a ewe called with a low bleat-

278

ing and was answered by a thudding of little hoofs on sod and stones.

Timothy held his watch to the glow of the fire. Past midnight. In an hour the moon would be up. By the traditional routine of this yearly expedition on the mountain with the Senior boys, he was to waken the sleepers to see the moon rise over The Wall. He knew what would happen when he did:—yawns, grunts, momentary openings of an eye, the blankets re-rolled more tightly around motionless forms. The teacher's life, he had often thought—continually waking sleepers to see beauties or meanings they cared nothing about, and watching them sink back to apathy.

Enough light fell from the sky, thick sown with stars, to show him that Mr. Dewey now stood up from his fire and, followed by his old dog, picked his way among the sleepers, along the Cobble. When he reached Timothy, "Do you feel like sleeping, T.C.?" he asked in a low voice. "If you do, turn in for an hour or so. I'll keep watch."

"Thank you, Mr. Dewey, I don't believe I will," said Timothy in the carefully natural voice he had been using for three months. "How about you?"

Mr. Dewey smiled, looked around him from the dusky stretch of the Crandall Pitch pasture to the mountains brooding under the glittering black sky, looked back at Timothy and shook his head. "No, I'm not sleepy," he said in a peaceful voice, and went back to his own small fire.

Timothy was not sleepy either, although he was very tired. But this is better, he thought, his weary wide-open eyes burning with sleeplessness, this is better than lying in that damned bed in that damned bedroom, staring up hour after hour at— A dreary inner voice said derisively, "If you think that using a great deal of profanity is going to make you more modern, more like Canby, you're mistaken."

He gave a rough animal-like shudder, as if to shake off a gadfly, and dropped his head between his hands. The night breeze, so mild as almost to be stillness, blew gently on one cheek, tilting the immaterial column of the smoke ever so little towards where the sun had last shed its warmth.

easily here. We will guard the piece with honor and discretion."

Murphy clapped his old friend on the shoulder. "Great. That's a relief. So you got a Pyramid Crawler for me?"

"Oh, yes. And I am very much looking forward to seeing it in action. The tomb robbers sometimes used young children or even midgets to get into these narrow passages." He shook his head. "Sadly, those unfortunates were often unable to get out again. Hopefully with the Pyramid Crawler we will be able to penetrate our pyramid's deepest secrets without any loss of life!"

"I hope so, Jassim, old friend," said Murphy, his face darkening. "I very much hope so."

SIXTY-THREE

WHEN THEY MET up early the next morning, ready to drive out to the pyramid in Jassim's equipment-laden Land Rover, Murphy got a sense that Isis had settled something in her mind. She didn't say much, but the measured, businesslike way she went about checking that they had everything they needed suggested an inner calm he had never seen in her.

As they took the Rodah Island bridge across the Nile and into the Shar'a al-Haram, running straight through the Giza district to the desert's edge, he wondered why he didn't feel the same way. After a few

With a bitter, doubled consciousness, knowing from the beginning of each remembered scene exactly how it would end, and yet living it through with the torturing intensity of suspense, he began once more to look at the faces and actions and to hear the voices which—night after night—filled the darkness of his bedroom as soon as he put out his light. Grotesque, tragic, absurd, violent, trivial —and all as inevitable as Fate!—he saw and heard again the sights and sounds that had brought him to where he was.

Old Mrs. Washburn's voice rising from the murmur of talk at the supper-table—how could any man have recognized so farcical an episode as the beginning of disaster? Or if he had, how could he have warded it off?—"So our little patient is well enough to let the nurse go? Well, we mustn't leave the poor child all alone in that darkened room. I'll bring my rocker down and sit right beside her bed, with my knitting."

Miss Peck had been the first to collect herself enough to speak. "The doctor doesn't allow anyone with her, Mrs. Washburn. He even had the *nurse* sit out in the living-room, with the door ajar. It's not only her eyes, you know. Nor the loss of blood. It's the results of shock. The doctor . . ."

"Oh, did he? Well, all right, I'll do what the nurse did then. If the door's ajar, I can sit close to it and talk through the crack. We must keep her cheered up."

Maddened by their ineffectualness, Timothy heard again the futile defenses they feebly tried to throw up. "The doctor says she's not strong enough yet to . . . Dr. Anson said she was to be sure . . ."

Mrs. Washburn quoted him firmly, "I *heard* him say that she's really convalescent now, and it would do her good to hear some cheerful talk once in a while, to keep her mind off this tiresome time of waiting for her eyes to be well enough to take off the bandage."

Yes, they had all heard the doctor say that.

Feeblest of all, his own voice. "But, Mrs. Washburn, for your own sake, ought you to try . . ."

"Why, I'd enjoy doing it, Professor Hulme. There's nothing I like better than being with sick people."

And to Miss Lane, "Oh, no, indeed, it wouldn't interfere with any

280

fretful hours tossing and turning in the grip of feverish dreams, he had given up on sleep and had spent the rest of the night pacing the garden at the back of their lodging.

Murphy had been hoping for something—a sign, perhaps, that he was doing the right thing, that it was part of God's plan for him to be there. But dawn had broken leaving him unrested and no wiser than before.

He looked at the Sphinx-like smile on Isis's face as she listened to Jassim's ridiculous stories of mummies' curses and haunted scarabs, and wondered if God had chosen to give her the sign, not him. Perhaps, like the prodigal son, she was the one God had favored. Not that he begrudged her. As long as *someone* knew they were on the right road.

Pyramid Road. He remembered that's what they called the approach to the desert. And when he had first driven along it in an old tin can of a Citroën with Laura, there had still been traces of the lush acacia, tamarind, and eucalyptus groves that had now totally disappeared beneath a tidal wave of urban sprawl.

plans of mine. I'm just a useless old woman, you know. I've nothing else to do."

Stunned by the extravagant unexpectedness of the danger, they sat silent in defeat. They had tried all the devices available to civilized people.

But Canby recognized neither defeat nor the limitations of good breeding. Here on the mountain, in the silence of night at its stillest, Timothy heard again the raw insolent rudeness of Canby's voice, battering down that door to which civilized manners had no key. "Say, that's a swell idea of yours, Mrs. Washburn! Too good for you to keep to yourself, by heck! I'll stay with you on that. I'll sit there too." And when the old woman, disconcerted, opened her mouth to protest, he closed it with an impertinent, "I'm just a useless young man, you know. I haven't got anything else to do either, see? Any more'n you have. Skiing's over for this year." Timothy once more saw Canby's impudent grin, as he looked around the table, careless of making a fool of himself.

Thus to the ghastly incongruity of a farce-comedy tune, Timothy once more heard the steel gates clang shut.

Even Dr. Craft, silent and sardonic as he was, and as little given to seeing anything at all entertaining in Clifford life, had laughed out loud, the first time he visited his patient after this, when he saw the two looking hard at each other across the door to the sick-room.

"Give us your orders, Doc," Canby had said flippantly. "We're the new nurse."

Anson Craft's doctor-face had lightened to hear a faint giggle float out from the darkened chamber. Timothy, coming in behind him, heard it too. But his face did not lighten.

"My orders," said the doctor crisply, "are that talk shall be limited to fifteen minutes in every hour—not a minute more. And not one calamity story out of you, Mrs. Washburn! Nor anything *in the least* exciting out of you, Hunter. Nor from anybody. Now, Mrs. Washburn, nobody is to go into the patient's room. She's strong enough to wait on herself." He raised his voice, "Miss Barney, do you hear me? When you're tired of them, just shut the door." He turned to the others, "And it's not to be opened one inch more than that crack till I say so."

As the concrete apartment buildings finally gave way and the three Giza pyramids appeared on the horizon, bringing a gasp of amazement from Isis and an accompanying chuckle from Jassim, Murphy wondered if the remarkable juxtaposition of ancient and modern was perhaps the sign he had been waiting for.

Here in Cairo, people rushed headlong into the future while the monuments of mankind's deepest past looked on, unchanging, as if to say, *If you want to know what really lies ahead, look behind you.*

The road climbed to the top of the square-mile plateau and curved around the Sphinx, with its thousand-year stare, and then the three awesome pyramids were there before them, housing respectively a royal father, son, and grandson. Clustered around the Big Three, the much smaller pyramids of queens and princesses only added to the sense of majestic scale. As the Land Rover continued on, circling to the northeastern edge of the plateau, the great pyramids started to shrink into the distance again. Isis craned her neck, trying to fix every fleeting detail of the extraordinary panorama in her mind, until Jassim tapped her on the shoulder and pointed dead ahead.

Standing aloof in this empty corner of the plateau, The Pyramid of the Winds could have been built yesterday, so perfect was its ancient geometry. Smaller than its more famous cousins, it was in its way just as impressive, its sheer walls of smoothly fitting stone blocks a testament to the timeless genius of its creators.

"It's amazing," Isis said, scrambling out of the Land Rover and squinting through the fierce haze.

"One of the world's great feats of engineering," Jassim agreed.

"It helps if you have thousands of slaves to drag the stone blocks into place," added Murphy.

"Of course. That is why our modern buildings are so puny in comparison," Jassim laughed. "You just cannot get the slaves these days."

Isis unrolled the three-dimensional map of the pyramid's interior while Jassim and Murphy checked that the Crawler's systems were in working order. "Perfect," Jassim pronounced finally as a crystal-clear image of the pyramid appeared on the screen of the laptop balanced on his knees. "And she seems to be responding correctly to all my commands." He patted the Crawler like a faithful dog and pointed toward the pyramid. "Go, fetch," he said sternly.

Tucking the Crawler under his arm, Murphy started clambering over the huge limestone blocks toward the entrance of the first air shaft. "The prevailing wind is from the south," Isis explained to Jassim, "so this shaft is likely to have the strongest inflow. It seemed like the most logical place to start."

Jassim nodded. "Let us hope the wind has not blown it full of sand."

Murphy jogged back over the sand and Jassim started the Crawler on its journey up the shaft. Over his shoulder, Murphy and Isis watched the grainy images slowly fill the screen.

"It seems to be clear. The Crawler's moving without any problem. I estimate it should reach the end of the shaft in about three minutes. So far there don't seem to be any objects in its path."

Three minutes seemed like thirty as they huddled in the Land Rover's air-

By the time he said so, March was over and for three weeks Canby had sprawled, hour after hour, all day long, every day, outside that door, like a watchdog on guard, oblivious as any dog of the passage of time. For the permitted quarter of every hour he brazenly outtalked Mrs. Washburn; for the periods of silence prescribed by the doctor, he sat with tightly closed lips, vigilant eyes fixed on her to see that she said not a word. When he ran out of talk, he read aloud, droningly, stumblingly, like a great schoolboy, unashamed of the poor work he made of it, calling out, "How *do* you pronounce s-l-o-u-g-h, anyhow?" Or, "Say, what does 'invidious' really mean?" with Susan's voice coming back in answer, faint, husky, but amused and natural—first antenna flung forward towards life.

And because he was there, always there, Canby was the one who welcomed her as she groped her way back to health. Everything that Timothy had counted on as a weakness of Canby's turned by a baleful magic into an advantage—that he was out of work and idle and futureless and irresponsible, all that Timothy was not, as he came and went in the few intervals of his sober, toilsome, exacting work. It was worse than that. Because he was Canby with no dignity to protect, no position in society to keep up, because he was a nobody who could afford (since it cost him nothing) to be as ridiculous as he pleased without injuring a prestige necessary to usefulness, he could ignore the presence of the loose-tongued old woman always in the room with him as Timothy could not. It was not long before Canby, throwing decent reserve, self-respect, good taste out of the window, said whatever came into his head to say to Susan, as though he did not know that Mrs. Washburn, now frankly detesting him, would at once set the party-telephone wires humming with foolish and malicious distortions of his confidence. These preposterous versions soon came back to his ears. He roared over them in the highest spirits, and brought them in for Susan to laugh about in Mrs. Washburn's very presence. One day when Timothy came in from supper to get the news, Canby was saying jocularly through the crack in the door, "Boy I saw down street yesterday told me—" he shifted his position to fix the old woman with a mercilessly amused stare—"that people are tellin' around that I been engaged seven times and married twice—or words to that

282

effect. Somebody must have been listening at the keyhole yesterday when I was telling you about Mildred. Next off, they'll have the Sheriff after me for failure to pay alimony to my wives." So he had been confiding in Susan about his emotional troubles, had he, thought Timothy, astounded and enraged, so they had come along to the confessional stage! And with that poisonous old parrot in the same room!

Confounded with surprise, his entire experience of what could be expected and what was impossible, thrown into incredulous disorder, he struggled vainly to keep his alarm and resentment out of his voice, and was stiffer than ever with his, "How are you today, Susan?" "*That's* fine. Keep it up."

It was nothing to Canby what Mrs. Washburn told people he said to Susan. It was something to Timothy—in his position, at his age, with his traditions. So Canby was the one who every day grew more and more wonted to the oddity of addressing himself to the crack of an ever-so-little opened door, Canby was the one whose talk grew more practiced, more fluent, more natural, more easy and intimate, and Timothy, his heart burning like fire, was the one to be awkward and bungling and left-handed, as in the presence of a detested, pitcher-eared village gossip and the irreverent young man, obviously (although unconsciously) his rival, he said self-consciously to a crack in a door, "How are you feeling today, Susan?" "That's fine. Keep it up." To such remarks, made in such a tone, Susan's faint answers were of course impersonal and remote. They might have been exchanging greetings in a crowd at a subway station. They would have been infinitely closer to each other there.

It had been like a long-drawn-out nightmare of helplessness. Day after day, his waking hours had been filled by the authentic, bad-dream inability to raise a hand in his own defense. Leaden-limbed, impotent, incredulous, he had watched the current setting away from him, faster and faster. The moment had passed—when had it gone by him? No, no, it had never been there—when, risking all on one stroke, he might have given Canby the peremptory order to drag the old woman away bodily, and leave him alone with Susan— but, no, he would not have been alone then, in the common room of a boarding-house open to constant coming and going. How could he have said to Susan what he could only say to her alone! More than that—there was the impassable barrier of the doctor's order.

Incredulous of the need for this order, urgent, impatient, he had followed the doctor to the street one day. "See here, Anson, if Miss Barney's well enough to have people—strangers to her—gabbling away all day in the next room, why isn't she well enough to have some of us who know her well, who really have a thing or two to say to her, step into her room for a quiet talk? She must be getting stronger all the time. Her voice sounds . . ."

Dr. Craft had at first said with his usual irritable rudeness, "When I'm ready to change the treatment of a case I'll say so. I don't need . . ." but after all, he was an Academy alumnus, had been not so long ago one of Timothy's students. "Listen, T.C.," he said more reasonably, "I'll tell you how it is." Standing by his car, he began to pull on his gloves. "There are two things to consider. One is this old hell-cat who'd go pushing herself in to hang over the bed, if I let down the bars. If you and Miss Peck could go in for a real talk, why, there'd be no keeping Mrs. Washburn out. And she's cold poison. It's hard enough for me to handle the situation as it is. Have a heart!"

He opened the door of his car and went on, "But that's not all. The fact is, that girl has had a terrific shock. 'Shock' in the medical sense, I mean. Not that we doctors know what 'shock' is. It's one of the many things we don't know. But let me tell you, it's one of the things we don't want to monkey with! I'm not at all sure she's really out of the woods yet, though I think her eyes'll be all right in a fortnight. Every medical man wants a good wide margin of safety when it's a question of shock."

He got into his car, saying over his shoulder, "What do you *want* to see her for, anyhow? What's the hurry?" Stepping on the starter, he answered himself, "If it's something about her position or her teaching—well, no matter what!—can't it wait? She's getting on all right now. Why not leave well enough alone? That combination of the cheerful young idiot holding the old idiot at bay—that's really *funny!* That's the kind of thing she needs now. Well, so long!"

Here on the mountain, once again, for the thousandth time, Timothy ran feverishly from one fast-locked steel gate to another, trying in vain to shake them, beating his hands against their bars.

He could not understand Canby's unconsciousness of what he

conditioned interior, trying to interpret the shadowy pictures the Crawler was transmitting from its miniature cameras. Finally Jassim pressed a key and brought it to a halt. "Far enough, I think. It must be near the lip of the shaft. We don't want to lose her. If there was anything in the shaft, we'd have seen it by now."

Murphy wondered when the Crawler had become a *her*. "Just let her go a few more feet, Jassim." He peered intently at the screen. "What's that? I can see something moving."

Jassim reluctantly moved the Crawler forward. "It could be a small animal, a rat perhaps, though I doubt there is much worth nibbling inside the tomb now."

"Okay, stop. There it is again. There's definitely something moving at the end of the shaft."

Jassim adjusted the focus of the twin cameras. "Let me see, is that any better?"

Murphy nodded. "It must be something beyond the air shaft. Something inside the great chamber."

"Like the head of a bronze Serpent floating in midair?" Jassim laughed.

was doing. How was it that no one told him? In a community alive with meddling tongues, why did no one meddle now? Everyone in town must have seen that he, that Susan—everyone, that is, at the Academy. At least all the students who came to the house on Sunday afternoons. Or had he been so damnably discreet and well-bred and middle-aged that their knowledge had gone only as far as half-conscious, unspoken recognition, the kind of dim perception which, because it has not yet been put into words, fades away to blankness before a more vivid and arresting impression? Canby was now certainly giving Clifford a vivid enough impression to blot out anything else. Everyone, not only the gossips, was following with guffawing sympathy the farce-comedy of his courting under the eyes of Mrs. Washburn! Yes, Timothy thought, that must be the reason —his own decent and decorous advance into sentiment, improbable in the first place, stupidly lacking in color and spirit, had been pushed from people's minds by one of the richest subjects of cackling that had ever been thrown to the town's pecking beaks.

And there was another explanation, a very simple and elemental one—the man leaning over the fire, his elbows on his knees, his face in his hands, quailed back from the last bitter drop in the cup he was draining, but drank it down and sickened. Since it was to be expected for a man of Canby's age to be in love, it took no perceptiveness on anyone's part to see it, but for a man of the age of Professor Hulme—

To live those days over again was so accurately like a nightmare, that as in a nightmare, a cold crushing weight pressed down on Timothy's chest and cut off his breathing. He struggled to wake himself up. Half-suffocated, he flung back his head to draw in a great gulp of the soft June air. His eyes were caught by the position of Orion. It had slid perceptibly lower since he had last looked up. With just that slow implacable shift, his star had sunk lower while Canby's mounted higher during those three weeks when he had in any one day more unbroken hours of talk with Susan than Timothy had had since that first twilight evening. He had had time and to spare, Canby had, to show himself to the girl with all the contagious ha! ha! of his confidence in life, which had brought the boys and young men of town swarming around him, yet which indicated nothing at all, thought the older man in a rage, save glands

Murphy gave him a steady look. "Only one way to find out."

While Jassim maneuvered the Crawler back down the shaft, muttering under his breath, Murphy checked that he had everything he needed. Rope, flashlight, utility knife. And his bow.

Jassim looked at him as if he'd gone mad. "What on earth do you need that for?"

"The last time I went down a hole looking for a piece of the Serpent, I could have used it. I'm not making that mistake again."

Isis didn't say anything as they walked over to the base of the pyramid, but as he prepared to climb to the entrance of the shaft, she put a hand on his arm. "Be careful."

He looked into her eyes. "I always *try* to be careful." But the devil-may-care grin he tried for wouldn't come.

"I mean it," she said.

With the bow strapped tightly to his body, and knees, shoulders, and elbows all wedged tightly against the walls, Murphy was beginning to understand why the tomb robbers had left it to children and midgets to negotiate the pyramid's air shafts. But a summer of caving in Mexico had taught him that even an average-sized man could worm his way through a surprisingly tight space if he could control his nerves. More often than not it was panic that made you stuck, not the physical dimensions of the hole you were squeezing through. He took a moment to slow his breathing, tried to relax his muscles, and inched forward, feeling the warm air being sucked past him. *I may never make it out of here, but at least I'm not going to suffocate,* he thought.

After ten minutes his knees and elbows were scraped raw and he was starting to wonder if taking the cumbersome bow with him had been a mistake. Without it, he'd have reached the lip of the shaft by now. He closed his eyes, knowing from experience that total darkness would paradoxically lessen his sense of claustrophobia, and slid forward again.

A few minutes later his fingers closed over the edge of the shaft and he opened his eyes. Pulling himself forward, he looked down at the abyss below. Somewhere in the darkness was the tomb of Queen Hephrat, but the incline of the pyramid's walls ensured that scaling them would be an impossible feat. He couldn't imagine how the orginal tomb robbers had managed it.

He squeezed out and rolled onto a narrow ledge. When he was sure he could stand safely without toppling into the dark, he raised his eyes. The winds were swirling all around him, seemingly from all directions. The power of the winds was not strong enough to blow him from his perch on the landing, but his hair and clothes began to whip every which way in the shifting air currents.

As he began to get used to the winds, he noticed that he was not standing in total darkness. A thin stream of light from one of the air shafts at the top of the pyramid shone straight down into the abyss. That light seemed to have been designed purposefully to produce the incredible spectacle that Murphy now found himself watching.

Probably no more than one hundred feet across the shaft from where he stood, high over his head, there was an object tumbling about miraculously in the void. The stream of light brought out a dull shine on what appeared to be a fist-sized lump of metal rolling about in midair. Just the right size,

Murphy guessed, to be the head of the Brazen Serpent.

Murphy didn't know how long he just stood there, transfixed by the sight of the Serpent's head, watching it dancing in air as it had been, unobserved, for thousands of years, but it seemed impossible to tear his gaze away. He knew he would never see anything so extraordinary as long as he lived.

As if his mind were being read, a voice shattered his reverie.

"A magnificent sight, Murphy. But you must ask yourself: Will it be your last?"

swollen to bursting with young blood. Canby had had time to tell Susan, as confidentially as though they were castaways together on a desert island, not only a thousand memories of his little boyhood and adolescence, but as her strength came back, to draw from her one story after another (which Timothy had never heard) of her childhood, of her life at the Academy, at the Normal School. "That girl thinks the world of you, Uncle Tim," he said one evening, happening to walk up the hill with Timothy. "As much as I do! We have great old times comparing notes about you! Telling stories of swell things we remember you doing. She told me today what you did and the way you looked when you found the kids on the school playground trying to kill a toad. And I told her about the mess I got into, time I had that helluva row with my step-father, and you yanked me away from him and took me in up here! And she feels just the same as I do about what you put up with from Aunt Lavinia. We'd give anything if we could somehow sort of make it up to you, help out somehow."

As Timothy remembered this remark, so casually made with its so-casual "we," the inner volcano broke again into flames—had Susan then repeated, trading confidence for confidence, what he had told her, her only in all the world, that Indian-summer afternoon on the frost-browned pasture? Suspicion, fury, indignation once more seared his tongue to silence. Again he must live through the momentary agony of an imagined betrayal before he could again remind himself that oh, no! no! Susan would never do that. It was not in her nature. And that idea about Aunt Lavinia did not need to come from her. Canby already had spoken about that. He had probably brought it out naturally enough as he went back in rambling talk to his days at the Academy, using it as he used everything, as a way to range himself with Susan—sympathy for poor Uncle Tim only a pretext for being on Susan's side.

Canby had even used Mrs. Washburn as one of the mediums for standing with Susan—two against one. For it had been impossible to quench the old egotist when reminiscences were being told. She had made an indomitable third, relentlessly capping their every escapade, adventure, or emotional crisis with one of her own. And Canby had turned that to his advantage! Like everything else! Before long Timothy was aware that an unspoken hilarious com-

286

munion of fun over Mrs. Washburn united the young people—two against one.

As they were openly two against his one on the evening when, breaking his paralyzed passivity, he himself brought a book to read aloud. Reading aloud was something Timothy did superlatively well and he had exulted in the idea of showing up Canby's illiterate awkwardness. He had read well, never better, with such feeling and spirit (it was Maupassant's "One Life") that Canby had fairly gaped at him, and at the end, said in humble admiration through the door, "Say, he certainly can knock the spots off yours truly, can't he? You're a whiz, Uncle Tim!" And Susan's voice, "Yes, isn't he *won*derful!" They were together again. Admiration made them two against one as surely as derision.

Mr. Dewey now stood up and picked his way along the rock to the other fire. "Moon's due to rise in three four minutes," he said. Wrenching himself away from his hypnotized glare back on the past, Timothy remembered where he was, got to his feet and stepped with the old man from one to another of the sleeping boys, giving each shoulder a shake, saying clearly in their ears, "The moon will soon be up. If you want to see the moon rise, now's the time." They grunted, nodded, and sat up, or propped themselves unsteadily on one elbow and looked around sleepily. All but Eli Kemp. He said clearly, although his eyes continued tightly closed, "What of it!" and pulled his blanket over his head to shut out the light. But Eli had been conditioned by his poverty never to think of anything but how to make another penny and keep from spending it, thought Professor Hulme, going back to his fire.

By the time he had sat down again beside it, he had forgotten Eli and the other adolescents, his eyes fixed in anguish on the slow thinning of the black velvet back of The Wall. Just so—how many times had he thought it—love had brought light to his darkness. Just so, instant by instant, his loneliness and apathy had been suffused with tenderness and hope. He began to tremble with the violence of sorrow repressed, clenching his hands hard in his pockets as he had clenched them before when shaken by the first gusts of passion.

287

SIXTY-FOUR

MURPHY LOOKED PAST the floating Serpent's head through the surrounding gloom to see where the voice had come from. On the opposite ledge he could barely see the outline of a human figure.

"Who are you?"

"My name is Talon. I told it to your wife, but I guess she never got to share it with you."

Finally the evil that struck down Laura had a name and a face. Every fiber of Murphy's being was screaming for revenge, and if anger alone could have powered him, he would have leaped the void in one

"Fine, isn't it?" said Mr. Dewey dreamily, watching with heart unwrung.

After a pause, "Yes, it's very fine," said Timothy, correctly.

The dark globe spun fast and smoothly under the feet of the watchers. The eastern mountains sank. The great disk, white with its heatless fire, swam up to its triumph. The twilight dimness of the pasture below the rock turned to silver. The sheep, as if the light had been a sound, stood up, drifted aimlessly about, talking to each other in sleepy, secret voices. Every weathern-worn knob and ridge of the Cobble's granite wave emerged from darkness to visible strength, and was transfigured from strength to beauty.

Mr. Dewey mused, "Doesn't seem possible—up here—now—tomorrow's newspapers will tell about the same old hellish goings-on of humans, does it?"

Timothy knew what he meant. He had been for months increasingly horrified by the statements of Nazi ideals in the news, and the evening before as they talked around the fire, he had asked the boys, "Don't it kind of make you wonder what General George Washington would ha' said? The history-books tell us he swore his head off at the battle of Monmouth. What cuss-words could he ha' found for Hitler!"

Timothy thought drearily, "Oh, he's trying to start that up again!" Wanting only one thing, to have the old man leave him alone in his pain, he made no rejoinder.

Mr. Dewey waited a moment, and then went back to his own fire, his dog stepping gravely at his heels.

Timothy sat rigid, horribly impervious to the night's apotheosis of peace. His mind tiptoed up timidly to remind him to look at the beauty around him, and shrank back, appalled by his suffering.

But presently his professional conscience, reaching him on a reflex of habit, bade him make sure that all was well with those entrusted to his protection. He turned his head to look and saw that, as he had thought, the boys had collapsed again into stone-sound sleep. No, one of them was stirring. Bending his eyes more intently, Timothy saw that the blanketed form nearest him was stirring. He rose to his feet, he took the two or three steps that brought him to the boy, stooped, put his hand on his shoulder.

It was Jules. Wide awake, he lay looking out over the silvered upland pasture and across the valley brimming with white.

Timothy asked, "Something the matter, Jules?"

The boy clutched at Timothy's arm and sat up. "Oh, Professor Hulme, I can't *stand* it!" He pulled the teacher down to sit beside him. "It's like that swell place in the Kreutzer—w-where the octaves . . ." He choked and rubbed his sleeve back and forth over his nose. Timothy pulled out his handkerchief and passed it to the boy, who blew his nose, handed back the handkerchief and pointing to a scraggly small bush near him said, his voice cracking grotesquely from treble to bass and back again, "Professor Hulme, maybe I'm crazy, but when that bush—when the light came—when that bush came out of the darkness it c-came *singing!* Honest! Do *you* think I'm crazy? Oh, gosh, I wish my darn voice would get through changing."

"You probably weren't quite waked up, Jules," suggested the teacher calmingly. "Sounds to me as though you were dreaming. Rather a nice dream."

The boy was silent, leaning against Timothy's shoulder, turning his head back and forth to look from the luminous bulk of the mountain above them to the valley where a river of white mist marked the course of the Necronsett. Timothy did not look at it with him. He had instantly forgotten where he was. He was far away, back in the past, hearing with a fresh shock the conscienceless levity with which Susan—child of duty though she had always been—airily excused herself to Miss Peck for being late for her work, as she was on almost every one of the many afternoons when Canby took her out in his car. He was sickening at her cool, frivolous answer to a question about the younger sister who had been the core of her heart. "Why, to tell the truth, I haven't written Delia for ages. I don't know just when her Commencement is. Oh, yes, she is going to be able to graduate this year. I think so, anyhow." His bruised heart ached and throbbed again in the unbearable pain with which he had watched her bored, blank, absent face in the teachers' meeting where he was putting all his ingenuity into expounding the idea about reading which she and he had worked out together with—for him—such exquisite pleasure— What was this stirring and nestling against him? Oh, yes, Jules, the little Jew boy

289

bound and gone for this Talon's throat. Instead, he tried to control his rage to focus on the standoff before him.

"You monster. So, I was right. You are the same man who is responsible for all of the horrors of the recent weeks."

"Yes, who would have thought an archaeologist would see this much action. You cover a lot of ground, Murphy, I'll give you that, but with enough money and power against you, there are no secrets, yours or the ancients', that can't be revealed."

"What do you want with the Serpent? How can it be worth murdering for?"

"I don't have to reveal *my* secrets to you, Murphy. All you need to know is that thanks to you, I will have the Serpent's head and then circle back to the American University, where you've locked up the middle piece."

"You are an awfully confident monster, Talon, I see that. But it doesn't look like you're any closer to grabbing the Serpent's head than I am over here. All the modern money and power you brag about doesn't look like it's any match for a clever ancient mind and a little wind."

Talon laughed. "That, Professor, is where you are wrong. It looks like you're the one who has no way to get out in the middle to grab the head, whereas I have a solution that is almost older than the pyramid itself."

Murphy saw a dark flutter of movement, and for a moment it was as if two objects were being tossed in the air in the center of the shaft. One was the head of the Serpent, the other was actually moving on its own, fighting the wind.

A bird, he thought. *Of course. A falcon.* Despite himself, Murphy had to concede that Talon had come up with an ingenious method for plucking the Serpent's head from out of the vortex.

Even in the uncertain light of the pyramid's interior, Murphy could see what a magnificent creature the falcon was. He could see the chestnut sheen of its wings, the dappled cream of its breast. A kestrel. Its ancient name, the windhover, came into his mind as he watched it miraculously keeping in place a few feet from the vortex's grip. *She is used to riding updrafts and crosscurrents,* Murphy thought, *but nothing like this. She must feel as if she's been caught in a blizzard. But she's learning fast. A couple of more passes and she'll have it.*

Without thinking, he slid his bow out of its case and notched an arrow.

He zeroed in on the falcon, which was now only a few feet from the floating head. Feeling his willpower drain, Murphy shifted his bow toward the target he could not resist. Talon. He drew the string back until every molecule of the bow was begging for release. With just a loosening of his fingers an arrow would streak across the space between them and through Talon's black heart.

Vengeance is mine.

Laura's killer just stood there. Was it Murphy's imagination, or was Talon smiling? *He knows I've got him in my sights,* Murphy thought. *Does he think I won't do it?* He felt his whole body quiver with the effort of keeping the arrow from loosing itself as if it had a mind of its own.

Time seemed to stop as he waited to see what his mind would do. The chamber suddenly echoed to the sound of Talon clapping his hands.

"Come on, Murphy. Do it! What's holding you back? It's just the two of us now. Your precious God can't see you! Do it!"

Murphy felt his bow finger trembling. He couldn't hold it much longer.

He swung the bow up and to his left and fired.

Despite the winds, the arrow hit its target. The falcon. Murphy could not take another man's life. Even the monster who had killed Laura. He also realized in the final second that Talon had been baiting him to distract his attention from the bird, who had grabbed hold of the Serpent's head.

And he could not let the monster Talon get the Serpent's head.

The kestrel plunged into the solid stream of air, talons extended. She gripped the head by the thin curve of bronze that would connect it to the middle piece and beat her wings furiously to turn toward Talon.

Murphy's arrow caught the falcon on the very edge of its left wing. With a horrible screech that echoed throughout the shaft, the Serpent's head was knocked out of the

from the city. He was whispering dreamily, "D'you suppose that mist hangs over the river like that every night, when we're asleep?" And dropping his voice to an even lower murmur, "D'you hear those sheep, Mr. Hulme? They don't sound like that in the daytime. They sound as though they'd put their mutes on to go with the moonshine, they're— Oh, *why* did Papa have to die!"

The insensitive sleepers had the best of it, thought Timothy, those with open eyes found only sorrow in their waking, the old man to see his ideals down under the hob-nailed boots of Storm Troopers, the boy in the memory of his irreparable loss, he himself— "Well, Jules, I think you'd better lie down again," he said. "Perhaps you can get to sleep now. Here, I'll leave my handkerchief with you, in case you get the sniffles again."

He tucked the blanket around the thin shoulders and stood for a moment watching with envy how the enormous peacefulness of the night flowed over the child, emptied now of his wonder and his sorrow, looking with envy at the other sleepers, not one of whom had wakened.

The fire burned low. He crossed two sticks over the coals and sat down, his eyes on the delicate column of smoke, bowing slightly in the faint breath of the night-breeze which so faithfully followed the setting sun, all around the world.

The impalpable lightness of the smoke reminded him—with one bound, memory had caught him by the throat and another of those intolerable scenes played itself out to the end, the first day when the doctor had allowed Susan to be up. Nobody had told him this was to happen. Nobody had realized his right to know before anyone else. When he and Aunt Lavinia had gone to supper, his heart had turned over to see her there in the living-room, wrapped in blankets, pale, her temples thinned to exquisite delicacy, lying back in Miss Peck's great rocker. He was there again, with the others, always all those others, standing around her chair. Near her, Canby fidgeted, half beside himself in the excitement of her actual presence. Timothy saw him again, as though he stood here by the night-fire on the rock, lean over her, heard him say impudently, "You've got the funniest-looking hair, Susan Barney, ever I saw. Looks like a fog.

What does it feel like?" and as he spoke, snatching off the blue fillet and burying his hands in the golden-brown mist.

"Give me back my ribbon!" Every time poor Timothy re-heard that angry, peremptory cry he heard more plainly in it the rich hot throb of a note he had not dreamed was in the range of Susan's voice. And then the tussle—as Canby stooped with the ribbon, her hand darted to his hair for a vicious tug that brought the water to his eyes.

"Let go! Ouch!"

She pulled again violently.

Canby struck at her hand, crying out, "Leggo, will you?"

He had torn himself loose, astonished by the pain, his face reddened in fury. "That *hurt!*" he told her indignantly, his voice as passionately out of control as hers.

"Who began it?" she asked in a rage, plunging her eyes into his.

On the other side of the little June watch-fire they faced each other again in intimate anger—the spark between them kindling visibly to flame. Oh, God! the fool he had been to think those gray eyes mild!

"Disgraceful modern manners!" Timothy's mind had instantly tried to range him with the other sedate, mature on-lookers, averting their eyes from this break in decorum as they turned their minds away from its meaning. "What a disgusting roughneck Canby is! He ought not to be associated with our decent country young people! It's a crime, his bringing up here his vulgar ideas of . . ." But Timothy's mind had long ago given up trying to drown out with its feeble chirpings the roll of thunder in his ears. Sitting there in the bright enchanted night he was lost in primitive rage that Canby's brutal young hands knew what his had so longed for as a delicate crowning joy, and he heaped up high around him—since it was his only defense—the self-righteous wrath of the man defeated by his own scruples.

He made an effort, finally, since he was suffocating in his own indignation, to break away from it long enough to breathe, and said anxiously to himself, "This won't do. I can't go on like this. I must think what I am to do."

But he could not think what to do. He could not think at all. Another memory had flashed up before his eyes—the worst! But

291

they were all the worst! Like a man caught in the first spasm of a recurrent wave of physical agony, he could only cower and hope to live through it, as his memory, spinning at lightning speed along worn grooves, set before him the familiar beginning, so harmless-seeming, so horribly charged with menace—the tea-table before the fire that April Sunday evening, Aunt Lavinia's gnarled hands lifting a cup, the students sitting cross-legged on the floor, Jules putting his 'cello away in its case—the astonished stir of exclamation over Susan's appearance, her first outside the sick-room—leaning on Canby's arm, brought by Canby—"the doctor was just in and said we might"—"we might"—we—we—the tea-kettle's gleaming copper belly, the little blue flame under it—the talk, the chatter, his counting one, two, three, four, five teaspoons of tea for the pot, and thinking, enraged, "Why didn't they tell *me* there was a chance she could come out? Why was *I* not the one to bring her?"—the pitched inner battle of his determination not to see the strange new different beauty in Susan's face, pale, worn, and rather plain in the after-effects of a long illness, and ravishingly lovely with a dazzled and dazzling light. The setting of his jaw, his silent oath that, come what might, he would take her home. "If I strangle Canby with my own hands, I shall put her in my own car and have her to myself—before it is too late. Why, I have not even *told* her yet—how can she be sure until I tell her—now, this day, this hour shall not go by until I have told her!" Gazing hypnotized at the first spurts of steam from the kettle, almost at the boil, he heard again the clatter of the young voices, the students drawing out Canby's tiresome wise-cracks, the question, "Well, for goodness' sake, Can, how many brothers and sisters have you got anyhow? You're always bringing out a new one!" Canby's voice, starting his usual quick-time patter-description of his absurd family, his manner anticipating the laugh which always followed, "Why, believe-it-or-not, I was my parents' only child. Fact. My father died when I was a baby, and my mother married a widower with three girls—I was only two then—and she died when I was three, and my stepfather married a divorcée with a boy and girl—and that made six children, halves and steps to each other, and our step-parents got divorced and my stepmother, my first stepmother I mean, married a man with one son, and my stepfather married a woman with an adopted daughter, and that made eight, and then the first step-parents and the second ones had children—and about that time I got sent to the Academy." His young listeners were in fits of laughter as Canby meant them to be. Tilting the tea-kettle to pour the boiling water into the tea-pot, Timothy thought, "Sordid, modern story!" and heard Susan's voice, vibrating in its purest note of beauty like a plucked 'cello string, say slowly and compassionately, "I think that's the saddest childhood I ever heard of!"

Timothy's head jerked up with a dreadful premonition of evil— why had he looked! Why had he seen! And there across the table, so close he could have touched her, Susan was looking at Canby, looking with the deep, soft, self-forgetting gaze of fathomless tenderness which was his . . . his! Canby looked too—and as their eyes met, it was not tenderness, no, not tenderness, that lighted those gray eyes to glory.

His horrified pain had been for an instant beyond his control. He had screamed out like a man run through. Canby had shouted, had sprung across the table to snatch at the kettle and turn its stream of boiling water away from Timothy's left hand. A clatter of breaking china and excited voices. . . . "Open a window! He's going to faint! Oh, his *poor* hand! Cold water—get cold water." Agonizing pain in his left hand—or was it in his heart? "Somebody telephone for Dr. Craft! Put it in cold water. Canby, quick! Get him upstairs!"

Wave after wave of nausea and a faintness that was like dying, that was not dying only because of his fixed certainty that his life depended on keeping Canby with him, on not letting him be in the same room with Susan.

He was in the bathroom now and violently sick, but it was all right, because his right hand had not loosened its clutch on Canby's arm. He was all but beaten into insensibility by the spasms of his retching, by the blaze of pain in his hand, but he was not defeated, he only tightened to rigidity the hand that held Canby to him.

They were in his bedroom now, Canby pouring cold water into a basin, holding his hand in it, pulling out the pillow so that he

293

bird's grip. It seemed to hang in the air for a moment, as if it had forever renounced the pull of gravity, then plummeted down into the dark. Somehow, having left the particular pull of its centuries-old rotations, the head was now free to plummet into the void. The wounded kestrel was falling almost as quickly.

Murphy watched it fall. It had almost been close enough for him to reach out and touch it. Now the Serpent could never be made whole again.

He wheeled back in Talon's direction, but the shadows had swallowed him.

Then he felt a sharp pain dig into the back of his neck and heard an even louder bloodcurdling squawk. It was a second bird. Murphy was able to recover in time to knock it away, and then it seemed distracted by the falling of the first falcon and flew off, perhaps to help it.

Murphy watched it fly away clutching in its claw Laura's cross, which it had ripped from around his neck.

SIXTY-FIVE

THE CLIMB BACK through the air shaft had the quality of a nightmare. Every inch seemed to take forever as Murphy imagined Isis and Jassim being butchered by the killer he had had in his sights. The thought tormented him as he forced his bruised and bleeding body through the shaft: *I could have stopped him. I could have stopped him.*

When he finally scrambled out and tumbled onto the sand, he couldn't see anything—the sunlight had temporarily blinded him. Then he felt arms around him, pulling him to his feet, and he could hear their excited voices. They were okay.

Back in the Land Rover, in between gulps from a bottle of mineral water, Murphy told them what had happened inside the pyramid.

"It is a good thing I know you are a man of limited imagination," said Jassim, rolling his eyes, "or I would be sure you had made it all up. A bird, you say, trained to snatch the head out of the air where it had been spinning for eons! Even now I am not sure I believe it."

"Just keep your eye out for another vehicle," Murphy said. "He must have approached the pyramid from the other side."

"How did he know we were here? That's what I don't understand," said Isis.

Murphy shook his head. "Beats me." He closed his eyes, suddenly exhausted. "I failed," he said more to himself than anyone else. "I thought that's what God wanted me to do. Find the Serpent. That was my task."

Isis was smiling her Sphinx smile. "What makes you think you failed?"

Murphy pounded his fist against the window. "I lost the head of the Serpent. It's at the bottom of the pyramid by now. No one will ever find it there."

"Maybe that's for the best," Isis said. "I think the Serpent—every bit of it—was nothing but evil. If God had a task for you, perhaps it was just to find the inscription. Dakkuri's final message."

"Well, guess what, that's at the bottom of the pyramid, too, in case you hadn't figured it out."

Isis ignored his sarcastic tone. "Not necessarily."

"What are you talking about?"

"The Crawler's camera was focused on the head for two or three minutes. The images may not be crystal clear, but the way it was moving in space, we'll certainly have it from every angle. If Jassim's lab has half the equipment he claims, we can reconstruct and enhance each frame. Perhaps we'll be able to put together a composite image— enough to read the cuneiforms anyway."

"Of course," agreed Jassim. "It is quite possible."

Murphy spent the trip back to the American University replaying the sequence of events inside the pyramid. He'd been about to kill Talon. He had no recollection of changing his mind. He didn't even remember aiming at the falcon—it just happened, as if the bow were aiming him, not the other way around.

That was always how a perfect shot felt. As if it were divinely inspired. *Well, maybe it was,* he thought.

Jassim was as impatient as Isis to see what the Crawler's tapes would reveal and kept the accelerator to the floor, even when the morning rush hour traffic started congealing around them. Isis kept her hands pressed together in her lap and her eyes closed. When they finally arrived in front of the elegant stucco building that housed Jassim's lab, he insisted on making everything ready while they showered and, in Murphy's case, changed the dressing on his knife wound as well as applying Band-Aids to his various cuts and scrapes.

Half an hour later they were hunched over a computer screen as Jassim's long fingers flew over the keys. After a few moments a grainy image of the Serpent's head appeared, glinting faintly in the murky light as it revolved on its own axis. "To think it had been there for two and a half thousand

could lie flat. His frightened blood, which had gone scurrying to the deepest recesses of his body, flowed back weakly to his brain, he remembered what he had seen, and cried out again in utter anguish.

"God! Let me get you some whiskey!" Canby said, shuddering.

And, "No . . . no . . . *no,*" he had panted. "You're not to leave me, do you understand? You are to stay here in this room with me." The doctor was there—when had he come?—saying, "Yes, Hunter, you'd better stand by while I put the tannic acid on and bandage it. How in hell did he ever get such a burn anyhow?"

And all that absurd horror of suffering and desperation for nothing! As everything he did was for nothing. The doctor went away saying to Canby as he went, "Don't bother about getting Miss Barney back, Hunter. I'll take her along in my car." But that went for nothing too. Still distrustful, although the house was in the profound silence of emptiness, Timothy kept Canby with him for long after that. Yet when, still too faint to walk alone, leaning on Canby, he went downstairs to the living-room he found Aunt Lavinia still up. Susan on the stool at her knee.

He had sunk into a chair then, too exhausted even to turn his head when Canby cried, his heart in his voice, "Oh, *swell!* I was afraid you'd gone!", as Susan answered, "I told the doctor he'd just have to let me stay till I saw how poor Mr. Hulme is!"

She had hovered near him then, compassionate, uneasy, yearning, remorseful—he could have sworn the shadow in her eyes was remorse—she had touched his bandaged hand tenderly, she had murmured like a dove, "Oh, if there were only something I could *do* for you!" and he had not, even at that, blazed out at her with a look of ironic rage. There was no irony in him. He had felt no rage, only utter weariness with sound and fury. His bodily reservoirs of anger-stuff were drained out to emptiness; for an hour's respite, he had used up all the raw material he had, from which his nerves could manufacture pain.

So he had not stirred. He had sat as still there as now on his ledge of stone. He had let her go without a word. He was glad to see her go, and take with her the mockery of that half-unconscious look of compunction.

294

years"—he made a clucking sound—"and now—*poof*—gone."

"We got the snapshots to show the folks back home, that's what counts," Murphy said.

"But they don't show anything. Not yet," Isis chided. "Move it forward—slowly."

Jassim advanced the film frame by digital frame until the underside of the head started to come into view. "Stop it there!" Isis commanded, and Murphy couldn't help remembering the effect she'd had on the idol worshipers in the sewers. "Give me as much magnification as you can."

Slowly the image grew until it filled the screen. Then, as Jassim magnified it still further, the outline was lost and all they could see was a scarred and pitted landscape of bronze, like the surface of a distant yellow moon.

Jassim shook his head. "That's about as much as—"

"There!" Isis shrieked.

Murphy leaned closer. She was right. What had seemed moments before like the random scratches and fissures of any

After they were alone, Aunt Lavinia said, "Tim, you *do* look ghastly! Were you so very much hurt?"

"Yes, Aunt Lavinia. I was a good deal hurt."

Well, it was over again—for this time. To live through it exhausted him, each time, to blessed apathy. He looked around at the lyric poem of the night and could not have told where he was. The moon was high now, straight over his head. It had blotted out all the stars which earlier filled the darkness with the pride of their glittering. Every twig, every bush, every commonplace pebble, every tree and blade of grass had put off the shifting many-colored mortality of daylight and stood transfigured in white peace. All but the man keeping his dark watch. From his anger and stubborn misery the light fell away, bathing the weather-beaten granite of the rock in glory.

There was no glory in the world where Timothy sat, holding hard to all he had left—for he had something left, he had found that out. He had the ability to make Susan unhappy with a blighting look, to undermine her confidence with a well-chosen insinuation wrapped in a pleasant phrase she associated with good will. He could still tarnish with doubt the brightness of her response to the torch held up by Canby. He could whirl over her head like a club that ignorant unsuspecting young trust of hers in his wisdom and good faith, and bring it down with all its shattering impact on her unawareness. He could do it! He hardened his heart, blacking out all its light, he trod resolutely down the path from one circle of his inferno to a lower, to a lower, to the lowest, and planned how he could do it. It had not been honorableness but middle-age that had betrayed him into the mawkishness of that dark hour of indecision in his office when like an idiot gentleman bowing and scraping and holding open the door to a cave-man intruder—would Canby in his place have invited disaster with that bloodless elderly weighing of civilized standards against the timeless savage hunger of the heart? Never! Never! Never! Canby was no such fool! And he was young. Canby would have struck out with those great fists of his, heedless if they battered down honor, rejoicing in the letting of blood.

Well, it was not too late for him to batter down scruples. It was not too late to do something! He had piled up, had he not—he knew he had—an enormous influence with Susan. He weighed in his memory like unexploded bombs, one after another, the hours with her that made him sure of this. She might not be in love with him—the breath went out of his chest as though he had been struck a blow—and came in again hot and swollen with the certainty that she loved and trusted him. Well, he could wield the power given him by that love and trust, he could stamp out as he would stamp out a treason, that damnable radiance in her face of which she was not conscious.

He shaded his eyes with his hand from another radiance, hating the moonlight, detesting the stillness and peace around him, and took out from its dark hole his dearest surest grievance, pressing its thorn deep into his outraged sense of justice—there was no sense, no meaning in all this. It did not come from the nature of things, but from blank idiot chance. It need not have happened. There was no inner logic or rightness in it, nothing but bad luck. He ran through his fingers the familiar rosary of chance sequence of chance events—if Susan had not happened to be away that week, if she had not chanced to come back earlier from her vacation—if Canby had not taken up ski-running, if he had not chanced to remember there on the Schenectady viaduct, or wherever it was, that Clifford existed—why, if Downer as a boy had not chanced to go to work in that office where he met the girl who was Canby's aunt, Canby never would have been sent to the Academy, never would—

"What's on your mind, T.C.?" Mr. Dewey was saying. "I been asking you for the last five minutes what time your watch says. Mine's stopped."

"Oh, I beg your pardon. It's"—he looked—"half past one."

Mr. Dewey set his watch, but did not at once turn away. He poked meditatively at the coals with the toe of his thick, lumberjack boot. "What were you thinking about so hard?" he asked again.

Timothy said bitterly, "I was thinking about luck—about chance, hazard—whatever you want to call it. I was thinking how imbecile we are to try to plan life, or make any sense of it, when everything in it is decided by mere brute chance. Something happens—or it doesn't happen. And that's all there is to it!"

296

Mr. Dewey sat down on the ledge to consider this. Don came around in front of him and with a sigh of happiness laid a grizzled head on his knee. Caressing it absently, Mr. Dewey remarked after a time, "Wa-al, that's only the way it looks to young folks. When you're my age, you'll have found out that there's no such thing as luck. Nothing ever just happens to anybody."

Timothy looked sidelong at him with a hostile eye, resentful of the dreamy quiet of his voice, as a man in great bodily pain is resentful of the cheap cheerfulness of good health. The old man lifted off his battered felt hat, laid it on his knee, and looked around him gravely. The moonlight, which took the warring chaos of color out of the world, replacing it by a patterned harmony of silver and delicate black, took the gray out of his thick hair and turned it to a line of shining white around his head. "What I mean is, I guess," he advanced, "that nothing can really happen to a person till he *lets* it happen. That's been my experience."

"I don't know what you mean, Mr. Dewey," said Timothy coldly.

"Wa-al," said the old countryman meditatively, "I'm not exactly sure what I mean, myself." He put his hat back on, stood up, and said very earnestly, "But I mean *some*thing!" and turned to walk towards his end of the rock. He had not taken three steps before he came back to say, "Now you try to get some sleep, T.C. You look to me as though you needed it! Unroll your blanket and lie down anyhow. I took my nap earlier."

"I must think about what to do. I must come to some decision about what I am to *do!*" Timothy told himself desperately. He could not have told what the old man had said. He thought he had not heard it. He thought he had forgotten it. But from his body, battered by the chaotic swirling of its deepest instincts, hurled back from rocky barriers it could not recognize, came now a muffled warning that it was about at the limit of its power to endure. The echo in his outer ear of the old man's compassionate counsel, although it did not reach his brain, stretched out his arm to unroll his blanket. The instant he lay down on it, his fatigue-poisoned muscles, the watchful weary nerve-centers which had kept those muscles taut, his very bones, abandoned themselves to that unheard, unremembered suggestion to rest. His sinews loosened, let his flesh

297

weather-beaten piece of metal suddenly took on the orderly form of written characters: the distinctive cuneiform etchings of Dakkuri.

Jassim prepared to print the image. "I expect it is something else I will find impossible to believe," he said, "but perhaps now is the time to tell me what this is all about."

Murphy put a hand on his friend's shoulder. "Wait until Isis has figured out what it means. Then I promise I'll tell you everything."

Jassim nodded as Isis practically tore the printout from the machine. None of them moved. However long it took, they weren't going anywhere.

"At least it's short," she said after a while. "I suppose he thought if the reader had made it this far, there was no point playing games anymore."

Her eyes darted back and forth across the piece of paper, and Murphy felt he could almost hear her brain working. Her lips moved silently, mouthing the words over and over until they made sense. Then she placed the sheet carefully down on the desk.

"Well?" Jassim seemed even more agitated than Murphy, who had stopped breathing.

She took a moment to compose herself, and began. "It starts with a ritual exhortation, as usual: *The servants of the snake have kept this secret. Honor to them and power hereafter.*"

She coughed. "Then comes the important bit.

> "*Babylon's great towers are dust, the wind blows them where it pleases.*
> "*But find the head and the body shall rise after, casting its shadow again over all the earth.*
> "*It is of gold and marks a king, the most powerful.*
> "*In Marduk's dwelling shall you find it.*
> "*O faithful servant of the dark, be commanded to raise it up.*
> "*From the dust Babylon shall be raised up also to rule again.*"

The silence dragged on, and Isis said, "That's it."

"It's enough," said Murphy quietly.

"But what does it mean?" asked Jassim.

"It means Babylon will rise again. At least, it will if the wrong people get hold of the Golden Head."

Isis looked at him thoughtfully, but Jassim was out of his chair, wringing his hands in frustration. "You're talking in riddles, Murphy. How can Babylon rise again? What is this *Golden* Head? I thought you were looking for—and just lost—the head of the *bronze* Serpent."

"I'm sorry, Jassim. Let me try to explain. According to Daniel's interpretation of Nebuchadnezzar's dream, the Babylonian empire was the most powerful the world would ever know. That power was symbolized by the Golden Head of the statue in the dream—the one he then had built. When Nebuchadnezzar saw the error of his ways, he had the statue destroyed. But I'm betting that the head was buried somewhere by the people who worshiped the Brazen Serpent."

"But why? If they didn't want to destroy it, why not melt it down? The gold must have been worth an unbelievable fortune."

"I'm pretty sure because they believed that if they preserved the head, then one day the right person would find it, and Babylon would rise up again."

Jassim rubbed his eyes as if he were checking he wasn't dreaming. "And what does this mean: *Babylon will rise up*? The old city will be rebuilt?"

"Not just that," Murphy said. "It means the power of Babylon will be rebuilt too. This time, as an evil power dominating the world."

Jassim turned to Isis. "I would like to know what you think of all this, Dr. Mc-Donald. You are a sensible person, like myself, I think. Do you really believe that an evil cult hid Nebuchadnezzar's Golden Head for two and a half thousand years, waiting for their chance to take over the world?"

Isis took her time to answer. "I'm not sure. My view of what's possible, what's real and what isn't, has changed recently. You see, I think I've seen evil at work now— genuine pure evil. Innocent people killed for a piece of brass." Her eyes caught Murphy's for a second. "I don't know what to believe about the Golden Head, the return of Babylon, all that. All I know is I'm afraid. More afraid than I've ever been in my life."

Jassim nodded solemnly, then turned to Murphy. "I am like Dr. McDonald. I do not know what to believe. But just to be on the safe side, I think it might be a good idea to find this Golden Head before anyone else does."

"I'll second that," Murphy said.

"So, where do you suppose Marduk's dwelling is?"

"That's an easy one," Isis said. "The temple of Marduk was in Babylon."

"So you're saying..."

Murphy nodded. "Exactly. For this one, I'm going to have to call in everybody: the Parchments of Freedom Foundation, the American University, and my friend Levi, to pull every string in the region. We've got to get into Iraq."

sink down to the support of the granite; even his proud pulse that was to know no truce with effort till the grave, slackened speed, beat low and murmured mildly as in a dream along the avenues still echoing to the roll of its loud insistent drumming. His eyelids, their lining inflamed with the long vigil, drooped over his eyes.

Yet he did not sleep. Or did he?

His vesture of decay lay heavy on the stone, gathering strength from old mysterious reservoirs of bodily renewal for the next bout with living. It lay so still, so rapt in unconsciousness, that his spirit, at the summons of the old man's other unheard, unremembered suggestion, floated free from the body—for the first time, the only time in his life—and, in careless effortless victory over time and space and death and mystery, went searching for its own old reservoirs of renewal, went looking for the meaning of meaningless chance.

It was in the past, the future, among the living, the dead, the forgotten, the remembered—it was everywhere at once in all that Timothy had ever known, as when the moon rose the light had been everywhere at once. His mother, his father, lived again before the man's eyes as they had lived before the little boy's—a year of their life no longer than one beat of his heart; and the man, living all those years at once, saw what the child had taken for granted, the great tree of honor spreading its shelter over their heads, its roots struck deep into a tradition ancient beyond the memory of man, the old honorable human tradition of protection due to the weak from the strong, due to youth from maturity. *Noblesse oblige*— how could he have taken the old motto as a silly expression of caste-vanity! Like all things that survive, it was the expression of a law of nature, the unbreakable law which enjoins upon those whom experience has taught, upon those who know what they do, who know where a step will take them and what a gesture will cost them, not to exploit but to stand guard over helplessness and ignorance—like that of youth, holding out its hands heaped with gold of which it does not dream the value. From every corner of his child-world—from all the hours of all his life, incidents, sayings, expressions, voices, happenings of which he had never spoken and others he had forgotten, came singingly together in a rhythmic whole.

It was the significance of things he saw in that hour, the weary,

298

SIXTY-SIX

"THE HANGING GARDENS of Babylon," Isis said dreamily, stirring her iced tea. "I can't think of five more mysterious and seductive words. They sound so familiar—but nobody actually knows what they looked like."

Murphy watched her catlike sips. "Are you sure about that? You don't have a memory of walking through them two and a half thousand years ago?"

Isis took out a piece of ice and threw it at him. "Stop that."

Jassim frowned. He had chosen the restaurant because it was quiet and it was

inflamed, flesh-and-blood of his closed eyelids transparent as crystal. All that he had ever known, seen, felt or been, emerged from the darkness of mere fact into the ineffable clarity of its true meaning. Yes, yes, he saw how nothing ever just happens, to anyone.

He pushed open again the door to the dirty, disordered hall bedroom, he was the adolescent beaten down by more than he could endure, and he was the man of forty-five staggering under more than was bearable—and there was Aunt Lavinia again, beautiful and vital as an angel in tweeds; but now the man saw her in the glory of universal light that gave meaning to her individual sacrifice:—Timothy's poor father had not lived up to the debt of honor of the strong to the weak, of the experienced and mature to the unprotected defenselessness of youth. Well, that was a debt that must be paid. Lavinia would throw her heart away and pay it, since someone must.

All its turbulence stilled in exhaustion, all its demands silenced in sleep, Timothy's body unloosed its troubled hold on the spirit, ranging far and weightless in its search for strength and understanding. His eyes were open, were they not—or was it only by glimpses that he watched the frail column of smoke rising from his fire and bowing itself towards where the sun had set, that he saw Mr. Dewey coming and going, noiselessly feeding the little flames? The old man was no more real than Susan, who came and went and stood there, silently begging him not to stamp out that radiance on her face of which she yet knew nothing. Or was that Canby, saying humbly, proudly, with his brown eyes clear as peat-water, that moneyless, futureless, nobody-in-particular though he was, he must be allowed to give Susan and take from her, what youth alone can give and take, what youth has a right to demand that maturity protect, since it is the core of life?

You are of no mean race—the proud challenge to which he had been brought up rang in his ears—what race? Humanity. From where his spirit soared, high above the body annihilated by fatigue, it had the one vision of wholeness without which no mortal should go down to death, saw the oneness of all and his part in that oneness—and burst into song, as a bird does when night ends and day begins.

It was a bird's song. From a stunted oak tree, clutching its roots into a crack of the granite, a white-throated sparrow was singing in his very ear.

For a moment he lay listening with his spiritual and with his fleshly ear to the two songs blending, before he thought that if a bird were singing, dawn must be at hand. He sat up and looked to the east. Yes, back of The Wall the sky was gray.

The bird, in a tranquil ecstasy for life renewed, swelled its tiny feathered breast and sang again. In the west, the moon hung low where the sun had gone down.

But it gave off no light. The earth had spun its great bulk all around its axis since light had come from the west. Not from there, from the east, brightness sprang to the zenith with one bound, paling the moon to silver.

Timothy looked at his fire. Night was no more. The night wind held its breath. The gray column of smoke, released from the night-long pressure, stood straight in the still of the dawn.

Over The Wall the sky brightened from gray to mauve to pink to scarlet. Timothy kept his eyes on the omen of the faery column of smoke. He did not breathe. The sun thrust one fiery shoulder over the mountain, and all the world gave a shout of color. Oh, what was peace with its pallor compared to the many-colored confusion of light!

The new day began. The day wind woke. The column of smoke slowly, gently, bowed itself to the rising sun.

"So be it," said Timothy Hulme, and got stiffly up to go on with the teacher's work of arousing those who sleep.

Chapter Twenty-three

RENEWED like eagles by long dreamless sleep, the troop of youth clattered up the trail. They jostled each other, yelling, laughing over nothing, till, broken by the extravagance of their mirth, they leaned against trees to gasp for breath. They strode recklessly with long legs over the rolling stones and gnarled roots of the steep, rough path, and when they tripped and fell, they rolled light-heartedly over and over on the moss and ferns at the side. They tried out echoes with whoops, they wrangled fiercely, and then in a sudden grave Apache silence, put their heads together over tracks of deer or fox in a patch of moist earth. They exploded every energy in senseless leaps into the air to snatch at a certain leaf like any one of thousands they could have plucked by putting out a hand quietly to one side, and the moment they had caught it, they flung it down, forgotten in the golden pleasure of the leap—finished bodies with the vitality of men, still capable, by gusts, of the almost unendurable child-ecstasy of being awake after having been asleep.

From time to time they looked back over their shoulders at the old and the middle-aged men soberly bringing up the rear, a grizzled elderly dog ambling at their heels. When, as often happened, they out-distanced their rear guard, the boys, enchanted to have a reason for screeching their lungs out, broke into a tempest of halloos, "Wai-ai-ait! Wait! Hold on, kids! Hey, you ahead! Everybody wait a minute!" Tumbling off their blanket-rolls they flung themselves down on the earth, reveling as sensuously in relaxation as, the instant before, in taut sinews and flexed muscles, and gazed up at the sun-flooded blue sky through the leaves of the birches, maples, and oaks. Those leaves, hanging limp and still in the windless air, were pale gold here on the mountain, not green as in the valley. They were tender and scarcely-opened baby-leaves, for the climbers were now far up on Old Hemlock and in altitude had gone

301

possible to find a table in an alcove where you could talk without being overheard. He was in no mood for games. "So that is where the temple of Marduk is located? In the Hanging Gardens?"

"Or above them. We won't really know until we get there," Murphy said.

"You make it sound so simple. Surely it is not possible to turn up at the site and just start digging. So many of Iraq's antiquities have already been looted."

"That's the point, Jassim. The best place for Iraq's ancient treasures right now is a museum someplace far away. When law and order have been restored, and Iraq's own museums are up and running again, then everything can be returned and the Iraqi people will be able to appreciate their ancient heritage without worrying that some hoodlum is going to take it and put it on the open market."

Jassim looked skeptical. "It is hard to believe that something so big—What did you tell me? Fifteen feet tall, six or seven in diameter?—could have evaded the looters. Either the ones who came after the war *or* the ones who were running the country for thirty years. I think perhaps it was melted down and turned into gold faucets for Saddam's bathrooms a long time ago."

"That's a lot of faucets," Murphy said.

"He had a lot of bathrooms."

Murphy sipped his water thoughtfully. "Dakkuri has proved to be pretty smart so far. He managed to hide a Biblical artifact so no one would find it until...the time was right. I'm betting he hid the head pretty well too."

"And now the time is right to find it?"

"I'm not sure there will ever be a right time to find a thing like that. But anytime is the right time to stop the wrong people from getting their hands on it."

Isis checked her watch and picked her backpack up from the floor. "Then, let's get a move on. Our plane leaves in two hours."

Jassim put a hand on her arm. "Wait just a minute, please, Dr. McDonald."

"Isis. Please." It was odd, but now that her goddesses no longer seemed so real to her, she felt more comfortable with her name. "What is it, Jassim?"

He looked uncomfortable. "You, Murphy, are a brave man. Or perhaps just foolhardy—but no matter. Perhaps it is all the same. And you, Isis, you have endured some truly terrifying experiences with an extraordinary fortitude. I, on the other hand, am no kind of hero. The people who want to get hold of the Golden Head are clearly very powerful and utterly ruthless. It is not a combination I like."

"I hear what you're saying, Jassim," Murphy said. "And if you don't feel comfortable coming with us to Iraq, I wouldn't blame you. I'll admit it would make our job harder not having you around to help with the logistics. But we could manage. However, two things make me think we won't be coming up against the likes of our birdman again. First, he never got to see the inscription on the Serpent's head, and you destroyed the film and deleted everything on the computer. We're the only three people who know where the Golden Head is."

"I wish I shared your confidence." Jassim looked nervously around the restaurant. "This terrible man, this Talon, seems to have been a step behind you every inch of the way, if you don't mind my saying so.

How can we be sure he isn't somehow listening in to our conversation at this very moment?"

"Maybe he is," Murphy admitted. "But here's the second thing. We're not going to be on our own when we get to the temple of Marduk. Right now, a unit of U.S. Marines is securing the site."

Jassim stroked his chin. "Well, I hope they have orders to shoot on sight any suspicious characters—and any suspicious birds of prey, for that matter."

"I'm sure they do, Jassim. So, are you in?"

"I believe I am making a very foolish decision," he sighed. "But I think if you did find the head and I was not there to share the greatest archaeological discovery of modern times, I would have to kill myself anyway. So, yes, I am in."

SIXTY-SEVEN

AS THE LAND CRUISER bumped its way slowly through the scattered ruins of the ancient city, Isis had to pinch herself to check that she wasn't dreaming. Since the loving presence of her father had departed, she'd lived her life in hiding. Her academic studies had been a way of avoiding all the things in life that scared her, and her little office buried at the Foundation was really a kind of bunker from which she had success-fully kept the outside world at bay.

Until Michael Murphy had turned up in her life, that is.

Now, in the space of a few short days,

back from June to early May. Lying so, chewing wintergreen leaves or black-birch twigs, their ears ringing in the silence, the boys heard dreamily the reasonable conversational voices of the two men as they plodded slowly up the path, composed and steady, like the ticking of a clock heard in an interval of wild bursts of bird song.

They had time for a good deal of conversation, the two shepherds of the flock. The Cobble was on the lower slope of Hemlock, and lay at the north end of the mountain, miles away from the look-out rock on Perry's Point which was now their goal. This annual climb after the over-night sleep on the Cobble was never done in less than three hours up and one down. They knew—Timothy Hulme from two decades of experience, Mr. Dewey from a life-time's—that when they finally pushed out from the thicket of spruce upon the gray weathered rock at the Point, the boys would be winded and tired and very glad to sit quietly, swinging their legs, chewing their sandwiches and looking down to the infolded heart of Windward Mountain, never to be seen except from here. So, both rather pale after their almost sleepless night, they took their time, leaning to the steep pitch of the trail, setting their feet down with caution on the stones which, loosened by rain and frost, rolled and shifted at a touch.

"We ought to have a Bee and come up here, a hull crowd of us, with pickaxes and shovels and fix up this path before it's *all* washed out," said Mr. Dewey, meditatively, as he did every Mountain Day at about this place.

"Yes, it would be a good idea," answered Timothy, as he always did.

He was like a man still slightly under the influence of an anesthetic, able to join rationally in talk, but unable to put his real attention on it. In his mind was a question not yet sharply defined, not yet desperately articulate, but clearer and more imperative, as the floating haze in his mind thinned and blew away in the day-time stir of ordinary life—"But now what? That was an ending. How do you go on after you've come to an end?"

Knowing that nothing would be done about the mountain trails this year any more than any other year, Mr. Dewey continued to talk purposefully about possible developments of this and other trails. They crossed the top of Dowling Hollow. This meant that they were halfway to Hawley Pond. "What-say we get our breaths?" suggested Mr. Dewey, sinking down on the huge trunk of an old fallen yellow birch. The boys ahead whooped the signal for a pause, and dropped down on the carpet of last-year's dry leaves, flattened and glued together by the great weight of the only-just-melted snowdrifts of the winter. Timothy lighted a cigarette. Mr. Dewey began rather anxiously to talk about a recent calamity at the Academy. Someone—impossible to find out who, and indeed they had not tried very seriously to find out who, since it was obviously a thoughtless, not a malicious, performance—had carelessly left a faucet turned on in the "Chemical Room" on the second floor, and all one night the water had dripped through a plaster ceiling, down over the shelves where the priceless irreplaceable old Encyclopedia volumes stood. The damage would cost nearly three hundred dollars to repair. Mr. Dewey had asked Timothy to write a report of this to Mr. Wheaton, hoping that he would either suggest referring it to the approaching Trustees' meeting, or possibly put his hand in his pocket to make it up. They had not yet had his answer. Mr. Dewey wondered aloud whether, when it came, it would be accompanied by a check. "You'd think he might! Just a half or a quarter of the price of one of those darned worthless old books of his. . . ."

"How can you call them worthless?" asked Timothy harshly, stirred to resentful irony as he was by any mention of Mr. Wheaton. "Nothing's worthless to him that somebody else wants. The more it costs him to get it away from somebody else, the more value it has. Of course. I'm surprised that you don't know that."

"I've heard funnier jokes than that," said Mr. Dewey, rather sadly. He fell to talking about Mr. Wheaton's health, said not to be very good of late.

"How old is he?" asked Timothy.

"Not old at all. Can't be more'n seventy. But by the looks of him, he's always et too much."

He got stiffly to his feet and snapped his fingers at the old collie. The boys scrambled up and started on along the trail which here, following the old wood-road, was wide enough for several of them to walk abreast. Jules began to sing the Academy song, and the

303

others joined in, bawling the sentimental doggerel of the chorus with that hearty lack of any suspicion of where the tune was, which always drove Aunt Lavinia to frenzy.

Mr. Dewey listened affectionately. "Sounds kinda nice out here in the woods, don't it?"

Timothy said nothing.

"I always thought a good deal of our Academy song," said Mr. Dewey.

"Does anybody know who wrote the words?" asked Timothy evasively.

After a blink of astonishment at Timothy's ignorance, " 'Twas John Crandall," said Mr. Dewey.

"The John Crandall? That gave the endowment? I never knew he wrote anything."

"Well, 'twas the only time, 'sfar's I know. He was Class Poet. I guess he had to. Pretty good, at that, don't you think, for just a farmer?"

"It certainly has become a part of life as much as any song I ever heard of," said Timothy, disingenuously.

The boys, loping rapidly along, were far ahead now, their voices softened by distance as they chanted,

> "Aca-á-ademy! Aca-á-ademy!
> The years with thee will strengthen me
> To stand for right, to hold the light
> Of Honor burning high and free."

Mr. Dewey hummed the air with them, under his breath. The boys vanished around a turn of the road. The two men walked soberly side by side. Mr. Dewey's thoughts went back to the question of Mr. Wheaton's health, and he asked, "D'you s'pose he'll remember the 'cademy in his will? You'd think he *might,* to hear him go on about how much he thinks of it and all." He asked as though Timothy could know, "D'you suppose he might think of leaving as much as ten thousand?"

Timothy shrugged his shoulders without speaking. He was thinking, "But of course it's only in novels—and movies—that you can stop when you come to the end."

"I say ten thousand," remarked Mr. Dewey, "because . . ." He

304

was silent, walking more and more slowly, looking down at the green and gray carpet of moss lichen, thrusting out his lips thoughtfully, and finally halted Timothy, laying a hand on his arm. "Say, T.C., why ain't this as good a time as any"—he looked around the empty forest—"to tell you that I've made my will to leave what I've got to the Academy. 'T'ain't much. It comes, take it all in all, wood-lots and mill and saving-bank books, to about ten thousand. That's what made me, I guess, think of that much as maybe coming from Wheaton too."

Scattering the remnants of the haze in Timothy's mind, his own intention about making his will for Susan shouldered its way into his memory. In a darting reflex of pain, he said, the words bursting from him, "That's what I'm doing too" (although the idea had never till that moment occurred to him). "Why not? I'm absolutely alone in the world. There's nobody close enough to me to be in the least dependent on me except my old aunt and I'll surely survive her. But I haven't much. It'll be no more than six thousand—even if inflation doesn't carry it all downriver. If only I had what I put into that stone house. What idiocy it was for me to buy that!" He spoke with passion, as though the purchase of the house had been a major mistake, ruining his life.

Mr. Dewey corrected the disproportion between what he said and his way of saying it, by a philosophic, "Oh, 't'don't amount to so much as that, does it? If you wanted to, you could sell it again, and get your money back—quite some of it anyhow."

"I'll put it on the market tomorrow!"

Mr. Dewey looked at him in a surprise which Timothy felt might in an instant turn to speculative curiosity. He added hastily in a surly voice, "When a man's made a fool mistake he wants to repair it as soon as he can, doesn't he, and forget about it?"

Forget about it, forget about it, forget about it—the words tolled in his ears. Was it only forgetfulness—not peace—that had been promised him at dawn? He hung his head sadly and plodded on in silence.

They came up with the boys waiting to take breath before starting up a part of the ascent tilted so sharply that Mr. Dewey, when he came to it, began frankly to use his hands as well as his feet. Nobody had any breath for talking. They all climbed more and

she'd been exposed to danger, to fear, and to death. She'd ventured quite literally into the unknown. She'd journeyed through the dark underground heart of a medieval city. She'd seen the inside of a pyramid. And now she was about to walk on the ground of Babylon itself.

On the walls flanking the famed Ishtar Gate, fierce dragons met her wide-eyed gaze, survivors of three thousand years of rain, wind, and sandstorms. But her heart didn't quite leap the way she'd expected. Perhaps after a lifetime of studying the multifarious gods and goddesses that men had worshiped through the ages, she had finally caught a glimpse of something greater.

"There they are." Murphy was pointing to a nearby hillside, where crumbling walls still rose from the stepped terraces of Queen Amytis's original design. At the top, the temple of Marduk was marked by a lonely pinnacle of sandstone.

As Jassim had predicted, the site looked as if the jackals had long ago picked it clean. Whole sections of the hillside had collapsed, covering what had once been the remains of ancient doorways and staircases with earth and rubble. Any remaining segments of stone with any sort of engraving or design had been taken, from hand-sized fragments to actual pillars.

Murphy was surveying the devastation when a tanned marine officer in aviator shades trotted up the hillside to introduce himself. "Colonel Davis, U.S. Marines. You must be Professor Murphy."

Murphy submitted to a bone-crunching handshake. "It's good to see you, Colonel." For the first time, he noticed the handful of soldiers in desert camouflage forming a loose perimeter around the hillside. "And your men."

"Our pleasure. Anything we can do, just holler."

"I don't know where to start," Murphy admitted. "We need to see what's under the rubble. We're looking for some sort of underground chamber."

The colonel grinned. "Figured you might be. So I did a little digging around when we got here. Seems the fellas who cleaned this place out left a couple of items they couldn't find a use for on the black market."

Murphy brightened. "Such as?"

"How would a sonar sled suit you?"

Murphy broke out laughing. "That would suit me just fine, Colonel."

Half an hour later Murphy and Jassim were dragging the sled—a lightweight plastic oblong the size of a child's mattress—slowly across the rockslide while Isis watched the images forming on Murphy's laptop computer screen a few yards away.

So far all she'd seen were the shadowy outlines of collapsed chambers and empty vaults. Then her attention was taken by the remarkable symmetry of a pair of dark parallel lines on the screen. "Hold on! Can you back it up a little?"

Murphy and Jassim steered the sled in a crisscross pattern over the rocks. There was no mistaking them now. Some sort of man-made object was down there, perhaps a dozen feet beneath the surface. And it wasn't small.

Murphy and Jassim walked over and looked at the screen. Jassim nodded. "A set of doors, perhaps? An entrance of some kind, anyway."

"But how are we going to get to it?" Isis asked.

Colonel Davis had been standing to one side, observing her at work. "Pardon me, ma'am, but would a bulldozer help?"

Without waiting for an answer, he marched off, and a few minutes later they heard the groaning of the bulldozer's engine as it crested the hill. It pulled up a few feet from where Murphy and Jassim had been working the sled. Murphy gave the thumbs-up and the bulldozer started to heave the rubble aside. Its first pass just seemed to skim the surface, but the fresh-faced marine perched in the bulldozer's cab soon warmed to his work and after twenty minutes Murphy gave the signal to stop.

He walked over to the area of newly excavated earth, then turned to Colonel Davis. "Now all we need is a few shovels."

Davis saluted smartly. "Coming right up. And I've got twenty men with plenty of experience digging holes, if you need 'em."

By the time they'd dug down to a depth of about ten feet, Murphy and Jassim were getting dizzy with the effort, but the half-dozen marines alongside them hadn't even broken a sweat. "Whoa, that sounded like metal," one of them said as his shovel

more slowly and came out together on the shelving ledge where Hawley Pond lay. They approached it with the usual astonishment to see it improbably there, its black water glistening in its rough granite basin. Ice was still floating on it. "No, you *can*not," the two men said firmly as they always did here to flushed and sweaty boys eager for a plunge.

By a reflex place-association and because it seemed a harmless speculation, Timothy's mind brought up a question which had occurred to him here on other Mountain Days:—What are the mysterious bases of authority? Why were twenty-five powerful young men—for physically they were that—held in check by two, whose combined strength could not have prevailed against any one of the boys if he had simply refused to obey? Why did they obey? Why did they, looking longingly at the cold water, docilely swing into single file on the path leading around the Pond?

But it was not a harmless speculation. "Why did the boys obey?" Timothy knew why. Because in his voice, his bearing, his look, there was the same gray dusty evidence of the passage of years from which Susan had fled at the first shout of Canby's unbridled youth, to race on ahead with those who leaped and ran and laughed at falls, leaving him to trudge behind slowly, cautiously, peering down at the ground, taking no step forward till he was sure he would not slip.

But after all—his thoughts, finding themselves on a familiar treadmill, began from wonted habit to plod forward, after all, he told himself, life lasts longer than mere youth; life is something more than excited headlong rushing forward along a path where a misstep might mean disaster.

He walked more and more slowly; Mr. Dewey passed him and went on ahead. He had sunk into a groove worn deeply in his mind by repetition. To have brought out one of those frayed old formulae brought the others with it. Had he the *right,* he asked himself wearily for the thousandth time, to let Canby seize Susan's hand and drag her at top speed away from safety into danger? Had he not a responsibility, as much as he had to forbid the boys that leap into icy waters, had he not a real duty to use the authority of his personality in the same way for Susan's ultimate good?

Mr. Dewey went around the turn of the road and disappeared.

306

Timothy was alone now, his mind stumping along from one stock idea to the next one, as mechanically as one foot swung forward ahead of the other.

And then, as if a clap of thunder had rolled through the quiet woods, everything in him stood still—his mind, his heart, his feet. He was shaken—all the world was shaken—by one great, muted, wordless pulsation from the song he had heard at dawn. It silenced his reflex relapse into the meagerness of good sense, like one noble throb from all the strings at once, silencing the whining prose of an oboe.

Oh, it *had* been a promise of peace—the glimpse he had seen of what was before him! It had been of more than mere forgetfulness!

His heart, with a wild rush, began to beat again. He waited to let it slow and steady, waited to let the vast reverberation that had pulsed through all the world die down to stillness, waited for the pale new leaves that had quivered as it passed, to quiet themselves once more to the tranced calm of the windless day.

When it was quite gone, when his pulse was again composed, he walked on along the wood-road, back into prose, asking himself, "Why, what was that?" But he knew what it had been.

Beyond the end of the Pond, he found Mr. Dewey leaning back against the first of the balsams. He waved his hand at it, "Here we are, you see, got up as high as the soft woods. I guess mebbe we'll live to the top."

"Yes, maybe we will," agreed Timothy seriously.

The boys were far ahead, hidden by the thick-growing spruce and balsams. One of them was yodeling with soaring accuracy.

"Nice kid," said Mr. Dewey, pulling himself up to his feet with difficulty.

It could be, of course, only Jules.

"I like him," said Timothy.

"Everybody does."

"Awful Jewish mother," Timothy added, as they started up the path.

Mr. Dewey let this pass for a while, and then asked, "Any worse'n Mrs. Washburn?"

307

Timothy tried to think of a way to parry this, could not, and admitted, "Well, no-o-o. Different."

Presently they came up with the boys, not lying around on the ground to rest as usual, but in a circle around Jules. "How do you do it?" they were asking him curiously, enviously. "Do it again! Go *slow,* so we can watch."

The two men stood to draw breath, watching the swarthy, ugly, intelligent face of the Jewish boy as he good-naturedly threw back his head and yodeled at slow speed, the others watching, mystified, the movements of his lips and tongue. He looked very cheerful and at ease, in the midst of his comrades. Timothy looked months back to the long hotel corridor, with the sad-eyed stooping adolescent shambling down the velvet carpet; looked back only to the night before to the one boy of all the twenty-five who had been moved by beauty to joy and sorrow.

Mr. Dewey murmured in his ear, "Wish old man Wheaton could see that!"

Timothy shook his head. "It wouldn't make any difference."

The boys broke up into groups now, moving forward up the trail more slowly, shrieking and screeching as they tried out their untrained voices in imitations of Jules' yodel. Theirs sounded so ludicrous that the attempt broke up almost at once in the wild spasms of hilarity which were the ending of everything they did on the Mountain Day climb. Only Eli Kemp's halloo showed any promise. "Say, Eli, you've most got that!" called Jules. "Listen! This is the way it goes!" Eli came over to the other boy and walked close to him, his head bent to catch the trick of the lilt at the end. Presently he laid his arm around Jules' shoulders, and leaning towards him tried out his yodel in an apologetic murmur. "Atta boy!" shouted Jules, enchanted. "You got it. Now let's do it together. Ready? Go!" With arms intertwined the two boys bent to the climb, yodeling "like wildcats," said Mr. Dewey, laughing.

They were on the last part of the trail, fighting their way up between dwarfed scraggy evergreens, over the steep broken ledges of rock, weather-worn to treacherous smoothness. This was the section of the climb for which they had all put on shoes with corrugated rubber soles—all but old Don, scrabbling and slipping and panting

308

bounced off something hard. On their hands and knees they brushed the last of the loose earth away and then stood aside.

Joined by Isis, Murphy and Jassim looked down on a huge set of bronze doors. Encrusted with mineral deposits and a patina of discoloring sediment, the sculpted panels still had the power to astonish, as images of Nebuchadnezzar's many conquests came into focus after an interval of three thousand years. And there, towering above even the great Nebuchadnezzar, was the image of Marduk, the warrior-god.

For moments, nobody spoke. Then Jassim said, "I'd say we were in the place where Marduk dwells, all right. Shall we go in?"

The nearly horizontal doors looked as if they had been sealed for all time, and even if the combined manpower of all present could pry them apart, they had no way of knowing whether there was anything more than earth behind them. The whole structure had long ago shifted from the vertical, perhaps in one of the frequent earthquakes the region was subject to, and it was possible the doors opened onto nothing.

beside his breathless master. Mr. Dewey stopped, sank to a sitting crouch to rest, looked ahead and shook his head.

"Don't get a mite flatter that I notice, as I get me more birthdays," he remarked and turning his head to Timothy, said, "Gosh, T.C., I wish't I was as young as you!"

"Ah, yes," said Timothy evenly. "I don't feel a day over sixty."

Mr. Dewey smiled at this witticism, wiped the sweat from his neck and forehead, loosed his collar and, bent almost double by fatigue, struggled on. His deeply lined old face, streaming with perspiration, was gray, not red like Timothy's and the boys'. Timothy thought in anxiety and exasperation, "He's too old to go along on Mountain Day—a sleepless night and a hard climb the next morning. He ought to give it up. Why *will* old people still persist in trying to do what . . ." and interrupted his thought with a startled, "Ha!" so audible that Mr. Dewey looked back in inquiry.

The boys had disappeared. The two men climbed in silence, occasionally giving a hand to the old dog as he slithered and fell, his toenails scratching vainly for a hold on the rock. "Why on earth bring the dog too?" thought Timothy. "As if a fine view were more to him than his bed in the woodshed!"

And then the rock flattened out under their feet, they were fighting their way through the green jungle of the stunted balsam and spruce on the summit, ferociously thick-set with branches to make up for the height they dared not have at that altitude. In the darkest nooks under the trees sunken drifts of snow lay, smelling of cold. A welcoming yell of "Academy! Academy! One! Two! Three!" greeted them as they stepped out on the bare open rock and sank down among the boys lying in the sun, breathing deeply in the cold wind which, no matter how stagnant the weather in the valley, always blew around Perry's Point.

"Everybody's sweater on," said Timothy with his first breath, pulling his own down over his head. Reluctantly they reached for their wraps, and not reluctantly at all fell like wolves on the sandwiches which Timothy extracted from the knapsacks. He looked at his watch. "Half an hour before we start down," he told them, and with a long sigh of fatigue lay flat on the sun-warmed rock, his arms up over his head. Mr. Dewey liked, on the few occasions when he went out with Academy students, to make as close a con-

Under Murphy's direction, three marines stood on one of the doors and attempted to lever the other one open with their shovels. Soon even they were sweating, and Murphy began to suspect the doors had been cunningly designed to suggest a chamber beyond that didn't in fact exist.

Then suddenly there was a wrenching sound and a shovel flew out of one of the soldier's hands as a crack appeared and a rush of stale air escaped from below. Grabbing hold of the door's edge, they heaved, and it slowly swung upward with a groaning of ancient hinges.

Holding on to one of the doors, Murphy eased himself down into the blackness, his legs hanging free in the empty space. So, the doors did open onto *something*. The fetid air was almost unbearable now, an acrid stench of decay more powerful than anything he'd ever experienced. He felt a wave of nausea and then his chest started heaving as his lungs convulsed. He heard Isis scream as his fingers slipped off the edge of the door, and then he was tumbling downward.

The moment seemed to stretch out, and Murphy thought of drowning men whose whole lives flash past them in a split second. Then a jarring impact sent a lightning pulse of pain shuddering through his legs. Before he could cry out, his head smashed against something hard and unyielding, and a black cloud ballooned inside his head, blotting everything out.

When he came to, he could hear voices from above. For a moment it was just noise, then the sounds turned back into words again and he understood it was Isis and Jassim asking if he was all right. He heard the second door being hauled back.

"I'm okay," he managed to say, hauling himself onto his hands and knees. Another wave of coughing seized him as more of the black air forced itself into his heaving lungs and he felt his eyes stinging with tears. He waited until the fit had passed, then wiped his face with the back of his hand. His head was ringing, but the pain in his legs had sub-sided to a steady throbbing. He opened his eyes.

Then closed them again as his head filled with an agonizing brightness. *The blow on the head,* he thought. *I've blinded myself.* Fighting down a wave of panic, he steadied his breathing and squinted through half-open lids. The golden light was still over-whelming, but he forced himself to keep his eyes open and gradually the fierce haze that filled his field of vision resolved itself into a solid object.

He was looking into the iris of a huge golden eye.

Still on his hands and knees, he shuffled backward in the dirt until the rest of the object came into focus. At first the powerful ridges and curving lines of sculpted metal didn't make any sense—like the jumbled features of a giant Picasso. Then his per-spective adjusted to its horizontal position and the face of Nebuchadnezzar glared at him across a chasm of two and a half thou-sand years.

Murphy shuffled back farther until he leaned against the wall of earth and looked into the face of the king. How faithfully the sculptor had managed to capture the king's features he had no way of knowing, but the sculpture definitely had an unnerving real-ism. The great eyes seemed to bore straight through Murphy like lasers, and the sneer of command etched into the huge mouth seemed to be saying, *Raise me up, you dog! I have lain in the dust long enough!*

He didn't know how long he had been crouching there, mesmerized by the imperious stare of the long-dead king, before he heard the thud of boots alongside him and the sound of excited voices raised in wonder and awe. Then strong hands hauled him upright and he closed his eyes again, grateful not to have to look anymore into the face of evil.

tact with them as he could, and it was Timothy's habit to stand aside and leave the talk to him. There were two or three things the old man always wanted to have a chance to say to youth. Especially now. He often told Timothy, "Every time I look at a newspaper, these days, I want to hunt me up another kid and tell him, 'Load your gun and cock it and stand guard over the Bill of Rights with your eye peeled, American boy!'"

It was probably to say that once more that he had toiled all the way up the mountain. Timothy had never thought the occasion especially favorable for serious talk. But there was no deflecting Clifford tradition, and Mr. Dewey's presence and moralizing on Mountain Day was of that tradition. Well, it relieved the Principal of responsibility for a half hour.

It was all just as it always was, the boys gobbling noisily, swallowing hard, passing the water canteens back and forth, and, as they emerged from starvation, beginning to look at the view with their usual topographical matter-of-factness. *"There's* the 'cademy tower," they said as eagerly as though they saw it for the first time, "and that green stretch south of it is Lundy Brook Hollow. Yes, it is too. Sure it is. And there's the Catholic Church. It is not, it's the 'Piscopal Church. Oh, Mr. Dewey, isn't that your sawmill—that red spot up where the rocks stick out? No, it's . . ."

Timothy closed his eyes against the light. When he opened them, he perceived to his astonishment that he had fallen into sleep, real sleep, not exhausted unconsciousness. He felt his mind rising slowly from a more complete rest than it had known for weeks. He listened, as one who has deeply slept and then awakened always does, to hear whether the world is still spinning true on its axis. The chatter of the boys was still. Only Mr. Dewey's voice in a monologue—Timothy rolled over, and saw the boys clustered around the old man on the other end of the rock. Mr. Dewey was looking down at a tiny pool of water, no more than a cupful, left from yesterday's showers in a hollow of the granite. Oh, yes, Timothy knew what he was saying—not politics and the Rights of Man this time, but the lesson in geology the old man liked to give young people up here, pointing out to them how water, although it looked so soft, yielding, and strengthless, would in the end get the better of the hulking rock carcass of the mountain. Timothy had often heard him thus, stooping over a shallow pool of rain-water in a depression of the rock, say to the Mountain Day climbers, "Ain't enough there to make your aunt a cup of tea, is there? But the mountain'd better look out!" The old man had always used it as a simple fillip to the boys' imagination, bidding them look from the humble pool along the great ridge of Old Hemlock's back, and guess which was stronger and more lasting than the other. But as Timothy listened, he heard that today even geology was tinged with Mr. Dewey's concern about the Rights of Man. Fascism and dictatorship were symbolized, apparently, by the mountain. The water—which could not but win in the end—was, he gathered, the resistance of free men to attempts to make them less than free. A good enough metaphor for a sermon, he thought (although what did boys from Vermont villages and farms have to do with Hitler?), and the better for Mr. Dewey's sermon because of being obvious. But were the boys listening? Did the young ever listen to the moralizings of their elders? In Timothy's gloomy moods of doubt he was sure they did not.

Still lying on his side, he shifted his eyes to the boys as they sprawled around the old man. But—as always, he thought—nothing can be learned about young people by looking at them. They might have been anywhere as they slouched down in their torn baggy pants and shapeless sweaters, their uncombed hair sticking out in tufts, their faces not very clean. Sometimes they looked at Mr. Dewey, sometimes they looked down at the tiny pool in the rock, sometimes their eyes went from the weather-beaten granite of the old man's face to the blue-and-gold immensity of the distant mountains and sky. During Timothy's sleep, some huge, heaped-up cumulus clouds had climbed up from behind Old Hemlock and hung over the Point, so that sitting here on the overhanging rock, they looked out from shadow across the valley at The Wall, vibrating blue in the sunshine.

Timothy sat up and looked at his watch. He had slept straight through the half hour they were to be on the rock. And he had not yet looked at the view. You could not come to Perry's Point and not look at the view. So he swung his feet over the edge and looked at it. The great white clouds over his head moved slowly forward till they shadowed the valley and the long line of The Wall on the

SIXTY-EIGHT

SHARI TUGGED AT Paul's hand. It was still weak from his long hospital stay.

"Hey," he protested, "the plaster came off only yesterday. You're going to pull it out of its socket."

"Stop fussing," she said. "Dr. Keller said too much sympathy wouldn't be good for you. It would impede the healing process. Look—there he is!"

He had let her drag him all the way to Washington, D.C., to wait at the airstrip where the Parchments of Freedom Foundation had arranged for the cargo plane to land. They had not arranged for the vast array of cameras and reporters, but it was hard to keep the arrival of such a spectacular artifact from the press.

When the plane touched down, Shari started waving frantically before Michael Murphy came bounding down the steps. "Professor Murphy!"

He turned with a quizzical expression, then walked over, beaming. "It's okay, Officer. You can let these two through. They've earned it."

The guard grudgingly stepped aside and Murphy and Shari hugged. Paul could feel the wordless communication passing between them.

They pulled apart and Shari said, "I can't believe you did it. I can't believe it's really here. In the States!"

Murphy grinned. "It wasn't easy. We had to persuade a lot of people it was the right thing to do. I couldn't have done it without my friends here"—he indicated a petite redhead with elfin features and an elegant, dark-complexioned man in a cream suit who were talking animatedly to the trucking crew—"putting the weight of the Parchments of Freedom Foundation and the

other side. Only the far-distant peaks beyond and the sky above them still caught the sun. It was a beautiful variation on the usual lighting. Timothy was aware of that. He also knew the view to be fine in all lights, especially to the right, where you looked down into those secret inner folds of Windward Mountain that could not be so much as guessed at from the valley. He looked down. Yes, there was the hidden heart of Windward . . . "And what of it?" he asked himself dryly. "Those far blue mountains shining under a gold-blue sky look as though they were the Abodes of the Blest. But they are not. They are in reality only an extra-poor corner of Windward County, Vermont. A lot of nonsense is talked about natural beauty. Has it, after all, any meaning?" He meant, any meaning to him, still quivering as he was in the shock of energies aroused to the explosion point—for nothing; like a runner crouched in terrific tension, waiting for the crack of the starting-pistol, who is roughly told off to stand to one side and watch the race.

It was time to go. He waited for a pause in Mr. Dewey's talk, and when the old man stopped to look at him inquiringly, he held up his watch. "Time's up."

The boys, made over by half an hour's rest and a few stale sandwiches, were ready to begin life all over again from the beginning. They rose whirring like a covey of game-birds, snatched up their blanket-rolls and were off. Part of the ritual of the day was the abandonment of group discipline on the way down the mountain. Nobody need wait for anyone else. The race was to the speediest. The elders, bringing up the rear, were held responsible for picking up things dropped in the scramble and for helping anybody with the sprained ankle or broken leg always predicted by older Clifford people, but never yet forthcoming after more than a century of annual Mountain Days.

Mr. Dewey laughed a little ruefully at the speed of their disappearance and shook his head over himself. "All-fired interested in my sermon, wa'n't they?" He tried to get to his feet, fell back, remarked resignedly, "I do what you don't do, T.C., I talk too much. All old folks do." He tried again stiffly to rise, accepted a heaving pull up from Timothy and stood for a moment to have his look at the view before starting back.

He gazed down into the secret heart of Windward Mountain,

his gray head sunk between his great stooped shoulders. Timothy, looking at the closed absent old face, asked himself skeptically, "Does it have any meaning for *him?*" The old woodsman might, from any expression in his face, have been calculating the amount of lumber to be cut from those slopes. He lifted his eyes—Timothy saw that they were intent, blue, and still under their shaggy brows —and looked beyond that lower mountain, beyond the valley dark in shadow, beyond the barrier of The Wall, off to the range after range of distant peaks golden in the golden light, a sunlit infinity of blue flowing above them. His face brightened. For an instant he was visibly there in the Abodes of the Blest. He drew a long breath, smiled, and nodded his head in grave agreement with an inner affirmation.

Like the instant's clicking open of a camera-shutter, Timothy was back in the first days after Susan's accident, when she lay between life and death, when in an agony of purified, nonpossessive love, he had been filled by only one hope, one prayer—that she might live, just that she might live. For that one instant his heart laid down its burden.

"We better get started down, I guess," said Mr. Dewey. The old collie hobbled to his master's knee and looked up adoringly at him. Mr. Dewey stooped, laid his hand on the grizzled head, and scratched it gently back of the ears. "Kinda nice up here, isn't it, Don?" he said in a murmur. To Timothy, after a moment's pause, he added in explanation of his florid emotion, with the apologetic tone demanded by Clifford good manners when taking up another person's time by chatter about oneself, "Mebbe the last time Don and I'll ever get up here."

"Oh, *no,* Mr. Dewey! How can you say such a thing?" asked Timothy.

The old man let this hypocrisy pass in patient silence, reaching into his pants pocket for his jack-knife. "I better cut me a good stout stick before I start down over those loose stones," he said mildly.

There was no breath left over for more than an occasional brief question and answer during the long climb down. Mr. Dewey was divided between fatigue, tense care lest he lose his footing and fall, and determination not to ask or accept any help from a younger

313

American University of Cairo behind it.
You know me, I'm not very good at playing
nice with bureaucrats."

"But you did it!" Shari said again.

"I even got some behind-the-scenes help
from a very special place, from someone
who had already helped us tremendously."
Murphy pulled a copy of a letter from the
pocket of his jacket. "Wait till you read this,
guys. As momentous as the arrival of the
Golden Head is today, this is even greater
reason for celebration. This letter was waiting for me when I got to the plane. Listen.

"My dear Professor Murphy—

"Thank you for honoring my home
with your visit, and for allowing me to
help you with your search for what I
now know was the Brazen Serpent,
which has in turn led you to the Golden
Head of Nebuchadnezzar. I am doubly
honored to have played some small part
in arranging for the exit for its
temporary home in your charge.

"But most of all, thank you for taking
the time to explain to me so clearly the

real reason why Christianity is the one true path to God.

"After you went to bed that night, I sat alone in my room contemplating what you had told me about the nature of God. For the first time, I understood that Jesus Christ had died for my sins and for the sins of the world. He then rose from the dead.

"That night, I received Him by faith, as you had urged, and I invited Him into my life.

"If I do not see you again in this life, I certainly will see you in the next, in heaven.

"Sincerely,
"Sheikh Umar al-Khaliq"

Shari broke out into a wide smile. "Oh, Professor Murphy, that has got to be such a great feeling, to know that you helped this sheikh in his search."

Murphy hugged her and noticed Paul again. He gripped his hand. "Hey, it's good to see you, Paul. You're looking well. And I understand you have a new scholarship from the Barrington folks. I trust that will allow you to really bear down and find some course of study that excites you more than business."

"Yes, sir. Shari here would not have let me agree to it otherwise. She's been a great help." He blushed, and Shari poked him hard in the ribs.

"Go easy on him, Shari," Murphy said. "He's still a young man. It will take a while before he realizes he's got to turn most of his life decisions over to God and a good woman, in that order."

She wagged a finger. "Professor Murphy!"

The lanky figure of Dean Fallworth sidled out of the hangar and blocked Murphy's path. Before he could react, Dean Fallworth grabbed his hand and started pumping it enthusiastically.

"Murphy—great to have you back. The faculty board and I, we're all tremendously proud of what you've achieved for the university. This is a proud day indeed for Preston, with one of our finest in the news." A sheepish look briefly supplanted his huckster's grin, and he lowered his voice so only

Murphy could hear. "I hope we can put our little misunderstanding behind us. My comments on that TV interview were taken totally out of context, you know. In fact, I'm considering a formal complaint against BNN and that awful reporter. She practically put the words into my mouth."

Murphy really couldn't think of anything to say. He would settle his account with Fallworth when the time came. Right now he was simply relieved that his position at the university was secure. When all the fuss and publicity died down, he'd be able to get back to his real job of inspiring his students. He knew that was what Laura would have wanted him to do.

He gave Fallworth a look to let him know he wasn't going to pick a fight now, but he wasn't necessarily letting him off the hook either. "Later, Dean." He brushed past him, leaving Fallworth standing, his fixed smile holding him in place.

"Isis, Jassim. I want you to meet some good friends and students of mine, Shari Nelson and Paul Wallach."

Jassim held his hand out while Isis delivered some last-minute instructions to one of

man; Timothy, between exasperation at the prickly vanity of the old mountaineer and a growing heaviness of spirit as the trail brought them lower and lower towards the valley life waiting for him, grimly unchanged for all his moment of exaltation at dawn. Suppose the first thing he should see as they came into the maple grove back of the Academy were Canby, lounging along beside Susan with his shambling powerful step, leaning towards her with that boldly intimate look which Timothy found so insolent? "Mr. Dewey, do let me give you a hand down this rock!"

"I was a-goin' up and down this rock before you were weaned, young man."

"Well, have it your own way, then."

"I guess I will, if it's all the same to you."

They were both of them irritable with an inner anxiety, with a secret pain. They hardly noticed what the other one said or did.

Hot and sweaty, their knees aching, Mr. Dewey's legs visibly shaking, they scrambled down the last steep stretch of the path, across the field back of the big maples of the sugar-bush, turned a corner and found themselves at the north end of the rock ledge on which the Academy stood. It was long past noon. They had not met Canby and Susan. They had met nobody. The tennis courts were empty. Not a soul was in sight. From the opened windows of the Principal's house, beyond the Academy building, the brass of the most vociferous part of the Aïda *March of the Priests* blared sonorously. Timothy thought with relief, "Well, here he is, and still alive."

Alive but excessively tired. With a pang of alarm for himself, Timothy noted that Mr. Dewey looked very old as well as entirely exhausted. His mind darkened in a familiar thought—the time could not be far off when the voters of Clifford would need to choose another Trustee to take his place. If they made another such choice as on the ill-fated election-day which had put in Mr. Wheaton— "Don't you want me to step ahead and get my Ford out, and take you home?" he asked, his solicitude too audible.

"No, I do not," said the haggard old man, nettled and belligerent. "I'm a-goin' to the office to see if there's a letter from Wheaton come in."

They limped on in dogged silence then, foot-sore, unshaven, their

314

coats over their arms, their faded shapeless Mountain-Day clothes stained brown and green by damp earth and moss, the played-out old collie dragging himself along at their heels. They climbed slowly up the worn marble steps into the echoing corridor with its musty smell of age and chalk-dust and mice, into the high-ceilinged, dingy room that was the Principal's office.

A good deal of mail was heaped on the pine table that was the Principal's desk. It was Saturday, the day for the weekly magazines, and it was near Commencement when catalogues from colleges, normal schools and "Institutes of Commercial Education" came in on every train. An untidy pile of second-class mail lay on the blotter, overshadowing the dozen or so letters waiting to be opened.

Mr. Dewey dropped his hat on the floor and sank heavily into a chair; Timothy put out his hand to sort over the letters. But at the same instant their eyes were caught by the cover of the weekly magazine on top of the pile—a reproduction of a colored photograph, with the raw realism of an unretouched snapshot. It showed a sort of rough wooden cage set on an open truck, in which were crowded ten or twelve men of various ages, collarless, disheveled, their heads shaven to the skull, large placards hanging down from their shoulders over their coats, dark, well-cut coats of professional men, torn, tumbled, dirtied. They hung their heads low in exhaustion, their hands, long-fingered and shapely, clutched hard at the bars. Below them, in the foreground, evidently standing on the street beside the truck, appeared a man in uniform, a swastika on his arm, a stocky, short-necked, cheerful-looking man, with a stubble of short blond beard almost to his eyes—small, deep-set eyes, they were, gleaming slits in his broad face as he grinned delightedly at the camera.

"Hell and damnation! Throw that thing in the wastepaper basket!" cried Mr. Dewey, reaching across to it and tearing it in two. "Makes me ashamed to look a decent dog in the face."

He flung the pieces down on the floor, put his hands on the head of his stick and dropped his chin on them, growling and cursing inarticulately.

With a shudder Timothy asked, "Doesn't it sometimes make you wish you could die and get out of the mess?"

315

"It does not!" said the old man vehemently. "What'd I want to *die* for? It makes me want to *do* something about it!"

"As if there were anything anybody could!" Timothy protested, as he began to sort the letters.

The one they were looking for came at once into visibility. The large square envelope of creamy thick linen paper with the return address and a coat of arms engraved in the corner was as different from the other commonplace oblongs of bluish-white as Mr. Wheaton's tailored tweeds and custom-made shoes were from the mail-order windbreakers and heavy boots so much worn in Clifford. It was addressed to Mr. Dewey. Timothy handed it across the table to the old man and tore open a letter in a cheap stamped envelope, postmarked from Boston, addressed to him in a handwriting that was vaguely familiar, yet not quite recognizable. It was signed Delia Barney—he blinked—who was that?—oh, yes—and it told him that she was now graduated from her Boston high school, having completed her course in three years, and would be glad to come on to Clifford for the special coaching for college entrance examinations which Professor Hulme had so "kindly suggested to my sister Susan."

Timothy was still looking down at this when Mr. Dewey said surprisingly, "Well, the damn dirty skunk," and laid the letter on the table. "Read it. Read it, T.C.," he murmured, dropping his head wearily back and closing his eyes till Timothy had finished.

It did not take long; the typing on the thick expensive paper was perfectly executed as always; the words, entirely legible in very black letters on white, leaped out to say that Mr. Wheaton had long ago and more than once told Hulme to get rid of that incompetent old Melville Griffith, and now was the time to do it. Anybody could see that he was the one who had left the faucet turned on; or if this could not be literally proved, it was so exactly like the kind of muddle-headed things he was always up to, it could be assumed he did. He certainly could not prove he had not. Here was the talking-point for dismissing him which Mr. Wheaton had long been waiting. "Here's your chance to take advantage of the depression and the unemployment situation. If you play your cards right, you can get a first-rate competent man who'd be a *real* janitor. Look around and locate a family man with young children who's been out of a

316

job for some time—there must be lots of them in Ashley since the shutting down of the chair factory—you could probably get him actually for less wages than Griffith. He wouldn't dare hold out for more anyhow, no matter what he had been earning."

The two men looked at each other in a long silence, Timothy's unshaven face stern, dark, disdainful; the old man in the chair, sagging under the weight of his years, slowly shaking his head from side to side. Finally Mr. Dewey remarked in a conversational tone, "Wa-al, I guess mebbe I could get a couple o'hundred for the oak on the Tyler lot. 'T'ain't really big enough to cut yet, but . . ."

"Oh, never mind. I've got nearly two hundred and fifty in the bank I could spare," said Timothy. It was what he always tried to save for his vacation travels—he had no sense of loss. What could he do with a vacation?

He laid the letter down. Mr. Dewey silently reached for it and dropped it into the wastepaper basket. As he turned his head to do this, he caught sight through the open window of someone on the far corner of the level ground in front of the Academy, and looked to see who it was. Timothy followed the direction of his eyes and saw a tall, red-headed boy pushing a bicycle up the hill from the village. He was in a faded checked shirt and cheap old Sears Roebuck pants, not in uniform, but both men knew that it was Burt Stephenson who earned part of his way through school by carrying telegrams from the Western Union office and special delivery letters from the post office.

Mr. Dewey said uneasily, "I'm just behind the times enough so it makes me kind of nervous to get a telegram. Don't it you?"

"Oh, this is probably from Jules' mother, changing her mind again about where he's to go this summer," Timothy told him. "She always telegraphs instead of writing. That's the New York of it."

The red-headed boy pushed his bicycle around the corner at the top of the hill, flung a long leg over the saddle, mounted, and pedaled along the short driveway to the Principal's house, dismounted there and started up the steps. Timothy went to the window and called, "Hey, Burt! If that's a telegram bring it over here."

"It's for Mr. Dewey. There's a special delivery for him too."

"Well, he's here with me."

The boy left his bicycle collapsed in a tangle of glittering wires

317

the crew preparing to open the crate. "The pleasure is all mine," he said. "I have heard many good things about you both. Preston University is truly fortunate to have such outstanding students of archaeology—especially considering the, shall we say, *unconventional* habits of your professor." He indicated Murphy with a wink.

Isis joined them. "Take no notice of Jassim. He's just making the most of being in the limelight. He thinks maybe some bigwig from the Discovery Channel is going to give him a series on the secrets of the pyramids."

"And why not?" said Jassim, doing his best to look offended. "I am an excellent communicator, I think, and I have the sort of face the camera likes. Miss Nelson, what do you say?"

"I'd tune in," she said, laughing. "After everything you two have done to help Murphy find the Golden Head, it's the least I could do."

Murphy coughed. "Speaking of which, let's start unloading."

It took the best part of an hour to unload the crate from the cargo bay and set it on a huge flatbed truck. Now the crate stood alone in the center of the truck like an enormous piece of modern art.

Murphy gave the signal, and the loading crew, evenly spaced around the crate, pulled at the ropes securing the panels on each of its four sides. The wooden panels crashed to the ground simultaneously. A team from the PFF raced over to cut the protective coats of fabric and plastic that had been fashioned around the head. As the last layer of wadding fell away, Murphy stepped up to the microphone set up alongside the head.

"Ladies and gentlemen of the world, there is much to tell about this great find, how we came to discover it, to reclaim it, and understand its significance. That will all have to wait until we have it safely in place in its temporary home, the Parchments of Freedom Foundation, which has generously put up the funds for this great artifact to be studied thoroughly and expeditiously. I want to thank God for His strength and guidance throughout the entire process. We look forward to sharing its wonders and secrets with you soon. Thank you."

In this moment of great professional triumph, Murphy was saddened by his thoughts of Laura and the guards at the PFF, and all the other terrible events that had led to this wondrous achievement. As if by reflex, he also shuddered when he thought about the man who was responsible for so much of that suffering, Talon, who was still at large, and would presumably be as keen to possess the Golden Head of Nebuchadnezzar as he was the Brazen Serpent.

Maybe even more so, because Murphy had thwarted his chances to put the Serpent back together. And if this mystery man Talon truly did have an interest in these icons for the dark powers many believed they still possessed, Murphy was beginning to have a feeling that as eventful as the last few weeks had been, the days ahead would present even greater challenges.

With God's help and protection, he would be ready.

SIXTY-NINE

THE SLAVES PULLED in unison on the ropes, straining with all their might. Finally, the massive piece of gold came crashing to the ground. The idol that had brought the king and his people so much torment now lay in ruins in the swirling dust, its disembodied head staring with betrayal at the man whose image it had been fashioned after. King Nebuchadnezzar then ordered that the pieces be gathered up and delivered to Dakkuri, the chief Chaldean priest, back in the city. The gold would be reused for sacred vessels, or so the king had been led to believe.

———

The king was mad, of that Dakkuri had no doubt. For seven years Nebuchadnezzar had groveled in the dirt, living like a beast in the shadow of his own palace, his wits scattered to the four corners of an empire that hung by a thread while jealous neighbors plotted its overthrow. And yet, now that the king's sanity had been restored, now that he spoke and thought and acted like a man once more, Dakkuri had a strange sense that he was madder than ever.

What else could explain his decree that all the idols should be destroyed? Somehow, Daniel and his God had the king under their spell.

Dakkuri shivered, and it was not just because of the damp air in his chamber. If the worship of idols was ended, who would the people turn to in times of danger and uncertainty, when plague and pestilence struck, when the crops failed or the rivers overflowed their banks? From whom would they receive the strength to destroy their enemies, to raze their cities and enslave their sons? Who would give them the power to rule the world?

More to the point, where would Dakkuri's own power and prestige come from? When he looked into the sacred fire, it was he—and he alone—who could interpret the shifting shapes of light. When Nergal, the fierce god of the under-

and started across the empty tennis court. He had a white envelope and a yellow one in his hand.

"Get off that court with those leather heels!" trumpeted Timothy in his loudest drill-master's bellow.

The boy gave a startled leap to one side and went around by the driveway. They heard his feet come clattering down the long corridor. He appeared at the open door of the Principal's office and handed the two envelopes to the Chairman of the Board of Trustees.

"Wait a minute, Burt," said Timothy. "Maybe there's an answer. Here, I'll sign for that special delivery."

Mr. Dewey had roused himself enough from his limp exhaustion to lean a little forward in his chair as he took the two envelopes from the messenger. He tore open the yellow one first, looked at it blankly, said, "What d'you s'pose that means?" and passed it on to Timothy. It read, "Sending important letter to you special delivery mail today. Gilbert W. Paine."

"D'you ever hear that name?" asked Mr. Dewey.

"Never," said Timothy, and then, "Oh, yes, I have. I think it's Mr. Wheaton's attorney."

Mr. Dewey tore open the letter, began to read, turned very white, brushed his hand across his eyes as if he could not see, and handing the letter to Timothy, said, "Here, you tell me what's in that."

They had forgotten the Academy Senior standing back of them.

Timothy began to read aloud connectedly, but by the end of the first sentence he was wildly snatching only at the salient word in each phrase, flinging them out without connection as if he were reading aloud a telegram, "George Clarence Wheaton found dead— apoplexy—will leaves Academy one million dollars for endowment —two hundred thousand for buildings—on condition name be changed—Wheaton Preparatory School—also exclusion all Jewish students—Jewish defined as person with any relative of Hebrew blood—codicil prescribes also that tuition be . . ."

Astounded to literal incredulity, clapping his hand wildly to his head, Timothy began to read the words again to himself, his eyes racing down the page. He was unaware that he was loudly exclaiming as he read, "Why! Why! Why! Of all the— For Heaven's sakes . . . ! Would you . . . ?" He looked up from the paper and

318

had the startled impression that Hemlock Mountain loomed there in his office.

Mr. Dewey was on his feet, had risen to his full height. Timothy had never seen him stand straight before, had never known how tall he was. His gray head seemed to graze the ceiling. He towered over Timothy's six feet like a cliff.

"What do you say to that, Timothy Hulme?" he asked, his face dark as thunder.

"I say it's infamous. What did you *think* I'd say?" shouted Timothy, crushing the letter together and flinging it down.

The old man's face cleared. He took a long step around the table and held out his right hand.

Timothy's hand clenched his, silently took the vow with him. It was done.

Their hands having spoken for them, fell apart. Mr. Dewey drew a deep breath and said in a steady voice, "Yes, now is the time, T.C., for all good men to stand up for their country."

Chapter Twenty-four

OVER the abyss between exaltation and everyday life, Mr. Dewey let down, as a bridge, the Clifford tradition of wasting no energy on heroics. "But let's get us something to eat first. I'm hollow as a drum." He stooped stiffly, picked up his hat and put it on.

Timothy, giddy with excitement, did his best to follow this Vermontish lead, "You're welcome to whatever Lottie has left for me at the house. Hash probably." His voice sounded odd and far away.

"Hash sounds all right to me." Shuffling towards the door, the old man suggested, "Better pick up that letter, T.C. No use spreadin' the news around before we've had time to think what we're a-goin' to do and how we're a-goin' to do it."

Timothy said with a tense uncertain laugh, "Oh, this is news there's no hiding." But he turned back, stooped over, picked up the ball of crumpled paper, put it in his pocket and was aware of an apologetic shuffling of feet behind him. Burt Stephenson stood there by the desk, embarrassed and troubled.

"Oh . . . !" said Timothy, and halted, entirely at a loss.

Mr. Dewey looked back, said, "Oh . . . !" and stood still. There was a short silence.

Then Mr. Dewey moved forward again, saying over his shoulder, "Well, Burt, come along with us to the Principal's house, will you?"

"Got to," murmured Burt, self-excusingly. "Left my bike there."

The three walked down the corridor at the old man's pace. At the front door Mr. Dewey halted, drew a rather quavering breath, and said forebodingly, "We got to move fast, T.C., if we're a-goin' to keep ahead of this." His eyes were fixed on the piece of western sky blue in the leafy frame of the two great sycamore trees. He was not looking at it, he was looking at his own old age.

In a moment, with a kind of controlled anguish, he put a question to Timothy, *"Can* I move fast enough, T.C.? Can I move fast at all, anymore?"

320

"The two of us together can probably get up quite a speed, Mr. Dewey," said Timothy.

Looking in concern at the old man's sunken eyes, darkly ringed in his pale, lined face, he added, "The first thing to do in a hurry is to eat. And to drink some coffee." He hesitated, "You wouldn't feel like taking my arm, would you, over to the house?"

To his surprise Mr. Dewey put out his hand to accept this help, and leaning heavily on the supporting arm, let himself down the high front steps.

As they took, very slowly, the length of the driveway between the Academy and the Principal's house, Timothy, still shaken to the core, looked around him, astonished to see that the day was still the essence of June—Vermont June—cool, bland, calm. The sprawling old Persian rosebush had bloomed overnight, and stood resplendent and secure, every burnished petal of its hundred flowers, every fragile grain of the gold-dust of its countless stamens as motionless as though it were set under an invisible glass bell. As they passed it, Timothy looked at its tranced immobility, thought, "That's where I've been for twenty years. That's where I was ten minutes ago," and could have shouted out like a man glowing under a cold shower.

He was aware of nothing but the indignation and the glorious combative rage in his heart. He gave not the slightest attention to his mind, distracted by the confusion of facts which it must sort out into order before a plan of action could be made. With no attention from him, it scurried from one corner of its task to another, crying out, "But suppose nobody else in Clifford, nobody at all . . ." and, "Oh, there's Aunt Lavinia to think of," and, "Vermont farmers can't be expected to . . ." and, "How much a month is the interest on six thousand, but, no, that Middle Pacific stock will never pay again," and, "Every merchant in town, *of course,* because of more business, will . . ." and, "There's the little stone house to fall back on!"

All this went on below the level of conscious thought. From its agitation, there came to the unshaven, ravenously hungry, furiously angry man stalking beside old Mr. Dewey, only a stimulating sense of personal danger, which was fuel to the roar of wrath in his heart. The words, ". . . on condition that . . ." were printed in

321

world, was angry, only Dakkuri could interpret the signs. If Nergal's wrath could be stemmed only by human sacrifices, it was Dakkuri who chose the victims. When demons entered the city, only he could decide who was possessed and who was not—who must be stoned to death and who spared. Sometimes, he flattered himself, the common people feared him more than their cruel king.

And the rewards were in keeping with his status. Robes woven with gold thread that glittered like the sun. The rarest sweetmeats, the richest wines, whenever he desired. And naturally he could take his pick of the temple dancing girls.

But in a world without idols, all that would be gone.

He lifted his eyes. Against the bare stone wall the lamplight flickered. And there, glinting in the shadows, was the Serpent.

He no longer remembered what impulse had led him to weld the broken pieces together again, to raise the Serpent up and give it an honored place among Babylon's many deities. But seeing it whole again, he had felt a dark power filling his body—like a goblet being filled to the brim with strong wine. His head had filled with light; a delicious, unbearable fire had bubbled through his veins. He felt like a giant. He could do any-

thing. A knife blade struck at his heart would have been melted by the energy that glowed through him. He was a god.

And from that moment on he was the Serpent's slave.

Breathing deeply and slowly, he focused on the sinuous bronze form before him. It seemed huge in the half-light, its shadow writhing on the wall like a living thing. He opened his mind, felt his will draining away like water from a broken pitcher.

As the familiar ecstasy crept into him, he smiled through closed lids. "Tell me what it is I must do," he whispered.

As far as Nebuchadnezzar was concerned, Dakkuri could be trusted. He had served many faithful years as a priest in the vicinity of the king's palace. But Dakkuri had a secret. He had become a devotee of the former angel of light who had rebelled against the Creator. Dakkuri, the Chaldean, belonged to, and was a servant of, the dark angel Lucifer.

Standing in the basement of the temple, Dakkuri addressed three of his most trusted disciples. The broken pieces of Nebuchadnezzar's image now lay alongside other sacred and profane vessels of worship in the dark and foreboding storage area. Most of these priceless items had been captured by Nebuchadnezzar's army during the raid on Jerusalem many years before.

Dakkuri spoke with quiet passion to his three Luciferian disciples. Each disciple had sworn an oath to carry out the task that was about to be assigned. It was a plan that would forever change the course of human history.

"Fellow servants of Lucifer, hear me. The Golden Head of Nebuchadnezzar must be hidden from the world until the time of the end."

Dakkuri picked up the beautifully formed Brazen Serpent, a fitting symbol indeed.

"I have inscribed on this Serpent the words to lead to the precise area where the head of gold is to be buried."

Dakkuri placed the Serpent on the vessel worktable and proceeded to break it into three pieces with a large hammer. He then handed one piece to each of the three disciples.

"Each of you is to travel to your predetermined areas and bury your portion of the Serpent as instructed. Each of the Serpent pieces will of course be useless without the other two."

One of the disciples stood and asked,

"*Master, why must the Golden Head remain hidden?*"

"*The world has no need for the head of gold at this time. But there is coming a time when the world's leader will have need of the Luciferian power that this Golden Head represents. That time is yet future. It is the time spoken of by Daniel the prophet in his interpretation of the king's dream. . . .*"

Dakkuri paused to reflect on the implication of his words.

"*It is the time when Babylon will rise a second time and rule the entire world.*"

SEVENTY

THE SEVEN SAT in their chamber deep within the castle. The man called Talon sat before them. Far from showing any fear at not having met their goals, he was showing annoyance at having to answer their questions.

"Murphy got lucky. He had the help of the U.S. Marines, and remember, you instructed me not to kill him or do any further harm to his circle."

"Yes." The British voice was doing the debriefing. "This has been a disappointment. We will never know what powers the Brazen Serpent might have had. A shame,

black all over the sunny world. "So he thinks we're for sale, does he, if he puts his price high enough?"

In front of the Principal's house, the bicycle still lay in a tangle. The long, red-headed owner of it stepped ahead of his elders, picked it up and trundled it to one side, out of their way. But he did not mount and ride off on it. He said, hesitatingly, "Say, Mr. Hulme—well—you see I get twenty-five cents for every news item I send in to the Ashley *Record*. I wonder if it would be all right to . . ."

The two men looked at him in silence, rather blankly. He took this to be disapproval and went on, extenuatingly, "I made a dollar in January, Professor Hulme, just off that one accident, down to the woolen mill."

"'At' the woolen mills," said the Principal mechanically.

"I mean 'at,' " said Burt hastily.

Timothy turned to Mr. Dewey. "What shall we do?" he asked.

Mr. Dewey thought for a moment, and said, "My great-uncle Zadok always used to tell me,

'What's got to be done
Better be begun.' "

"That's so," said Timothy, and went on gravely. "Burt, this is about the most serious thing that ever happened to our old town. You're a Clifford boy. It's up to you as much as anybody to help do the right thing. Had your lunch? No? Well, go on in the house and telephone your grandmother that you'll have it with us. And we three Clifford men can talk this over afterwards. I'll help you get your news item ready. You'll probably get more than a quarter for it too."

"Yes, Professor Hulme," said the boy, in a subdued voice, following his two elders into the house.

Timothy motioned the boy to the telephone, got Mr. Dewey down to the table—set for one—found the dish of hash in the warming-oven in the kitchen and put it before him, started the coffee making, opened a can of corned beef, poured some milk for the toothless old dog, showed Burt where the knives and forks and dishes were kept, and stepped upstairs to speak to Aunt Lavinia. He found her about to lie down for a nap, asked her in what he thought was a quiet casual voice, "All right, Lavvy?" and told her,

322

but whatever powers it had, we do not need them in order to move forward."

"Well, it served its purpose," Talon replied offhandedly, seeming to be concentrating more on the object he toyed with in his hand, poking it with his sharpened fingertip, than on his words. "It led Murphy to your precious Golden Head."

"Indeed. It led Murphy there. Not you. Now we must adjust our strategy. Now that the Golden Head is known around the world because of his discovery. That will require some careful rethinking and planning. But the good news, Talon, which is why you are still in our good graces, is that with all this notoriety, when we do take control of it—and we will—it will be a symbol of even greater power and glory."

Talon rose. "Good. You let me know how to proceed. You can have the power and glory." He turned to leave, swinging the object he had been preoccupied with as he walked away. It was a leather strip holding a cross, one he had once broken into three pieces, but which was now glued together.

"I've got a personal interest in this now."

AFTERWORD

I hope you have enjoyed *Babylon Rising*. As noted in my introductory message, I am having a great time creating this adventure, and I can't wait for you to read the next book in the series. I'm in the middle of writing it now and I'm having even more exciting times working on the second book than I had on this first one. And that's saying something.

Look for the second novel in the Babylon Rising series in hardcover in fall 2004.

In the meantime, please share your thoughts with me about this first book and

"I just wanted to let you know we're back. Mr. Dewey's going to eat something here before he goes home." But after one look at his face, she slid off her bed, crying, "What's happened, Tim? What has happened?" He shook his head, tried to smile. "Tell you later," he said with what he intended to be a reassuring intonation. It startled her so that she huddled a dress on over her wrapper and, half-buttoned, her hair straggling, came hobbling down the stairs as Timothy and Burt came in from the kitchen with the big pot of coffee and more bread and butter.

"You're hiding something from me, Timothy Hulme," she cried, over the stair railing. "Somebody has died and you're not letting me know." She was thoroughly alarmed and spoke her own pure straight English, with no trace of the whimsically put-on Scotch burr.

"Mr. Wheaton has died, Aunt Lavinia."

Halfway down the stairs she halted, astonished, relieved, resentful. "Why, you crazy loon, that's *good* news," she exclaimed with her bald disregard of conventional decencies. She sat down where she was, looking through the banisters at the three men below.

Timothy did not contradict her. He pushed the beef and bread towards the boy, he poured out the coffee and drank his own cup down, black.

The old woman called crossly to them, "Will you tell me why anybody in his right mind should look calamity over such a death as that?"

Speaking both together, Mr. Dewey said to her, "The point is, Mrs. Henry . . ." and Burt Stephenson cried out in utter bewilderment to Timothy, "But see here, Professor Hulme, that letter said that there is a lot of money coming to . . ."

Aunt Lavinia raised her voice rudely to drown out theirs, "Haven't you wit enough to see that . . ."

The telephone rang. With disciplined twentieth-century submission to that summons, they all went into a trance of suspended animation while Timothy, chewing hard on a mouthful of food, went to answer. "No," he said thickly into the receiver. "No, Mrs. Merrill, I cannot. No, not any time at all this afternoon. I shall be occupied all the rest of the day." He hung up the receiver. As though

323

released from a spell, they instantly went on where they had stopped, Aunt Lavinia's voice the loudest as she said scornfully, ". . . that all it means is that you won't have to fight his uncivilized ideas about education any longer."

Timothy, back at the table, told her curtly, without stopping his famished chewing and swallowing, "He's left the Academy some money on condition that no Jewish students ever be admitted."

"Why, Jules would have to be sent away," cried the old woman.

Exasperated at the incurably personal way in which women take things, Timothy said dryly, "He certainly would."

"But . . ." began Burt Stephenson, and stopped, looking from one face to another.

"Well, wouldn't ye know the old rascal'd think up some dir-r-rty trick as his last act in life?" said Aunt Lavinia conversationally. "And a stupid trick too. To be fool enough to think he could bribe self-respecting English-speaking men to pull their forelocks to his money. . . ." She was struck by the trouble in the faces below her. "You're never thinking of taking it!" she cried.

Their faces darkened. Each waited for the other to speak.

She stood up, leaned over the rail, gave them a long piercing look and put into one foreboding phrase her lifetime of observation of human frailty. "Oh, it's a *great deal* of money," she said sadly.

"More than a million dollars."

It was worse than she had been able to imagine. She cried out in dismay. Her legs failed her. She collapsed on the step where she stood, gathering her legs stiffly up under the twisted, badly-put-on skirt, her elbows on her bony knees. Presently she put up a hand to hide her eyes.

The hungry men forgot her and ate on in silence. All at once, perhaps with food in his stomach and normal bodily processes beginning again, Timothy had stopped feeling and begun to think, issuing an imperative order to work such as his mind had not received for months and putting his whole attention on it as it swung zestfully into action, enchanted to be of importance in his life again. "The first thing, the very first thing," he thought, "is to see that Burt's news item for the local press sets the right note. That'll mean taking time really to talk to Burt. After that, look out for the way the news is telegraphed in to the Boston and New York papers.

324

After that, find someone who will be willing to be candidate for . . . a letter to the alumni . . . a mimeographed statement to . . . and then . . .”

The food on the table was all eaten. Timothy got up mechanically, went into the kitchen, brought back what was left of a custard pie, cut it into three pieces and served the others. But although he took a fork into his hand, his own piece lay untasted on his plate. His brows drawn together into a frown of concentration, he sat looking down unseeingly at the long fingers of his hand. They did not lie relaxed and upperclass in slim distinction on the tablecloth. They clutched the fork tensely as though it were a weapon.

Mr. Dewey reached for the coffee pot and poured out a cup all around. When he pushed Timothy's towards him, Timothy glanced up and asked, “It *is* two months, isn't it, that . . .”

Mr. Dewey, unsurprised, nodded. “Yep. It'll come on—what's today?—it'll come on August 16th.”

Timothy sank back into his trance. He had forgotten where he was and presently looking up was surprised to see that Aunt Lavinia stood by the table, putting back the strings of her white hair to peer into his face. He thought absently, on a reflex of habit, that she wished to be helped upstairs, got to his feet, and offered her his arm. But she shook her head, and stepped back, saying, “Tim, dear lad . . .” Her voice was gentle and serious as he had not heard it in years.

“Yes, Aunt Lavinia?”

“Tim, look at me.”

He looked at her.

“Because you have an old woman hanging around your neck like a millstone you're not going to be less than you were brought up to be? Tim, I'd starve—and happy to—rather than stand in your way now.”

He was pleased with her, kissed her cheek lightly, told her with a smile, “You'll be allowed to starve, Lavvy dear, when I do.”

She brought her hands together with a clap. “Then you'll resign? Oh, *Tim* . . . ! Good for you!” She laid one hand on his shoulder. “Do it this minute, Tim dear!”

He flung off her hand roughly with a shake of his shoulders, shouting, “Resign? I'm not going to resign! What makes you think

look for additional information and news updates from me at my website:

www.timlahaye.com

I also invite you to visit www.babylon risingbook.com, the official website of the series. In the coming months on this site, you will find additional background information about the series, the characters, and the revelations in the novels. You can sign up for the Babylon Rising newsletter, read excerpts of forthcoming titles, post comments, keep in touch with the Babylon Rising team, and send a Babylon Rising electronic postcard with your own custom message.

Again, thank you for reading *Babylon Rising.*

I'm going to take this lying down? I'm not going to hand over the Academy to that bandit without firing a shot. I'm going to fight!"

At this, Burt Stephenson's mounting bewilderment and alarm burst into speech, "Why, Professor Hulme, you're not going to fight this *gift,* are you? Good gosh, Professor—why, we can have the gymnasium like we've always wanted to!"

"As we've always wanted to," corrected the Principal.

Aunt Lavinia was as bewildered as the boy. "But, Tim, you can't fight it. It's done. What can anybody do about it now?"

"Ah, that remains to be seen. We're going to put our heads together on that point this very afternoon. Burt, what classes have you?"

"Only a lab period from two to four, but see here, Professor Hulme, it would be simply *terrible* for the 'cademy if you— You don't mean you're . . . ?"

"You're excused from lab this afternoon for more important business," said Timothy. "How much time before you have to mail your news item to the *Record?*"

"Why, I always try to get them in on the five o'clock train north."

Timothy had his watch in his hand. He put it back in his pocket, saying, "Plenty of time then. Let's go. Mr. Dewey, can you manage the stairs to my study? We won't be interrupted there. And I've got the file of Academy catalogues up there and some clippings and other papers with the dates and figures Burt will need to have." Trying to eliminate the complication that Aunt Lavinia would certainly be, he said to her pleadingly, *"Why* don't you go on back to your nap?"

She did, as usual, what she pleased. "I'm in this too, Tim!"

"Yes, that's so," he said resignedly. "Well—Burt, take Mrs. Henry's arm and help her up the stairs, will you?"

He himself ran ahead quickly up the two flights of stairs, leaving the two old people and the boy to climb pantingly and slowly, and stop often to get their breaths. On the third floor, their voices a hum behind him, Timothy pushed open the door to his study, found the air inside close and hot, opened the windows, slid the papers on his desk into a drawer, pulled out a pasteboard letter-file from those on a shelf and dropped it on his desk, swept off to the floor a pile of books he had laid down on the couch.

326

Then, his preparations finished, he stood still in the middle of the room to await the arrival of the others. His gaze was turned inward. Plans and plans and plans spun in his head at top speed, with an ordered hum of controlled purpose. He put his right hand up to his head, turned his eyes downward to the floor on the left, his mind, collected, cool, gathering momentum as it surged forward.

Someone was calling to him. Above the babble of talk on the stairs Aunt Lavinia's voice rose, shouting, "Tim-o-thy!"

He blinked, came to himself, stepped to the landing and shouted back, not too patiently, "What do you want, Aunt Lavinia?"

The others gave her a moment's silence, but he could not catch what it was she was asking.

"What did you say?" he called and leaned to listen. The slowly mounting elders had not yet reached the turn in the steep attic stairs. Timothy could not see them, but from around the corner Aunt Lavinia's voice came clearly audible now, "Canby's here. I've told him. He wants to know can he come up too?"

"*Who?*" asked Timothy blankly.

"Canby. Canby Hunter."

"Oh . . . ! Oh, yes," said Timothy. "Sure, if he wants to."

Chapter Twenty-five

IT had been Timothy's intention, as much as he had any one plan clear in the stream of plans pouring through his head, to use the first part of this "talking over" for orderly, reasoned presentation to Burt Stephenson of the ideas he and Mr. Dewey would have to explain a thousand times to everybody else in town. But it did not turn out that way. There was nothing orderly about what was done.

He had heard their voices talking all at once while they were still on the stairs. Once they were up and inching along the hall to his study, behind Aunt Lavinia's slow limp, he could make out the words of their broken exclamations. Burt was asking, more and more insistently as nobody answered him, "But what *difference* would it make! We don't *have* any Jew students anyhow—not to speak of." Aunt Lavinia, breathless with her climb, was panting, "How ever does Tim think he can fight it? He can't get at Mr. Wheaton now!" Back of them Canby said loudly to Mr. Dewey, "Hell's bells, a poor town like Clifford would never—why, Uncle Tim is *crazy!*" And Mr. Dewey was repeating steadily like an incantation, "Over my dead body, I tell ye! I'll sell out and move to Ioway, first."

By the time they were in the study and had seated Aunt Lavinia, they had bungled and shoved a disorderly way into the middle of what Timothy had meant to take up at the beginning. He stood waiting for them to quiet themselves, using the grim, taut, impatient silence which was part of his technique for quieting uproar at the Academy, and in the first pause reminded them gruffly of what they had come up to do, "Mr. Dewey, do you want to say something to Burt about his news item? Or shall I?"

Mr. Dewey, letting himself down slowly into a chair, shook his head, "No, I'm too mad to talk. You start in, T.C."

Canby stood leaning against the door-jamb.

Timothy sat down at his desk and motioned Burt into the chair

328

on the other side, wondering where to begin. The boy's intelligent, blunt-featured, freckled face, under the rough, reddish hair, was intensely serious and utterly puzzled. He gazed silently at the Principal of his school, attentive to what he might say, his eyebrows drawn together over his young clear eyes, his mouth—still a child's mouth in spite of his six feet—hanging a little open. As Timothy looked across his desk at the young mountaineer, intact, innocent, ignorant—in danger—he found himself stirred to the depths by an awareness of the moment's meaning. Back of those clear, intelligent, life-ignorant eyes, he saw all Clifford—in danger—and knew with astonishment that he loved it. Leaning across the desk, "Give me your hand, Burt," he said. When the big, angular young hand was in his, he gave it a great clasp like the one with which he had made his promise to old Mr. Dewey. "Burt, I've known you for—well, since you were a little boy in the first grade, and I've respected you just as long as I've known you—" He took another vow, "I make you my promise now, Burt, that I'll do my level best—no matter what it costs me—to see that nothing is done, now, that an honest Vermont boy like you will ever be ashamed of."

"Yes, Professor Hulme," murmured Burt, abashed to have his self-controlled Principal give him that warm look of affection, shaken by the tremor in the well-known harsh voice. "Yes, Professor Hulme. But . . ."

Timothy released the boy's hand. "Yes, of course, Burt, that 'but' of yours is what we're here to answer."

Aunt Lavinia said impatiently, "What I want to know is what *can* be done. You and Mr. Dewey haven't the say-so, have you?"

Timothy explained, marveling anew at her ignorance of all the mechanisms of Clifford life, an ignorance she had kept intact after twenty years of Clifford, "Everybody in town has a say-so, Aunt Lavinia, that has a vote. Don't you remember, eight years ago when Mr. Merrill died and after two months Mr. Wheaton was elected? The Town will have to choose another Trustee to take Mr. Wheaton's place."

"Good Heavens, have we got to wait two months before this can be decided?"

"How else, Aunt Lavvy? Everything, you see, will depend on who is elected as the third Trustee."

329